FINDING KATARINA M.

FINDING KATARINA M.

ELISABETH ELO

Hardcover ISBN: 978-1-947993-43-3
eISBN: 978-1-940610-98-6
Library of Congress Catalog Number: 2018962650

First hardcover publication:
March 2019 by Polis Books LLC
221 River St., 9th Fl. #9070
Hoboken, NJ 07030
www.PolisBooks..com

POLIS BOOKS

Russia is the land where things that don't happen, happen.

—Czar Peter the Great

Surely all art is the result of one's having been in danger,
of having gone through an experience all the way to the end,
to where no one can go any further.

—Rainer Maria Rilke

PROLOGUE

Kolyma region, northeastern Siberia, 1951

She had seen prisoners commit suicide by running through the leafy birch forest, drawing the expected bullet in the back. Taking any sharp thing imaginable—on one occasion, the jagged edge of a broken metal bucket—to gnaw at their wrists until a vein opened. Ever since the death of her infant son, she'd imagined different ways to kill herself and mentally rehearsed the steps of each until she was sure she would succeed. But when she finally threw the end of the thick rope she'd made from torn strips of fabric over a beam in the deserted barracks, her resolve drained away.

How stupidly dramatic she was being. As if choosing the time of her death proved some kind of mastery. As if a self-inflicted end was somehow better than the starvation, disease, or violence that would find her in due course. Her suicidal plan was nothing more than a hapless tinkering with the trivial matters of when and how death would make its inevitable claim. There was no solace in it, only the humiliation of having turned against herself.

Kicking the rope under her cot, she took stock of herself. Her body was a pitiful relic of what it had been, but it was still capable of movement, and her mind was still capable of thought. She counted two additional advantages: evil did not shock her anymore, and mortal fear was gone.

Vera, the infant daughter pulled from her arms on the day she was arrested, would be three years old now. For that child's sake, she would use what was left of her strength to attempt escape. Her chances of success were slight. Even if she managed to slip away from the camp, winter was closing in, and the distances were vast. But she would be dreaming of a warm reunion with each homeward step, and when death found her, it would be no more than what was bound to happen anyway.

1

"There's one more person to see you," my assistant said, peeking her head into my office. Her straw purse hung from her shoulder—a sure sign that she intended to head home after we spoke, which she had every right to do since it was an hour after closing time. We'd had a busy afternoon, with patients backed up in the waiting room, most of them needing routine care, one person, unfortunately, very sick.

"Not another emergency, I hope." I had a work function that evening and had to get home in time to change and take a cab downtown. Also, I was tired.

"Doesn't look that way. But how would I know? She won't tell me her name or what she wants, only that she needs to see you. She's been waiting all afternoon."

I groaned, fearing a lengthy consultation. But I was also intrigued. People who stubbornly wait for hours to get what they want tend to impress me.

"All right. Send her in."

The young woman who appeared in my doorway was tiny, no more than a hundred pounds, early twenties maybe, with Eurasian features and glossy black hair that fell freely across bare arms. Her yellow cotton dress was wrinkled and quite plain compared to what the generally well-off patients at the medical center usually wore, and she teetered on the kind of high platform sandals that were in vogue that summer and that were probably keeping the orthopedists busy. One of her toes was wrapped in a grubby band-aid.

She was fidgety, could barely meet my eyes. My first thought was that she must be a shy former patient with symptoms that embarrassed her, yet she didn't look familiar.

"Are you Mrs. Natalie March?" she asked softly, managing even in that short sentence to insert several guttural consonants where they didn't belong. A Russian accent.

"I am," I said in a light tone, hoping it would help her relax.

She blushed. "I am sorry for problem. I am sorry English language is not good."

"We could speak Russian if you prefer." I'd grown up speaking Russian with my immigrant parents. My fluency made me a popular physician among Russians living in the Washington, D.C. area—business people, embassy workers, diplomats and their families. But none called me *missus*.

"Da. Spasiba."

When I asked if she was a patient with the practice, she said no, that her business was personal. Her Russian was spiced with a subtle regional accent I couldn't place.

"Have a seat," I said, indicating two leather chairs facing my desk.

She perched gingerly on the one closest to the door and began twisting a small silver ring on her finger. Her hands were well-made, with tapered fingers and defined muscles. In fact, every part of her anatomy was beautifully formed and proportioned: slender ankles, toned calves, sleek arms, elegant neck. Her body gave the impression of having been sculpted by a master craftsman with a keen appreciation for the beauty of the human form.

"My name is Saldana Tarasova," she said, so quietly I could barely hear her.

I remained silent, knowing there was more to come.

After a long pause, her dark eyes, flourishes of eyeliner accentuating their rising slant, flicked up to meet mine. "I am cousin."

I offered what was probably a rather stiff smile. To the best of my knowledge, I didn't have any cousins, and now that I'd had a closer look at her, was certain we hadn't met before. The thought flashed through my mind that she might have a psychiatric disorder, in which case I'd be there all night finding the proper care for her. Or that she might be dangerous, despite her innocent appearance. I pictured the red security buzzer, now standard equipment for medical personnel at the center, tucked under the lip of my desk.

"Cousin?" I repeated. "I don't think so. You must be looking for someone else."

She dropped her gaze abruptly, blushing so deeply that her tan cheeks shaded to burnished copper. The nervous ring twisting resumed, even more torturous this time. She appeared to be fighting back tears.

I saw that my response had upset her and tried again. "I'm sorry…Saldana, is it?"

She nodded briefly and miserably, her eyes still downcast.

"You've caught me by surprise. I don't believe I have any cousins. Maybe you could say a little more."

"My grandmother, Katarina Melnikova, is also your grandmother."

"Ah." The words were like a gentle slap across my face. Melnikova was indeed the name of my maternal grandmother who'd been sent to the gulag with her young husband in 1949.

"Yes, I know that name," I said, "though I haven't heard it spoken in a long time."

Not since I was fourteen years old, when my mother, in an awkwardly formal ceremony, showed me an old photo album she'd been keeping hidden somewhere, possibly in shame, or in the Russian penchant for secrecy that I, an American teenager, couldn't hope to understand. She had turned the old pages slowly, finally stopping at a black-and-white photo of a young couple with easy, confident smiles standing with arms linked on a city street. The woman was dressed in a wool travelling suit with a belted waist and a jaunty felt hat that perched on the back of her head; the man wore a tweed overcoat, unbuttoned, over a white shirt and thin dark tie. There was blurry Cyrillic lettering on one of the shop signs behind them.

"Those are your grandparents," she said.

I stared at the photo in bewildered surprise. I'd never seen a picture of them before and had been told almost nothing about them, only that they were Ukrainians who died when my mother was an infant. I'd always assumed that her reluctance to speak about them was due partly to the pain of having lost them and partly to the fact that, as a consequence, she knew very little about them. I'd also assumed, with no basis at all, that they'd died from natural causes.

That day, my mother told a different story. Her parents were Jehovah's Witnesses who'd been rounded up in one of Stalin's many mass deportations, forced onto a train, and shipped to the Siberian gulag where they'd presumably perished.

My surprise gave way to a potent mix of horror and grief. We were studying European history in school, so I knew that the Russian gulag was a network of prison labor camps where millions of people—some estimates as high as eighteen million—were worked to death mining gold, uranium, and tin; felling trees and shipping lumber; and building thousands of miles of roads and railways to fuel Russia's modernization. The conditions in the camps were horrible: most of the prisoners died of starvation, exhaustion, disease, exposure, or abuse. I'd read about the gulag as something that had happened long ago and far away, never dreaming that my own grandparents were among the victims.

I felt dizzy from the shock, then angry. Why had my mother not told me before? Maybe she thought I was finally old enough to know something as serious as this. In that case, I wanted to respond maturely, so she would know that her faith in me was not misplaced. In those hard days after my father's death, I was always trying to be strong for her, so she would have one less thing to worry about.

The photo album was on the table in front of us, closed. My mother's eyes were misty with tears. I swallowed hard and told her that I was sorry I would never meet her parents, that I was very sorry for what they'd suffered, and what she herself had been through as a result. I said that I loved her and wanted her to be happy, and that I wanted to help her be happy however I could.

She smiled at me tenderly, brushing a strand of hair off my face. "What did I do to deserve you, Talya?"

"I love you, Mom," I whispered. I often said those words to her, and I've repeated them frequently since.

"If you want to make me happy," she said, "there's one thing you can do. I know you like to ask a lot of questions. You're only happy when you're finding things out. But I've told you everything I know. So, please, for once, just let things be. This subject is difficult for me, and I don't want to talk about it again."

I promised, of course, and kept my word. But the horrifying knowledge lived and burned inside me nonetheless. I found myself pushed into a close personal relationship with the gigantic Stalinist horror, and I knew I'd never be the same.

Now, twenty-five years later, as I sat in my corner office at the George Washington University Medical Center, the idea that one of my grandparents had survived the gulag seemed impossible, unreal. It was probably a hoax— some kind of weird new identity theft. A demand for money was probably coming next. But how could the obviously frightened young woman sitting before me have unearthed a name that had so little history attached to it, and that I barely knew myself? And why go to so much trouble? Certainly there were easier ways to extort money from a stranger.

I studied my visitor more closely. She had high round cheeks and a small jaw, narrow dark eyes and honey-brown skin. I saw no family resemblance at all. I was on the tall side, and my features were angular.

"Where did you say you were from?" I asked.

"Yakutsk."

"Yakutsk," I repeated, utterly blank. "Where's that?"

"Northeastern Siberia."

I tried to picture Siberia as a relatively normal—if chilly in winter—region of the world where young women like Saldana Tarasova ate and slept and shopped and went to school. But I couldn't manage it. My vision of Siberia was too tainted by its ugly history. To me, it was a mindscape of impenetrable darkness and killing cold; the vast icy crust at the end of the world where a good portion of history's nightmares were stored; where, until this moment, I'd been sure that my grandparents' skeletons were layered with those of many others in an anonymous mass grave.

I said, "I was under the impression that Katarina Melnikova and her husband died in a prison camp."

"Grandfather did not survive; Grandmother escaped."

Escaped. The gulag camps were considered virtually escape-proof. The thinking went that if winter temperatures didn't kill people, the sheer, ungodly distances would. I couldn't help feeling a surge of interest in any person, related or not, who'd managed such a nervy, desperate feat. "She's still alive?"

"She lives in a village on the Tatta River. She's eighty-nine."

I tried to imagine this, too. The young married woman in the photo had seemed vital, energetic. There was a simple, straightforward light in her eye and a trace of pleasant humor around her mouth. Apparently, this same woman now went about her business in a Siberian village. At age eighty-nine.

"Katarina Melnikova," I repeated musingly, feeling the heavy Russian weight of the syllables on my lips. It was possible I'd never spoken her name out loud before. It was melodious and beautiful, but still nothing more than a name to me.

"How's her health?" I asked, because it was something to say.

"She has the problems old people have."

"She had more children, then. One? Two?"

"Just one. My mother, Lena. Lena Tarasova. My father lives in a different city. He has a new family," Saldana confessed quickly, getting it out of the way.

"Is your mother in Yakutsk with you?"

"Yes, we have a flat there. I have a younger brother, Mikhail, who lived with us until recently."

"Well…" I said in a tone of finality, placing my palms flat on my desk as I usually did before I stood up. But I couldn't just end the conversation, as if it were a standard medical consultation. I had to respond differently. But how? I wasn't yet willing to accept Ms. Tarasova's statement as true. And if I did accept it, what then? It was all a little baffling.

"Well," I hemmed. "Well, I really don't know what to say. This does come as a shock. My mother will be so…surprised. Why…?" I tried to keep the reproach out of my voice. "Why was she never told?"

Saldana looked down at her hands. A few seconds of awkward silence passed.

There'd been some kind of messy family business, I guessed, for which the young woman in front of me—she didn't look to be more than twenty-one—shouldn't be held responsible. But anger prickled my skin nonetheless. My mother had spent her life believing her parents were dead. She'd dragged this weighty tragedy through, so far, sixty-six years of living, as if it were a soldered ball and chain. Why on earth had Katarina Melnikova chosen to remain unknown? Didn't she care about the baby daughter she'd left with her brother in Kiev? And even if she had no maternal feelings at all—I saw plenty of examples of this baffling phenomenon in my practice—hadn't she been the least bit curious? I knew it wasn't fair to jump to conclusions about Katarina Melnikova, whose situation had been desperate, to say the least. Still, I was upset for my mother's sake, worried about how she would react to the good news that Katarina was alive and well, and the bad news that she'd waited until now to make herself known.

"How did you find me?" I asked my visitor.

"We knew that Grandmother left her first child with her brother in Kiev when she was arrested. My mother tracked him down, and he gave us your mother's married name. We couldn't find her address, but we found yours. Your work address, that is."

Saldana looked at me directly, her dark eyes anxious and hopeful. "I'm sorry. I should have called first, but I didn't know how you'd feel. I was afraid you wouldn't want to meet me, and I didn't want to email for fear you wouldn't reply. I couldn't risk not talking to you."

I blinked at her slowly, my mouth agape. The detail about the brother in Kiev had clinched it for me: Saldana was, must be, for real. It was simply too much to think that she would know where my mother was raised, and by whom, if her claim wasn't true. A wave of strong emotion passed through me—joy. Then another emotion poured in behind it—fear. Fear that the joy wouldn't last, that it would be stolen or destroyed somehow, before it had a chance to flower.

"How long are you in town?" I asked.

"Until tomorrow afternoon. My train back to New York leaves at four o'clock." She explained that she was in the States to perform with a ballet company as part of a cultural exchange program. The dancers had been in rehearsal all week. Their show opened on Friday, one week from today. It had a two-week run, after which she would return to Russia.

"I'd love to take you to dinner, but I have something to do tonight, a work thing I can't get out of. Can I meet you tomorrow?"

She nodded eagerly.

"Where are you staying?"

She named a cheap hotel on Rhode Island Avenue.

"That's very near the Capitol Building. I'll meet you there at nine tomorrow morning, on the lawn outside the west entrance, at the bottom of all the marble steps. In the meantime, if you need anything, please call." As I jotted my cell number on the back of my business card, it occurred to me that my new-found cousin had gone to great lengths to meet me, that showing up in my office unannounced had been a risk, that she was a young person alone in a foreign country and might well be scared to death.

"I'm very glad you found me, Saldana," I said warmly. "We'll have a nice time tomorrow, yes?"

She accepted the card with two hands, as if it were a precious gift, and looked gratefully into my eyes, apparently convinced at last that she wasn't going to be turned away. "*Spasiba, Natalya Marchova*," she said.

The sound of my name in Russian sent an unwelcome chill through me—I had no love for the country my parents fled, despite my fluency in the language, which I saw merely as a skill I could use to reach more patients and serve them better. Like many children of immigrants, I deeply cherished my American identity.

"Call me Natalie. Come on, I'll give you a lift back to your hotel."

⠂ ⠆ ⠐ ⠄ ⠠ ⠂ ⠠ ⠄ ⠐ ⠆ ⠂

The evening was brilliant, all crystal and floral centerpieces, white wine flowing and waiters weaving among the guests. What made it so magical was the fact that virtually everyone present really did wish the guest of honor well. For nearly thirty years, Dr. Andrew Solomon, my retiring mentor, had been the medical center's standard bearer and moral compass, a brilliant, dedicated physician who'd managed to make us all a little better than we really were. I couldn't count the number of times I'd knocked on his door with a question, a problem, or simply the need to talk unguardedly to someone who understood the kinds of things that troubled me. Not once did he make me feel small or stupid; I always left feeling stronger and more clear. You cannot put a price on that; you cannot say thank you enough. That's what I said in my little speech, and the words, being heartfelt, came easily, no notes required. At the end, I could tell by all the smiling faces—some of the women even tissue-dabbing their eyes with care—that I'd done him justice, and that made me glad.

Afterwards, there were pictures, and some whispered nudges about how I was one of several candidates being considered for Dr. Soloman's job. Then quite suddenly, in a flurry of flashing bulbs, I found myself standing between Dr. Solomon and Dr. Joel White, my arms lightly encircling each of their waists, and my inner world quickly crumbled. When the picture-taking was over, I excused myself shakily, found an empty table at the back of the room, and sat down among the balled-up linen napkins and lipstick-smeared coffee cups. People smiled at me from a distance, and I smiled awkwardly back. The dance band started up, the party rolled into full swing, and I was relieved to be left alone.

I saw Joel reach out to his brand-new wife, Melissa, and pull her onto the parquet. Joel and I had been medical students, interns, and residents together. We'd helped and stood by each other all that time, sharing notes, gripes, sandwiches, the flu, our heady successes, devastating failures, and the sheer addictive exhaustion of our work. We'd made love, too, using sex in all the ways it shouldn't be used: as an antidote to loneliness, a sedative for anxiety, a novelty to break the boredom, a way to obliterate ourselves. We'd talked about marriage a few times, in a polite, obligatory way, but we were almost too close, too familiar, to take the idea seriously. For a few years, we lived in different cities completing fellowships, then found ourselves together again at GW, where we'd been close colleagues for the last decade. Now, with Joel graying at the temples, and my once-long hair cut in a short, simple style, we had an intimacy that was in some ways more profound, more crucial to our lives, than mere romantic love. We could almost read each other's minds.

Melissa was not of our world. She was untested—coddled, in my opinion— superficial, as lucky people tended to be, and effusively light-hearted. She teased Joel in public about his work habits, as if they were a charming flaw. It was clear that she planned to cure him of workaholism with regular doses of social events, dinners and movies, and weekend getaways. The perfect confidence she brought to this task was just another of her delightful traits.

In my opinion, Melissa was naively miscalculating the depths of her husband's dedication to his career. But how could a woman as protected as she truly understand a man like him? Had she ever seen an anesthetized patient stretched out on an operating table, or reached into that person's liver to pull out a golf-ball-sized cancerous tumor? Had her after-work ears ever burned with the echoes of children crying from chronic pain and wretched, innocent bewilderment? Had she ever attempted to relax before a crackling fire, only to close a novel and grab a textbook she'd pored over a hundred times before because she needed to be absolutely certain, right then and there, that there wasn't a single detail she'd overlooked?

As I watched her gracefully twirling at the end of Joel's arm, in a lovely dress that fit her so well, that managed to be both tasteful and flirtatious, I felt my lips curl with unwanted envy. Young Melissa probably didn't smell like antiseptic even after she showered. She could still enjoy the sweet feminine luxury of doting on the cuteness of babies because she'd never had to watch one die.

I'd tried not to see Joel's marriage as a betrayal. I'd *worked* at not seeing it that way. But ever since that sunny winter wedding, when the smile on his face glowed brighter than any smile I'd seen on it before, there had been a sharp new pain in my heart and a grating tension between us. He'd taken to lecturing me in a friendly way on what he was learning from Melissa about the all-important work/life balance, on the apparently critical need to get out and enjoy yourself once in a while, and, to my horror, I'd heard resentment quivering in my retorts. I believed I knew only too well what he was trying to say: I was supposed to find someone, too. He needed that to complete his own happiness. It would free him up somehow, in some complicated way, if he could confidently release me into someone else's care.

But it wasn't that simple for me. Men had never really looked at me very much, and lately, they didn't look at me at all. It had been a long time since I had a date.

The truth was that I'd managed to become what the Chinese call a "leftover woman," a woman who'd traded the best of her child-bearing years for power and status. It was an ugly term, conjuring stale smells and lumpy textures. Moldy food items that no one really wanted, that were kept around just until they could be guiltlessly thrown away.

This was obviously an unhealthy way to see oneself, so I was glad that the dark thoughts came only in the middle of sleepless nights, which, due to my chronic state of fatigue, were rare. For the most part, I succeeded in not giving my situation much thought. I was only aware of it in unexpected moments like the one that had just occurred, when, my arm encircling Joel's waist, I felt his taut, graceful body under his suit jacket, and his familiar smell rose to my head like the world's most excellent wine.

A hot sun—fat and round like the exaggerated yellow orb in a child's drawing—was climbing the eastern sky when I arrived at the National Mall the next morning. The city had been in the grip of a heat spell for the last week, brutal even by Washington standards. I'd slept badly, my dreams crowded with images of wooden sentry towers and bedraggled prisoners shuffling across snowfields, and my early morning run had been an arduous, discouraging affair. Before leaving my condo, I'd donned big dark glasses and a Washington Nationals baseball cap.

Saldana appeared at the top of the marble steps a few minutes after nine, wearing the same yellow dress and ungainly platform sandals she'd had on the day before. The only difference was that her glossy black hair was woven in a long braid that fell across one shoulder. She caught sight of me when I waved, and began descending the stairs with effortless grace. There was something magnetic about her that drew the eye, that made the sneakered tourists turn and stare. I was reminded of a line from Byron, *She walks in beauty, like the night / Of cloudless climes and starry skies.*

"Come and sit," I said as she approached. "It's a glorious morning, even if it is beastly hot."

"Sorry I'm late."

"It's only a few minutes. Have you had breakfast yet?"

She nodded a bit timidly, as if worried that eating breakfast had been an etiquette mistake.

"Good. So have I," I lied. "Why don't we walk for a while, before it gets even hotter. We can head up to the Washington Monument. There are a lot of wonderful museums on the way, and we can stop in one of them if you'd like."

"Thank you. That would be very nice," she said with perfect politeness, leaving me with no idea whether she meant it or not.

The mall was filling with hikers and lawmakers, mothers with running toddlers and dog-walkers tethered to several leashes at once. Saldana and I strolled to the Washington Monument, chatting all the way, past sprinklers spewing a fine rain on parched lawns. Then it was on to the Reflecting Pool, and all the way to the Lincoln Memorial, with Saldana gradually becoming more open and relaxed. When I asked what she liked best about the United States, she replied without hesitation: the cars.

"There are so many, and they all look brand new," she said. "Where I'm from, only the richest people can afford them; everyone else has to take buses. I've spent half my life on street corners waiting for buses to come. It's the worst in winter, because some days there's so much moisture in the air that you're in a fog of frost and can't see very far in front of you. You don't know the bus is coming until you hear the motor; then it looms out at you all of a sudden. Buses used to scare me when I was little." She offered me an incongruously bright smile, pleased to have offered up this little intimate fact, and happily added, "If I lived in America, I'd buy a convertible and drive it all the way to Beverly Hills!"

I smiled at her enthusiasm. "What else do you like about America?"

"The handicap ramps," she said more soberly. "So people in wheelchairs can go wherever they want. In Yakutsk, they mostly stay inside."

Her impressions of the US weren't all positive, though. She was displeased with the dance company she was performing with because, as she haughtily explained, they practiced sloppy techniques that a Russian ballet master would never tolerate.

"They rehearse too much," she said. "It's not necessary. If you know a piece, you know it. You don't need to keep repeating it over and over again, until you hate every step and just the sound of the music makes you cringe."

The museums we passed hadn't interested her, but she was very keen on the Botanic Garden when I mentioned it, so from the Lincoln Memorial we strolled all the way back towards the Capitol Building, except on the other side of the mall. By this time, heat was radiating up from the ground in palpable waves, and the air was a nearly unbreathable soup of stifling humidity. Saldana's bare arms had grown pink from the sizzling rays. I hastened our steps, eager to reach air conditioning.

The main hall of the Botanic Garden was like an oasis when we finally entered it: cool and lush, its light softened by a soaring glass dome. The place had just opened for the day. A noisy, excited throng of tourists was milling about, snapping group photos and grinning selfies. Saldana looked a little wilted from our hike.

I led her through glass doors into the tropical rain forest, which was hushed and cool, despite the thick humidity. A dense earthy fragrance greeted us, and there was a greeny dimness to the air, as most of the light was blocked by the thick jungle canopy overhead. We wandered for a while in companionable awe before taking a seat on a wooden bench tucked into a corner. Tangled ropey vines dripped from branches, and the ground was lushly carpeted with flat-leaved ferns in varied shades of yellow and green. I knew—and I think Saldana knew it, too—that with so much friendly, superficial banter behind us, the time had come for her to honestly explain herself—the long train ride, the surprise appearance, the urgency. What she really wanted.

"I love that you're here, Saldana. I love getting to know you. But I wonder if there isn't some reason for your visit you haven't told me yet," I said.

She froze a little, then swallowed hard enough that I could see her neck muscles move. "I have something to ask."

"Go ahead." I wondered if she wanted money, which I was prepared to give, up to a point.

"I'm very proud to have been sent to the United States as a representative of my country. This is a wonderful opportunity for me to share the artistry of Yakutia with American audiences. Now more than ever, when there's so much hostility in the world, it's important to promote understanding between our two countries. Whether Russian or American, we're all the same underneath our skin. Don't you agree, Natalie?" She produced a tortured-looking smile.

I nodded, wondering what on earth was prompting such a stilted speech.

"It's very unusual for a Russian citizen such as myself to be granted a visa to the United States. I'll probably never have such luck again. I'm scheduled to return to my country soon, as you know. But..."

"But...?"

"But everything's so nice here! America is a good place to be a dancer! And if I couldn't be a dancer, I could go to school! There are a lot of schools in America. My English is not good right now, but I would study very hard and soon have a job to support myself." Her smile folded into what it had wanted to be all along: a grimace. "But my visa is only for thirty days."

An Indian family passed in front of us, the woman in a brilliant sari and two children trailing wide-eyed with wonder. We remained quiet until they were gone and for some moments afterward. I had a sense of where this was going and was hoping I was wrong.

"Have you looked in to getting your visa extended?" I asked.

"Not possible," she said quickly. "It was issued for cultural exchange, not work or study. I would have to have a job here to get it extended, and even then, it's very difficult. The rules are very strict."

"You might try calling the US State Department."

"I'm a principal dancer at a respected ballet company in Russia," she whispered in a low voice, as if revealing a state secret. "I am…what you call…a national treasure. My country will never let me leave."

"Are you sure? I could put you in touch with someone—an immigration lawyer or someone like that." But even as the words were leaving my mouth, I knew they were hollow. I was just trying to create some cover for myself. If I could pass Saldana off to someone else, I might be able to slip away from any involvement. "A professional will give you the best advice for your situation. I'm sure there are some legal avenues open to you."

Saldana stiffened, and spoke the next words with surprising steel. "I'm not returning to Russia when my visa expires. I will remain in the United States. Things will be very difficult for me at first. I'll need so much—a place to live, US dollars, food. It would be much easier if I had someone, an American citizen, to help me out."

My cheeks grew warm with rising blood. So this was the reason for the surprise visit. I was being asked to help her defect. I could forgive her opportunism; I even admired it. What I couldn't abide was her naïveté.

"Saldana, listen to me. Before you go too far down this road, you'd better think long and hard. Maybe you've got some picture in your head of what America is like. Picket fences, apple pie—I don't know. But whatever you're imagining, I'm going to tell you right now you're dead wrong. Life here isn't easy for undocumented aliens. You'd be hiding in the shadows, always looking over your shoulder. And you, of all people, have so much to lose. I doubt you'd be able to dance in a company here without papers. Are you really willing to give up your career?"

"I was told there are jobs in hotels," she said staunchly.

"Hotels? Are you serious? How could working in a hotel possibly be good for you? Long, exhausting hours for low pay. Being treated like a servant constantly—and still not able to make ends meet. You're a ballet dancer, Saldana. An artist starting out on a wonderful career that you've worked very hard to achieve. Do you even know what you're saying?"

Tears pooled in her eyes. "Please, Dr. March. Natalie. Please…"

But I wouldn't allow myself to be swayed by emotion, not in this case, where there was so much to lose. "I'm sorry. I can't in good conscience support your choice to do something that I know would be difficult and dangerous, and that I honestly believe you would live to regret. And then there's the not-so-small matter of the law. What you're proposing is illegal. You must know that. If there's some other way I can help you, I would certainly like to do it. But you can't expect me to intentionally break the law. I'm very sorry, Saldana. It grieves me to say this. But I won't help you defect."

A few tears spilled over her lower lids. She brushed them away quickly, before they could roll down her cheeks. "I was hoping…since we're cousins…"

"You thought our being related would make a difference?"

"Yes," she said in a small voice.

"It makes no difference, Saldana. If anything, it only makes me care about you more. And what about your relatives back in Russia? Your mother and brother, your grandmother. Have you thought about them?"

"My mother is the one who sent me here! She says I have to stay, no matter what. I *can't* go home!"

"What do you mean, *you can't go home*?"

She fairly spit out the next words in a mix of bitterness and despair. "I never wanted to come here, but when my mother found out I could get a visa through this cultural exchange, she said I had to take it. That it was an opportunity I wouldn't get again, that I'd be sorry all my life if I didn't get out of Russia when I had the chance. She told me to contact you, that you'd help me because we're family. And she promised that she and my brother would join me here soon."

She was madly twisting the ring. "But I think she was lying to give me courage, because she never said a word before about wanting to leave Russia. She loves her country, as I do! And I know for a fact Misha would never come here!"

Her face reddened and crumpled, and fresh tears streamed down her cheeks. She swiped them away with her small, perfect hands, tried to control the heaving of her breath.

At a loss for words, I tried to put my arm around her shoulder but she pulled away slightly, not wanting to be consoled, and continued in a rush, "Something is happening to my family, something bad. I didn't speak to my brother at all before I left. My mother said he was away on a trip, but where would he be that he couldn't call to say goodbye? And why would he have gone on a trip without telling me? When he moved away, we stayed in touch, then I didn't hear from him at all. That's not like him! My mother was trying to act normal, but it was obvious she was upset. I begged her to tell me what was happening, but she only kept repeating that America is a wonderful country, that I would be the first to go but soon we'd all be here together, happier than before. Yet she looked so sad!"

Saldana grabbed my forearm with fingers strong as talons. "I only agreed to come because I could see how much it meant to her, and because I thought she might be telling the truth—maybe she and Misha really would come to America! Now I'm sure I made a terrible mistake. It was wrong for me to leave the country when they might be in trouble. What if they need my help? But now I'm here, so far away, and I don't dare go back because my mother worked so hard to get me here—she used all her money to pay a bribe for my visa—and if I go back it will ruin everything she tried to do. Maybe this really *is* what she wants for me—to be happy in America. But how can I be happy if she and Misha aren't with me? I don't want to be here alone!"

She broke down into unfettered tears, her thin body wracked by more sorrow and confusion than I could readily imagine. I succeeded in putting my arm around her quaking shoulders, murmuring "I'm so sorry" several times. Eventually, she quieted, rubbing her reddened cheeks roughly with the heels of her hands like children do.

My mind was racing with questions, sympathy, fear. I had no idea how to respond or what to do. "I wish I could help," I murmured, as much to myself as to her.

"You can! Let me stay with you for a little while after the ballet, just until I get settled here."

I didn't have the heart to deny her again, but I was still a long way from saying yes. Playing for time, I said, "Come on, let's walk some more."

We glided like two ghosts toward the next exhibit, as if just the talk of defection had made us both a little shadowy. Through a set of glass doors fogged with humidity, we emerged into the Orchid Room, moist and dim and thick with vegetation. Hundreds of vivid pink, purple, and orange flowers clung to the tangled limbs and trunks of their unwitting arboreal hosts, and sprouted impossibly from the crevices of mossy rocks.

Too preoccupied to pay attention to the beauty, I led Saldana silently to the next exhibit room, where the dry heat of the desert accosted us. Rows of paddle-armed cacti rose stiffly from the drained, monochromatic landscape, giving testament to the stunning adaptability of lifeforms.

I was painfully aware of the tiny dancer trailing behind me, of her terrible hope and profound vulnerability. I feared that she was already doomed, like a patient with a fatal illness who didn't feel sick yet but whose days were numbered nonetheless. I knew I had to honestly describe the risks and the probable course of events to her, just as if she were a patient facing tough choices and tougher odds. But what did I know about immigration, really— either legal or illegal? It wasn't my specialty. There were experts out there who were in a much better position to advise her. I realized with a relieved sigh that I had no business counseling her until I'd checked with them and ascertained the facts. A second opinion, if you will.

In the medicinal plant section, we sat down again. The species arrayed around us were mostly small, each one tidy and unique and a little odd. The light was clean and white; the air held a subtle astringent bitterness. Saldana was fidgety, awaiting my verdict.

"Saldana," I began, "I think that before we go any further with this, we should talk to someone who knows the ins and outs, the loopholes, of the whole immigration process. An immigration lawyer, for example. There's got to be a way for you to get what you want legally."

She looked frightened and completely skeptical.

"We have to give it a shot," I urged. "What if there's a solution that neither of us knows right now? Don't you see? This whole thing could be simpler than we think."

"I don't know," she said fretfully. "What if they turn me in?"

"They won't. Everything you say to a lawyer is held in the strictest confidence. They're not allowed to share your information with anyone else or do anything against your will. They're just there to lay out the facts and give you the best advice."

"You know people who do that?"

"Not personally, but I can find someone. Just give me a few days. Your name won't be mentioned, I promise."

Her face was pale, and she was twisting her silver ring back and forth erratically. "I don't want to get in trouble."

"You won't."

"I should talk to my mother first."

"Yes, good idea. Call her, and tell her what I said. Tell her I want to help you, but I don't want to break the law, and I can cover your legal fees. Do you want me to talk to her, too?"

She was biting her lower lip. "Maybe later. I'll let you know."

"You have my card, right?"

She patted her small purse. "Right here."

"All right, so I'll come up to New York next weekend for your performance—I'd love to see it. By then I should have some answers for you, and we can talk about everything again and decide what to do."

She let out a sigh of capitulation, but her eyes remained clouded with anxiety.

I reached for her small hand and gently squeezed it. "Please don't worry. You have three weeks before your visa is up. That's plenty of time for us to figure this out." I was starting to convince myself.

"And if we don't?"

"Let's take one thing at a time."

"Natalie, please. I need to know the truth. What if I can't stay legally?"

"First things first," I replied evenly, putting her off again. Her face fell in disappointment, but she seemed resigned.

After lunch at a little restaurant near the Capitol, we picked up her bag at her hotel and walked over to Union Station in time for her four o'clock departure. She was quiet as we stood side-by-side in the cavernous, echoing hall, in a thick press of travelers. When the loudspeaker announced that the New York train was boarding, and passengers began thronging toward the designated track, she turned to me and said quietly, "Please hurry. There's not much time."

"Don't worry. I'll see you soon."

We kissed three times on the cheek—left, right, left—as Russian women sometimes did, and she dashed off to join the jostling queue. I watched her disappear into the crowd of busy Americans, just as she hoped to do.

I turned away with troubled thoughts. No part of me wanted to break the law by harboring an illegal alien. But Saldana clearly had no intention of returning to Russia. She would be alone and vulnerable in New York City or wherever she chose to go. How could I justify not offering her help? But if I did decide to help her, it wouldn't be as simple and straightforward as she seemed to think. There would be many challenges that neither of us could foresee. It would be cruel to go only part of the way with her and then let her fall. I'd have to be willing to stand by her for as long as she needed me to.

I was in what seemed an impossible quandary. The best I could do was hope that I discovered a way to resolve it before I saw her again.

2

My mother was waiting in her wheelchair inside the glass doors of the Arborway Rehabilitation Center. She parked herself in that spot at ten a.m. every Sunday, her keen eyes scanning the parking lot. The instant she caught sight of me, she waved eagerly, looking like a disabled child about to be rescued from a dull week at boarding school. Multiple sclerosis had put her there—first in the rehab, then in the chair. For most people, the disease was capricious: it ebbed and flowed, responded to some treatments and not others, according to its mysterious whim. Vera March's MS was—so far—remarkably predictable. It didn't rush or lag, surprise or devastate—it just kept fulfilling its promises at a steady rate. First, numbness, weakness, muscle spasms; then deteriorating coordination and balance, followed by speech and vision problems, unstable mood, respiratory weakness, and so on.

She'd arrived at the center a year ago when difficulty swallowing made it dangerous for her to be alone. Medicare partly covered her private room; I made up the rest. She knew she probably wouldn't go home, and didn't fight it. My companionship—two hours every Sunday—was what she lived for now.

That, and the changing of the seasons. At the end of her life, Vera March had become a nature lover, had learned the flora and fauna of the bucolic Maryland suburb in which the center was located. There were binoculars on her windowsill through which she occasionally spied hawks. Sometimes deer grazed in the meadow outside her window. Sightings of fawns last spring had been a special delight.

I leaned down and kissed her cheek. "Morning, Mom."

"Sweetheart. So good to see you."

Heat was bad for multiple sclerosis patients—Uhthoff's phenomenon, medically unexplained—but nothing short of Armageddon could dissuade my mother from her weekly jaunt. I ducked into her room to put the flowers I'd brought in a vase of water, and to deposit my other gifts: Toblerone bars and a couple of new mysteries and thrillers. Then, recapturing a bit of the enterprising spirit we used to share in the old days, we ventured outside, where the heat hit us with force and the manicured grounds offered not a single shade-bearing tree.

A concrete walkway skirted the parking lot and looped back, a twenty-minute walk if we were slow. We stopped, as usual, at the point farthest from the rehab center, where there was a wooden bench next to a desiccated sapling tethered to a stake. I sat down and pulled the wheelchair close. We always discussed my life first, because talking about her world was too hard at the beginning of the visit. I had decided not to mention Katarina Melnikova until later. For now, I wanted it to be just the two of us, re-bonding after a week apart.

Cicadas droned in the hot, heavy air as we finished catching up. I stood and pushed the wheelchair again, stopping one more time at what Vera called "the garden," currently nothing more than a rectangle of scorched marigolds in dried clumps of dirt. A bead of perspiration rolled out of her hairline and meandered down the side of her pink, overheated face, and I was glad when she agreed to be wheeled back to the air-conditioned center.

The common room was furnished with couches and a piano no one played.

My mother always chose to conclude our visits there instead of her room because she preferred to be "out and about." We arranged ourselves in a corner for private conversation, though at the moment no one else was in the room.

"You'll never guess what happened," I began. "A young Russian woman named Saldana Tarasova came to my office. She said we're cousins."

"Really? How astonishing. I wonder who it could be. Your father had two siblings, so I suppose it's possible. But he didn't keep in touch. How on earth did she find you?"

"She wasn't from his side, Mom. She was from yours."

My mother frowned, trying to assemble the possibilities. Her mind was often foggy. "Let's see…on my mother's side, there was only Uncle Sergei, who didn't have children of his own. Maybe someone from my father's side? It's been so long, I can't remember."

"Well, this will come as a shock, Mom. But it turns out that your mother, Katarina Melnikova…"

Vera startled a bit at the sound of the name.

"…is alive and living in Siberia. In a little village on the Tatta River. Not that I know where that is." I paused to let the information sink in, took my mother's hand. "Apparently, Katarina survived the camps. Escaped, actually. She married and had a daughter, Lena Tarasova, and it was Lena's daughter, Saldana, who came to see me."

Vera's face had turned completely white. I pressed her hand—cold and limp—between my own. She gazed fixedly into the middle of the room, as if witnessing the bizarre spectacle of her mother's buried ghost struggling back to life. I started to say something, but she shook her head.

"I just need a moment," she whispered.

Across the room, there was a banquet table covered with snacks and water bottles and a plastic dispenser filled with watery lemonade. I brought back two cups of lemonade and handed one to her. She held the cup unsteadily. Before she could drop it, I gently took it away. In a few minutes, when she was more composed, I'd hold the cup to her lips so she could sip the drink.

Minutes ticked by. Footsteps and voices echoed from the hallway through the open door. A cart of metal lunch trays rolled past, pushed by a worker in green scrubs. I wondered, too late, whether telling her had been a terrible mistake.

"You did the right thing," she said, reaching out to touch my knee.

"Are you sure?"

"I always want to know the truth. I'm too old to be afraid of it."

I took her hand again, felt the weak pressure of her squeezing back.

"I love you, Mom."

She nodded, wobbled a smile. "Well, of all things to happen at my age…I never expected this."

"Saldana's in New York now, but I could probably arrange to have her visit, if you want."

She was still a bit dazed.

"We need to think a bit about what we want to do. It's perfectly okay to do nothing for now. Maybe just let all this sink in. You might decide to contact Katarina Melnikova eventually, maybe even meet her at some point. It's entirely up to you. If you want to get in touch, sooner might be better than later, as she's in her late eighties."

"She's eighty-nine," Vera answered. "I do the math every year on her birthday." She gave a girlish laugh. "Her birthday is in June. June fifth. I never told you that."

"Mom…"

"I used to dream about her—what color hair she had, what her voice sounded like. I knew she was probably dead, but that didn't make a difference. I kept believing we'd meet some day when I least expected it. That she would phone, or send me a letter, or simply walk up and sit down beside me and say, *Look, after everything, I'm here.* It's funny, but that dream never left me. I still carry it, right here." She tapped her chest with her fingertips. "When you were born, it was stronger than ever. I wanted so badly to share you with her."

"Mom, please..."

"I want to meet her, Natalie. It's all I've ever wanted."

"Are you sure?" A trip with her would be difficult, but not impossible, if it was carefully planned.

"I've never been surer of anything." Her eyes were shining with joy and hope.

With some alarm, I realized she had automatically assumed that Katarina Melnikova was reaching out to her in love. I knew the situation was more complicated than that: Saldana wasn't acting as Katarina's emissary; she'd had a far less exalted motive for making contact. Who knew what Katarina's place in all this really was?

I should have told my mother the truth right then and there, but the smile on her face was so beautiful, almost transcendent, that I couldn't bear to disappoint her. It was easy to imagine what this news meant to her. It probably felt as if her life had come full circle, in a sort of muted triumph, as if a small part of everything she'd so painfully lost—her parents, her past, her own identity—was being magically restored.

"I'll talk to Saldana and see if it can be arranged," I said, smiling despite my misgivings. "I trust that Katarina and your half-sister, Lena, will want to meet us; at least I hope they will."

"Not *us*," she said. "*You*."

"Me? You just said—"

"Oh, for goodness sake. I can't go. You see me sitting in this chair, don't you?"

"That's not a problem, Mom. The airlines make allowances for wheelchairs."

"Please. Let's not kid ourselves. I can't travel anymore. Lately—I wasn't going to mention this—lately I'm incontinent."

I balked at this latest indignity, but managed to keep my expression smooth. "We could bring a health worker along."

"Out of the question. It would be humiliating for me. It's bad enough that I have to have my bottom scrubbed, that some days I can't hold a spoon. The last thing I want is for my mother to see me like this." She pressed my hand between hers. "I want her to meet *you* instead. You're strong and healthy; you're the best thing I've ever done."

"Mom. What would be the point? You're the one who wants to meet her."

"I can't go, Natalie. How often do I have to say it?"

I sighed. Vera was unbending when she wanted to be, and in this case, she was probably right. She was far too proud to play the role of invalid publicly. And there was no telling what travel and accommodations were like in northeastern Siberia. Probably not superhighways and Holiday Inns. But the thought of going by myself cast the trip in an entirely different light, and cut my enthusiasm down by half. I was suddenly conscious of my packed work schedule and an upcoming medical conference I'd pledged to attend.

"You should contact them right away," Vera was insisting. "If there's any possibility you can go, I want you to take it. It's rather miraculous, when you think about it. All those years." Her eyes shone with happy excitement. "Take a lot of pictures, will you? You can bring pictures of me, too. But not the way I am now—when I was younger. My wedding picture perhaps. And write down everything that happens, everything she says. Take a tape recorder—that's a good idea. I want to know every last detail when you come back." She smiled broadly, imagining her dream coming true.

"I don't know, Mom. It might be hard for me to get away from work. Maybe we can arrange for them to come here."

"No excuses, Natalie. This is for me, okay?"

"But my patients…"

"No, no, no!" she cut me off with sudden anger. "Your patients *don't* need you. They need a doctor, but it doesn't have to be *you*. It's time you got off your treadmill, Natalie. Your career has been entirely too important to you— too demanding, too consuming. It's not healthy for you, and never was. You're almost forty years old, for god's sake. You've reached your goal; there's nowhere higher to climb. How much success does one person need?"

I felt frozen in place, shot through with little needles of emotional pain. I'd always known that my mother thought I worked too hard, but she usually wasn't so blunt. And it hurt that she assumed I worked only for success. That wasn't my motivation at all, at least not entirely.

"Now's the time to stop and look around," she went on, the pent-up words tumbling out. "Ask yourself what kind of life you really want. I swear, if you don't adjust your course soon, while there's still time, you'll never be truly happy. Not happy the way you deserve to be."

"While there's still time?" I repeated accusingly. I knew full well what she was referring to, but I wanted to make her say it directly, instead of packing it into a sly little clause.

"While there's still time to start a family," she said baldly, looking me in the eye.

"I'm not even married," I said, trying to diffuse the tension with a droll tone.

"You don't need to be, not anymore. One of my friends said her daughter ordered sperm from a catalog."

"Mom, stop!"

A few moments of charged silence passed. I could tell she wanted to go on, now that the third-rail subject of my childlessness had been broached, but she held back and eventually managed to find a soft look for me. "It all goes by so fast, sweetheart. You'll be where I am sooner than you think. I want you to take this trip, okay? Not just because it will mean a lot to me, but because it will mean something to you, too. You'll get away, far away—do you even remember the last time you got away?—and when you come back, you'll have a perspective you don't have now. You need that so you can move forward in your life. In a new way, if that's what you decide you want. Trust me, darling. This trip will be good for *both* of us."

I felt a little betrayed, like my usually supportive mother had seen an opportunity to air a hidden grievance at last, and had kicked the door wide open, guns out and blazing. Especially galling was the way she'd managed to tie our emotional needs together in one big Siberian bow.

"I can't promise anything right now," I said woodenly. "First, I need to talk to Saldana to find out if this trip is even possible, and then I have to check my schedule to see when I might be free."

"Call her right away, darling. Katarina Melnikova is no spring chicken, and there's not much time left for me either, as you know."

· ·   ·   ·   ·   ·   ·   ·   ·   ·   ·

That afternoon, I retreated to my couch with a glass of iced tea and my laptop, and started searching the internet for immigration lawyers who could advise Saldana. I ended up nodding off, and was jolted awake at around four o'clock when a shrill noise erupted from one of my devices. I sat straight up, like a suddenly activated robot, and swung my legs over the side of the couch. If there had been army boots on the floor, I would have slipped my feet into them and marched in whatever direction the hospital lay, through a wall if need be. I was entirely capable of issuing orders while half asleep—such were the fruits of medical training. But this time it wasn't my pitiless beeper with breaking news of a patient in distress. It was the jangling cell phone on the coffee table.

The caller identified himself as Detective Carl Ruggeri, New York City Police Department. His voice was thick and sweet, like sugared porridge.

Doesn't sound like a cop, I thought immediately, and tartly demanded proof of his identity.

Ignoring my request, he asked if I knew a woman by the name of Saldana Tarasova.

"Why? Is she under arrest?" I couldn't imagine what illegal activity a girl like Saldana could possibly be involved in.

No, that wasn't the reason for his call. My business card had been found in Ms. Tarasova's purse. What exactly was my connection to Ms. Tarasova?

I admitted to being her cousin, the little-used word feeling clumsy on my lips. The fog of sleep was dispersing. Something bad had happened. I reached for the glass of iced tea on the table, changed my mind.

"Are you the closest family member in this country?"

"I believe so. She was visiting from Russia."

Detective Ruggeri regretted to inform me that Ms. Tarasova had been the victim of a homicide.

"What?" I said, though I'd heard him perfectly well.

He repeated it. *Victim of homicide.*

I sent a stream of gibberish into the phone: *No, that can't be. I just saw her. You have the wrong person*, and so on. Hastily building a wall of denial that just as hastily crumbled.

He waited patiently for my reactions to subside before asking if I would come to New York to identify the body. Barely pausing for my answer, he gave me the address and hours of operation of the city morgue—closed Sundays, open nine a.m. to five p.m. Mondays through Saturdays. He instructed me on such particulars as which door to enter and whom to ask for. I rifled for pen and scrap paper, copied everything down in crabbed, spiky handwriting I could barely read afterward. He said I should proceed to the police department for an interview with him directly afterward, and provided his phone number, which I was asked to call shortly before my arrival there. His mellow, slow-measured tone was sickening, as it indicated how many times he'd recited the litany before.

I ended the call feeling as if the floor had dropped from under me. Through eyes made glassy by tears, I saw Saldana sitting across from me in her yellow dress, her glossy braid falling over one perfect shoulder. There was gentle sympathy in her eyes, as if I were the injured party. I almost spoke to her. *How can you possibly be dead?* But the vision gently dissolved, leaving a coldness, an emptiness, in the air. An absence. A desperate wail started in my chest. I wanted her to come back.

My next reaction was horrified guilt: I'd let her down. She'd thrown herself on my mercy, pleaded for help. She'd been alone in this country—alone and scared—barely speaking English, forced to run away from home, from a nameless threat powerful enough to rip her from her mother's arms. And what had I done? Scolded her, kept her at arm's length, allowed her to return to New York with nothing but a hazy, half-assed plan to make some phone calls and meet again in a week's time. If only I'd listened with empathy instead of a legalistic mind, I might have heard her desperation, truly fathomed the dangerous and terrifying position she was in, and taken immediate action to keep her safe. If only I could do it over again.

I'd been trained to deal with crises: the greater the stress I was under, the cooler my head became. So I didn't give in to my feelings right away. I had to function, perform necessary tasks. I phoned my office manager at home and told her to cancel my Monday appointments. *A personal day*, I said, because I couldn't explain something that I didn't believe yet myself. Then I opened my laptop to check the Washington-New York shuttle schedule—a flight departed from Reagan every hour—and booked a 6 a.m. departure. That way, I'd beat the worst of the rush-hour traffic and be at the morgue when it opened. I marched into the bedroom and selected the clothes I'd wear the next day: a linen sheath with a light sweater and flats. I packed my large leather tote with Advil, an extra set of glasses, and my phone charger, and slipped in a few unread medical journals as well.

Frantically, I cast about for other little jobs I might perform. I emptied the dishwasher, watered the African violet on the windowsill, put on a load of wash. And when there wasn't one more task to do, not one more distraction to be found, I sat on the edge of my bed and wept.

Detective Ruggeri looked like a Renaissance cherub who'd expanded gigantically, shed its wings, and sprouted facial hair. He had a large head covered in thick black curls, and oversized features with thick, curvaceous lips. Loose abdominal fat interfered with the fit of his pants. He was seated across from me at a metal table in a drab interview room, stroking his chin with the darkly distracted air of someone whose mind was pursuing several hopeless ideas at once.

"Shame," he murmured, eyes at a lazy slant. "Nice Russian girl. Ballet dancer."

If he was worried I'd be uncooperative, he needn't have been. I was eager to talk. I'd just come from identifying Saldana's body, and there was a scream in my chest that decorum prevented me from releasing.

Saldana's throat had been slit—an expert cut through the trachea, vocal chords, and esophagus. One perfect slice all the way back to the spinal vertebrae. There would have been searing pain followed by shock and unconsciousness. It would have been over quickly. Which was better, I supposed, for her. But not really. There was no *better* here.

"She came to my office Friday evening, said we were related through a grandmother I thought was dead," I told the detective.

"You must have been surprised."

"Very much so."

"Any proof of the relation?"

"She knew my grandmother's name."

He raised one bushy eyebrow and held it aloft long enough for me to take its meaning. Maybe he was right: maybe Saldana Tarasova *was* a con artist who'd found an easy mark in conscientious Dr. March. But I didn't believe that for a second.

"Saldana was for real," I said.

He nodded reluctantly, as if willing to grant me a minor delusion or two. "Okay…so the long-lost cousin shows up out of the blue. Why? You think she just wanted to meet you after all this time?"

"Of course not. She wanted my help to defect."

Somewhere in the pouchy eyes, a gleam was born. "Yeah. Now that makes sense. What'd you tell her?"

"I said it was a bad idea."

"Smart. I would have said the same." His tilted smile leaked wry amusement. "*Then* what'd you say?"

"That I needed time to think about it."

He chuckled. "Of course you did. Young woman—all alone, scared. I probably would have said that, too." He paused: a different idea had got hold of him. "You want a coffee?"

"No, thanks."

"Not a coffee drinker, huh?"

Why is he wasting time? Sharply, I said, "I am, actually. But I just identified a young woman's murdered body, so I'd rather skip the refreshments, if you don't mind."

"Don't mind at all," he said, ignoring my tone. "By the way, what'd you think of the body?"

His manner was so flippant that I felt like slapping him. Glaring, I said, "I can tell you that she was attacked from behind by someone who knew how to apply tremendous force at exactly the right place. The windpipe is not exactly easy to sever."

"Really? How do you know?"

"I'm a surgeon. I cut into bodies for a living."

His eyebrows went up and down in a short-lived bushy flight. "Always nice to have an expert on board." But his tone was more annoyed than grateful.

Maybe he saw me as just another clueless civilian playing the game of sleuth. "Any other observations while we're at it, Doc?" He wanted me to get my investigative aspirations out of my system fast.

"The weapon was a wire garrote, not a knife. A knife serrates the skin; a garrote compresses it. There's less blood flow because the vessels are squeezed shut."

"Interesting," he dead-panned.

"It would have been a silent death," I continued. "Gurgling, maybe; some kicking. But that's all. And over pretty fast."

Ruggeri leaned back, linked his hands behind his head, and stared at me a few beats too long. Skeptical, but curious. "Okay, Doc. You want to solve a puzzle? Try this one: computer and cell phone missing, passport and some cash in a drawer, purse with her wallet and your card still in it on the floor. No rape, no signs of struggle. What do you make of that?"

"How do you know what he took?"

"From two charging cords on the desk, both plugged in. Why did you assume it was a man?"

"Habit, I guess. And the fact that the murderer would have needed physical strength to make that cut."

"Are you saying a woman couldn't have done it?"

"No. A woman could have done it, too," I admitted. A dim memory started to stir but quickly settled back into the dark, untraveled recesses of my mind.

Ruggeri grinned and brought his chair upright, leaning forward in a fluid motion until his elbows landed on the scratched surface of the metal table, and his face was only a few feet from my own. "I've been in this business a long time, and there's one thing I've learned. One thing I can always rely on. People tell you who they are. They can't help it. They're telling you all the time. You just have to listen."

"Where is this going, Detective?"

"What I'm saying is, I like you. You stick to the facts, you get pissed off if someone changes the subject, and you can admit a mistake. You know how rare a person like you is? These days, most people don't care about facts. You tell them something true they don't like, and they just argue like arguing will change it. I don't even bother talking to people like that. With you, a conversation is possible."

I said, "I'm glad I passed your smell test, Detective. But so far you haven't passed mine. How do you intend to find my cousin's killer?"

He laughed a little. "Right you are, Doc. Time for business. So, off the top of my head, I'd say we're looking at an interrupted burglary. She entered the hotel room and caught the guy in the act; he panicked, strangled her, grabbed the computer and phone, and ran away without finding the cash."

"Would a common thief use a wire garrote?"

Ruggeri tried to grin, but it was more of a disturbed leer. "You want to know some of the weapons I've seen used to murder people in my career?"

"Ah…no thanks."

"By the way, where were you Saturday night?"

"You can't be serious."

"I'm always serious," he said with a small, incongruous smile.

I shook my head at the stupidity of it. "I was in Washington, D.C. I went home after I left Saldana at Union Station and didn't go out again. My doorman saw me come in."

He pulled a small spiral-bound notebook out of his pocket and slid it across the table to me along with a cheap plastic pen. "I need your address and the doorman's name."

"I can give you his direct line if you want." I had the number stored in my phone.

"Even better."

As I jotted down the information, my fingers started to tremble like they never did in the operating room. I'd seen television shows where the wrong person was accused—surely that couldn't happen to me. But that's what every wrongly accused person believed at first, wasn't it?

"You're wasting your time," I said, pushing the notebook back to him.

"Procedure," he said smoothly as the tattered little book disappeared into his pocket. If he really was the expert he claimed to be, he'd probably noticed my involuntary swallowing and the dilation of my pupils.

"There's another piece to this whole thing, a pretty important one," I said, trying to regain my footing. "My cousin came to this country against her will; her mother pushed her into it. Told her that she and Saldana's brother would be joining her in America before too long. But Saldana didn't believe it. She was convinced her mother was getting her out of Russia because of some trouble her brother was in."

"What kind of trouble?"

"She didn't know. He'd gone AWOL, apparently."

Ruggeri shrugged. "So what are you suggesting?"

"Only that a burglary gone bad isn't the only possible explanation. She felt strongly that something bad was happening at home. Maybe she was right, only whatever it was, was far worse than she imagined. Maybe someone followed her from Russia and—"

"Assassinated her?" His eyes rolled.

"It's possible." I paused. "Isn't it?"

"Damn those Russkies. Always with the espionage."

"Please stop with the stereotypes, Detective. My parents were Russian immigrants, and I'm a little too familiar with the usual slurs."

"Okay. I apologize. And I won't rule out your theory. But without more information, there's not much I can do. By the way, did you mention this possibility to anyone else?"

"You're the first."

"You ought to keep it that way."

"Why?"

"It's a sticky situation, isn't it?" he said, wagging his shaggy head. "Folks from the Russian Consulate will be showing up here any minute asking for a report. They're good people—I got nothing against them personally—but they're not what we would call transparent. No way of knowing how they'd react to your information that the victim was planning to defect, that the mom back home was behind the plot, and was planning to do the same, with the brother in tow. I sure don't like hiding relevant facts, but it'd be a shame if the folks back home got in trouble. Lots of unanswered questions here. Know what I mean?"

I clamped my mouth shut. I definitely didn't want to make anything worse for Saldana's family.

"You ever been to Russia?" Ruggeri asked benignly, our little collusion already swept away.

"No."

"Really? Never wanted to visit the homeland, and all that?"

"My parents fled that country. I don't have a good feeling about it. But now that I know I have family there, I may decide to visit after all."

"Better hurry, before Putin shuts the whole place down," he said without noticeable concern. He glanced at his watch and gave a big sigh. "Thanks for coming all the way from D.C. on short notice, Dr. March. If I have any more questions, I'll be in touch."

"Who notifies the family?"

"When a foreign national dies on US soil, their country's consulate takes care of that. Of course, there's nothing to stop you from contacting them as well."

"What about the body?"

"We keep it for autopsy, then it goes to the consulate and they follow their procedures."

He stood up heavily—there was some arthritic stiffness in his joints—but I made no move to join him. It couldn't be right to just walk away, leaving Saldana's corpse on a slab in the morgue, awaiting the grisly hack job known as autopsy.

"What happens now? How are we going to find the killer?"

"*We?*" he repeated.

"You," I amended.

His hands disappeared into the pockets of his jacket. "I'll keep you posted."

"Will you? Really? Because I'd like to stay informed."

A business card was produced and set in front of me with a snap of authority. "Call whenever you want. Just remember, these things take time."

I had to play a frantic game of catch-up the next day—dashing over to the hospital for bedside visits, squeezing disgruntled patients whose appointments had been cancelled the day before into already tight office hours. I was in full-on work mode, which meant that lunch was a cup of Dannon yogurt and a Keurig coffee at my desk, and my personal feelings, including my feelings about my murdered cousin, were, of necessity, swept aside.

Mid-afternoon, I dialed Ruggeri's direct number during a break between patients, got no answer, and left a voicemail. I knew I was pushing it: how much could he have accomplished in the twenty-four hours since we'd talked? Hadn't he said, *These things take time?* But time was a luxury we didn't have, because with every passing minute, Saldana's killer was getting further away. *Getting away with it.* That could not be allowed to happen. I churned with rage just to think of it.

My next call—to the Russian Consulate in New York City—was answered by a thickly accented receptionist. Identifying myself as Saldana Tarasova's cousin, I asked whether the Tarasov family had been notified of her death. I planned to contact the Tarasovs personally, I said, but not until they'd heard the news through official channels.

My call was transferred to an office inside the consulate, and after explaining myself a second time, I was put on hold. A stirring Russian folk song thundered on speakerphone for many minutes until the call was either automatically or purposefully disconnected. I redialed immediately, and this time got a long automated menu. When the recorded message ended, I pressed zero to speak to an operator, got dumped into voicemail, and requested a callback. I knew enough about Russian bureaucracy that I didn't actually expect to hear from them, and I wasn't wrong.

That evening, at my condo on the fourteenth floor of a downtown apartment building, I poured a glass of pinot noir and leaned wearily against the frame of the sliding glass door that opened onto my small balcony. The heavy clouds that had been amassing all day opened up as I stood watching, and a drenching rain began to fall. The potted geraniums soaked it up, their reds and pinks turning vivid in the watery gray light. Washington Monument, where I'd walked with Saldana just three days ago, was a tall shadow in the distance.

An image of Saldana's remains laid out on the stainless steel bed took shape against this dismal backdrop. Her skin waxy, drained of blood; her lips pale, nearly white; yet her beautiful hair still richly black, still with a silky shine. The cut across her neck drew and riveted my appalled attention. I'd sliced into living flesh with sharp knives many times, and had forgotten the wounds almost immediately, because they were merely the entrance into the body, no more important than a door was to a house. The murderer's cut was different—brutal, aggressive. It had been opened to let blood drain away, to let life escape. It went against everything I stood for, everything I believed. It made every cell in my body revolt.

Why hadn't I taken my vulnerable young cousin at her word, opened my door and my heart immediately, willingly provided the safe haven she'd clearly needed? Why, instead, had I hastily erected a wall of cold words and colder procedures to separate us? What was wrong with me?

I chugged the rest of the pinot noir, went into the kitchen, poured another big glass, and rifled clumsily through a stack of take-out menus by the phone.

Sometimes it's better not to think too much. Decided on Thai. Again. I was about to dial the restaurant when the intercom buzzed. It was the doorman, calling to say that I had visitors—two men who'd given their names as Jason Zelnick and Mark O'Mara. The names meant nothing to me, so I told the doorman not to send the men up: I'd take the elevator down to meet them instead.

The lobby was spacious and glassy, decorated with sleek modernist furniture and inoffensive abstract paintings in neutral tones. Two clean-shaven men were seated next to each other on one of the smooth leather couches, not talking, not thumbing phones. They wore jackets and ties, and couldn't have been more than thirty. Collapsed umbrellas dripped on the floor next to their polished leather shoes.

My stomach soured a little. Ever since Detective Ruggeri had asked for my alibi, the spectre of becoming a suspect in the investigation had been hovering over me. I'd told Ruggeri that the doorman had seen me entering the building that evening, but, in fact, there was a good chance he hadn't, as I'd hurried past the reception desk to catch a waiting elevator, and couldn't remember if I said hello to him. An alibi wasn't an alibi if there was no corroborating witness, and I hadn't seen or talked to anyone else that night.

The men rose to greet me, introduced themselves in subdued voices, and showed me badges. CIA. A chill went through me. Not for my own sake this time, but for Saldana's family's. Was the idea of a Russian plot not so far-fetched after all?

I invited the agents up, figuring I had no choice. They remained silent in the elevator, flanking me in a way that made me tense. I wondered if they were carrying guns. I ushered them into my living room, where the glass door was still open. The rain was pounding the concrete balcony, and the sheer curtains billowed in gusts of fresh damp air. I switched on a couple of lamps and offered the men coffee, which they politely refused. They'd taken seats next to each other on the couch, both leaning forward, elbows planted on knees, presumably unwilling to let soft cushions distract them from their important business.

"What's this about?" I asked, taking a seat on the other side of the coffee table.

"We understand that you met with a Russian national a few days ago," O'Mara said. His cheeks were rosy and his blue eyes were calm. He had a large square head that sat bluntly on his shoulders like a boulder at rest in its appointed place.

"You mean my cousin, Saldana Tarasova, who was murdered Saturday night."

"That's correct, ma'am. We'd like to ask a few questions about your relationship with Ms. Tarasova and what transpired during your meetings with her on Friday, July twenty-second, and Saturday the twenty-third."

"You must have spoken to Detective Ruggeri of the NYPD."

"If you'd just answer the question, ma'am."

"I'd be happy to. But first, what's this about?"

Zelnick broke in. "Perhaps you could start by telling us when you and Ms. Tarasova first met." His voice was deeper than O'Mara's. His eyes were hooded, hard to read. One of his shoulders dipped a little; it was almost a slouch.

"Friday night," I said.

"You mean to say that you had no contact with her before that time?"

"None whatsoever. She showed up at my office sometime Friday and waited hours to see me. I met with her at around six p.m. I'd never seen her before. I didn't even know she existed." I sounded defensive, I realized. I took a deep breath and tried to relax.

"Why don't you walk us through that evening," O'Mara suggested mildly.

"Well, she came to my office Friday, as I said." And just as I'd done the day before, I spilled everything I knew.

"She was scared," I concluded. "But she couldn't say why. She sensed something was wrong, and was terrified she'd never see her family again."

I paused. O'Mara had been scribbling notes as I talked, while Zelnick had kept his hawkish eyes trained on my face. His unwavering gaze was starting to unnerve me; without thinking, I flashed him a hostile look.

"You didn't know anything about this Russian family until Friday night? Never heard of them before?" he said, making it sound ridiculous.

"Correct."

Zelnick and O'Mara exchanged a glance.

I said, "Look, can I ask what this is about?"

O'Mara piped up. "This is a routine procedure, Dr. March. When a foreign national dies in suspicious circumstances on American soil, we usually write a report."

"Wouldn't it be the FBI who did that?"

"In these kinds of cases, our jurisdictions often overlap," he replied.

"These kinds of cases? What does that mean?"

Zelnick cut in, "Dr. March. We appreciate how cooperative you're being. We have a few more questions, and then we'll leave you alone. Did Ms. Tarasova give you anything? A package or envelope?"

"No."

"Did she allude to any sensitive information she had, information that others might want?"

"No."

"Did she say anything about the Russian government?"

"We didn't discuss politics."

"Is there anything you want to add about your conversation with Ms. Tarasova? Anything that seemed strange or unusual to you?"

This is what they always say. A routine script.

I said, "No, I have nothing to add. But I do have some questions of my own, if you don't mind. The NYPD detective thought my cousin's death was probably an interrupted burglary. I know I'm not a specialist in this area, but a couple of details don't make sense to me. The murder weapon, for example, and the way it was used. How many petty thieves carry wire garrotes and know how to kill with them so efficiently? Why was her computer stolen, but not her money or jewelry? And what about the fact that she was planning to defect?"

I expected O'Mara and Zelnick to react somehow, if only to share a glance or jot a note, but they kept their eyes trained on me impassively, their expressions perfectly neutral.

Zelnick finally said in a humoring tone, "What specifically is your question?"

"I'm asking if it could have been an assassination. By the Russian government. Or someone."

"We have no reason to suspect that, Dr. March," O'Mara said placidly.

"If you did, would you tell me?" *Stupid question. Of course they wouldn't.*

Neither one replied.

"Okay, guys. I get it. But be straight with me for a minute. My mother wants me to go to Russia to meet these new members of our family. She's sick and dying and I'm inclined to humor her. Should I be worried? Is there any reason I shouldn't go?"

O'Mara gave a wide smile, happy to have good news to share. "No, ma'am. As I said before, this is just a routine inquiry. Feel free to go about your business as usual."

I looked to Zelnick, who seemed to be the one in charge. "And you agree?"

He nodded curtly. "You're fine to travel. If something changes, we'll let you know."

He stood up, and O'Mara closed his notebook.

I showed them to the door, took their raincoats out of the hall closet. "If there's anything I can do to help…"

After shrugging on his belted trench coat, Zelnick reached into his pocket and handed me a business card. "If you remember some detail later on, you can reach me at this number."

They took their umbrellas and walked down the carpeted hallway to the elevator.

I closed the door, affixed the chain, and went out on the balcony. The rain had let up; drops were plopping intermittently on my railing from the balcony above. The sky was a turbulent dark gray, the lights of the city lending a faint orange glow to the cloud cover.

Zelnick and O'Mara emerged from under the awning over the front entrance and walked in lock-step along the discreetly lighted walkway to the street. They crossed the street and turned right. Parking was horrendous in this area, and I wondered where they'd left their car. Or had they taken the metro from their CIA office, wherever that was?

I glanced at the business card I was still holding. It showed only Zelnick's name and phone number, no CIA insignia. It occurred to me that I actually knew nothing about the two men who'd just been in my apartment. They could have been anybody: their quickly flashed badges could easily have been fakes.

Careful. Your imagination is running away with you.

Nevertheless, a part of me was tempted to run down and follow Zelnick and O'Mara through the foggy streets, just to see where they went. Luckily, the saner part of me realized that spying on spies was bound to be folly. I was simply overwrought from the whole affair. I slid the door closed against the damp night and went back to ordering Thai.

I called Ruggeri again the next day. Patients were backed up in the waiting room, but they could wait.

To my relief, he picked up the call, and launched into a progress report. Interviews with the small number of people who'd known Saldana in New York hadn't turned up any promising leads, and the crime scene hadn't yielded much information either. When I pressed him to share the autopsy and forensic results, he bluntly informed me that my expertise was not required. The NYPD had a well-trained staff of experts and was perfectly capable of handling homicide investigations on its own.

"By the way, did you talk to the CIA about this case?" I asked.

"I passed on your concerns to them as a matter of course."

I was relieved: my suspicions about Zelnick and O'Mara could be put to bed.

"Take my advice and go on with your life, Dr. March," Ruggeri counseled. "I know that can be hard for people who are used to being in charge. But there's really nothing more you can do."

"Will you be sure to call if there are any developments?"

"I absolutely will," he said in a tone of finality.

Too much finality, I thought.

I decided to try the Russian Consulate in New York City one more time. I was put on hold, transferred to another department, and another, and another, each time repeating my simple request. Had Ms. Tarasova's family been notified of her death? The bureaucrats seemed to find my inquiry both bizarre and nonsensical. At no point did anyone admit that they even knew who Ms. Tarasova was. Maybe they were seeking to avoid international legal wranglings, or maybe they considered the incident to be dirty national laundry best kept to themselves. Maybe they just didn't care, maybe they were covering up, or maybe a gag order had been issued from above. Or maybe they truly had no clue what I was talking about. The possible reasons for their apparently colossal stupidity were endless. But one thing was certain: a lone American citizen was not about to penetrate the consulate's thick defenses. Eventually, I was instructed to submit my concerns in writing to the Office of the Deputy of Public Affairs at the Kremlin, and that was the end of the goose chase for me. I expected to get answers from Putin's Kremlin about as much as I expected to ride a unicorn to Narnia.

There was nothing left to do but contact Saldana's mother directly, trusting that the consulate had done its job. At first, I was stymied because I didn't have her number. Then it dawned on me that I could Google NYC dance companies until I found one presently hosting a visiting Russian artist. This eventually brought me to the Marcus Glasson Dance Company, where the artistic director, badly shaken by what had befallen his guest artist, was more than willing to cooperate. He said he'd spoken to Saldana's mother the day before: she had indeed been informed of the murder, though he couldn't say by whom. As her English was rudimentary, and his Russian was nonexistent, their conversation had been short. Nevertheless, he found her to be remarkably calm, under the circumstances. He gave me her number, and the next morning at 6 a.m.—7 p.m. Russia time—I took a deep breath and made the call.

The initial reactions of parents who lost children ran the gamut from unrelenting hysteria to catatonic depression. There was no way to predict how any individual would respond. Lena Tarasova seemed to fall squarely in the middle of the spectrum. She was simply sorrowful, which was, I thought, the most painful place to be. She knew who I was right away and accepted my condolences graciously. I talked about the day I'd spent with her daughter, how much I'd enjoyed her company. Opening up a bit, she described Saldana's kindness, her remarkable talent in dance, how hard she always worked, and how much she loved her family and friends.

Then the conversation took an unexpected turn. Apparently, the Russian Consulate had given Lena hardly any information about the homicide. She'd called the NYPD, but her English wasn't good enough for her to understand what she was told. Could I provide her with the details?

I gently shared what I knew, conscious of how upsetting some of the facts might be. She listened without interruption, then pressed me to elaborate on certain aspects of the crime: Was I sure Saldana was garroted? How did I know? Was the murderer in the room when Saldana entered, or had she been followed there? Had the door been jimmied open, or had the murderer somehow interfered with the electronic lock? Which items were stolen, and what was left behind? Were any other rooms in the hotel burglarized that night?

The questioning was so thorough and specific that I felt like I was being professionally debriefed. I couldn't help wondering whether Lena had the same suspicions I did.

I decided to venture in. "The police are treating it as an interrupted burglary, but they can't be sure. Some details do seem unusual."

After a long pause, she said, "What do you mean?"

What should I say? *Is there any chance your daughter was assassinated by your government?* I settled on, "Saldana told me about her plan to stay in America after her visa expired."

"I don't know what you're talking about. There was no such plan," Lena said.

So that's how it was. My aunt was going to keep her secrets, and I supposed I had to honor that.

I said, "I just want you to know that…I wish I'd done more to help. I mean, right away—the day we met. Instead of putting her off." It was embarrassing to hear myself babbling my guilt. Was I looking for absolution from this bereaved mother? Was that fair?

"You couldn't have known what would happen," she said in a gentler tone.

"It was brave of her to come. I was surprised to meet her, of course. It was, well…astonishing to find out about you and your son and…your mother." A flush crept up my face. The fact that they hadn't contacted us until they'd needed our help still rankled a bit. I had no idea whether they wanted a relationship with us at all. And now, with Saldana gone, the situation was even more complex. Nevertheless, I blundered on.

"Saldana said that your mother, Katarina Melnikova, is still alive. My mother—her name's Vera, by the way—was so surprised and happy to hear that. It meant a lot to her. To me, too."

When Lena didn't answer right away, I figured the conversation, and any chances of a relationship, were about to end.

But I was wrong. When she finally answered, there was a smile in her voice. "You really ought to meet her. And Mikhail, too. We call him Misha."

"Misha," I repeated. "That's a nice name."

"He's a nice boy. Though he's nineteen now, so I should probably stop calling him a boy."

Given the way my previous probing questions had gone, I decided not to mention that Saldana had been worried about him.

Lena said, "I was meaning to ask you this after Saldana had settled in a bit. But I suppose I might as well ask you now. Would you and your mother consider visiting? I know it's a long trip."

"That's very kind. Actually, we talked about it already. My mother would like nothing better, but she can't make it, I'm afraid. She has multiple sclerosis and is confined to a wheelchair."

"Oh, I'm sorry to hear that."

"But I could come," I heard myself saying.

"That would be very nice. It would be good to meet you. Especially now. Saldana's death…" My aunt's voice grew thick with emotion. "I want something good to come from it. If that's possible. It's the only way I can—" The words caught raggedly in her throat. "Saldana would want it, too…for something good to come of…this."

"I think she would," I said softly.

"Let's talk again soon," Lena said, her voice husky with grief. We exchanged information, and she promised to call in a couple of days.

Her word was good. She phoned that weekend and proposed a two-week trip. The plan was for me to spend some time in Yakutsk with her. Misha, she said, would join us there. Then she and I would travel out to the country so I could meet Katarina Melnikova.

I firmly stifled all the usual concerns about my patients that had prevented me from taking vacations of more than a few days in the past. Life was short and precious, and opportunities like this usually came but once. Saldana's death had put that much in perspective for me at least. If I'd needed any more motivation, there was always Vera. She talked about nothing else. When I finally confessed what had happened to Saldana, the shocking news only strengthened her commitment to reach out to her Russian family through me.

It took a couple of weeks to settle the details. Lena and I talked on the phone a few more times and exchanged emails. There was a passport to renew, a tourist visa to be granted, and coverage at the hospital to be arranged. As luck would have it, Joel agreed to take most of my patients, an act of generosity that I found bittersweet.

I flew from Washington D.C. to Moscow's Domodedovo Airport—a loud, dirty, and confusing place. Taxi drivers accosted me as I made my way through the terminal; pamphlets were shoved in my face. Clumps of people moved about in surges that seemed to have no direction or destination, like schools of fish. As I had a six-hour layover before my flight to Yakutsk, I thought I might have lunch, then find a quiet place to dip into the novel I brought. But the few cafes were crowded, and I didn't see an open seat in any of the gates I passed. Finally, I found one in an odd balcony area overlooking a roiling sea of heads. I tried to read, but my concentration was broken every two minutes by a woman's heavy voice loudly announcing departing flights and gate numbers. The voice seemed quintessentially Russian, a blend of brash indifference and jaded carelessness—a far cry from the sing-song, saccharine tone of corporate reassurance that I was used to hearing in American airports.

I felt a bit anxious as I sat there, unavoidably eavesdropping on the conversations happening all around me. I had always felt a deep connection to Russia, if only because of my parents and my ability to speak the language. But what did I really know about the land of my forebearers? Just the usual stuff Westerners learned: Russia as Cold War adversary, as present-day bad actor, as a sham democracy barreling toward outright dictatorship. Mixed in with that, a hodge-podge of random images gleaned from novels, history books, and the media: the Romanovs, Rasputin, the pogroms, Doctor Zhivago, the bombs in Chechnya, the oligarch Khodarkovsky, oil pipelines, Matryoshka dolls, endless silvery green forests, and Putin's pale-faced scowl. It was alarming, really, the paucity of my knowledge. My brain had been little more than a lint catcher.

By the time I was finally seated on the Siberian Airlines jet to Yakutsk, I was clumsy and dull-witted from fatigue and a quiet unease. It seemed the day had ended hours before, leaving behind a strange pointless trailing in which I was caught. The plane was flying against the planet's rotation, and it felt like going back in time. When the drinks cart came, I ordered two shots of vodka, and finally, at thirty-thousand feet somewhere over the Urals, I fell into a twilight sleep. The rumbling of the jet engine became the shuddering of the earth as in my dream masses of people, massive plodding armies, churned and grated west to east across the steppes like a human tectonic plate, accompanied by the rhythmic *clack-clack-clack* of train after train speeding along the newly laid iron tracks of the Trans-Siberian railroad, people crammed inside the filthy cars so densely that they didn't lean in the turns—all betrayed, disowned, rendered useless to themselves and others, barreling toward the frozen catch-basin of Siberia, toward unimaginable suffering and near-certain death. The horror startled me awake, and I felt something in my psyche shift. I understood more deeply what I'd known only superficially before: that my grandparents had been among those nameless masses, two real people caught and swept away like specks of dust in a thundering maelstrom. I couldn't imagine what they'd felt, and didn't want to try. But it seemed important to me suddenly—

crucial, even—to find out from Katarina Melnikova when I met her exactly how she had managed to escape.

3

Night was dissolving, stars winking out in a violet wash of dawn. With a couple of dozen other passengers, I stumbled sleepily across the tarmac toward a one-story building made of cheap concrete. The air was cool and mild; it smelled of mud and something sweet. Inside the terminal, a group of people with dark, Asiatic faces stood patiently behind a flimsy rope, peering eagerly around and behind me, breaking into wide, occasionally gap-toothed smiles when they caught sight of whomever they were waiting for.

I scanned the terminal, looking for Lena. It was the kind of place you could take in at a glance: one gate, one baggage carousel, one ticket counter, and a couple of soda and snack machines. Two police officers in black uniforms stood near the main entrance, billy clubs fastened at their belts. Disheveled travelers waited for bathrooms along the side wall, where there was an administrative office and, further along, a corridor leading somewhere.

I'd seen a poor-quality snapshot of Lena on Saldana's Facebook page. With her square-ish face, short haircut, and rectangular black glasses, she'd struck me as stolid and plain, the kind of person you wouldn't pick out in a crowd.

And I certainly wasn't picking her out now. Luggage from the flight started appearing on the moving belt. My leather duffel was conspicuously expensive and intact among the battered valises tied with twine and the cardboard boxes wrapped in swaths of plastic. I grabbed it and made my way to the front of the terminal. I'd sent Lena my itinerary a couple of days ago, and she'd replied with an enthusiastic promise to meet me at the airport at the appointed time. Maybe she meant at the main entrance or outside on the curb.

There was nowhere to sit on the concrete apron in front of the terminal building, so I plopped down on my bulging duffel and finished off some bottled water I'd bought eight hours earlier at Domodedovo. I'd been travelling for over twenty hours and was bleary with exhaustion. It was just after five a.m. Once the travelers who'd disembarked with me had dispersed to waiting cars and sped away, I was left alone to contemplate the airport's huge empty parking lot, a dreary moonscape of potholes and broken asphalt. I figured I'd give Lena fifteen minutes before I called.

When the time came, I tried her cell, got bumped to voicemail, and left a message. She'd probably gotten the time wrong and might still be asleep. Just after six, I dialed her landline and got no answer. I called her cell again and said that I was heading to a hotel and would try her again later that day.

A taxi had pulled up while I was waiting and was idling by the curb. The driver seemed to have sensed my situation because the minute I pocketed my phone he emerged from his cab and went around back to open its trunk. A fat-cheeked man wearing a grease-stained nylon jacket, he approached and pushed a business card under my nose.

"I work for hotels sometimes, but mostly for myself. Call this number when you have to go someplace." He jabbed a dirty finger at the card. "I work days, nights, weekends—any hour. If you want to take a long trip outside the city, I will take you myself or arrange it for you. If you want to bring your friends, I will rent a van. I am very safe, very trustworthy. With me, you are assured of a fair price. All you have to do is call that number, and I will come for you right away."

"Aysen the Taxi Driver," I said, reading the name on the card.

He nodded, his black eyes thin as slits above his mounded cheeks.

He drove canted forward, hugging the wheel of a battered Land Rover Discovery. The windshield was streaked with dirt, and the radio played tinny Western pop remixed with a syrupy beat. High-rise concrete apartment buildings backed up to both sides of the highway, broken by on/off ramps and billboards advertising such things as washing detergents and fruit-flavored drinks. In one, a pasty-faced campaigning politician with a bad haircut and ill fitting suit grinned down at passing motorists, menacing in his enormity. Everything was hovering behind a scrim of dust.

Traffic into the city was light. But Aysen stayed glued to the car in front, speeding up and slowing down as it did, as if driving were a matter of not letting the distance between bumpers expand. Finally, he swerved onto a ramp, and soon turned onto a wide city avenue.

"You see all the construction?" he said, waving his hand. Steel cranes rose here and there like long-necked birds, and scaffolding rigs covered several facades. "Yakutsk is growing all the time. It's the gold, the oil, the diamonds— all of it making the politicians and businessmen rich. And foreigners—they get rich, too. The rest of us? Not so much." He turned to me. "What are you here for?"

"Visiting family."

"Oh." He laughed with disappointment.

Eventually, the SUV jerked to a stop in front of a yellowish building with a high windowless facade—the North Star Hotel. A flashing neon column ran up its face, exploding at the top in a red, five-pointed star that managed to salute the Kremlin and Las Vegas equally.

I paid Aysen in rubles I'd acquired at the currency exchange at Dulles, the transaction prompting him to assure me once again that the fastest taxi service in Yakutsk was at my immediate service with a direct call to his private line.

I checked in foggily at the front desk, too tired to notice much of the hotel decor—worn red carpeting, fake flowers, a lot of gleaming white tile—and bumped my luggage up three flights of stairs, step by tedious step, because the elevator was broken. The room was stuffy and overheated; the triple-paned window wouldn't budge. A sign over the sink warned me not to drink the water, so I screwed the plastic top off the bottled water that had been provided and chugged half of it.

Fatigue was overtaking me with delayed vengeance, as if my jet-lagged body was catching on to the fact that it wasn't supposed to be awake. I propped two thin pillows against the headboard and half-reclined on a pink-fringed double bed. I couldn't sleep just yet—I had to call Vera and let her know I'd arrived safely.

The guide book I'd read on the plane had cheerfully reported that cell phone reception in Yakutsk was excellent. I had my doubts about that, but when the night nurse at the rehab, Caitlin O'Donnell, answered the phone, the guide book was proved right. Caitlin's voice was loud and crystal clear, even clearer, it seemed, than when I called from Washington.

"Hi, Caitlin. It's Dr. March."

"Dr. March! Your mother said you were in Russia."

"I am. It's seven a.m. here. What time is it there?"

"Nine p.m. How's your trip so far?"

"Fine so far. I just got to the hotel. Is Vera up?"

"Ah, no. She's sleeping right now. Actually...she had a fall. No broken bones, but she was a little shaken up."

"A fall? When?"

"A couple of hours ago. She got out of bed somehow and was trying to use the bathroom by herself. She wasn't there long."

"There?"

"On the floor. She was able to reach the emergency buzzer."

I groaned, picturing the scene: Vera crumpled on the bathroom tiles, not calling out right away because she wanted to get up by herself. Only after many minutes of fruitless, silent struggle would she have alerted the staff. Thank god she was all right. It could have been much worse if she'd hit her head or the emergency buzzer had been out of reach.

"You said she was upset?"

"A little shaken up, yes. Dr. Branson prescribed Xanax as needed. I hope that's okay with you?"

"Fine, Caitlin. But one dose ought to be enough." I trusted Dr. Branson, but I also kept a keen eye on how he managed my mother's care. I wasn't about to sanction regular use of an addictive psych med.

"Of course. Do you want to leave a message?"

"Yeah. Tell her to use her call button the next time she wants to get out of bed. That's an order." Vera knew she was supposed to notify staff when she wanted to get out of bed. But now and then she liked to test herself, just in case any of her functions had been miraculously restored.

"Will do, Doctor."

"And tell her I arrived safely and will phone again in the morning—your morning."

I ended the call with a worried sigh. I hated being so far away. If there was a crisis while I was gone… But the care at the rehab was first rate. I'd made sure of that before Vera was admitted. Still, I'd feel better when I was home.

I woke a little after noon. There were no messages from Lena on my phone.

After a quick shower and change of clothes, I went down to the lobby, where a skinny concierge wore an expression that seemed expressly designed to warn away irritating travelers. I bravely asked if anyone had tried to contact me. She raised aggressively tweezed eyebrows at me, as if it was a rare and stupid question, which in the age of cell phones, it probably was. Nevertheless, she obliged me with a cursory glance at some papers on her desk before delivering a neatly clipped *nyet*. She probably hated Americans, or everyone. I still wasn't too worried about Lena. I figured the problem was nothing more than a simple miscommunication, which would be straightened out soon enough with a bit of embarrassment and a friendly laugh. After lunch at the hotel restaurant, and two more unanswered calls to Lena's landline and mobile, I decided to walk to her flat.

It was hot out. Not as bad as D.C., but hotter than I'd expected. The sun was a whitish disc, indistinct and low-hanging, oddly searing. A breeze raised reddish-brown dirt and swirled it through the air, so that every parked car, every sidewalk and curbstone, was copper-tinged. I stood under the hotel awning next to an animated group of Asian businessmen carrying identical briefcases, and brought up the street map on my phone. Lena's address appeared as a blinking blue dot over a mile away, diagonally across the city, on the edge of a river that bore her name. When the driver of a taxi idling nearby gave me a pointed look, I shook my head to signal that I didn't want his services. After so much time cooped up in planes, I needed exercise, and I was curious to see the city.

As I reached into my bag for my sunglasses, I felt a touch on my shoulder and turned to see a woman about my age in a beige linen pantsuit with a large leather tote slung over one shoulder. "Excuse me, but I'm in a bit of a hurry. If you're going downtown, would you be willing to share your cab?" She had a strong, brassy voice. Huge sunglasses covered half her face.

"You can have it," I said, stepping aside. "I'm going to walk."

Swiping off the glasses, she blinked at me with a trace of something—

familiarity or amusement—and said in English, "Don't tell me you're American."

"Is it that obvious?" I answered in English.

"Afraid so. But your accent isn't too bad. I'm a Yank, too, actually. Meredith Viles." She reached out her hand, and my eyes caught the gleam of a large diamond on her finger, larger than any I'd seen.

"Natalie March," I said. Her hand was dry and thin, with a firm grip.

"Business or pleasure?" she asked in the abrupt manner of busy people who are eager to get to the point. She brushed over-processed blond hair away from heavily made-up eyes, giving the diamond another chance to dazzle.

"Pleasure. Family," I replied, matching her succinctness.

"Ah, nice," she said meaninglessly as she opened the door to the cab. She tossed her tote onto the backseat and, as she slid in after it, called over her shoulder, "Enjoy Yakutsk." The door slammed, and she immediately craned forward to speak to the driver. I got the impression that she went about her business in a chronic state of urgency like I did back in Washington. It ocurred to me that for the next few weeks I had no appointments, no scheduled surgeries. It felt odd to be so footloose.

· ⸱ · ⸱ · ⸱ · ⸱ · · ·

The buildings in the downtown area were either drab concrete boxes preaching the Soviet utilitarian gospel, or modern glass-and-steel towers bragging about their newfound capitalist wealth. Mixed in to the architectural argument were some elegant old wooden structures, relics of nineteenth-century Czarist Russia. Painted in soft pinks and blues, with folksy pointed shutters, they added a bygone romantic aura to the city streets, even when their flat roofs were crammed with silver satellite dishes and spurts of shooting antennae.

I strolled along among a mix of ethnic Russians and native Siberians, eventually arriving at a canal of dark water separating the city proper from the residential neighborhood where Lena lived. Pedestrians were crossing over on a wide arched footbridge whose railings were festooned with bright cotton ribbons and plastic trinkets that created a riot of color in the dust-filled air. I fell into line, a matted, feral dog trotting calmly beside me.

A warren of Soviet-era apartment towers rose on the far side of the canal—severe concrete monoliths, structures so lacking in imagination that my imagination would have been hard-pressed to envision them. Their drab faces had once been painted fanciful shades of turquoise and tangerine, but the paint had faded so much that only a wall here and there showed any color at all. Small square windows punctured the facades in lonely rows. There was precious little greenery anywhere, only spindly weeds and the occasional emaciated tree, its branches permanently bowed from yearly traumas of heavy snow.

Like every other man-made structure in Yakutsk, the apartment towers were set on pilings designed to absorb shifts in the permafrost lying just below the earth's surface. The pilings in this neighborhood compared badly to the ones in the city proper: they were thin stilts that hardly seemed capable of holding aloft multiple stacked floors of concentrated humanity. If I'd stooped, I could have scurried among them across an apocalyptic landscape of rocks, hardened dirt, concrete chunks, and blown garbage. But first I would have had to duck under a trio of fat steel pipes that ran chest-high alongside the street, bringing heat and hot water to each building and taking away sewage. The old pipes were patched in places; a tear in one of them emitted a human stench.

A couple was just emerging from the door of Lena's building. I sprinted up a set of steps, but it banged shut before I could grab the handle. I rang the buzzer and waited. No one came. In time, an old woman carrying a tiny, scrawny dog and a thin plastic bag overfilled with groceries tottered up the steps. She wordlessly handed me her grocery bag and swiped an electronic pass card to unlock a metal door that was almost too heavy for her to manage. I held it open for her and followed her inside.

The lobby was a dank, windowless area with a wall of broken wooden mailbox cubbies. I trailed the old woman up a dim turning stairway whose shadowy walls were splashed with spray-painted graffiti. She passed the second floor where the Tarasov apartment was located, and slowly ascended to the fifth floor where, her little dog crooked in one arm, she began the tedious process of unlocking three deadbolts on the door to her flat. It finally swung open, revealing another door behind it—also metal, also painted black. This one opened with a single key. Taking back her grocery bag, the old woman favored me with a placid smile devoid of curiosity.

I headed down to the second floor, found Lena's door, and knocked. When no one answered, I knocked again. Then put my ear to the door—no television or kitchen sounds. I tried a few more times, glancing up and down the drab corridor—perhaps there was someone I could ask—but the place seemed deserted.

I checked my phone, but there'd been no text or email from my aunt since I'd left the hotel. Was it possible she had the *day* of my arrival wrong? I scrolled through my inbox. There was our thread, *Flight info* in the subject line. The date and time I'd given were correct. *See you soon!* she'd replied.

Something must have happened. Something serious enough to have prevented her from picking me up at the airport and contacting me to explain. It occurred to me that she might have taken ill, that she might have had a heart attack or stroke, and could be lying helplessly on the floor of her apartment at this very moment, unable to come to the door or make a sound.

I hurried across the hall and rapped sharply on her neighbor's door. The drone of a television was just audible. "Hello?" I called out urgently. "Hello?"

The door was opened by a small man with a broad dark face and wire-rimmed spectacles. Before I had a chance to introduce myself, a tabby cat darted between his legs and ran into the hallway, and the voice of a little girl shrieked, "Dima! Dima! Come back!"

The cat ran straight to Lena's door and stopped, so I was able to scoop it up and bring it back to a girl of about seven or eight, now standing by the man's side with her arms plaintively outstretched. She immediately cradled the pet safely to her chest.

"What do you say?" the man prodded.

"Thank you," she murmured shyly, and immediately withdrew.

The man smiled at me. "Dima is still getting used to his new home."

"Did he used to live…?" I gestured to the door behind me.

"Yes. He's really our neighbor's cat. We're taking care of him while she's away."

"She's away? Lena Tarasova is away?" I repeated, stunned.

He furrowed his brow, seeming to realize he'd never seen me before.

"I'm her niece from America. I didn't know she was away."

"She went to visit her mother a couple of weeks ago. You probably know that her daughter died recently."

"Yes, I do. That's partly why I'm here. I was expecting Lena to meet me at the airport this morning. She said she would."

"Hmm. If she said so…maybe there was a mix-up?"

"It looks that way. Did she say when she'd be back?"

"A few months. She left it vague."

"I'm sorry. Did you say *months*?"

He nodded.

"And she left a couple of *weeks* ago?"

He nodded again, obviously perturbed by my incredulous reactions.

"*Two* weeks, would you say?"

"About that."

Maybe I had the wrong Lena Tarasova. Both her first and last names were fairly common. There could easily be other Lena Tarasovas in Yakutsk. But how many would have a recently deceased daughter?

I gave a great, long exhale. At least now I knew why I'd been stranded at the airport. My aunt had left Yakutsk shortly after Saldana was killed, apparently intending to stay away for months.

I cleared my throat. "Do you happen to know where her mother lives?"

"A little village. I didn't catch its name. She said something about getting to the ferry on time, so it's probably to the east, across the river."

The area between Yakutsk and the Pacific Ocean was about the size of Canada.

I must have looked upset because he said, "I'm sorry I can't be more help."

"Oh, thanks. This *is* helpful, actually. Do you happen to know what the cell reception is like out there in…" I stopped myself from blurting *the god-forsaken wilderness*. "…in the country?"

"Depends. In some places, very good; others, maybe none."

So there was another puzzle piece falling into place: Lena could be out of cell phone range.

I thanked the man again and tottered out of the building, light-headed with confusion. None of this made sense.

Lena had told me that she worked as the secretary to the president of Alrosa Corporation, one of the largest diamond mining and processing companies in the world. Tomorrow was Monday. I supposed I could try to call her at work. But what would be the point of that, if she'd already left town?

．· ·· · ·· ·· · · ·

The sullen concierge shook her head before I even asked—no messages. Was it my imagination, or was she sadistically pleased? I tromped up the three flights to my room and tried Lena's phone numbers again half-heartedly. Nothing.

I'd barely noticed the room that morning, but now I took a good, long look. It was remarkably ugly, even by hotel standards. Green shag carpeting and burnt orange wallpaper gave it a garish circus look. The furniture was cheap and thin, and a stuffed armchair exhaled dust when I sat on it. The air had a dense, stale quality, as if the exhalations and evaporated sweat of previous guests were still hanging about.

I tried to raise the window again, perching one butt cheek awkwardly on the ledge to get my shoulder into the upward push. It wouldn't budge. Maybe it wasn't supposed to open. There would be reasons for not opening windows in this part of the world. Ungodly cold in winter, hordes of spring mosquitoes, swirling summer dust. Other factors I was presently unaware of. I gave up on the window and switched on the wall-mounted air conditioner. It wheezed and stuttered before settling in to a loud, rattling drone, expelling lukewarm gusts.

I was still trying to grasp my situation. I desperately wanted to keep an open mind about my aunt, but the facts kept getting in the way. Those times when we spoke on the phone, those emails—she'd already left Yakutsk by then! Why wouldn't she have said that? The agreed-on plan was for her to show me around Yakutsk for a few days before we went out to the country to meet Katarina. In fact, she'd specifically promised to take me on a tour of an Alrosa processing plant, where I could see the diamonds being cut and polished, and even buy some at a deep discount. Why would she have mentioned that when she'd already informed her neighbors that she'd be away from home for several months? Had she intentionally deceived me? If so, it was an odd lie. I couldn't imagine what she'd been trying to hide.

I thought back to how she'd sounded on the phone. She'd come across as sensible and grounded, intelligent and caring, and there'd been absolutely nothing in her speech to make me question her sincerity. Despite her recent bereavement, or maybe because of it, her enthusiasm for my visit had seemed warmly authentic. But I also recalled our conversation about the crime scene, when her cold curiosity had struck me as more professional than maternal. At the time I'd chocked it up to the fact that people grieve in mysterious ways; now the strangeness of her reaction assumed a foreboding tint.

A disturbing pattern was emerging: Misha possibly in some kind of trouble, which then seemed to have been resolved; Saldana wanting to defect, then murdered; Lena leaving the city even as she encouraged my visit. The members of the Tarasov clan seemed to be disappearing one by one. My head spun, concocting various scenarios to explain it all, each one more absurd than the last. It was like trying to recreate a recipe when you had only half the ingredients.

It's not my job to figure this out. I was just a distant relative, a virtual stranger, whose place in these opaque machinations was tangential at best. Whatever else might be true, Lena had left me stranded without a word of explanation, and now it was up to me to take the hint and withdraw. I felt damn foolish about the whole clumsy mess. What Kool-Aid had I been drinking when I thought it was a good idea to travel halfway around the world on the basis of a couple of phone calls and some emails? And the saccharine dream of a joyful union with relatives who hadn't sent so much as a postcard until they'd needed a very big favor?

I opened my laptop and checked return flights. I'd come in on a Washington-Moscow-Yakutsk route, which had been as direct as I could get. Now I saw that there was no way to get back to the States early without adding a few legs to that journey, incurring a cancellation fee and dramatically increased ticket prices, and enduring some very long layovers. Nevertheless, I hobbled together a workable itinerary. But held off on booking, as I needed time to cool down.

. ⠂ . ⠄ . ⠁ . ⠂ . ⠈ . ⠂

I called my mother late that afternoon, fully intending to announce that I was coming home.

"Hello?" Her voice sounded weaker than usual.

"Mom? Are you okay?"

"Oh, sweetie. I'm glad you called. Yes, I'm fine."

"I heard you had a fall."

"Oh, it was nothing. I got a little bruise on my knee, that's all."

"You know you're supposed to use your call button when you have to go to the bathroom, right?"

"Of course. I do that. Usually."

"All the time from now on, okay?"

"Please don't dwell on it, dear. Your mother isn't made of glass. Now tell me about you," she said, sashaying out of the spotlight. "You landed safely, I heard. Have you met up with your aunt?"

"Well, as it turns out, things haven't gone as planned."

"Oh, really?" A tone of dismayed surprise.

"Yeah, she didn't meet me at the airport, and I haven't been able to get in touch with her. I left messages and went by her apartment. And she hasn't contacted me. I guess we got our signals crossed. I'm sorry, Mom."

"Oh, I'm sorry, too, darling. That must be frustrating after your long trip," she said, trying to bury her disappointment in concern for me. "I'm sure it's nothing to worry about."

"The problem is, Mom, I found out she left Yakutsk weeks ago. It's crazy. I have no idea what happened, and I can't think of what else to do."

"What are you saying, Natalie? Are you saying you're coming home?"

"Well, there aren't many options, are there?"

"It's only been a day or two. You shouldn't give up so easily."

"I don't really see it as giving up. More as accepting the facts."

"Nonsense. I'm sure she'll reach out to you soon."

"Mom. She knows I'm here. She has my phone number."

"I know, darling. But something might have happened."

Of course something happened, I thought.

She continued, "Give it a few more days. I know how impatient you can be, but you can certainly use the time to your advantage. After all, you're in a very remarkable city! I was just reading about it. Let me see…I bookmarked it…" The sound of rustling pages. "Yes, here it is. There's a place called the Permafrost Institute, which does some very interesting scientific research that I'm sure you would enjoy. There's also a Mammoth Museum, where you can find life-sized stuffed mammoths, whatever they are. And there's a khomus museum, the only one of its kind in the world!"

"Khomus?"

"I'm sure you've seen one, Nat. It's that metal instrument that people hold against their lips, and then they pluck a reed that vibrates at different speeds? Apparently, there are a lot of excellent khomus players in Yakutsk. And did you know that our own President Abraham Lincoln was quite a good khomus player himself? He's even featured in the museum's Hall of Fame!"

"Gosh. I didn't know that, Mom."

"See? There's always so much to learn about a place."

I sighed, knowing I was beat. Vera would never forgive me if I left Yakutsk so fast. In a few days, maybe she'd see things differently. After she'd had a little more time to prepare herself psychologically for what she would probably experience as a personal rejection, though I would do my best to talk her out of that.

"Okay. You made your point. There *is* a lot to see here," I said, trying to work myself into the tourist spirit.

Vera paused. "Are you sure you're okay with this? It's not too much to ask, is it? A few more days, just to be sure there hasn't been some simple mix-up that will be straightened out soon?"

"It's fine, Mom," I said. "It doesn't make sense to have come all this way just to turn around and go home. And who knows—I may get a call from Lena tonight."

"I hope so. I truly do."

"So do I. Now you take it easy, okay? No traipsing up and down the halls in the middle of the night."

"You make it sound like I'm out on safari."

"Love you, Mom."

"Oh, Natalie. I love you, too."

The restaurant on the ground floor of the North Star Hotel was reputed to be one of the best in the city. It was certainly lavish. Red damask wallpaper with a raised felt design, ornate brass sconces, velvet draperies dripping with silken tassels. A white grand piano worthy of Elton John occupied a corner of the room, next to a raised platform for a band or performer. Gold-veined mirrors doubled and tripled the dim interior of flickering candles on white-clothed tables. The place looked like a cross between a cabaret and a nineteenth-century bordello.

I was waiting for the hostess to seat me when a diner at a shadowy corner table waved. It was the same woman who'd asked to share a cab earlier that day. The jacket of her linen suit was slung over the back of her chair, while the leather tote occupied the seat across from her, papers sticking out. She had the wilted look of someone at the end of a long work day.

"Not eating alone, are you?" she asked in English when I went over.

I admitted that I was.

"Then you absolutely must join me. I haven't ordered yet, so the timing's perfect. Come, sit down."

It was undeniably good to hear someone speaking English.

Seeing me hesitate, she added, "Just put that bag on the floor."

I complied, happy to avoid another solitary meal, and searched my memory for the name she'd given earlier. "Meredith Viles? Did I get that right?"

"You certainly did. But I don't remember yours."

"Natalie March."

Her friendly smile revealed prominent, slightly yellowed teeth. She turned to catch the waiter's eye. He was already approaching. "Caviar and another menu, Sergei. And a bottle of my favorite. You know the one—Cuvee D'Amour."

She had a lean runner's build, a long face with deep creases from nose to lips, a wide, expressive mouth, and admirably square jaw. Her make-up was a shade darker than her natural skin tone, giving her the artificially tanned look of a Palm Beach socialite. Dirty-blond hair, worn long and loosely curled, was stiffened with styling gel and teased at the crown.

"Where in our United States do you hail from, Natalie?"

"Washington, D.C."

"Oh, I *love* Washington. I went to school there—Georgetown. Foreign Service with a specialty in Russian affairs. If I'd know I'd end up spending months each year in Siberia buying diamonds, I might have switched to French or Italian." She gave a throaty laugh.

"I didn't know buying diamonds could take that long," I replied.

"It does if you work for Tiffany." Tiffany purchased a large percentage of its diamonds from Siberian mining and processing companies, she explained. Her job was to evaluate the gems, supervise the cutting procedures, maintain good relations with Russian diamond suppliers, and generally keep her ear to the ground. On the basis of her reports, Tiffany estimated yields for the upcoming year and renegotiated its annual contracts accordingly.

"It sounds more interesting than it really is," she said. "I spend most of my time inspecting the mining operations of Alrosa subsidiaries and the other, smaller companies. Needless to say, accommodations in the Russian Far East aren't what you'd call deluxe: I'm lucky if I get a decently cooked chicken breast and vodka that isn't home-brewed. When I'm not travelling, I'm usually here in Yakutsk attending horribly long meetings and very dull cocktail parties."

I'd perked up at the name of my aunt's employer. "I wonder if you ever met Lena Tarasova," I said. "She's secretary to the president of Alrosa."

"Oh, him," Meredith groaned. "Boris Mendevez. A total sleaze who kisses me on both cheeks and slips his hand over my ass whenever we meet. He works hard to keep me happy, I will say that for him. Tiffany is one of his top buyers, along with DeBeers and a few others."

"Did you ever meet his secretary?"

She frowned thoughtfully. "I don't think so."

I was beginning to wonder if Lena even existed.

"Why? Is something wrong?" Meredith asked.

"I was supposed to meet her, but the plans got screwed up somehow."

"You poor thing," Meredith said with a sympathetic shake of her head.

Sergei appeared with a bottle swaddled in a linen napkin. I didn't have much patience for the smelling of corks and the swirling of wine in the bottoms of glasses, but Meredith Viles seemed in her element. "Fabulous," she concluded, smiling up at suitably nondescript Sergei, who poured the wine and disappeared.

Turning to me, she raised her glass, the diamond on her finger magnifying the candle's flicker. "Cuvee D'Amour is a very unique vintage—the grapes are native to southern Siberia and northern China. It's bold and fragrant like a Bordeaux, but with a crisper finish. Tell me what you think."

Its dark red color, almost black, gave me the slightest hesitation. I tasted it, and it was good.

"You like?" Meredith asked.

"I like."

"*Horosho*," she said in triumph, the ubiquitous Russian term of approval.

The caviar arrived in a crystal bowl set on a plate of shaved ice, with small squares of buttered toast and a flat spoon made of reindeer antler. With Meredith's encouragement, I seconded her order of reindeer steak. Sergei took our menus and went away.

Meredith leaned forward, her voice dropping to an intimate timbre. "If you don't mind my asking, what happened with your aunt?"

"I don't mind at all. The whole thing's making me a little crazy, actually, and I'd just as soon get it off my chest." I only meant to explain my immediate quandary, but Meredith was a keen, empathic listener, the kind of person who made you feel sane and perfectly reasonable however zany your tale might be. She asked one good question after another, and before long I'd spilled the entire story, starting with my mother's apparently orphaned state and ending with my apparently ruined trip.

"What on earth are you going to do?" Meredith asked.

I shrugged and gave a helpless laugh. "Sightsee for a few days and see if anything changes. Then, I guess I'll just go home. I dread seeing my mother. This is going to be hard on her."

"I can imagine," Meredith said.

We talked about Russia after that. Meredith didn't hold back. "It's a maddening, exhausting country. You spend half your life waiting in one place and the other half waiting someplace else. Bureaucracy changes on a whim. And the Russian people, you may as well know, have two very different faces. The public one, which is cold and inscrutable. And the private one, which can be very warm and loyal if they like you. You can't blame them for being wary, though. They've faced so many hardships and betrayals; I don't think we in the West can truly fathom it. Raped by the Soviets for seventy years, then wrung out by the oligarchs. And now? Well, now, global capitalism has come storming in. Did you know that sixty percent of Alrosa is owned by foreign investors? You can't tell by looking, but billions of dollars are changing hands in this part of the world. Right here, in fact. In Yakutsk. In this hotel."

She topped off our glasses. "There's no trickle down, by the way, unless you're talking payoffs to corrupt officials. That's the one thing that hasn't changed in Russia: the people are left to rot. They mine the resources at low wages—not just diamonds, but gold, titanium, timber, oil—while the billionaires fly in and out, and the politicians live like kings. Meanwhile, apartment buildings all over the city are crumbling to dust, the schools and healthcare are below horrible, and you can't even rely on the utilities to work properly. Even in this hotel, the best in the city, the heat may suddenly fail. If you complain, they tell you to put on a coat. Gas is controlled by the city, you see, so there's nothing they can do."

I listened, fascinated by the stories she went on to tell of her exploits in the Russian Far East, which she compared to the old American West. Lawless, violent, everything up for grabs. Yet for all that, she seemed quite at home. The reindeer was surprisingly good—like beef with a hint of venison—and the flavor of the wine grew richer with each glass. I noticed that the edge of her left hand was lightly ink-stained. Southpaw, I thought. The ink smudges as they push the pen from left to right.

She sipped her wine. "Now you. What do you do?"

I described my work at the hospital, and we spent another leisurely span of time over coffee and dessert, sharing our life stories. She'd been raised in Las Vegas by a single mother, a croupier at one of the big casinos. After Georgetown, she went on to a career at the US State Department and the American Embassy in Moscow before moving to the private sector. She was married briefly, no children, and described herself as happily addicted to her work. I was struck once more by her resonant voice. She had a kind of earthy charisma, the ability to effortlessly cast a spell of intimacy, and I found myself easily drawn in. Her different facets flickered like the diamonds she trafficked in—hard-nosed grit vied with cultured sophistication, friendly warmth with aloof independence, Las Vegas glitz with Manhattan elegance. I was willing to bet that she was ruthless in her business dealings, and probably a loyal friend.

Back in Washington, I spent most evenings either on-call or exhausted. Usually alone, and in company limiting myself to one or two glasses of wine so as to be clear-headed the next day. This night was a welcome novelty for me. There was no bothersome black pager hooked to my belt, and to the extent that my mother was being taken care of, no patient to worry about. I returned to my room pleasantly inebriated, my head full of the wild stories of a woman who seemed a lot like me but whose life was so richly different from my own. As I flopped onto the anemic mattress in the circus-colored room, it occurred to me that I'd had a wonderful night despite my troubles. Maybe being a tourist in Siberia for a few days wouldn't be so bad.

I slept late for the first time in ages and blithely skipped my morning run. After a leisurely breakfast in the dining room, even more garish in sunlight, I consulted my guidebook and plotted out my day. I decided to put Lena out of my mind. If she wanted to reach me, she could call. In the meantime, I would trek around Yakutsk like a typical American visitor, in Nike sneakers and a baseball hat.

The eerie turquoise ice caves at the Permafrost Institute were worth the trip, and the woolly mammoth replicas at the Mammoth Museum were fearsome indeed. I decided to skip my mother's third suggestion, the allegedly world-famous Khomus Museum, in favor of lunch at a cozy restaurant in the historic section of town and a two-hour boat ride on the sparkling Lena River. On my way back through the downtown area, I saw a banner advertising The Festival of the Northern Peoples, which was taking place that very day in a festooned public squre. Drawn in by the bright spectacle, I wandered amid hundreds of short, dark-haired Siberians who were ducking in and out of teepees made of stretched animal hides. Tourists fingered handmade goods arranged on tables, and a small crowd sat before a low stage, on which grandmothers in elaborate beaded and fringed costumes banged drums and chanted long, haunting phrases. The air was filled with the earthy smells of dung, cured hides, and hay.

I bumped into a herder standing between two reindeer, holding the bridle of each. "Excuse me," I blurted in English. And corrected myself, "*Izvenitya.*" He remained impassive, his face brown and leathery, with grime in the creases and an oily sheen. He wore an old wool cap from which tufts of black hair stuck out like feathers, and had soft, thick-toed, animal-skin boots on his feet. The reindeer flanking him seemed placid enough, but I knew from my guidebook that these animals had snarly, unpredictable dispositions. One stepped forward and bumped me with its long, bony snout, bowed low by the weight of elaborate antlers. It blinked bulging, fly-swarmed eyes at me, its long, curling eyelashes giving it a disconcertingly coquettish air. Startled, I said *izvenitya* to the reindeer as well, and saw the herder smile.

In the middle of the plaza, a pair of newlyweds was being paraded around in a red cart pulled by two reindeer. The bride was resplendent in wedding white, the bashful groom in a stiff gray suit and slightly askew lavender tie. A herder carrying a long switch led the plodding animals forward, while wedding guests and random passersby clapped and cheered. Sitting rather dazedly amid the hoopla, the young couple wore happy, innocent expressions on which no trace of self-consciousness could be found. Before I left the festival, I purchased a silver bracelet for my mother and a horsehair talisman—the kind of campy thing I never usually bought—for myself.

It was after six when I arrived in the lobby, sore-footed and just the right amount of tired. To my surprise, the stone-faced concierge waved me over and wordlessly presented me with a dainty cream-colored envelope.

I tore it open eagerly, hoping for an apologetic explanation from Lena. Instead, the handwritten message read *Drinks at 8? Suite 501. Meredith.*

4

The bar was well-stocked with fresh ice and cut lime, the lights were low, and smooth jazz guitar—Pat Methany, I guessed—was emanating softly from an iPad on the coffee table next to a flickering candle. The stage appeared to be set for a seduction. I felt a quick flush of embarrassment—had I given out the wrong vibes last night? Should I start talking about a boyfriend back home?

"How was your day?" Meredith asked, handing me a vodka over ice. She was wearing tight white jeans and a white sleeveless blouse set off by a long turquoise necklace and a stack of gold bracelets. And the ring, of course, glittering like a miniature beacon on her long-fingered, manicured hand.

Perching on a gaudy white vinyl sectional, I recounted my tourist adventures, helping myself now and again to to cheese and olives from an hors d'oeuvre plate set on an incongruous blue-tiled coffee table. Meredith's penthouse suite was just as ugly as my single room: brown shag rug, saggy gold curtains, a murky abstract painting comprised of numerous pointy angles staring down from an otherwise barren wall.

We talked for a while pleasantly, sharing a few laughs over some of the odder (to us) aspects of Russian life. But I continued to feel uneasy. Was it just my imagination, or was she gazing at me a little too intently, as if unwilling to let me out of her sight? Just as I was about to mutter something about not being able to stay very long, a key turned in the lock, the door swung open, and a man entered the suite.

In his late sixties with a bald head and a long gray beard that fanned out onto a stained T-shirt, he had the gnarled, ancient look of an Old Believer—the Russian orthodox who'd escaped the Bolsheviks a century before by wandering far into the Siberian wilderness, building wooden shacks by streams, and subsisting on berries and bear meat. Broken capillaries spread like webbing through his ruddy cheeks and up the broken terrain of his bulbous nose. His pot belly was high and taut, like a pregnancy, while his arms were thinner than you'd expect a fat man's to be. There was a tincture of yellow in the whites of his bleary eyes. Cirrhosis, probably. I wished I could order a liver function test— the whole battery of blood tests, in fact, plus an electrocardiogram.

Meredith introduced him as Oleg. She didn't introduce me, which likely meant that Oleg already knew who I was. He stared at me with a weird sense of ownership, as if I were a prize pig being hauled to a county fair. I glared at him to get him to back off. Our eyes met and locked. He was practically leering.

I looked at Meredith, who sat swirling her drink so that the ice clinked in the glass. "What's going on?"

"I'd like to talk to you, Natalie, about something important."

A quiver of nerves ran through my body. "What?"

She gave a long, capitulating sigh, like someone embarking on an unpleasant task. "There's nothing to worry about."

The words slammed into me like a punch. There's nothing to worry about meant there's everything to worry about.

"What?" I repeated.

"I need your help. Your country needs your help."

"What are you talking about?"

"I know you have some questions—suspicions—about your cousin's murder. Well, I have the same questions and suspicions. I'm hoping we can work together."

"Who are you?"

"I work for the CIA."

I had a rush of emotions: fear, mostly. Then relief: at least we were on the same side. Then anger: she'd lied to me last night. Then fear and relief combined: Saldana. This was about justice for Saldana.

"So you're not really a diamond merchant." She'd done a pretty good job convincing me.

"I am, actually. I'm also a CIA case officer."

I jerked my thumb at Oleg. "And him?"

"A foreign agent. We've worked together for years. I trust Oleg completely."

"I thought handlers and their spies weren't supposed to be seen together."

"There are exceptions to every rule, especially in this part of the world. Oleg's my driver, pilot, protector, assistant. He helps me get around and generally takes care of things."

"Can you get him to stop staring at me?"

She laughed a little and told him to mix himself a drink. When he went to the bar, she said quietly, "He's got some rough edges, but he's one of the good guys, and a lot smarter than he looks. He's motivated to work with the US out of ideology, not greed or revenge like most others are. You may come to appreciate him in time."

"That depends on whether I ever see him again, which hasn't been decided."

She leaned back, crossing one long leg over the other. "First let me say that if there were any question about your character or loyalties, any at all, this conversation would not be taking place."

"What do you mean? You did a background check?" Whom had they talked to? How much of my life had they ransacked?

"You passed with flying colors. You're a very straight arrow, Natalie. No criminal record, no history of drug use, no extremist political activity or questionable companions. Your colleagues think highly of you. Most everyone thinks highly of you. You're hardworking, honest, ethical. Completely dedicated to your profession. You're almost as clean as they come."

Almost? I blinked. Too rapidly. *Don't react. It's just a word.*

She continued, "You live well but not extravagantly. No debt, other than your mortgage, which you pay on time each month. You don't do social media, and most of your internet searches are medical topics." She looked at me deeply and thoughtfully, as if I were a rare species to be studied and admired. "You're a remarkably independent woman, Natalie. Almost solitary, in fact. Your only deep relationship appears to be with your mother. You're unmarried, no children. No lover. No church. Not even a book club. You have a few old friends, but you don't make time for them, do you? You wait for them to reach out to you." She smiled with what looked like admiration.

"You seem pleased by that."

"There are times when a lack of connections is an asset."

"I suppose this is one of those times."

"It could be. That's up to you."

"What else did you learn about me?" I said, trying for nonchalance. *She must know. How could she not?*

"Let's see. You're in excellent health. You eat well, jog every morning, lift weights three times a week. Minus the one day you spent in New York to ID your cousin's body, you haven't missed a day of work in years." She sipped the vodka. "You're also fluent in Russian—a critically important skill from the agency's perspective."

"Right. Is that all you've got?"

"Is there more?"

"No. Nothing more." I let out the breath I'd been holding. *They'd missed it, thank god.*

Oleg returned with a bottle of beer. He sat and tipped it up, glugging. Wiped his mouth with the back of his hand. He had tattoos on each knuckle. When he clenched his fist, they probably lined up and made a statement I wouldn't be interested in.

"I'm sure you understand why we had to take precautions. The important thing is, I believe we can help each other, and I think that when you've heard what I have to say, you'll agree. What I'm about to tell you has to be kept in complete secrecy. No one must ever know what's said here today. That includes friends, family, lovers, even a future spouse. Do I have your word?"

"If I say no?"

"Then our little drinks party will be over, and Oleg and I will leave you to enjoy a few days of sightseeing before you return to the States. Without locating your aunt."

"Does that mean you know where she is?"

"She's safely with your grandmother, Katarina Melnikova, in the village she grew up in. It's quite remote, not listed on any map. It would be impossible for you to find it on your own."

"But if I cooperate, you'll tell me where it is."

"I'll do more than that. I'll help you get there and bring you out. You'll be well taken care of."

"Sounds like a bribe, Meredith."

"Think of it as a win-win." She gave me a level, businesslike look. "Do you agree to maintain complete secrecy?"

I hesitated. The quid pro quo was bothersome, but I wanted to help solve Saldana's murder; I'd wanted that since the beginning. And I desperately wanted to meet my relatives, if only for Vera's sake. Also, though I'd never thought of myself as much of a patriot, I couldn't say no to serving my country. But perhaps the most persuasive factor was that if I didn't find out what all this was about, I'd never stop wondering.

Meredith interrupted my thoughts. "I need you to give me a verbal *yes*, Natalie, recognizing that your word is your oath."

"Yes," I said, feeling unsure.

I reached for the glass of vodka on the table and took a long swallow. My fingers were trembling. What on earth was I doing? I was a doctor, not a spy. I looked in people's ears by pulling gently on the lobe. I warmed the stethoscope under my armpit before I listened to their hearts.

"Good. Then let me get you up to speed." She started talking faster. "Your aunt, Lena Tarasova, is one of the few foreign agents we run in Siberia. Like Oleg here. Her position as an executive secretary at Alrosa gave her access to information we found useful."

"So you do know her."

"Very well." She pursed her lips. "I didn't tell you that last night because my goal is to protect my agents. First, last, and always. Nothing is more important to me than that. Which brings me to your cousin, Mikhail. Or Misha, as he's known. After his graduation from the state-run ballet school, he became a foreign agent as well. I sent him to Mirny in mid-May on his first covert mission. Two months later, he disappeared."

"Mirny?"

"About eight hundred kilometers west of here. Not very big—forty thousand people maybe. There's a famous diamond mine there, the Mir Mine, and a chemical processing plant."

"Okay. Go on."

"When Misha went missing, I had to face the possibility that under harsh interrogation he might expose himself and Lena, too. If Lena was arrested, the FSB might use Saldana as leverage to get either her or Misha to talk. I urged Lena to go into hiding with her daughter, but she refused. Instead, she found an opportunity to get Saldana out of the country, and unwisely insisted on staying in Yakutsk in case Misha showed up there. It wasn't until Saldana was murdered that she agreed to return to her village."

"Why did she pretend to want to see me? She was already in hiding, yet she encouraged me to come."

"We thought that once you were in Russia, you'd be more...amenable."

"To working with you?"

"Exactly."

"Then why not pick me up at the airport instead of going through this charade?"

"Because I wanted to get to know you a bit before we spoke. Also, I needed you to behave like a tourist to please the FSB."

"The FSB? Are they watching me?" I said with a gulp. The FSB was Russia's internal security force, equivalent to the FBI.

"Possibly," Meredith said with an oddly reassuring smile. "They sometimes keep tabs on solo American travelers. When you bore them, they go away."

Oleg was watching me keenly, the brown bottle clutched in one fat hand. He looked a tad less hostile than before, but I got the impression that if I tried to leave, he'd block the door.

I tried to collect my thoughts. Everything was happening so fast. "I'm guessing you think the two things—Misha's disappearance and Saldana's murder—are related."

"That's one of the things I want to find out. At this point, there isn't any evidence to suggest a link. According to Lena, Saldana had no inkling that her mother and brother were spying for the US, and she posed no danger on her own account. As far as I can see, there's no reason why the Russian government would have wanted to assassinate her."

"But you suspect it."

Meredith shrugged. "I really don't know. If I had to guess, I'd say she was murdered in an interrupted burglary, as the NYPD concluded. But the fact that the two events happened so close together does make me wonder. There could be a hidden connection, in which case I'm missing something important. Not just a puzzle piece, but possibly an entire puzzle, if you know what I mean."

I stuck my finger in my glass. The vodka was cold and almost gone. I drank down the rest. "What do you want from me?"

"I want you to find Misha."

I laughed out loud. "Me? You've got to be kidding."

"Not at all. I want you to go to Mirny, ask questions, track down leads. Investigate."

"Why don't you get one of your own people to do it?"

"Believe me, I'd much rather use one of my own. But it's not that easy. With the exception of Oleg and your aunt and a few others, I haven't had much luck recruiting in the Russian Far East, especially among the native peoples, who distrust ethnic Russians and Westerners alike. In short, I don't have a man or woman in Mirny. That's why I sent Misha up there in the first place."

"But there must be someone in your organization who could do this better that I can."

"As you'll soon see, if you decide to accept this assignment, Westerners are very conspicuous in the smaller Siberian communities. Any Westerner showing up to ask questions about Mikhail Tarasov will be news immediately. It's hard to provide effective cover in that kind of situation." She looked at me with a sort of languid force, a soft insistence that was both sultry and powerful. She was clearly used to persuading people to take risks. I was starting to feel like putty in her hands.

"But you, Natalie," she continued, "you don't need a cover. You're the real thing—an actual relative of Misha's, a caring American doctor with a true, searchable identity. His sister was just killed in a shocking incident of apparently random violence, an incident publicly recorded in newspapers and online media sources, so you have a valid reason to be in Mirny. Like anyone in your situation might, you want to connect with your cousin, console him, create a family bond. You'll naturally be shocked to discover that he's missing— you'll want to do everything you can to find him, both for yourself and for his mother, who's inconsolably bereaved. Family bonds are sacrosanct in that community. You'll have the sympathy and support of almost everyone you meet."

"*Almost* everyone. Just not whoever may be behind Misha's disappearance. The bad guys, so to speak."

Meredith uncrossed her legs and leaned forward confidentially. "Natalie, I'm obviously privy to more information than I can give you at this time, and I can assure you that we wouldn't be having this discussion if I thought there was significant danger. In the very unlikely event that there's the slightest bit of trouble, you'll have the full resources of the world's most powerful intelligence agency at your back."

She glanced at Oleg, who pulled a mobile phone from his pocket and sent it spinning across the coffee table to me. It was a small flip phone, cheaply made. He tapped a cigarette from his pack of Ducats, slipped it between dry brown lips, and began patting his pockets for a light. The end of the cigarette wobbled up and down as he gave me instructions. "That phone has tracking device, so we always know where you are. When you want to contact us, you text or leave voicemail to number programmed in. We reply quickly, maybe ten minutes, hour at most." Having found what he was looking for, he struck a match and put the flame to the cigarette's tip, which flared red as he inhaled. His eyes narrowed to beady slits in the haze of smoke. "That phone number is only possible communication so you memorize number in case you throw away phone."

"Why would I do that?"

He shrugged blandly, waving out the match. "Eh? How should I know? Maybe to keep others from finding?"

Meredith interrupted in a reasonable tone, "What Oleg means, Natalie, is that if there's ever a question in your mind about whether you should have this phone in your possession, dump it right away and call us from a landline when you can. Don't use your personal phone to contact us. Ever."

A buzz of tension jumbled my thoughts. I looked in quiet disbelief at the burner resting lightly in my hand. I hadn't agreed to anything. Yet I felt as if I were plummeting down a rabbit hole with Teflon sides, nothing to grab hold of.

"What exactly am I supposed to do?"

Meredith smiled and leaned back, sensing that my resistance was crumbling. "Nothing too difficult. Just ask the obvious questions of whomever you meet in the normal course of events—neighbors, friends, co-workers. When was Misha last seen, did he say where he was going, is there someone you could talk to who might know where he is? Did he seem upset in the days before his disappearance? Did he do anything unusual? Did anyone make a police report? If so, have the police investigated, and what did they conclude?"

I must have had a doubtful look on my face, because she went on, "Remember, as a doctor, you've dealt with all kinds of sensitive situations— you're probably better than you realize at judging emotional states, and your own instincts will let you know how far you can push before you set off alarm bells. At the end of the conversation, you'll leave your card and ask your contacts to call if they remember anything or learn anything new. That's it. Simple and natural. Nothing more than what any concerned relative would do. The only difference is that you'll report your findings to me."

My palms were sweating, and my shirt was sticking damply to my back. I was being sucked into something I didn't fully understand and couldn't see the true perimeters of. I only knew, as I did when I was pulled into Saldana's orbit, that getting out wasn't going to be easy.

Meredith coaxed gently, "I'm giving you an opportunity to help your country, and your Russian family. And your mother. I know how badly she wants contact with her past."

"Oh, no. Keep my mother out of this," I warned. But I was beaten. Meredith Viles had outmaneuvered me from the beginning. Which I didn't appreciate. But she had her reasons, just as I'd had mine for doing what I was glad was still hidden in my past.

"One more thing," I said hesitantly, trying to put my finger on something important I needed to ask. "Oh, right. What was Misha doing in Mirny? What kind of covert operation was it?"

"Sorry, Natalie. The CIA operates on a strict need-to-know basis. It's for your own safety."

"Right." I hadn't really expected her to tell me, but not knowing made me uneasy. It meant I'd be blind to potential dangers. I'd have to trust Meredith to keep me safe—a dubious proposition given that she'd been playing me all along—but I couldn't see a way around it.

"You in?" she asked, as if it were a poker game.

"Yeah. I'm in," I said.

"Good. We're a team now." She held her glass aloft. "To our success!"

Oleg leaned in and the three of us clinked glasses. The seduction had occurred.

Meredith and Oleg were waiting for me at the airstrip the next afternoon, having made the final checks on the four-seater, single-engine Cessna that would take us to Mirny. Oleg tossed my duffel and backpack into the storage area behind the backseat and we all piled in. Our flight path followed a winding gray line of highway running northward, then veered off over dark green taiga stretching hypnotically in every direction, broken only by flashes of silver streams.

Eventually, the city of Mirny appeared on the horizon—dirty and ugly and vaguely round, like a brown scab on the earth's healthy green skin. Its southern edge was cleanly amputated by what appeared to be either a gargantuan black meteor crater or an enormous lake of very dark water.

As we got closer, the city materialized into a gritty warren of densely packed two- and three-story buildings with the standard Soviet apartment towers rising from its midst like dingy, oddly-colored stalks growing from a concrete bog. The massive, weirdly blue-black crater turned out to be the Mir

Mine. Its stunning size, sharp rim, and apparently bottomless depth made me dizzy, even from a distance.

When Meredith looked back and saw me gaping, my nose pressed to the glass, she yelled over the engine din, "About a mile in diameter and seventeen hundred feet deep. Visible from space. We won't fly over it because the downdraft can suck a small plane right out of the sky."

"That's got to be the biggest hole in the world," I yelled back.

She laughed. "It's not. There's an even bigger one in Utah. The Bingham copper mine. Which just goes to show, anything Russia does, we can do better."

I glanced over to see how Oleg would react to that dubious brag, and saw the two of them exchange a cozy smile.

We landed at a small airport outside the city, taxied to an area designated for private planes. As Oleg unloaded the luggage, I was sweating from more than just the heat emanating from the sunbaked tarmac. I felt totally unqualified for what I was about to do. I'd spent most of my adult life in controlled environments—schools and hospitals—where I'd absorbed large amounts of scientific information and learned to follow standard medical protocols exactly. I was used to having answers, to knowing beforehand what I was supposed to do in a given situation, and when and how to do it. Now I felt stripped of both knowledge and skill. I couldn't say what the next hour would bring, much less the next few days. The information I had was sketchy, and my training was nil. From now on I had nothing but instinct to rely on.

My face must have shown my unease because Meredith nudged my shoulder playfully, saying, "Hey, don't worry. You're going to do fine."

"Easy for you to say."

"Just trust yourself." She leaned in, and we air-kissed on both cheeks.

After watching Meredith and Oleg ferry their luggage down a gravel walkway to a paved lot where they had a car parked, I shouldered my backpack and duffel and headed to the terminal building where I would call a cab. The plan was for them to stay in Mirny on business while I looked for Misha. Meredith had been frustratingly vague about how long she expected the mission to take. When I'd pressed her, she'd said, "Let's just see how it goes."

In the backseat of the beat-up taxi taking me to Misha's flat, I stared anxiously out the window. Mirny was a Soviet industrial city, hastily built at the edge of the diamond mine to service the miners and engineers. Far north, and far out of the way, it was the opposite of a tourist spot. We drove past concrete office buildings and an empty Soviet mega-plaza. Traffic lights blinked through their paces for a couple of cars at a time—no traffic jams here. City Hall slipped past the window—a long concrete rectangle with all the charm of an ice-cube tray. Then a small Russian Orthodox church with gold onion domes sprouted unexpectedly, like a flower out of rubble.

We turned onto a main thoroughfare, heading east. A small horse bearing a large man plodded down the middle of the road. The driver swerved around them without slowing down; in fact, I had the impression he'd speeded up. I glanced through the rear window at the man's brown, lined face and tangled mat of dark hair. His little horse, with its long swishing tail and sunlight-colored mane, was sturdy and pretty, like a carousel pony. An incongruous sight in the desultory urban landscape.

"Where do you think he's going?" I asked the driver.

He shrugged. "Evenki. Reindeer people. Who knows where they go."

I gazed back curiously at the horse and rider. The sun was sinking dramatically behind them, still enormous, still blazing, bloody and distended at the lower fringe, as if tearing from its own weight.

The taxi turned onto a side street and rumbled past a few of the usual apartment towers with their washed-out turquoise and tangerine facades. At the end of the road, backing onto a forest and low hill, was a row of nicer-looking, three-story apartment buildings with shingled roofs and brown clapboard siding. Some architect had been granted rare license for self-expression, because the two upper floors had long casement windows opening onto small balconies, lending the place a vaguely European charm.

The driver stopped in front of one. I paid him and got out, clutching my belongings. Looking up nervously at the building, I silently rehearsed the name Ilmira Nikulina. Ilmira Nikulina was Misha's roommate, a high school teacher with a quiet life, according to Meredith, who was usually home at this time. She would be my first contact, and possibly the most important one, as she'd likely know Misha's daily routines, his social life, and, depending on how close they were, his state of mind in the days before he disappeared. My job was to gain her trust and get her to confide in me, while keeping in mind that she might have seen through his cover and outed him as a spy to the authorities.

Don't overthink it, I told myself. I quickly ascended a few steps to the door, pressed the outdoor buzzer, and waited. The door unlatched with a weak vibrating hum, and I made my way up two flights of worn but clean wooden stairs. At the end of a linoleum corridor, a woman was peering out of an open doorway, only her head visible. Her hairstyle was a contradictory mix of short blond curls and bangs slicked sideways and affixed to her scalp by a bobby pin. Her most noticeable feature was her mouth—the upper lip thin as a pencil line and the lower lip full and drooping.

I explained that I was looking for Mikhail Tarasov.

"Who are you?" she asked suspiciously.

"Natalie March. An American relative of Misha's. Sorry to just show up like this. Misha was supposed to meet his mother and me in Yakutsk a few days ago, but he never showed, and he isn't answering his cell. We're worried. Is he here?"

After a quick glance down the hallway, she waved me inside, whispering, "Thank god you've come. I didn't know who to call."

She was in her late twenties, square and muscular, dressed in an old T-shirt and sweatpants, with bare feet that were short and thick, like fleshy paws. Back home, she might have been a former college rugby star who still played in a weekend league. She ushered me into a kitchen at the front of the apartment and motioned for me to sit down, introducing herself as Ilmira Nikulina—which I already knew.

"Tea?" she asked, running water into a kettle and placing it on the stove without waiting for an answer. She sank heavily into the chair opposite me, a pained look in her pale blue eyes. "I have some very bad news for you. I haven't seen or heard from Misha in over six weeks."

"Are you serious?" I said, acting surprised.

"I'm so sorry. I wanted to notify someone, but Misha was a very private person: he said almost nothing about himself. I tried his mobile dozens of times. I called the chemical plant, but they said he hadn't shown up for work. The phone number he'd put on his job application was the same one I'd been calling, and he'd given no prior address or emergency contact. I had no one to notify. All I could do was pray that someone in his family would come looking for him, but no one did, until you, tonight. Thank god."

"I can't believe it," I said in feigned distress. "Six weeks? And you have no idea—"

"None." Her lopsided mouth screwed into a tragic pout. "But I can tell you something else. On the day he went missing—July twelfth, it was—two men pushed their way into this apartment and searched his room. They refused to tell me anything. They were very rough, rude men. I thought they might hurt me, so I backed off. They left with his computer."

"Do you know who they were?"

"Policemen, they said."

"Police? Did they say if he'd been arrested?"

"No, they gave no more information."

"Did you call the police station to see if he was there?"

"Yes, right after the men left." Her eyes slid sideways. "They said they never heard of Mikhail Tarasov."

I paused, trying to square the contradiction. "So the men who said they were policemen?"

"Were not. Local, I mean. They were maybe a different kind of policemen." Her voice lowered to a whisper. "Secret police."

"Are you sure?"

She shrugged. "How can anyone be sure?"

"Well, did they show ID?"

She looked at me askance. "If they did, I'd have known they were lying. Instead, they lied about being policemen. That's how I know."

She got up to turn off the whistling kettle, and I was left to ponder this most Russian logic.

If Ilmira's suspicions were correct, the situation might be as bad as Meredith feared. Which led to other questions. If Misha had been captured as a spy, who had outed him? Now that I'd met Ilmira, she seemed an unlikely candidate, unless she was a very good actress. And where was Misha now? Imprisoned? Executed? But there was no proof that the men really were "secret police"— which I assumed meant FSB agents—other than Ilmira's fearful assumption.

She returned with mugs of steaming tea. A bowl of crusty sugar and a vase of limp yellow wildflowers occupied the center of the wooden table. Ilmira sipped the hot tea quickly, without pleasure, and turned her head away, fingers splayed across her mouth.

"Things are getting worse all the time. At night, I lie in bed and think, This must be what it was like before, under Stalin. You get your name on a list, or you have the wrong friends, or someone accuses you—and the next thing you know, you're disappeared."

I pressed her, "Is it possible that these men were not FSB agents? Could they have been anyone else?"

She gave a blasé shrug. "Sure. It's possible. They could have been criminals, mafia. Thieves." There was no conviction in her voice.

"Did Misha gamble, deal drugs—anything that might have gotten him into trouble with those kinds of people?"

"You don't know him, do you?" she said with pity in her eyes.

"No, actually I don't."

"Then let me be the one to tell you—Misha's the sort of boy who gets into trouble in school, the sort you worry will never amount to anything. But he wouldn't hurt anyone, not even a dog. He is *not* the sort to get into drugs or crime."

"Then why would anyone want to hurt him? What could he have done?"

With bitter resignation, Ilmira said, "Anything. Nothing." After a pause, she added, "It's not right. But that's how it is."

Letting my head fall into my hands, I said, "Oh god, what will I tell his mother? She's going to be devastated." I took a few deep breaths, as if trying to quell my panic. "I have to give her more information, Ilmira. She'll never be satisfied if all I can tell her is that he's missing and the FSB took his computer. She'll be sure to wonder what he could possibly have done. Most of all, she'll want to know where he is now. Maybe you can help me. I need to talk to people who knew him. Go to his workplace. And we should go to the police—or did you already do that?"

"I did, but the local cops don't actually look for missing people. It's just in case a body turns up. Then they notify you."

"This is horrible. Is there anyone he might have spoken to? Did he have any close friends?"

She shook her head. "Not really. He'd only been here a few months. There's a couple on the second floor—he used to go down to their apartment nights and come back drunk. I'd hear him banging around in the kitchen, looking for something to eat. They also work at the chemical plant—he probably met them there. Those are the only friends I know of."

"What are their names?"

"Bohdan Duboff and Tanya Karp," she said with a sneer in her voice. "Loud, flashy people who pretend to be jetsetters. Jetsetters in Mirny. What a joke."

"Did you talk to them after Misha disappeared?"

"We don't get along. I know what they think of me, and they know what I think of them."

Night had fallen beyond the open window. Cooler air was spilling over the sash. I sipped the strong black tea. My heart was pounding wildly. I was playing my part well, I thought. But I was also facing the stark fact that Misha was gone, most likely not through his own choice, and even though I'd known that coming in, seeing the fear on Ilmira's face brought the reality home in a new and terrifying way. I was almost convinced at this point that Ilmira knew nothing of Misha's real identity and that she'd played no role in his disappearance. She seemed too open, sincere, and innocent to have busted a spy and turned him in. But Meredith had told me to trust no one, a rule I intended to live by for the brief time I was in her employ.

Ilmira drained her tea and set the mug down firmly, indicating the end of our conversation. "I'm sorry you came so far only to hear such terrible news." She pushed herself up from the table with solemn weariness, plodded to the sink, washed and toweled off her hands with slow deliberateness. With her back to me, she said, "I don't know how long to keep Misha's room for him. If I get another roommate, and Misha returns…that would be awkward. But I can't afford the rent myself. I paid his share last month. Another month's rent is due next week. I can't pay it again."

I saw what she wanted. "I'll pay what he owes, and this month's as well. And stay here for a few days, too, if you don't mind."

She nodded in obvious relief. "Yes, that's a good solution. Come with me, then." She marched off down the hallway briskly, as if my offer might not last, scooping up my duffel on the way. I grabbed my backpack and followed her, passing three doors on the right that opened into a living room, bathroom, and bedroom.

The door at the end of the hallway was closed. She dropped my luggage on the floor outside it. "When you leave, would you pack his things and take them with you? I shouldn't be the one to do it."

Musty air and the stale smell of dirty socks. A twin mattress on the floor, partly covered by a rumpled sleeping bag and cast-off clothes—T-shirt, sweatpants, underwear. On the floor, a pair of muddy Nike sneakers and a nylon backpack with a water bottle stuffed in the mesh pouch. I reached for a framed photo on the desk, his sister and mother standing close together in front of a body of water that might have been a lake. Saldana's innocent smile, her simple, natural beauty, brought back the familiar flood of sorrow and anger. I quickly moved my gaze to Lena. Her short haircut and black-rimmed glasses gave no indication of a clandestine life: she might have been any working middle-aged mom. I returned the photo to its place next to an opened jar of peanut butter crossed by a crusty knife. Scattered across the desk's worn surface were sunglasses, neon green ear buds, a computer charging cord, a phone charging cord, and a backup battery charger. A coffee cup was half filled with a liquid made unidentifiable by a thick scum of mold on its surface. It was obvious that the person occupying this room had intended to return.

I rifled through the desk drawer. Pulled out a paystub from the Mayadykovsky Chemical Plant, pens, stamps, and a large serrated hunting knife with a curved ivory handle.

I searched the closet. Misha had a typical teenage boy's wardrobe of jeans, sweatpants, and zippered hoodies. Most of it was on the floor. Nudging the pile with my toe, I uncovered a pair of old hiking boots lying on their sides, yellowish dirt caught in the rubber treads.

I dipped my fingers into the pockets of every article of clothing, finding nothing more interesting than a couple of rubles and lint. I peered under the mattress, checked for loose floorboards. Finally, I sat on the bed and visually scanned the room. The walls were dirty white, empty of pictures or posters. The only ornamentation was a horsehair talisman, similar to the one I'd bought at the festival a few days before. It was hanging on a suede string from a gooseneck lamp beside the bed.

His photos and emails, his music and web searches, would have been on his computer. What remained was telling me nothing, except that Misha was a real person. A trace of his masculine odor still lingered in the folds of the sleeping bag. I could almost feel his presence in the room.

Strange, but I felt like I knew him. We were both grandchildren of Katarina Melnikova; our cells carried the same DNA. There would have to be a few shared traits. I wondered what they might be. He was athletic enough to have been a serious student of dance. I had no special abilities in that regard. We didn't look alike either. I knew from Saldana's Facebook page that he had a striking, rugged quality, while my features were unremarkable. Maybe I was trying to read too much into the family connection, scrounging around to find a worthwhile reason for having put myself in danger. It hardly mattered at this point. I was here in his messy room, in a stark industrial city near the top of the world. The only way out was through.

I gently fingered the silky horsehair talisman. His lucky token, a constant reminder of his Sakha roots. Had it kept him safe?

I called Vera a little later, my nightly ritual. I couldn't tell her where I was or what I was doing, so I concocted a trip to the Archeology Museum of Northeast Asia, where I reported having laid astonished eyes on human artifacts dating back three million years.

She burbled a laugh. "And you enjoyed that?"

"Very much!"

"Three million years—amazing. I can't begin to fathom it." Her voice softened to its warmest tone. "It's so nice to hear you're having a good time, sweetheart." A pause. "Any message from Lena?"

"Not yet. We'll give it a few more days."

She sighed. "Do take care, Natalie."

"Of course, Mom. You know me."

After the call, I felt more distant from her than I ever had before. It wasn't just geography; it was the lie, and how smoothly I'd told it.

5

Ilmira was gone when I shuffled into the kitchen the next morning at nearly ten o'clock. There was clotted gray porridge in a saucepan on the stove. I'd read somewhere that porridge was Vladimir Putin's favorite breakfast, a fact that made the gooey substance even less appetizing. I opted instead for a bruised banana and cup of chai.

The apartment was baking, so I opened the kitchen window, but there was no breeze. Just humid, gritty air that hung motionless, oppressive. I took my tea and banana into the sparsely furnished living room, kept dim by drawn mustard-colored curtains. I opened the curtains and the windows, and turned on the TV—anything to breathe life into the drabness. The news show that came on was slow and somber, stern announcers plodding heavily from one topic to another against an eye-straining backdrop of blue and gray chevron stripes.

I switched channels. A boxing match between two bloodied, bare-chested hulks popped up on the screen. I watched the grotesque spectacle of skull-jarring frontal face punches and pounding jabs to the torso, noticing the fine horizontal rain of sweat and blood droplets spewing off the bodies, and thought about concussions, contusions, infections, broken bones, chronic pain, and brain damage. Someday, these men would show up in a doctor's office asking to be made whole. Good luck with that.

Next, I wandered to the bookcase, reading titles with my head at a slant, until I came across a stack of unopened mail on a shelf. Four or five envelopes were addressed to Mikhail Tarasov and postmarked after July twelfth. Ilmira had probably been putting them aside for his hoped-for return. Flipping through them, I found a credit card offer and an advertising flyer, nothing special. Then the return address of one caught my eye. *Novaya Gazeta*, a newspaper with a Moscow address. I sliced it open, and a half piece of paper with a printed message slipped out.

Dear Journalist,

Thank you for your submission to Novaya Gazeta. We regret that your article is not suitable for our publication and wish you luck in placing it elsewhere.

The Editors

Below that, a handwritten note: *Be careful. You can get in trouble with a subject like this. –MG.*

I tried to fathom what it meant. Misha was a journalist, as well as a dancer and a spy? Well, why not? I traced my finger over the blue-ink scrawl on the bottom of the form: *Be careful.* Whoever wrote those words had pressed down hard on the pen, making shallow indentations on the thin sheet, as if he or she were feeling especially adamant. I checked the postmark, almost illegible over the highly colored Russian stamp. August fifth.

What kind of dangerous article had Misha proposed? And why would he do something that reckless while he was working undercover for the CIA?

If *Novaya Gazeta* was a typical magazine, it received dozens, maybe hundreds, of submissions a week, so the chances of getting more information about Misha's story were slim. Still, it was worth a try. I pulled out my laptop and connected to the internet with the password Ilmira had jotted down for me the night before, navigated to the magazine's website, and skimmed the masthead for an editor with the initials MG.

There was a features editor by the name of Maxim Gusev. I scribbled down the newspaper's main number, turned off the TV, and paced around the living room, swinging my arms, clearing my throat, rolling my Rs against the roof of my mouth, and flapping my lips with my index finger to make the drone of a puttering motor boat—exercises I'd learned from the play-to-win coach of the debating team at Rockville High. On the inhale, I envisioned my voice being pushed down into my diaphragm where it belonged; on the exhale, I brought it forth in the long, round *Ohm* of the lowest register possible. I might not be able to fully disguise my American accent, but I felt pretty confident about passing for a man.

A pleasant-sounding woman answered.

"Maxim Gusev, please."

"Who's calling?"

"Mikhail Tarasov, journalist."

"What is this regarding?"

"A story we're working on. He told me to call."

"Just a minute, please."

A minute later, Gusev came on the line. "*Who* is this?" He had a dry, gravelly voice that conveyed both impatience and a certain good-humored openness. I pictured a man in his fifties who was used to being pitched, who gave a writer thirty seconds free of charge, not a heartbeat more, to say something interesting.

"Mikhail Tarasov. You read my manuscript recently."

"Tarasov. Hmmm. Don't remember the name. Remind me what the subject was."

"It was…ah, controversial. You were worried it might get me into trouble."

After a lengthy pause, he said, "Oh, yes. I remember now. The abandoned gulag camp in Siberia. The one the herders discovered."

"Yes, that's it."

"In a valley, as I recall. Very remote. What did they call it again?"

I had no idea what the herders called the valley, so I punted. "Would you mind discussing the story with me for a minute, Mr. Gusev. You see, I'm not sure where to go from here, and if you could share more of your thoughts…"

"Russia isn't ready for your story, Tarasov. It may never be. People want jobs, food, opportunity; they don't want to read about the gulag. Most Russians don't know what went on there in the first place, at least not the full extent of it. Don't forget that Stalin is still a god among many, and Putin has made criticizing him a traitorous act. And, frankly, Tarasov, even if your story wasn't so controversial, I still wouldn't publish it. The allegations you made weren't supported by your evidence. Those photos could easily have been doctored. You'd need better proof than that to make the story credible, and I have no idea where you'd find it."

I started to say something but he barreled on.

"I'll tell you something, just between the two of us—I believe you and I'm not surprised. But I'm an old liberal whose days are numbered. I worry about you young ones, you idealists. Fact is, Tarasov, there's little hope of change. I never thought I'd say that, but it's true. Why risk yourself pushing boundaries that can't be moved? Take my advice, and be careful what you say."

"I understand, Mr. Gusev. But this story is very important to me; I'm not sure I can give it up."

He lowered his voice. "You're being very stupid now, Tarasov. You do realize that *Novaya Gazeta* is closely monitored, don't you? Anyone who writes for us goes on a list; even the submissions aren't safe. Which is why I destroyed your manuscript and the photos that came with it. And why I wrote you that note: I thought you should be warned. What's your accent, by the way?"

"American. I grew up there. My father was a diplomat."

"Well, that's another thing you should keep under your hat. But it does explain your naïve attitude." He paused. "You want a story idea, how about the herders? What were they called again?"

"They were…Evenki," I said, the old man on the shaggy horse popping into my mind.

"Right, right. Interesting people. You can take photos of *them*, and nothing will come of it. Especially if you stress the healthy and productive lifestyle they're enjoying. If you want to send me *that* story, I promise to give it a good look."

"Thank you, Mr. Gusev. You've been a big help."

* * *

A baby's monotonous wail drifted through the open window. I paced the living room, piecing together what I'd learned: Reindeer herders had discovered an abandoned prison camp and given it a name. Misha took photos and made "allegations" that his photos didn't support. That means he'd been to the place. But where was it, and what were the allegations? More importantly, did his foray into journalism have anything to do with his disappearance? If that were the case, Gusav had been right to warn him. But what could be dangerous enough to warrant the arrest of a nineteen-year-old Sakha man whose exposé wasn't going to be published anyway?

My plan was to visit Misha's friends, Bohdan Duboff and Tanya Karp, that evening after dinner, when they were likely to be home. In the meantime, a long, hot afternoon stretched ahead of me. Out of curiosity, I googled Evenki herders and abandoned gulag camps. Nothing came up, but I started reading articles about the Evenki—their history and geographic distribution, their ancient customs and modern-day herding operations—and before I knew it, an hour had passed. I discovered that Mirny was home to the Evenki Historical and Cultural Museum. The museum didn't have a website, but the Mirny visitor page gave its address and hours of operation: Wednesday and Saturday afternoons between two and four p.m. I checked the map; it was on the outskirts of town, about a half mile away. I had time to shower and find a decent lunch somewhere. Then I would enjoy a culturally enriching afternoon.

The Evenki Historical and Cultural Museum was sandwiched between a liquor store and hair salon. Its name was carefully hand-painted in fanciful lettering on a pretty wooden plaque decorated with reindeer, horses, and a crescent moon. The plaque was affixed to the center of a rusted metal door that might have been salvaged from a derelict prison or military site. I tried the handle. It didn't budge. I pressed a buzzer and waited.

A second floor window opened, and an old man peered over the ledge, tufts of white hair sticking out from his head. His face was burnished to a ruddy brown, the skin pulled taut over high cheekbones.

"Are you here to visit the museum?"

"Yes."

"Wait a few minutes, please. We're almost ready."

A short while later, I heard a light step on the stairs, and the creaking door was opened by a young woman resplendent in a reindeer-hide tunic embroidered with tiny multi-colored beads. Her face was flat and pale, heart-shaped, astonishingly pretty—framed by silver ornaments dangling from a silver headdress. The black hair falling loose across her shoulders and down to her waist was like a silky second garment. Close to her chest she held what appeared to be a warrior's shield—an animal skin stretched on a round frame decorated with beaded horsehair tufts. She bowed slightly, too bashful to meet my eyes.

"Welcome to the Evenki Museum. I am pleased to be your guide today. May I ask what country you are from?"

When I told her, she announced that she would conduct the tour in English. I explained that she didn't have to do that, as I spoke Russian quite well, but she demurely insisted.

I followed her up a narrow stairway to a long, cramped room with a scuffed wooden floor and a single window, the same one from which the old man had looked down. He stood smiling in the doorway to a side room, wearing a wrinkled suit jacket, a tailored white shirt, and a western-style string tie. He was small and genial, apparently content to observe the proceedings with kind, indulgent attention.

The museum consisted of a counter with a glass case running along the left wall. Inside, dozens of small artifacts were arranged on green felt cloths. The right wall was crowded with photographs of varying sizes in cheap plastic frames—mostly black-and-white, some sepia-toned, many hanging tilted, all of them dusty.

The young woman introduced herself as Emmie. Her grandfather was named Tolya. With a graceful Vanna White gesture, she directed my attention to the glass case and began to speak in slow, rather tortured English sentences. It didn't go well. She stumbled over every other word, blushing with each mistake, but showed no signs of letting up, until with a lightly rueful shrug she suddenly reverted to her native language. Tolya grinned, perhaps in support of her brave linguistic attempt, and she couldn't suppress a proud teenage giggle. She then proceeded to describe the origin and uses of each artifact displayed on the green felt, working her way across the first shelf before moving down to the second.

I quickly got bored—I was not, it turned out, particularly captivated by artifacts such as clay pots and beaded headdresses, however authentic they might be. I would much rather have scanned the shelves on my own for a bit, and then talked informally with Emmie and Tolya, who seemed quite nice. But when I tried to politely interrupt Emmie's memorized spiel, the girl appeared crestfallen, so I held back and let her finish. When every item in the glass case had been fully explained, I again tried to initiate a two-way conversation, but

Emmie gracefully swirled to the wall of photos and began explaining those. I resigned myself to enduring the performance, even managing a smile and several interested nods of the head. By the time she'd finished naming the six people in the last photo and explaining the important event that the photo commemorated, I was ready to cheer with relief. But the treasures of the museum hadn't been exhausted yet. Jangling the silver ornaments on her headdress, Emmie floated to an ancient saddle mounted on a log base, and proceeded to instruct me in the process of its construction from reindeer hides and sinews, her delicate fingers tracing the intricate workmanship.

At long last she favored me with a lovely smile and said in letter-perfect English: "Admission is free, but donations are welcome."

I opened my wallet and pulled out a generous wad of rubles, which I slipped into a glass jar on the counter labeled for that purpose. "I have a question I'm hoping you can answer," I said.

"We'll be glad to help if we can," Tolya replied. One of his eyes was dark brown, almost black; a cataract in the other eye had turned it milky beige.

"I heard that an abandoned gulag camp was discovered recently, perhaps by herders from around here. Do you know anything about that?"

He furrowed his brow. "Do you mean Death Valley?"

"Possibly. I don't know its name."

"Why are you interested?"

"I'm looking for someone who might have gone there."

Creases appeared in his forehead as he thought about that. He asked if I'd like to sit down, and led me through a doorway into a studio apartment with one twin bed, one mattress on the floor, a sink, small refrigerator, and a stove on which a dented kettle sat. Clothes were crammed into a broom closet and folded in piles on the floor, and there were piles of books and papers everywhere. A dining table pushed against a wall was covered with a vinyl cloth; a vase in its center held sprigs of poplar. Emmie trailed after us, grabbed some clothes that were lying on the bed, and quietly left.

The old man began, as Russians inevitably did, by making tea. We engaged in pleasant small talk about my trip, the weather, and so on. It went on long enough that I started getting impatient again, until, finally, he began talking about an abandoned camp that an Evenki brigade travelling along the Dentin River had discovered this past spring. They'd come across a huge field in a shallow valley and stopped to let the herd graze. The reindeer started showing signs of illness within a few days. First the fur on their legs came out in clumps, then they became very tired and refused to walk. Alarmed, the herders drove them down the valley as best they could, and were surprised to come across the remains of a mining camp. A uranium mine, by the looks of it, so they figured there was radioactivity in the grass, and that was what was making the animals sick. They called the place Death Valley.

I frowned as I processed the information. It was no secret that the Soviets had mined uranium in Siberia to make the bomb; any number of such places would have been in operation during Stalin's brutal regime. I doubted that the discovery of such a site would be considered controversial; it might not even be particularly newsworthy.

"Herders must come across a lot of abandoned prison camps in their travels," I said.

"Yes, but they're usually marked on maps, and if there's radioactivity, signs are posted. Warnings not to drink the water or eat the berries, and so on. This camp was unknown until the herders stumbled across it, and there weren't any warnings."

"What do you make of that?"

Tolya shrugged. "Don't know. There were so many prison camps in the Kolyma Region during the gulag era, it's possible one was forgotten."

"Did the herders report it?"

"You mean to the government?" He grimaced bitterly. "We have as little to do with the Kremlin as possible. If the Russians overlooked one of their death camps, what is that to us?"

"I see. How might someone local—not an Evenki—have found out about it?"

"There was a notice in the Mirny paper, in a section called Evenki News, that described the camp and warned other herding groups to stay away." He sipped his tea, and when he put the cup down on the table, he said, "Now tell me who this person is who went to Death Valley."

I told him as much of my story as was needed—a death in the family, a desire to meet my relatives, arriving in Mirny to find that my cousin had vanished without a trace. I explained that he'd been trying to sell a story about an abandoned gulag camp recently discovered by herders to a newspaper, that the camp was probably one of the last places he visited before he disappeared.

Tolya looked askance. "You think he might be there now?"

"From what you say, I hope not. I just know that something important must have drawn him there, and if I knew what it was…"

Tolya pondered, shook his head. "I can't imagine what it would be."

"You didn't happen to hear about a young man going out there, to Death Valley, did you? It would have been in June, most likely. Mikhail Tarasov is his name."

"No, I heard nothing like that."

"Would you let me know if you do?" I produced my card and put it on the table. "Thank you, Tolya. You've been very kind. And I certainly enjoyed the museum."

His smile revealed worn-down stubs of stained teeth. "I don't think so. But it was nice of you to let Emmie conduct her tour. She practices very hard, and her English is getting better all the time."

. · · · · · · · ·

On my way back to the flat, I stopped for groceries at a little mom-and-pop store painted bright yellow with an off-kilter screen door and a couple of old cars parked in a dusty lot. The cashier glanced up briefly, seemed to take me in for a moment as a bit of an oddity. I smiled, which probably only served to confirm my strangeness in that generally unsmiling country, and the cashier looked away quickly, as if recoiling from the excessive friendliness.

I scoured the aisles, picking up anything that looked good, with a mind to stock Ilmira's empty refrigerator and cupboards. There were various cheeses and yogurts; beets, tomatoes, and cucumbers; and, of all things, frozen Purdue chicken breasts. No sodas or processed junk foods from international food companies, who probably hadn't found a way yet to turn a profit in this faraway corner of the world.

When Ilmira returned from work and opened the refrigerator door, she gave a squeal of delight. We sat down to Bulgarian wine, pickles, olives, cheese and crackers, followed by a simple dinner of chicken and rice. I think she was relieved to see that I wasn't going to be a slacker, that I intended to pull my weight in cooking and chores.

As daylight faded and shadows lengthened in the room, we talked together easily, exchanging stories of our lives. She was a person of puzzling contradictions: one on hand, pragmatic and literal-minded. On the other, moody, fatalistic, and full of old superstitions. In another circumstance we might have become friends, but I was sharply conscious of my duplicity. My goal was just to do my job and get out of Mirny as quickly as possible.

I eventually steered the conversation to Misha, explaining what I'd learned about his interest in the gulag, reindeer herders, and journalism. She said he hadn't mentioned any of that to her. But she did recall him taking a weekend trip in late May, shortly after he moved in. I checked off the days in my head: he would have had plenty of time to write and submit the article between then and July twelfth, when he disappeared.

Had Gusev's warning come too late?

Around eight-thirty p.m., after Ilmira and I cleaned the kitchen, I went down to the second floor and knocked on the door of the Duboff/Karp apartment. It had three deadbolts, so a fair amount of metallic clicking and sliding attended its opening. A thin sylph of a woman peered out at me. Her hair was jet black with a bluish sheen, cut in short spikes moussed straight up. Heavy make-up bruised her eyes, and a small purple tattoo of a Russian Orthodox cross nestled in the indentation at the base of her neck. Her skin was the near-translucent white of many sunless winters.

"Tanya Karp?"

"Who are you?" She was in her late-twenties maybe, toughened and wary, but curious.

I introduced myself and explained my reason for being there. "We're all very worried. We haven't heard from Misha in quite some time. His roommate said you were friends, and I was wondering if you have any idea where he might be."

A gruff male voice interrupted. "Tanya, who's at the door?" A man appeared and edged her aside with his bulk and self-importance, dark eyes glowering from under thick black brows. He was dressed in a white, blue, and green athletic suit about twenty years out of date, its top zipped over a slightly protruding abdomen, tufts of curling chest hair blooming almost to his neck. His hair was slicked back from his low forehead with some kind of oily gel. He looked to be my age, maybe a few years younger—a once-strong man going soft with time, but still, in his puffed-out chest and bandy-legged stance, exuding the hostile arrogance of a fiery youth.

Tanya spoke to him in a low, confidential tone. "Misha's cousin. Looking for him."

"We don't know where he is," the man said bluntly. He turned away, and

Tanya moved to close the door.

"You must be Bohdan Duboff," I interjected. "Please, could you spare a minute or two? Misha's mother is very worried. We all are."

He turned to observe me keenly. "Where are you from?"

"The United States."

"I thought so," he said, proving the minor fact of his accent prowess. He looked me up and down until it was blatantly rude, and, either incorrectly guessing that I was harmless, or curious about how an American had arrived on his doorstep, stepped aside. I was ushered into a small dimly-lit room overfilled with furniture—brown polyester couch threadbare in spots, rattan chairs scattered about, an old exercise bike crammed in a corner, and a wall of pine bookcases stuffed with books, papers, and photographs that were either cheaply framed or taped to the shelves. An ashtray on the coffee table brimmed with cigarette buts, half-smoked joints, and a roach clip, while spindly plants in clay pots kept close company on a windowsill. A gorgeously colored Turkish rug that most Westerners would have coveted warmed the dusty wood floor.

A frenzy of shrill squawking erupted as a large green parrot lunged off its perch and attached itself to the bars of its ornate metal cage, leaving the vacated swing to sweep back and forth, squeaking on an unoiled hinge.

"Hush," Tanya told it, using her index finger to flick the bird's talons off the bars one by one. The bird croaked some outraged Russian-sounding words before repairing to its swinging perch, where it bobbed its yellow-crested head in what looked like keen excitement.

I took a seat on the couch, keeping up my anxious patter—Misha's been gone for so long, it's unlike him not to call, he's never done anything like this before, etcetera.

Duboff scoffed paternalistically. "Come now. Don't be so dramatic. Why do you think the worst? He's a young man feeling his oats. Probably just gone off somewhere—maybe on a trip or with a woman. Tell his mother not to worry. He'll show up soon."

"It's been over six weeks," I insisted. "Did he say anything to you before he left? Was he seeing anyone? Did he mention any new friends?"

"Nothing that I recall," Tanya said, frowning. "Six weeks? I didn't realize it's been that long since we've seen him."

If they knew anything about Misha's covert activities, they were hiding it well. Bohdan's masculine condescension and Tanya's bewildered concern seemed genuine and unrehearsed. I picked up no shared glances or fleeting expressions of suspicion or fear. But I was a neophyte in the spying business, and my instincts might very well be wrong. They could still be Misha's snitchers, or even his abductors.

"His clothes are still in his room," I continued with breathless worry. "His roommate says he always told her where he was going—then suddenly, with no word to anyone, he disappears!"

"Oh, you can't listen to Ilmira Nikolina. That woman is always complaining and finding trouble," Bohdan said. "Last month, she told a neighbor there were ghosts in the hallway. Ghosts! Can you believe it? No, she's not to be taken seriously. She's a…" Here he used a Russian word that had no real English equivalent—something like *old biddy* with a twist of *virago*.

"I just don't know what to do," I said mournfully, letting my shoulders slump.

"Let it go," Duboff insisted, this time with a touch of sympathy for Misha's distraught relation. "What are you so worried about anyway? You think he was murdered? There's not a chance of that, if you ask me. We had him down here many nights to talk and drink and listen to music; I think we'd know if he was into some bad business that could get him killed. There was nothing like that. I tell you, Misha's a good kid. Likes to laugh and tell stories—smart, too, very interested in politics. I'd be surprised if he had a single enemy."

It looked as though Misha had done a masterful job of keeping his cover with Bohdan and Tanya, just as he had with Ilmira. But what if they were the ones spinning lies right now, and I was the one being played?

"Look," Bohdan explained in his labored, pedantic way, "if Misha's being held for ransom, your family would have heard from the kidnappers by now. But who would bother with a kid who doesn't have two cents to his name? He might have died in a car crash, or drowned, or something like that—that would be very sad. But what would be the point in hunting for his body? There's not much chance you'd find it if you don't even know which direction he went in, and the snow will cover it up in a few months in any case. My advice is to bring his picture to the police, so that if they find his body, they'll know who to call."

I filed away the fact that Bohdan was showing precious little concern for his missing friend. He continued, "What else is there? He got lost in the taiga? No way, too smart for that. He's part Sakha—you can see it in him. They might live in villages now, but herding's in their blood. Thousands of years of nomad life doesn't go away in a few generations. So, in my opinion, there's not much you can do to find your cousin. My guess is he doesn't want to be found, which means you're just wasting your time. But, like I said, he's a good kid, and if he's alive, he'll turn up soon, if only to keep his mother from worrying."

Bohdan seemed quite satisfied with this airtight reasoning, and I sensed that any challenge would only lead to argument. The subject was closed for now.

He gestured to Tanya, who obediently left the room and returned a moment later with a bottle of vodka and three shot glasses. Leaning forward, he splashed the vodka into the glasses, and lifted his glass to me, as if a toast were the only reasonable response to life's insolvable problems and maddening mysteries. "*Za vstrechu!*" To our meeting!

"*Za vstrechu!*" Tanya followed her boyfriend's lead with a delighted smile, in which I detected a trace of relief. The vodka meant we were going to be friends.

"*Za vstrechu!*" I added.

We all downed the first shot. It was cheap stuff that burned my throat.

Bohdan immediately poured another round and raised his glass again, calling out with equal gusto, "*Vashe zrodovye!*" To your health!

"*Vashe zrodovye!*" Tanya chimed in.

"*Vashe zrodovye!*" I held my glass aloft. The second one went down a little easier, given that the burn of the first one had anaesthetized my throat.

No sooner had I plunked the empty glass on the table than Bohdan was refilling all three.

"Oh, no. Wait a minute," I protested with a polite laugh.

But Bohdan pressed the third shot on me, at the same time magnanimously announcing, "To our American visitor!"

"To Natalya!" Tanya added warmly, hoisting her glass in the air.

"To new friends!" I obliged with a smile, only this time, when I put the glass down, I covered it with my hand. Refusing a toast was considered bad manners in Russia, but I felt that I'd done my duty as a guest. "I'm sorry. You're being very kind, but I'm not used to this. I really can't keep up."

"One more for now. Then I promise we'll take a break," Bohdan said reasonably.

I removed my hand, and the fourth round was poured. This time, Bohdan nodded at me shrewdly and lowered his voice to a more intimate register. "To the beautiful woman who flew halfway around the world to search for her Siberian cousin."

"To Misha! May he return to us soon!" Tanya said with an odd giggle.

I raised the glass containing what I fully intended would be my last few ounces of vodka that evening, and met Bohdan's glinting eye. Was I imagining things, or did he suspect me? Or was he coming on to me?

I said, "To happy endings. May we all find what we're searching for." I swallowed the vodka in a single gulp and coughed at the after-burn.

Bohdan leaned back in his chair with his hands behind his head, elbows spread wide—a classic dominant pose. Having worked among ambitious men for most of my career, I knew better than to let such body language go unchallenged. I adopted the same position, inhaling deeply to expand my chest, and did him one better by crossing one leg across the other, ankle to knee. We stared at each other for a few seconds longer than was comfortable, sizing each other up.

"So. You are American," he said in a studiously neutral tone that nonetheless contained a hint of challenge.

So this is what he wants, I thought.

I bluntly admitted my nationality and added a couple of provocative opinions, thereby launching the kind of interminable political discussion that Russians love. Over the next hour, the three of us thoroughly aired our ideological differences. We didn't spare each other's feelings, thus engendering trust, and took to raising our glasses each time one of us made an especially cogent point. Soon, we were being unbearably brilliant in our own and each other's estimations, and the emptied bottle was replaced by another.

The first four shots having worked their magic, I couldn't recall why I'd so prudishly resisted vodka's obvious charms. Vodka was nothing less than the national drink of Russia, the ax that broke down barriers and the glue that held the huge federation together. It was nourishment for the moody, oft-neglected Russian soul, as elemental as mother's milk and as necessary as water. Russians let out their true warm-heartedness when they drank—their true opinions, too. With any luck, either Bohdan or Tanya would drop their guard just enough to let important information slip, if they had any.

"In Russia, we have all the parts of a democracy—elections, parliament, laws—but it's all big joke," Tanya asserted. "Everyone knows we have an authoritarian system that doesn't care about the citizens at all."

"As long as you have elections, you can change that," I pointed out.

"Bah, elections. They put the ballot box on the outside, while behind the scenes the votes are being destroyed," Bohdan said disgustedly.

Tanya added, "And even if you elect new politicians, it makes no difference. One's the same as the other, and they're all corrupt, especially Putin, the little madman. He's been lining his pockets all along."

"There must be someone who can stand up for the people," I said, my voice trailing off. My idealism was fading fast in the corrosive atmosphere of my hosts' total political disillusionment.

Bohdan wearily shook his head. "You Westerners don't get it. If you want to truly understand Russia, you have to think of it in two parts: the government and the people. The two parts don't speak to each other at all. They don't have the same language; they don't even like each other. The government acts the way it wants, and the people do the same. It's always been that way. We have a saying in Russia, *God is far up, and the Tsar is far away.* The Kremlin thrashes around like a huge stupid ape with a stick up its ass. And what do the Russian people do? We endure."

The conversation wound through several more topics, and all the while the toasting didn't let up. Apparently bent on displaying a wit that nature had not endowed him with, Bohdan was a font of shop-worn aphorisms. *Teaching a fool is the same as treating a dead man. Little thieves are hanged, but great ones escape.* He insisted on counting the shots and further insisted that even numbers were unlucky; we had to end each round on an odd.

"But you're only counting in even numbers!" Tanya protested, covering a belch with the back of her very white hand.

Bohdan leaned forward to look deeply into my eyes. "Dr. Natalie March, my very good friend from Washington, D.C., here we have an ancient saying: *When a visitor leaves Siberia, he will dream of returning, but he will not know why.*"

I gave a sincere, if bemused, smile. The night had become so warm and comfortable for me that I believed it might be so. I'd started to like Bohdan and Tanya; their honest, uncompromising cynicism hinted at a rich core of unfailing idealism underneath. They wanted a better world—who could blame them for that? If they ever visited Washington, I would invite them to dinner at my condo. At which I'd be damn sure to serve something better than the crap-ass fermented potato water that was presently corroding my stomach and making my eyes cross.

Vaguely aware that this natural impulse toward affection was dangerous, I dutifully reminded myself that Duboff and Karp were quite possibly my cousin's abductors and enemies of the United States. But maintaining suspicion was an arduous task after so much friendly conversation and so many vodka shots. Thirteen maybe? An odd number, of course, and unlucky, to boot! Was that a sign? Was it all going wrong? And did anyone know what the hell *to boot* meant? Truth was, I'd always been a mushy, emotional drunk—in college, I once threw my arms around a dean who had unwisely appeared at a tailgate party, and gushed in his ear that he was a Very Great Man before slobbering a kiss on his cheek. Sometimes it is just so much easier to love the ones you're with.

Russians have a word, *nedoperepil*, that describes having drunk more than you should have but less than you absolutely could have. An hour later, I was at the far edge of *nedoperepil*. My eyes kept drifting of their own accord to the surreal spectacle of the large multi-colored bird and his mechanically bobbing tufted head; to the ornate scrolls in the thick Turkish rug; to blurry brown stains under the window in the shape, I thought, of mating frogs. What had caused those unsightly blots? Water stains from a leaky roof? A splattering of wine or coffee? Blood? Were they a clue I ought to pay attention to? I mustn't forget to be on the constant lookout for clues, I reminded myself. Maybe I should snap rapid-fire photos of the stains surreptitiously and send them off to a CIA lab for analysis. Then I'd be a Very Great Spy! As if from a distance, I heard Tanya's voice rise in an aggrieved lament.

"Three- and four-year-old children complaining of pains in their legs! Why should little children have pains in their legs? Why?"

The doctor in me came to a wobbly sort of attention. "What's this, Tanya?"

Bohdan's thick eyebrows knitted together. "The process we use to decontaminate was never tested. The experts warned it wasn't safe, but the Kremlin insisted we get the job done as fast as possible, so we were told to go ahead. Now the whole city is poisoned. There's phosphorous in the water and plants—we can't help but consume it. Almost every family has someone sick with cancer. And the little kids complain of pains in their legs."

"And how do you suppose the great Russian government has answered our complaints?" Tanya said, rising in fury from her seat. "Let me show you how!"

She grabbed two bizarre-looking gas masks off hooks by the door and held them aloft. "We're told to carry these with us to and from work each day; on the job, we're supposed to keep them over our shoulders at all times in case of an 'incident.' Ha! They say *incident*, but what they mean is *accident*."

"Three men were killed by a gas leak a few years ago," Bohdan said.

"Here. Try it on," Tanya insisted, shoving the mask in my face. The rusted zipper required some tugging, and I had to loosen and re-connect the stiff leather straps. Then I held up the grotesquely misshapen thing, puzzling over which way to put it on. Tanya helped, but the instant the mask covered my nose and mouth, I believed I could smell an acrid burning dust, so I whipped it off and dropped it on the floor.

"See?" Tanya said. "The authorities brag they've given us protective gear, but these masks are a joke."

She and Bohdan began to talk over each other in their rush to describe just how bad things were.

Bohdan said, "Mirny didn't used to be this way. We had the mine; we had the chemical plant. We were a poor city, sure, but we were proud of the work we did before they converted the plant. Now the government says it's going to close the plant for good once the decontamination work is done. That's less than a year away. More than a thousand people will be out of work."

"How do they expect us to pay for our food if we don't have jobs?" Tanya demanded in a red-eyed frenzy. "Do you think they'll give us unemployment checks like they do in the United States? No way. We'll just rot here with nothing to do, half starving like the old people! Yes, it's true: we're going to starve! First poisoned, then abandoned. The people of Mirny are no more than dirt under the government's feet." The purple cross at the base of her neck throbbed with her agitated breathing.

Bohdan glanced over at his girlfriend and said, "Don't excite yourself, Tanya. You know it won't be like that for us."

"Not for us maybe. But everyone else will suffer, as if they haven't done enough of that." Tanya's eyes flashed when she explained to me, "We're leaving Mirny. Soon." She glared defiantly at Bohdan, adding, "With my mother."

"Oh, your old mother," he said gruffly. "Do we have to talk about that again? She'll be fine here, just as she's always been. I tell you, she comes here too much. You're tied to her apron string."

"Really? Is that what you think?" Tanya retorted with an upward tilting chin. "Don't you notice the cooking and cleaning she does? Do *you* want to do that work when we get to Batumi? Because I won't do it all myself. And if we have children, shall we live on one less paycheck so I can stay home to take care of them when my mother would do it for free?"

Bohdan had sunk a bit under the barrage. "All right, all right. Let's not argue. Your mother can come, too."

The parrot squawked, and Tanya balled a wad of paper and threw it at the cage. "Not you. You are ugly and you smell."

Bohdan looked at me dolefully, in need of sympathy, which I obediently gave. At the same time, I was struggling to carve out some memory space in my alcohol-sodden brain. *Batumi*? Where was that? I'd never heard of the place before.

"When are you leaving?" I asked—the most innocuous question I could think of.

"As soon our stupid car is fixed," Tanya said, her feistiness slightly subdued by Bohdan's capitulation.

"The mechanic is waiting for a part," Bohdan said.

Tanya rolled her eyes. "In Russia, we grow old waiting for parts."

By then I'd given the conversation about as much attention as my addled brain could manage. A couple of photos taped to a shelf of the bookcase were swaying before my eyes, coming in and out of focus. I rose and carefully traversed the short distance. One was of Tanya and Bohdan in bathing suits, standing ankle deep in the lacy waves and sinking wet sand of a beach. Other bathers in bright suits surrounded them. Further out on flat blue water, a woman in a bathing cap floated peacefully on her back.

"Look at you two bathing beauties," I teased.

The parrot nodded and grunted.

"Is that Batumi?" I asked.

"No, Baku," Bohdan said. "Batumi is in Georgia, near the Turkish border. It's warm there, even in winter, full of beautiful birds and trees."

"Like nightingales and turtle doves. And green warblers, which are my favorite," Tanya said excitedly. "And the trees? There are so many different kinds. They say the pink blossoms of cherry trees drop right onto the streets." She sighed dreamily. "It's on the Black Sea, very beautiful. We're going to move there soon."

Then, glaring at Bohdan, she kicked ineffectively at the legs of his chair, and added in a fresh wave of dissatisfaction, "But first we have to drive nine thousand kilometers to Baku. And you said we'd never go back!"

"This is the last trip, I promise," Bohdan replied tersely.

"I despise Baku," Tanya confided to me. "The Muslims hate Russians, and we hate them back. We're only going because we have to, because *Bohdan* says we have to, and of course we women are always expected to do just what the man says! What he does there is very secret. I only know that he leaves me to sit on the beach by myself for hours, and when the wind comes up in Baku, as it always will, the sand swirls in little cyclones and stings your eyes. You have to run indoors just to get out of it. Then Bohdan shows up and says, 'Quick! Let's go!' and I'm expected to jump to my toes."

"Tanya. Enough," Bohdan said in a low voice.

A secret, I thought. Must keep them talking. "I hear Baku is a fascinating city. The cultural center of Azerbaijan with Western and Middle Eastern influences combining. I'd love to go there someday."

"Oh, do! You can meet us there. We'll shop together on Nizami Street and go to the beach while Bohdan's working. Who knows, you might meet a man!" Tanya gushed.

Bohdan shot her a cold, hard stare. Their eyes locked for a few seconds until Tanya looked away.

I said lightly, "I'm not sure about the man, but the rest sounds like fun." What to say next? I decided on the direct approach. Keeping the light tone, I added, "Bohdan, what *do* you do in Baku?"

"Nothing," he answered woodenly.

"*Nothing*? Is *that* why you've dragged me there twice already?" Tanya said with as much outrage as she dared.

Again, that harsh, restraining look from Bohdan.

I said, "Well, if I do visit Baku someday—can you recommend any good hotels or restaurants?"

A few stony seconds passed while Bohdan and Tanya stared at each other pointedly, with Tanya seeming to hover in a confused place between defiance and submission. Not taking her eyes from his face, she said, "We like to stay at the—"

"Enough!" Bohdan said sharply. "Be quiet, Tanya." He tossed back the few last drops in his glass, and smacked it down on the wood.

Tanya picked sullenly at her sweater.

The mood in the room had completely changed.

I confessed to being exhausted. Long trip, my worries about Misha, and so on. Thanking them for their hospitality, I said I hoped I could return the favor someday. Tanya showed me silently to the door.

"Maybe we'll visit you in Washington, D.C.," she whispered, without much hope, and I said that would be nice.

The hallway seemed unduly long and shadowy. In the stairwell, I kept one palm on the wall, planted my feet carefully on the steps. It was a challenge to find the right door.

Ilmira answered my knock, the TV screen glowing in the living room. She surveyed my disheveled state with a dour frown. "See? It was the same with Misha. They plied him with alcohol and sent him staggering back here late at night. He had to drag himself out of bed in the morning. That's not right. A person who works with dangerous chemicals needs to be alert."

I blinked slowly at Ilmira's features until they found their correct places. "You are perfectly correct!" I said with rudely mocking enthusiasm, while the words *old biddy* and *virago* echoed in my mind. Then, just as suddenly, sympathy overcame me, and I surprised her with a big warm hug. "You are so good, Ilmira! You worry about everyone!"

She drew back, a little startled and a little pleased.

"*Spokoynoy nochi!*" I called over my shoulder. And that motley crowd of mismatched syllables felt so warm and earthy on my tongue that I shouted them a few more times.

In Misha's bedroom with the door shut, I dropped like a sack of rocks onto the bed, murmuring, "Look at me, spying like a pro." And passed into sleep with two seemingly unrelated words spinning around in my head: *Dangerous. Chemicals.*

My head boomed with pain, a severe pounding directly behind my eyes, and my mouth was a sand-filled trough. Outside Misha's bedroom window, the day was well-established, the sky an iridescent blue expanse with feathery filaments of cirrus. I shuffled to the kitchen. There was another pot of oatmeal on the stove; it gave me the dry heaves. I downed two glasses of water with aspirin I found in a cabinet and went back to bed.

It was after noon when I woke again. A mounded white cloud with a gray underbelly was drifting across the sky. Rain, I hoped, to finally break the beastly heat. All was quiet inside and out, and I floated for a while in blessed semi-consciousness, until a troublesome thought began to nag. There was something I needed to do, something important. Then it came to me. I needed to pass on the intelligence I'd gathered to Meredith Viles. Reaching an arm over the side of the bed, I fumbled for the crappy spy phone in the pocket of the jeans lying crumpled on the floor, and texted the following:

Ilmira N. says two men ID-ing as police (but really not) came to flat day M went missing and took his computer. Ilmira believes they were FSB.

Local police said M not arrested.

M wrote news article about radioactive gulag camp, sent to Novaya Gazeta. Editor rejected, calling topic "dangerous."

Camp recently discovered by herders, named Death Valley.

M friends with neighbors who also work chem plant. Names: Bohdan Duboff, Tanya Karp. They plan to move to city in Georgia (Batumi) and traveled by car to Baku twice (?) on unidentified mission.

What to do next? Please advise.

I took a shower and was pulling a comb through my wet hair when the spy phone pinged. The message was from Meredith: *Check for black Lada parked on street in one hour.*

I finished dressing, cooked up eggs and toast, forced myself to get them down. More aspirin, more water. Headache persisting. Most likely stress at this point, coming from a creeping dread that things might get worse before they got better.

I was waiting at the kitchen window when the boxy little car appeared. I hustled down the stairs and across the quiet street, and piled in to the passenger side seat. Meredith was behind the wheel, wearing big dark glasses and an olive-green headscarf over her hair. She pulled away from the shoulder, and drove six or seven blocks into a congested neighborhood of apartment towers, then turned into a pot-holed gravel lot behind a tiny food market, and backed the Lada into a space by a rusted fence. Advertisements for the day's specials—beets, chicken stock, yogurt—were plastered on the store's rear entrance. The engine of the old car continued to ping and wheeze for a few moments after it was shut off. The hot sun blazed through the dirty windshield.

Meredith took off her sunglasses and angled her body to face me in the cramped space. "Talk to me about Duboff and Karp."

I said I didn't think they were involved in Misha's disappearance. They'd seemed too natural, too surprised, when they learned how long he'd been missing. As the words were leaving my mouth, I heard their naivete.

"They charmed you," she said disapprovingly.

"I wouldn't call it charm."

"You lost your objectivity."

"I guess. I don't know. They just don't seem like bad people."

"Natalie. Listen to yourself."

"Okay, okay."

"Tell me exactly what they said about Baku and Batumi. Think back. Their exact words. Take your time."

I closed my eyes and recreated the scene in my mind, starting with the photograph of Bohdan and Tanya in their bathing suits at the edge of the shallow lacy waves, their Russian bodies pale as winter in a blazing Azerbaijan sun. I recited our entire conversation about Batumi, and then Baku, as precisely as I could.

She sighed with satisfaction. "This is very good work, Natalie. You made some real progress. Now there's something I need you to do." She reached into her purse and pulled out some black molded plastic gizmos, three of them, each about the size of a book of matches. She held one up, pinched between two fingers.

"This little device is fitted with a SIM card. If there's a sound above forty-five decibels within ten meters, it calls our number, and we listen in. I'm giving you three: bedroom, kitchen, living room. All you have to do is conceal them." When she tried to drop them into my hand, I folded my arms across my chest.

"Are you crazy? I'm not trained for that."

"It has to be done. We need more information, and we need it as quickly as possible."

"Forget it, Meredith. There's no way I can get into that apartment again. I've already used up my only excuse for dropping by."

She gave me a reproachful look. "Please. You're better than that; I know you are. I've seen what you can do, what you've already done. Now take the devices."

I didn't. Instead, I looked into her eyes. "What's all this about? What was Misha doing here?"

She sighed with undisguised impatience. "Nice try. But as I said before, this is a strictly need-to-know operation."

"Baku? Batumi? What's the significance?" I said, undeterred.

"We don't have time for this. You want to get on with your life? Get away from all this stuff? Then plant the devices. That's all. A simple job."

"Simple but not easy. Because even if I did manage to get inside their apartment a second time on some pretext, how am I supposed to conceal those things without them noticing? In the bedroom, no less."

"You'll think of something."

"What if I don't?"

"You will. You're a problem solver. You like the hard challenges."

"Is that what it says in my psych profile?"

"Yes, actually. That's exactly what it says."

The air conditioning had shut off with the engine, and the sun was heating up the car's interior. I felt claustrophobic, and cracked the window to get fresher air. Sounds streamed in on the draft: mostly passing cars and, somewhere, children shouting.

After a while, I said, "So what you're telling me, without telling me, is that Duboff and Karp are probably up to some shady business in Azerbaijan. And what you're flatly refusing to tell me is whether that business is in any way connected to what Misha's objectives were. Which, if it were, would make Duboff and Karp prime suspects in Misha's disappearance. And, therefore, rather dangerous."

"Correct," she said, eyes trained on the back of the market.

If I could have boarded a plane to the States right then and there, I probably would have. But Meredith, with her unerring psychological acumen, cut off that impulse before it had a chance to grow.

"What's your answer?" she asked sharply.

"You're asking me to risk my life. That's a lot more than I bargained for. Too much, I'd say. Plant the devices yourself."

She cut in harshly, "Okay, Natalie. I didn't want it to come to this, but you've given me no choice. You see, I *could* use what you did in medical school against you. But I really don't want to do that. Especially when your name's on the short list for chief of surgery."

I groaned without surprise. It was like hearing the second shoe hit the floor, the one I'd been waiting to drop. How wishfully stupid it had been to imagine that the secret episode from my past could have slipped by the CIA.

"It was self-defense," I said woodenly.

"Come on. Own it. You rode an elevator down eight floors to the basement, then took it right back up to the classroom where you and the other student had been studying. You had plenty of time to leave the building and call the police. But you didn't. Because that would have put you in the limelight, wouldn't it? It would have given you a reputation as a troublemaker in a very competitive program in which you were determined to come out on top. So you decided to take justice into your own hands. Borrowed a sharp little scalpel from the cadaver room. Sheer luck that you didn't slice his jugular."

"It wasn't luck. I knew exactly what I was doing. I wanted to scar him close to the artery, and that's what I did. So he'd have something to remember me by, and would always know what I could have done."

"Thank god for your steady, well-trained hand. But, of course, he didn't see it that way. He filed charges. Attempted murder. He got cold feet when you started squawking rape, and you both slunk away before you could destroy each other's brilliant careers."

"No, Meredith. That wasn't what happened. He dropped the suit because he knew the truth—that *he* was the criminal, not me."

"You want to talk about truth? Okay. Here's a question that's been bugging me: was it rape or attempted rape?"

I drew in a sharp breath. How did she know? Had there been something in the record, or was she just digging? I could lie, but I found that after all these years, I didn't want to. I wanted to come clean. I looked her in the eye. "Attempted. I was stronger and faster than he thought I'd be. But, Meredith, if it had been some other woman—"

"I get it, Natalie. You don't have to justify your actions to me. I'm a woman in a man's world, too. You wanted to teach the bastard a lesson—that the good old days of getting away with that shit were over. But you made a rookie mistake: you got too hot, let your emotions lead the way. You didn't think it through. There were police photographs of the guy's bloody neck and witnesses who could place you in the room with him. There was no way he wasn't going to charge you for what you did. You had to lie—make a counter-charge of rape days after it was too late to be proven—to get him to back down."

My mouth was dry, and my heart was pounding. I knew where she was going, and there was nothing I could do to stop her.

She said, "If that police report from twenty years ago were to leak..." the sadness and disappointment on her face looked completely sincere, "...it would ruin your career."

"This is blackmail, Meredith."

"I don't want to resort to that."

"You just did."

"Yeah. I guess I did," she said without regret. She squinted at me curiously. "Tell me. Do you think you could ever do something like that again?"

"What? Intentionally hurt someone? Of course not."

"If you knew you could get away with it?"

"What a terrible question to ask."

She nodded. "Yes, it is. A terrible question. Still, all things considered, is it fair to say that in certain rare circumstances, you're capable of premeditated violence?"

I snorted. "Apparently."

She didn't reply, and I started to sweat profusely, my fists curling inward. My cortisol levels had rocketed—like a cornered animal's, my eyes roamed in every direction, scanning the environment for threats. The only threat I could find was the one sitting next to me in the tiny overheated car: Meredith Viles. But she was my lifeline, too.

She said, "I promise this is the last request I'll make. As soon as you plant the devices, you're out of here."

"The same day. No delay. That's the deal."

"Agreed," she said. "Absolutely."

I opened my hand, and she pressed the three plastic wafers into my palm. They felt hard and cool against my skin. A flutter of panic coursed through my body. I was officially out of my league.

6

The brunt of the hangover had drained away. In its place was acute anxiety about the job in front of me, and a large doubt about whether I'd measure up—a feeling not unlike pre-surgery jitters, which had never abated, not even after years of practice, because only an idiot wouldn't be scared as shit about cutting into living flesh. Over the years I'd learned to handle the ferocious stress. You had to kick it to the ground, more than once if need be, and if you had to stomp on it to keep it from getting up again, you did. Because you were the boss—you had to remember that. You stayed calm and analytical, even if you were faking; you rehearsed each part of the procedure in your mind over and over until it was like reciting lines of dialog in a play you'd performed a hundred times before. Once inside the surgical theatre, you didn't think beyond the moment. You focused on the first small step, then the next, and the next, losing yourself by degrees in the act, until about halfway through, with surreal clarity, you realized that you'd surrendered to something beautiful.

It was two o'clock when I got back to the apartment. Ilmira was at work, as were most other tenants, it seemed, because the building was hushed and serene. The day had grown hotter; dense, humid air flowed into Misha's bedroom through the open window as I laid down to rest for a little while. There was still a gentle, painful squeezing around the periphery of my brain, alcohol's last caress, but it was bearable, and I drifted off, hoping that when I got up I'd have an answer, or the inkling of an answer, about how to go about doing what I had to do.

Sometime later, I woke with a start to the blaring of a car horn. I plodded to the long casement window next to Misha's desk and began to crank it closed, glancing out to see what the commotion was. The driver of a small sedan was gesturing rudely to a woman who had dropped a torn bag of garbage in the parking lot and was walking away from it. The woman paid him no mind, and after a few more blasts of his horn, he got out of the car and picked up the messy bag himself, tossing it atop an overflowing dumpster, where it did not stay, but rolled down to the ground, bursting along the way.

There was a balcony below the window I hadn't noticed before, similar to the ones overlooking the street. *Balcony* was a generous term to describe the odd structure: it was more like a narrow fire escape, about five feet long and three feet wide, without the retractable stairs. Floor and sides consisted of thinly spaced iron bars capped by a low rail.

On a whim, I cranked the long thin window as wide as it would go, and squeezed out gingerly onto the iron bars. They held my weight easily. My eyes fell on the matching balcony below, where a stretched clothesline was draped with drying dish cloths and towels. It occurred to me that at least part of Bohdan and Tanya's flat must lie directly under Misha and Ilmira's. Given the different layouts of the two apartments and the fact that the front doors were at different ends of the corridor, that hadn't been clear to me before.

The small parking lot, which had been nearly empty when I lay down to rest, was now half full. Residents were returning home from work. As another car entered the lot, I clambered back through the window, not wanting to be seen.

My personal phone pinged. A message from Toyla:

I talked to a helicopter pilot who remembers taking a guy to Death Valley a couple of months ago. He didn't remember the guy's name. Said he was young, new in town, worked at the chemical plant. Stayed at the camp for a couple of hours. Didn't say why. Hope that helps.

I wrote back, thanking him for the info. I copied his message into the spy phone and sent it to Meredith, following that text with one of my own:

Confirmation that Misha went to Death Valley. Obviously found something there editor thought was "dangerous." Someone should check it out.

At least that person wouldn't be me, I thought gratefully. I'd be leaving Mirny as soon as I got these devices off my hands.

A few minutes later, Meredith replied:

We're on it. You stay focussed on Duboff and Karp.

⠂⠄⠂⠄⠂⠄⠂⠄⠂⠄⠂⠄⠂⠄⠂

"Who is it?" came Tanya's lilt through the closed door. The deadbolts slid open one by one, and the door swung wide. Her face fell when she saw me standing in the hallway. "Oh, it's you."

I held out a bunch of vividly dyed chrysanthemums that I'd bought from a street vendor. "I wanted to apologize for last night. I drank way too much. I actually don't remember what happened after about ten o'clock. Hope I wasn't rude."

She cracked a hesitant smile. "Oh, no. You were fine. Nothing to worry about."

"Whew. I'm glad to hear that. Anyway, the strangest thing happened. I ran across something in Misha's room that might be a clue to where he is. Ilmira couldn't tell me anything about it—I wonder if you could. Can I come in?"

She looked uneasy. "It's not a good time. Bohdan will be back soon."

I made an embarrassed face. "Did I do something to make him mad?"

"Nah. He just gets this way sometimes. Moody, you know. Typical guy."

I rolled my eyes. "Tell me about it." They'd probably argued after I left—him criticizing her for gabbing too much, warning her to keep her mouth shut around the American.

"It'll just take a minute," I insisted in a friendly tone.

She swayed a bit, grimacing. Her chapped lips were almost as pale as her face. Anemia? Fatigue? Something.

"All right. Just a minute, though. Come into the kitchen. I'm making dinner."

Potatoes were boiling in a pot on the stove, their bland smell wafting through the room. A cutting board was covered with uncooked chicken breasts, which Tanya had apparently been pounding with a heavy meat tenderizer lying nearby. She didn't offer me tea, a sure sign of her ambivalence.

"Sorry to bother you," I said, taking a seat at the table while scanning the room for a good place to stash a thin object about one-and-a-half inches square. My sweeping glance took in potted plants on a windowsill trailing dried-out vines, cracked dishes stacked on open plywood shelves, and walls plastered over with posters of rock bands and hostile, craggy landscapes.

"What are you looking at?" Tanya asked.

"Oh, the posters…fascinating." I heard my insincerity, and she looked unconvinced. "It seems Misha was writing an article…" I said, waiting for an answering glimmer in her eyes. It didn't come. "…about an abandoned prison camp that was discovered by herders—did he ever mention that to you?" Even though Meredith had taken over this line of inquiry, I figured I could still use it. It had the advantage of being true, and I might even learn something I could pass on to Meredith.

"He liked history," Tanya said off-handedly. "But I never heard him talk about such a place. We don't usually talk about those things."

By *those things*, she probably meant the gulag camps and prisons. "Evenki herders? Did he mention having Evenki friends, or taking any trips with them?"

"Don't think so." She turned to the counter and resumed pounding the meat.

I slipped one of the listening devices out of my pocket, concealing it in the snug palm of my hand. What if I laid it on the inch or two of floor behind the refrigerator, an area people rarely cleaned? I rose quietly from my seat. Tanya was hammering like a madwoman. The metallic clatter of a key turning in the front door reached us, and Tanya whirled around, the blocky tenderizer held aloft.

"He's early. You have to go. I can't explain right now. Just, please, go out this way—"

She swept across the room, and opened a door beside the refrigerator, waving the tenderizer in a rapid sweeping gesture to encourage speed. I slipped through, found myself on the landing of a dirty stairway that descended one flight. Yellow kitchen light illuminated it, but as soon as Tanya shut the door, I was swamped in dark. I slipped the device back into my pocket, groped for a light switch that I couldn't find. My hand brushed against a railing. I felt my way down the steps, careful not to make noise, lest Bohdan hear. The smells of dirt and mold rose to meet me as I descended. At the bottom, I put my hands out and inched forward in the dark until I touched a door of clammy, half-rotted wood. I ran my fingers along its edge, felt a deadbolt, which I turned, and a metal chain, which I unleashed. The door groaned open, and I stepped outside into a warm, gloomy twilight, loamy dirt under my feet, the edge of the parking lot ten feet ahead. The sickly aroma of the untended dumpster filled my nose.

I walked around to the front of the building, almost certain that Tanya wouldn't welcome me into her home again. I'd have to find another way. As luck would have it, I'd just been introduced to the well-hidden back entrance to their flat. Now if Tanya would just forget to slide the bolt and hook the chain…

At two a.m., I slipped out of bed and pulled on sweatpants, a T-shirt, and sneakers. I ghosted along the dark hallway past Ilmira's room, down the poorly lit stairs, and out the front door. There was a nip of cool in the air; a profound silence, broken by the soft crunch of gravel under my rubber soles. The moon was peeking from behind thin clouds, shedding a pale glow on the access road. Parked cars were shadowy hulks.

I found my way to the apron of packed dirt behind the building, and when the dumpster reek reached me, I followed it through the gloom. Scuttling, scratching sounds rose up suddenly—foraging animals scattering amid the soft rot and trash. There—the back door to the Duboff/Karp apartment was visible in the feeble moonglow. I approached and gently turned the handle, gently pulled. It didn't budge. Pulled harder, and this time felt its slight motion arrested by the deadbolt. Yanked it fast and sharp, just to be sure, but all it did was creak and strain against the steel.

Clever Tanya didn't forget.

The night murmured outside Misha's bedroom window. A pale trapezoid of moonlight cut across the floor. I was frustrated, restless, still buzzing with adrenaline from my failed attempt, when it occurred to me that I hadn't called my mother. What's more, I'd been too drunk to call her last night, and hadn't even thought of calling her all day. The challenges I was facing were occupying my mind so completely that the Western world, my real one, had slipped into insignificance.

My call took a long time to connect. I started to think it wouldn't, when, suddenly, Nurse O'Donnell's voice filled my ear with enough volume to startle me.

"Caitlin. Hi. It's Dr. March. Is Vera awake?"

"I should hope so. It's four thirty in the afternoon. What time is it there?"

"Oh, let's see. Past two a.m., I guess."

"I hope you have a good reason for being up in the middle of the night," she said with a tease in her voice.

"As far as I'm concerned, there aren't any. But that's me. How's Vera?"

"Steady. Recovering from her fall. She went to the flower arranging demonstration in the common room this morning."

"Really? Did she like it?"

"I'll let her tell you, Dr. March. I know she'll be glad to hear from you."

Vera was agitated. A terse tone and abbreviated answers were payback for my negligence. She obviously sensed that something beyond simple forgetfulness was going on, that I wasn't being completely honest with her—a breach of trust that she didn't state explicitly, but her hurt was evident in her querulous tone. I heard the strain in my own voice when I cheerfully asked about the flower arranging class. Ignoring my question, she demanded to know if I'd heard from Lena. When I said no, she insisted that there had to be a way I could meet Katarina Melnikova without my aunt's help.

I reassured her as best I could, and kept the call short. Afterwards, I vowed to myself to finish my work in Mirny as quickly as possible, so the CIA could make good on its promise to deliver me to my aunt and grandmother in their remote village, and I could get home to Vera soon, with lots of photos and happy news to share.

The next morning, Ilmira's freshly laundered underwear was draped over a clothesline that stretched across the bathroom. She must have hung it before she went to work. One end was tied to the shower head, the other to a towel rack, with a long spool of unused rope lying underneath it on the floor. The sight was annoying at first, as I would have to take the clothesline down in order to shower, and then hang it again when I was done, but as I was laying Ilmira's wet things on a towel temporarily, an idea occurred to me.

I brought the clothesline to Misha's room, climbed out the window as I'd done the day before, and peered over the railing. One floor below, Tanya and Bohdan's window was open. I lowered one end of the clothesline, and watched with satisfaction as it plopped onto their balcony. There was plenty to spare, enough for it to be folded into a double strand, which, when looped around one of the bars on the balcony's floor, would yield four thicknesses of rope, which ought to be enough to hold my weight for the brief time I would be suspended between balconies. I aligned the lengths, tied a knot one-third of the way down, another two-thirds of the way, and a last one to gather the loose ends, and let my primitive ladder drop through the bars.

My heart was battering my rib cage, and my palms were leaking sweat. The challenge seemed beyond my physical strength, if not my nerve. It was an impulsive, probably stupid idea, but was actually a little less crazy than ones I'd sleeplessly considered the night before. The fact that it scared me only meant that I needed to do it quickly, before I had time to psych myself out.

It was just before 10 a.m., so Tanya and Bohdan were probably at work. There were a few cars in the sun-dappled parking lot, but no signs of life. The warm air hung heavy and still.

I dressed quickly, stuffed the three devices, masking tape, my mobile, and the key to Ilmira's apartment into my pockets, swung one leg over the railing, shifted my weight to the other side. Relying on nothing but the strength of my arms, I lowered myself just enough to wrap the dangling rope around one leg the way I'd been taught in summer camp. By pressing the sole of my free foot against the rope where it rubbed against my ankle, I could stop myself from slipping, and a good portion of my weight was transferred to the clothesline. In this way, I was able to lower myself gradually, until my feet touched the railing below and I could balance on it with help from the rope. I dropped onto Tanya and Bohdan's balcony, landing in a crouch.

I squeezed through their open window, and found myself in their bedroom. An unmade bed, clothes strewn about, jewelry and make-up on the dresser. I listened—nothing. The closet was gaping open, stuffed with clothes on hangers and piles of shoes. I slid a chair over to the closet door and climbed onto it. Feeling for the edge of the inside doorframe, I taped one of the devices to the wall above the narrow ledge, then slid the chair back to its usual place.

I headed quietly down the corridor, past the kitchen on my right, into the living room. The parrot erupted into a shrieking diatribe, flapping aggressively against the bars of its cage. I murmured sweet nothings to it, as Tanya had done, and stroked its crabbed talons gently until it settled down. The room was just as I remembered it—every available space taken up by sundry items such as CD towers, snowshoes, dusty vases, and stacking dolls.

"I am a very fine parrot," the parrot informed me in perfect Russian.

I whirled to stare at it, so surprised that I almost didn't hear a key turn noisily in the front lock, sliding one deadbolt open. I glanced around frantically, but there was no place to hide. A second key turned in the second lock. I darted into the hallway, raced back to the bedroom. A few seconds later, I was hovering behind the bedroom door, listening to slow, shuffling footsteps—a woman's—enter the apartment. It wasn't Tanya because Tanya's steps were quick and light. The woman turned into the kitchen.

Water splashed in the sink; the refrigerator opened and closed. A low humming commenced and slowly rose into a melancholy song: "Katusha," a famous folk song about a girl pining for her soldier at the front. The old woman—Tanya's mother?—had the kind of rough, ancient voice that did justice to mournful ballads.

The apple and the pear tree bloom,
Fog lay above the river.
There went Katusha onto the shore,

Onto the tall, steep shore.

As the song unfurled, I retreated to the balcony, where the true seriousness of my position dawned on me. Getting back up to Misha's balcony would be a lot harder than getting down had been. I could probably shimmy high enough to grip one of the floor bars, but wrapping my hands around the top rail would require strength I didn't have, and hoisting my body over that rail would be all but impossible.

Since the old woman was busy in the kitchen—doing dishes, it sounded like—I figured I could sneak past that room and slip out the front door. But as I was tiptoeing down the hall, she bustled out of the kitchen, still singing, and disappeared into the living room. The parrot produced a civilized *Privyet, babulya.* I slunk back to the bedroom and let out my breath. Tanya's mother—it had to be—hadn't seen me, and I'd seen her only from the back—fat and very short, in a sack-like brown dress. Thinning gray hair with some scalp showing through. Edema in her ankles where they disappeared into heavy black shoes.

I crossed to the window with a new idea. If I could untie the knots, pull the clothesline down through the bars of Misha's balcony, make it a double strand instead of a quadruple, and reattach it to Tanya and Bohdan's second-floor balcony, I might be able to lower myself to the ground.

The mournful ballad stopped abruptly. The sudden silence rang out like a warning bell.

I froze, fully expecting the old woman to storm into the bedroom and confront me. Instead, she shuffled mercifully out the front door and closed it behind her. The clicking that accompanied the relocking of each noisy bolt was audible in the bedroom.

I counted to sixty slowly. And did it again, in case she was coming back. Then I slipped down the hall and into the kitchen and glanced out the window. She was trundling down the sidewalk, headed back toward town. I breathed a few times deeply, until my pounding heart slowed.

The kitchen had been nicely tidied up. Dishes and pans were drying on a rack, and the vinyl tablecloth was wiped clean. It looked like Tanya's mother truly was doing her part to bring order to her daughter's messy abode. She'd even arranged some sorry-looking apples in a bowl.

I squatted down next to the refrigerator, reached into the narrow space behind it, and tucked one of the bugs in the half-inch of space underneath it.

On to the living room. The parrot shrieked when it saw me again. I hissed at it in English to shut the fuck up, as I was too jacked on adrenaline to go through the business of soothing it. It fell silent right away, having apparently taken my meaning. Then I stood in the middle of the chaotic room, searching for a good hiding spot for the last device. The crammed bookcases looked promising, until I realized that any book could be opened at some point. If I slipped the device into the hem of the curtain, the sound would be muffled. If I taped it to the underside of the coffee table, it could be dislodged. My eye fell on nesting Matryoshka dolls on an end table. I eagerly opened the rosy-cheeked grandmother at her waist, and removed her four progressively smaller daughters, but the device was too wide to fit inside the newly hollow space. My frustration mounted. There were probably a hundred places in that room to conceal a small plastic square, but for the life of me I couldn't find one. Every spot I laid eyes on was subject to being handled at some point.

The only truly unmoving object was the couch. I knelt and felt under the upholstered skirt for the squat wooden leg. It wasn't big enough to accommodate and conceal the device, assuming I could have taped it to the back somehow. I was running out of patience. It occurred to me that I should just slide the device a couple of feet under the couch and be done with it. The vacuum couldn't reach that far, and I doubted that Tanya or her mother was in the habit of picking up heavy pieces of furniture to clean underneath. I laid down on my stomach and proceeded to stretch my arm under the skirt into the roughly six inches of space between the bottom of the couch and the floor. A metal object was in the way, so I shimmied a few inches further along and tried again. My hand encountered another metal object, which rolled into a third with a dull clang. I picked up the skirt and peered into the under-couch darkness, but couldn't make out what was there. So I pulled one out.

It was a steel canister, about eighteen inches high and five inches wide. With a dull red-painted stripe around the base and a faded hammer and sickle.

My head suddenly seemed to be floating above me.

I pulled out the others. There were eight altogether—identical but for letters near the tapered tops that looked like they'd been etched with a small knife. OPA on four of the bottles. DF on the other four.

Abbreviations, obviously. They seemed familiar, but I couldn't recall where I might have seen them before.

A gun at my head couldn't have forced me to open one of those bottle shaped containers. I didn't even want to touch them. I sat stupidly on my ass on the floor and tried not to hyperventilate. Finally, sense dawned. I pulled out my phone and snapped some pictures of the eight canisters huddled together in front of the couch like a little battalion of dwarf soldiers. From every angle, top and bottom as well. Then I slid them all very gently back under the couch.

My hands were trembling, and my breath was shallow. I feared I might pass out. To hell with planting the third device. I needed to get out of there fast. I stumbled past the beady-eyed, blessedly quiet parrot to the front door, terrified that a tenant would see me leaving the apartment, but the corridor was clear. I didn't have keys to lock the door behind me, but that wouldn't necessarily be a tip-off, as the old woman had been there and could take the heat for forgetting to do it.

Back on Misha's balcony, I reeled the dangling clothesline up through the bars, quickly untied the knots, and began coiling it around my arm. A car drove into the parking lot as I finished. The driver peered up at me through her windshield. Did she think it odd to see a person standing on a balcony with loops of rope around her arm? I didn't know. But what difference did it make? I'd done my job—most of it—and I'd be leaving Mirny soon.

I remembered, from chemistry class: *OPA* stood for isopropyl alcohol, the rubbing alcohol commonly used for disinfecting cuts. *DF* had me stumped, so I grabbed my laptop and looked it up on Wikipedia. It was methylphosphonyl diflouride—a kind of insecticide, only orders of magnitude more toxic than anything farmers used. The Germans developed it for chemical warfare in 1938. They mass-produced up to ten tons of the stuff before the war ended, but for reasons no one knows didn't use it on Allied targets. DF didn't do much by itself, but mixing it with OPA incited a chemical reaction that transformed it into GB, better known as sarin.

My entire body broke into a sweat. I knew what sarin was, but my fingers automatically entered it in the search field anyway. A clear, odorless liquid twenty-six times deadlier than cyanide that rapidly evaporated into a vapor and was lethal at extremely low concentrations. Death usually occurred within one to ten minutes of inhalation.

I slammed the laptop shut, as if I'd just seen Satan's ghost. Everyone knew that Syrian strongman Bashar Al-Assad was using sarin on his own people. Just a few months ago, the news had shown footage of corpses lying in the streets of Douma with eruptions of foam at their mouths, and screaming children who'd managed to survive the attack being drenched with hoses. I remembered a *Sixty Minutes* segment on a sarin attack in Syria in 2013. Assad's soldiers had filled rocket launchers with the deadly nerve agent. The bombs exploded across a densely populated area, releasing clouds of poisonous gas. Over 1,400 civilians experienced an agonizing death. At least 426 of them were children. I had noted the exact numbers because I kept trying to imagine that many critically ill people being rushed to hospitals at once, and felt some of the helpless despair those Syrian doctors must have experienced.

The news show had gone on to explain that sarin attacks were relatively low-tech warfare, the kind of thing that even a poorly trained terrorist group could pull off easily if it had the materials.

When the segment was over, I immediately did exactly what anyone who knows me well would have predicted I would do. I had looked up the effects of sarin exposure on the human body, in case I was ever called upon to treat victims of an attack. Sarin blocks the enzyme that allows muscles and organs to relax after exertion. Essentially, the body convulses to death. Initial symptoms are tightness in the chest, constriction of the pupils, uncontrollable drooling, and tearing of the eyes. Loss of bodily functions follows: victims vomit, urinate, and defecate. Their eyes and lungs blister and burn. Their muscles jerk violently, and they have ongoing epileptic fits. Usually, death comes from asphyxiation stemming from the loss of control over respiratory muscles.

There's nothing a doctor can do.

I began pacing Misha's narrow room, my heart pounding through my chest. One floor below was a weapon that could kill everyone in the building and countless others before we even had a chance to run away.

I texted the photos to Meredith and waited for her response in an agony of impatience, the cheap spy phone cupped in my hand.

So this was what Bohdan and Tanya were up to—stealing sarin from the chemical plant where they worked and selling it to buyers in Baku, Azerbaijan.

I almost couldn't believe it. To think I'd spent hours the night before getting drunk and swapping tales with them, getting to know and sort of like them, all the while perched above a stash of deadly WMDs. How wrong my instincts about them had been.

How could they do it? What weird, twisted logic were they using to justify their acts? I hadn't noticed any signs of religious fanaticism or bloodlust on a massive scale. They weren't Russian nationalists either, as far as I could tell— they were too bitter about what was happening in their city, too cynical about government in general, to be on Putin's payroll.

The only motivation that fit was greed, born from despair. They saw themselves as trapped in a dying community, with only poverty and unemployment to look forward to. It made sense that they'd be tempted to sell whatever valuable commodity they could get their hands on to the highest bidder, especially if the payoff was life changing. And what could be more life changing than permanent relocation in a foreign country? Turtle doves cooing in pink-blossomed cherry trees and a little white house with a picket fence.

But no, it didn't work. I simply couldn't get my head around the fact that they would trade WMDs for a tired domestic dream. Even though I knew full well that there were plenty of sickos in the world who would happily swap sarin for a bottle of vodka and a pack of smokes.

The phone vibrated. "Excellent work," Meredith said breathlessly. "Where did you find them?"

I described their location. Not much of a hiding place.

"They probably weren't going to be there very long."

"How much destructive power is that?"

"Eight canisters? That's enough for four artillery shells. Enough to kill a village."

The scientist in me took over. "How do they handle the stuff without killing themselves? I mean, they might be relatively safe now, but at some point, those chemicals have to be combined."

"Right. Those metal containers can be transported and handled in relative safety because as long as the DF and OPA are kept separate, there's no problem. Once in the field, the fighters put a canister of each chemical inside an artillery shell, separated by a thin rupture disk. When the shell is fired, the disk breaks and the spinning of the shell mixes the two chemicals, producing liquid sarin, which is released on impact."

I said, "And when the liquid sarin hits the air, it evaporates instantly. Into a gas so dense it doesn't rise into the atmosphere but spreads along the ground in a yellow cloud."

"You know your chemistry, Doctor."

A wave of nausea came over me, as if I myself were a spinning artillery shell. I kneaded my forehead uselessly with my fingers. *Think, don't feel.* So much needed to be done, all of it dangerous. The metal containers had to be removed from the flat and disposed of somehow; Duboff and Karp had to be stopped before they could steal any more nerve agent from the plant. Were there only eight canisters, or had others been hidden in other places? How much had been smuggled already? Who were the buyers, and what were the intended targets?

"Meredith?" I said, my heart in my throat. "What happens now? Who's going to deal with this mess? And, just in case you have any crazy ideas, I absolutely won't do it."

I could feel her smile on the other end of the phone. "Don't worry, Natalie. You're off the hook. Our people will take it from here."

"Oh, thank god. When can I leave?"

"I'm going to move very quickly to get you out of there. You'll get a text soon with instructions. You may have to leave immediately, so be prepared."

"I'll be ready. Count on it."

The minute we hung up, I started throwing my stuff into my duffel. I wanted to warn Ilmira and everyone else who lived within a half-mile radius, but knew I couldn't. *As long as the DF and OPA are kept separate, there's no problem.* No problem. I repeated that several times until I believed it enough to function.

An hour passed, then another. The afternoon dragged on. I made tea and let it get cold, turned the TV on and off. All the while a thought was nudging the edges of my consciousness: Had *this* been Misha's objective in Mirny—finding stolen WMDs? If so, Meredith would have known that she was delivering me into a serious danger zone when she recruited me.

I recalled how she and Lena had lured me to Siberia, how Meredith had let me flail about until I was ripe for persuasion. It wasn't out of the question to think that Meredith had outright lied about the danger when I asked. I needed to prove my suspicions false; otherwise, how could I trust anything she said from now on? I sent another text: *I need to talk. Call me.* A few minutes later, my phone vibrated.

"Did you know there might be sarin in that apartment?" I asked tersely. I was clutching the phone with a sweaty palm, pressing it hard against my ear.

A pause. "What's going on, Natalie?"

"What do you mean, *what's going on*? Nothing's going on. I have a question, that's all. Did you know there might be sarin in that apartment?"

Another pause, this one longer, followed by a long capitulating sigh. "All right. I'll tell you as much as I can. Mayadykovsky Chemical Plant is one of several facilities that's supposed to be destroying Russia's enormous arsenal of chemical weapons, in compliance with a 2006 international treaty. The stockpile at Mayadykovsky originally included about forty thousand aerial bombs and missile warheads stuffed with toxic nerve agents like saran, soman, and VX. A few years ago, the Kremlin announced that the plant had disposed of ninety-eight percent of its materials. Not a word since about the remaining two percent, which is enough to wage massive chemical warfare anywhere in the world." She took a breath. "Are you following this?"

"Yes."

"We've long suspected that Russia's been supplying Syria with chemical weapons, or the means to make them. Naturally, we want to keep a pretty close eye on Russian stockpiles and figure out how the material is being moved, and by whom. Last winter, we received intelligence indicating that small quantities of a nerve agent were being smuggled out of Mayadykovsky and sold to some bad actors in the Middle East."

"So you recruited Misha to go undercover at the plant."

"Correct. We had a list of suspects, Duboff and Karp among them, but no evidence. Misha's job was to get close to the suspects and dig up whatever he could."

"So you *did* know that Duboff and Karp might be smuggling WMDs. But you didn't mention that to me."

"Natalie, in this business, there are secrets inside secrets. Are you really that surprised?"

I didn't say anything. Finally, I asked, "You think Misha was on to them?"

"Without him here to tell us, there's no way to be sure. My guess, probably."

I swallowed hard. "So maybe they figured out he was a spy and got rid of him."

"Makes sense, I'm afraid."

If the thought of Bohdan and Tanya selling sarin to terrorists was hard to accept, the thought of them murdering Misha was harder. In the case of sarin, the actual killing would be done by others in a different country. With a pile of fancy rationalizations, they just might succeed in convincing themselves they weren't really responsible. Murdering Misha was different—it would have been up close and personal. They would have had wet red blood on their hands, a real person's body to dispose of. They were damn expert liars if they'd done it. *If.*

I said, "Let's not forget the other option that's in play. The gulag camp, and whatever was going on with that. Misha could have earned himself some enemies there."

Meredith cleared her throat. "I should have told you this before, but whatever Misha was doing relative to this gulag camp wasn't part of his CIA mission. I don't have the manpower or the resources—or the mandate, frankly—to look into that."

"What? You said… I thought you wanted to find him."

"Of course. But there are limits to what I can do."

"You're giving up on him," I said coldly.

"I wouldn't call it that."

"No? What is it called when a nineteen-year-old goes missing, and the people responsible for putting him into a very dangerous situation won't expend the so-called 'resources' to try to find him? You recruited him, Meredith. You knew at the time he was just a kid. If he's gotten himself into trouble, you owe him more than a bureaucratic brush-off. Especially when it's perfectly clear that *something* is going on with him and that gulag camp. Don't tell me you don't have the money. How hard can it be to check the place out?"

I remembered Misha's messy closet, the hiking boots with yellow dirt caked in their treads. Why yellow?

Meredith's voice was as smooth and distant as a flight attendant's. "I appreciate what you're saying. Truly, I do. I'll take another look at Death Valley, I promise. Right now, I need you to pack your bag and be ready to leave. You've done an outstanding job, Natalie. You should be very proud."

· ∴ · ∴ · ∴ · ∴ · ∴ · ∴ ·

The morning air was cool and humid with incipient rain. I'd received my marching orders late last night via text: the black Lada would come for me at seven a.m. and take me to the airport. It was Saturday, so Ilmira was still asleep. I wrote a note:

Dear Ilmira,

Sorry to leave so abruptly. I got a call—there's been an emergency with my mom, and I have to go home right away. Here's money to cover the back rent; I'll leave the key under the mat. Sorry I can't take Misha's stuff: feel free to sell it or get rid of it however you want. Please let me know if he shows up or you hear anything new. I've given your info to his mom—I hope that's okay. I don't know what she intends to do now, but she'll be in touch if she needs anything.

I really appreciate your hospitality, Ilmira. You've been terrific. Thank you for everything. Come and visit me in the States if you possibly can. I mean that.

Warmest wishes,

Natalie

My purse was on my shoulder, backpack and leather duffel by the door. I waited at the window, dressed in jeans, short boots, and a light jacket, and as soon as I saw the car take the corner, I high-tailed out the door.

I very much wanted to see Meredith Viles behind the wheel. Instead, it was crusty Oleg, smelling of days-old sweat and tobacco smoke.

"Ms. Viles couldn't come. She sends best wishes for safe trip," he said. There was a tremor in the red, swollen fingers gripping the steering wheel. Hangover? Anxiety? Early Parkinson's? I tamped down a surge of anxiety by telling myself that as long as I got to the airport on time, it didn't much matter who drove.

Oleg checked his mirrors carefully before pulling away from the curb.

We turned onto the main thoroughfare. The entrance to the Mir mining complex came up a few minutes later. A uniformed security officer stood sentry while first-shift workers trudged through the gate, their clothes the color of mud, and trucks waited to be inspected, both going in and coming out. Further on, successive blocks of windowless industrial buildings slipped past the Lada's dirty window. I wondered what went on behind their blank, imposing walls. Diamond cutting and polishing? The mass production of engagement rings? Odd to think of these drab factories creating coveted symbols of romantic love.

Oleg lit a Ducat and held it pinched between sausage fingers. I cranked open my window to escape the wreath of smoke. He checked his rear and side mirrors, which I'd seen him do a couple of times already.

"Looking for someone?" I said.

"Looking and not finding. This is good."

"That's not what most people would say."

"I am not most people," he replied with a smug smile, pleased with his own supposed mystery.

The airport came into view—a few paved landing strips with a single terminal building and three large hangars. Oleg turned in, made a slow circuit of the gravel lot, and parked at some distance from the terminal. He turned off the engine.

Adjusting his heavy body to face me in the cramped interior, he said, "I must ask you now to please open compartment in front of you and remove envelope."

I popped open the glove compartment and took out a large manila envelope with a string closure. It was bulky with irregularly shaped items. I stared at it for a moment, sensing that I wouldn't like whatever it contained.

"Open it," he said.

I unwound the string and poured the contents into my lap: a passport, license, credit card, airline tickets, and a fat stack of rubles held together by a thick elastic. Also a smartphone in a brown leather case, with charging cord and earphones. I opened the passport. My face stared back at me over the name Anne-Marie Phipps.

"What's this about?"

He sucked down a plume of smoke and, lungs expanded, choked out a comment clearly meant to be ironic. "So you will have safe trip home." On the exhale, a phlegmy cough rumbled in his throat. "In few minutes, you will board plane to Novosibirsk, where you will pick up flight to Moscow. From there you will take the American Airlines to your Dulles airport outside Washington, D.C. It's long trip. Twenty-two hours. But when you travel west in partnership with sun, you gain a day. Think of that—destiny is giving you extra time to live. As thanks."

I was shaking my head vigorously. "No, that's not right. I'm not returning to the States yet. I'm going to the village where my relatives are. Meredith arranged it; she must have told you that." I unfolded the travel itinerary and checked what it said. To my surprise, it was as Oleg described: three flights, landing me in Washington that evening. I refolded it quickly. "No, sorry. This is wrong."

He held the cigarette close to his face. There was a tincture of leer in his wistful smile. "I am sorry to tell you that new plan was made. Is much better for you to return to USA."

"That's not what I agreed to," I said hotly.

He shrugged his heavy shoulders. "It does not matter what you think you agreed to. This is instruction now."

"No, this is crazy," I said, shoving the passport and other things back into the manila envelope. "I need to talk to Meredith."

"She is not available."

"What? Are you kidding?"

"She wants me to say she is sorry if you are disappointed."

"Disappointed? *Disappointed* doesn't come close. She said I'd be taken to see my relatives if I did what she asked. Well, I did it. Now it's her turn to live up to the bargain."

He pinched his eyebrows together with mocking sympathy. "You are wasting time with this talk, my friend. Your flight will depart soon. So now I ask you to leave behind anything connected to your real identity. Phone, license, credit cards, passport. Also, please, your laptop computer. And, of course, the small phone you were given to use."

"You want me to give you my passport? Are you kidding? There's no way I'm doing that. And I'm not giving you my personal phone or my computer either."

"Please try to understand clearly. You have no choice in this matter. I must ask you to do this very quickly."

"This is ridiculous. I'm calling Meredith." I punched speed dial number one on the spy phone and listened through four rings. There was a click, and the phone went dead.

Oleg held out his meaty palm.

"Okay," I said, dropping the burner into his hand. "I can't get through. But I'm sure *you* could reach her if you want. I demand that you do that now. Get her on the line immediately, and let me talk to her. I really must insist."

"I am very sorry, Doctor. You will please notice that you are being treated with respect."

"Respect? You break your promise and call it *respect*?" I glared into the small pig's eyes drowning in puddles of flesh. He smelled, actually. He carried the smell of sick in the folds of his flesh. My anger flared, cold anger. "You really don't get it, Oleg. I'm not getting out of this car until I've spoken to Meredith Viles."

Oleg carefully placed his burning cigarette in the Lada's tiny plastic ashtray, already overflowing with butts, and leaned his massive bulk toward me, his damp, sour breath wafting in my face. He grabbed my left wrist in his heavy hand and squeezed it to the point of pain.

"What are you doing?" I yelled, trying to yank my hand away.

His grasp tightened. With his other hand, he bent my wrist back as far is it could go. Stripes of searing pain shot up my arm. "A surgeon cannot perform operation with broken wrist. Maybe you know this." He added more pressure. The pain was intense. I could feel the bone start to crack.

"Stop! Let go!"

He loosened his grip. There was a slight sheen of sweat on his upper lip and a snakey glint in his eyes.

I wrangled my wrist out of his hold and started rubbing the tender joint. "They're going to hear about this back at Langley," I said. It was a pitiful remark, but the best I could come up with. With my good hand, I rummaged angrily in my leather purse and dropped the things he'd asked for unceremoniously on the car floor. Then I stuffed the bulging manila envelope into my purse.

In a voice slick with authority, Oleg said, "You will have no more contact with CIA until you are in Washington, D.C. You will have no knowledge of Oleg the driver or Meredith Viles of Tiffany Co. And, of course, you will know nothing about our work in Mirny."

"Fuck you," I said.

A tiny smile of satisfaction hovered at the corner of his mouth. "Go now. Plane to Novosibirsk departs in twenty minutes."

"No worries, Oleg. I like to cut it close. Before I go, I have a couple of questions you better answer very quickly and very honestly if you want me on that plane. First, what's going to happen to the canisters?"

"You weren't told?"

"I want to hear it from you. Specifics, please. What's going to happen to them?"

"They'll be removed."

"Duboff and Karp?"

A short inhale, a rapid blink. "They will be watched."

"And Mikhail Tarasov? What about him?"

Oleg looked utterly blank, maybe a little frightened.

"The clock is ticking, Oleg. Say something."

"He should have been more careful."

I balked at the way he said it. It sounded so final. "Is he dead?"

"No one knows."

"But you assume?"

"Yes."

My mouth went dry. "How long have you assumed this?"

"Hmm. Some days, weeks…?"

"Exactly how many days and weeks?" Good god, had they believed he was dead all along?

The tip of Oleg's cigarette glowed red as he pulled a long drag into his lungs, buying himself time. "This I am not so sure about."

"Yeah. I bet you aren't." I got out of the car.

. . . .

A uniformed man at the security gate shoved his hands roughly into my duffel bag. He wasn't going to find anything there but clothes. A television on the wall blared the morning news. Truths, half-truths, lies. Bleary travelers yawned at the newscaster, and went on with their business unperturbed. *We're sitting on top of a tinderbox. Chemical, biologic, nuclear—how close to Armageddon we all are.*

I moved sideways a few feet to the next uniformed man, who flipped through the pages of my fake passport, glanced down at the photo, up at my face, down at the photo.

"How did you enjoy your stay in Mirny?"

"It was delightful."

"Sightseeing?"

"Yes."

"Did you purchase any diamonds?"

"No."

"Most tourists come for the inexpensive diamond jewelry."

I fake-smiled. "Next time."

He snapped the passport closed, handed it back to me. "Have a safe trip, Ms. Phipps."

I gathered up my baggage and proceeded to the gate—not hard to locate as there were only four in the airport, and three were vacant. A scattering of passengers were waiting for the Novosibirsk flight to board. Everyone looked tired, disgruntled. There were, as yet, no children or babies among them, so chances were good we would all be able to sleep on the plane.

I hadn't been waiting long when an announcement came over the loudspeaker: departure was delayed by thirty minutes. Mechanical trouble. I shrugged. What was an extra thirty minutes when I was going to be in transit for twenty-two hours? Still, I wanted to get out of there soon. There was nothing to distract me in the terminal, not even a newspaper stand. I was left with nothing but my own turbulent thoughts.

Vera would be so disappointed when I arrived home empty-handed. What would I tell her? Some story, I supposed, which she wouldn't entirely believe. The lie would cast a shadow between us, which nothing but total honesty could displace. But that would never happen, as I was sworn to secrecy and would uphold my oath, though the CIA hardly deserved my loyalty, having so little of its own.

I pictured Meredith Viles—her flashing diamond ring and strangely skeletal face. Meredith Viles trafficked in deception for a living. And I'd believed everything she'd said. How many times had she lied to me, starting with the very first night?

Had the promised family reunion on the banks of the Tatta River ever been a real thing? Maybe not.

Was the CIA really going to investigate Misha's connection to Death Valley? Unlikely.

Travelers on the delayed Novosibirsk flight were scattered around the terminal in various stages of boredom or fatigue. Nearby, a fat man dozed sitting up, softly snoring, his multiple chins pooling on his chest. I felt heavy and rooted like him, mired down in circumstances out of my control. I wondered how much Lena knew. Would Meredith tell her about Misha's foray into journalism? Somehow, I doubted it.

Right now, I was the only person in the world with a hankering to know what Misha had been doing at that abandoned gulag camp. The only person willing to follow the trail of breadcrumbs he'd left. Didn't that make me responsible in some way? But what could I do?

How futile everything seemed. Saldana, Misha, Lena, Katarina Melnikova. Who were they anyway—these people for whom I'd traveled so far and risked so much? I'd had such high hopes, been so suckered by the dream of a happy extended family. But common DNA was never meant to stretch this far.

I'd never be sure of anything now. Never know what really happened to Misha, or whether Vera's lost mother really was living in a Siberian village at the age of eighty-nine. I'd never stop wondering about them, my mysterious Russian family, never really be clear of it. And Vera's heart would break. Again.

So why had I surrendered my passport and accepted the unwanted airline tickets? Why was I letting Meredith Viles call the shots, when she'd glibly deceived me so many times, and now was shipping me home like unwanted baggage, against my stated desires? Through a proxy, no less.

If I got on that plane, I'd live to regret it—of that I was sure.

What if I didn't?

What if I went back to Mirny and kept looking for my cousin? There was a chance I'd find him, and if I did, I might still get to Katarina Melnikova's home. Because, even though I didn't know the name of her village, Misha would. In solving one problem, I'd solve two.

And even if my search was fruitless, as it likely would be, I'd at least be able to return to the States with no regrets, having done everything I possibly could to make things come out right for Vera and myself. Then, whenever I recalled this whole debacle in the future, I'd at least have some pride and peace of mind.

I stood up and shouldered my luggage, made my way out of the gate area, more crowded now than it had been earlier. The official who'd checked my passport looked up as I passed. "Change your mind, Ms. Phipps?" he said archly.

I wished I were in America, where no one remembered your name. "Yes, as a matter of fact, you got me thinking…I really do need a pair of diamond studs."

7

A taxi took me back to Ilmira's apartment, its wipers flapping in the first weak drizzle of rain. The key to the apartment was still under the mat. Ilmira's bed was unmade, her purse gone. She was probably out shopping on this Saturday morning, or off to visit friends.

I would have to explain why I was back. *Gosh, I'm so relieved: it was a false alarm. My mother recovered completely!* Another wearying lie.

I fried an egg, made tea and toast. I still hadn't quite caught up with what I'd done, but I did feel better, freer, more like myself. Taking my breakfast into the living room, I switched on the TV. *Die Hard* was playing on one of the stations. The dubbing was atrocious, but Bruce Willis's all-American face was comforting. Even the assault rifles splaying bullets into bad guys, and the roof of the Nakatomi Building exploding into flames had a welcome familiarity. Eventually, almost everyone was dead, an eerie quiet enveloped the charred skyscraper, and a different kind of sound reached my ears. Dim, rhythmic. What was Bruce up to now? But the sound wasn't coming from the TV. I lowered the volume—it was coming from the back of the apartment. I followed it into

Misha's bedroom, then to the balcony. When I opened the casement window onto the wet morning, the sound grew loud, vivid, piercing. An old woman's anguished keening. Deep and ancient, like the sound of suffering itself.

A terrible dread enveloped me. I walked slowly out of the apartment and down the stairs. A small group was gathered outside Tanya and Bohdan's door. Medics were carrying a stretcher out of their flat. There was a body on it, covered by a sheet. I pressed myself against the wall of the corridor to let them pass. Next to me, a balding, middle-aged man was squeezing his eyes closed; his heavy lips mumbled a prayer. A tall, official-looking woman emerged from the apartment, followed by medics carrying another stretcher.

"What happened?" I asked urgently as the woman passed.

"Two murders. A single bullet to each head."

The body on the second stretcher was smaller than the first. A strand of black hair escaped the covering sheet.

I turned to the balding man. "When?"

"Don't know. The old woman found them," he said.

I quietly returned to Ilmira's apartment.

The wail of Tanya's mother followed me up the stairs and rang in my ears long after I shut the door.

. . . .

I was numb with shock. What had Oleg said? *They will be watched.*

I'd let the lie pass without comment, without even noticing. What a fool I was not to have guessed. Of course they'd be assassinated. Of course. There was blood on my hands now. I was dirty with spy work. With collateral damage and all the other euphemisms. Were the murders necessary? Possibly. But a life was a life, and doctors didn't take lives, even to save others. At least that's what I'd always told myself.

Ilmira burst into the apartment, hair dampened from rain that was falling steadily now. Her eyes grew round when she saw me leaning against the kitchen counter. Raising her hands to the sides of her face in stiff-fingered horror, she cried, "You can't be here! You have to get out right now!" She rushed to the rain-streaked window and glanced down to the street. "Did anyone see you come in?"

"I take it you know what happened," I said.

"Everyone does! The neighbors are all talking about it." Her face was livid. "What madness made you come back?"

"I didn't know."

"*What?*" She slumped down at the table. "I took you in, treated you like a friend. And all the time, you were…you were…"

"It wasn't me, Ilmira. I didn't do it, I swear."

"Do you think I'm just a stupid Russian that you can lie to my face?"

"I'm *not* lying—"

"I *know* you are! Do you want to know what someone was saying about you just now? That they saw you on the balcony, holding a heavy rope in your arms. Why did you have a rope on the balcony, Natalie? Why?"

I shook my head in horrified disbelief. How quickly things came undone.

Ilmira continued breathlessly, "How long do you think it will be before the police come here, to this apartment? Until they question *me*? And I'll tell them everything—I promise I will! I'll tell everything I know about Dr. Natalie March, and how she lied to me."

The blood drained from my head so fast I thought I might pass out. I was as good as dead if I were caught. But I couldn't succumb to panic. First, I had to deal with Ilmira, who, at any moment, might pick up the phone and turn me in. There was no point in denying what she was saying. The evidence was too strong, even if it was wrong. I had to get her on my side somehow, make her *want* to cover for me.

"Ilmira, wait, please calm down. I have something to tell you. I promise, if you'll just listen…"

She made a violent hand gesture halfway between *fuck you* and *hurry up*.

"Yes, I broke in to their apartment," I said, trying to appear calm. "I thought Tanya and Bohdan might be involved in Misha's disappearance, and I was looking for clues, evidence, anything that might help me find him. I climbed down from his balcony to theirs. I did that. But when I didn't find anything, I left. That's it, Ilmira. I swear. I had nothing to do with the murders, absolutely nothing."

I suspected that the last part, the *absolutely nothing*, painted me as a liar and wished I hadn't said it. But there was nothing to do but wait to see how much, if any, of my story she believed.

Her eyes glimmered darkly. "You didn't say anything about leaving Mirny last night. Then, this morning, I wake up and you're gone. Why so sudden, Natalie? Why today?"

"But I didn't go, did I? I came back! I wouldn't be here if I were guilty, would I?"

"What *are* you doing here?"

"I was about to get on the plane when I got a message from the hospital saying my mother was fine. It was a false alarm. So I came back. I didn't know about the murders, Ilmira. I swear to you. I had no idea."

She looked away. I sensed that she wanted to believe me, but after the shock of the murders, she wouldn't easily surrender what she thought she knew.

"It could have been anyone," I continued urgently. "It could have been… whoever took Misha. It's frightening, I know, to think there might be someone out there. But it wasn't me, Ilmira. I swear it wasn't me."

She swallowed, her throat visibly constricting.

"We've only known each other a little while. But you *do* know me, Ilmira. I'm not a total stranger. Think for a moment, please. You must know in your heart I'm not capable of murder. That I could never in a million years do anything as horrible as that."

She flicked a tear from the side of her face. She was silent for a few moments.

Finally, she said, "You're right. I don't believe you're the killer. I believe you didn't do it, but…"

"But what?"

She stared at me with bald accusation. "I think you know who did."

"I don't," I said quickly, too quickly. I could feel the lie emblazoning itself on my face, in the muscles I couldn't control.

She saw the truth and immediately turned away. "Leave now. Just go."

"I didn't want it to happen," I said, the words tumbling out of my mouth. "I didn't know it was going to happen. There was nothing I could do to stop it. I'm not…" What was I trying to say?

She whirled around, her face contorted. "I'm connected to you, don't you see? As soon as they start putting the pieces together…"

"What pieces? Someone saw me standing on the balcony. So what? It doesn't prove anything!"

"They'll know you could have gotten in that way. It makes you an obvious suspect!"

"But I wasn't the one in the flat late last night or this morning or whenever the murders took place. The real killer got in some other way. He left traces— he must have. A jimmied door, a broken window. Something. And *he* might have been seen as well. All the evidence isn't in yet, Ilmira. It won't necessarily point to me."

She emitted a low moan. "Oh god. This is horrible."

"Wait a minute," I said. "No one knows I was in their apartment the other night, do they? No, just you and me and them. And they're dead. So there's nothing connecting me to them. Other than standing on the balcony, which isn't evidence of anything. And since I left early this morning…you could say I left then, as I did…and the murders probably took place later…"

"Oh, how you grasp at straws, trying to convince yourself that things aren't so bad! Do you really think Tanya and Bohdan didn't tell the world about their American visitor? Of course they did! They probably bragged to everyone they saw. Said you invited them to your penthouse apartment in Washington, and promised to take them to dinner at the White House, and made up a hundred other lies." Her voice rose to a wail. "Don't you see? It doesn't matter if there's evidence against you. It's just the fact that you were here! The police, the neighbors…they'll all suspect me of working with you or taking money from you. I'll be brought in for questioning. My name will go on a list. I'll never be trusted again!"

I felt sick to my stomach. "I'm so sorry, Ilmira. I would do anything to make this up to you. What can I do? There must be something—"

"You can leave right now. That's what you can do for me. Just *get out of here*."

"Yes, I can do that." I nodded in dumb obedience. I ought to go right away, before someone came in and saw me there, before the police started their questioning. I looked up, expecting to see terror and rage on Ilmira's face. Instead, there was grief. She had trusted me, shared her secrets, and now she was more alone and burdened than before.

"I'm so sorry. I didn't want it to be this way."

She shrugged off the apology with an icy taunt. "Where are your friends now, Natalie? Your murdering friends."

"They're not my friends. They never were."

She looked at me hard. "Are you a spy?"

If I lied, she would know it. I paused too long before answering.

"Yes, you are." She turned toward the window, took a few deep, audible breaths. "Tanya and Bohdan…?"

"Were involved in something very bad."

"Tell me."

"You don't need to know." *But why shouldn't she?*

"Tell me."

"Sarin."

She nodded slowly. "Stealing it, selling it."

"Yes."

"Well, then. I'm glad they're dead."

Neighbors huddled on the sidewalk under dripping umbrellas, murmuring among themselves, turning anxious faces toward the faded brown apartment building where the murders had taken place. The rain was fine and warm, the sky a low gray sheet.

I brushed past the small groups, wearing a wide-brimmed rain hat pulled down around the sides of my face. The hat had been donated by Ilmira, who wanted me gone, completely and irrevocably gone, who would insist she'd not laid eyes on her American guest since the night before. The duffel bag on one shoulder and the backpack on the other were dead giveaways, but Ilmira had refused to let me leave my luggage behind. I expected to be stopped and identified at any moment. A sense of frightened chaos reigned among the bystanders, who were milling about, uncertain of the facts. Had there been one death or two? When had it happened? Why? A police car sped noiselessly up the street, its silence more ominous than a blaring siren would have been. It made a sharp turn into the parking lot behind the building. The ambulance and other vehicles were back there, their pulsing, glowing lights visible in the moist air. Local voyeurs streamed in that direction. I walked on alone.

I reached a commercial street on the edge of the city ten minutes later. Here there were shoppers, families on Saturday outings—people who wouldn't have heard about the murders yet. A vendor outside a store offered me a bunch of chrysanthemums wrapped in cellophane. I waved her off, but she followed aggressively, prattling about the pretty flowers. She seemed to know I was a tourist. Was it really that obvious? Did I walk like a Westerner? Or was it my clothing that set me apart? All I knew for sure was that if I didn't want to be instantly pegged as American, I had better not open my mouth.

The flower vendor trailed off, and I walked a little slower on the wet sidewalk, putting distance between myself and the scene of the crime. Another silent police car sped past. Stay calm. It might have nothing to do with the murders, I told myself. Clear thinking was needed now, not fearful reactions. First question: where to go?

The airport and hotels were off limits. If not now, then very soon, airport security and hotel personnel would be on the lookout for an American woman travelling alone. The CIA's false documents wouldn't be much help if I were questioned because I didn't have a cover story to back them up. I had no idea who Anne-Marie Phipps was supposed to be. If I were detained, Ilmira would be called in to identify me, which she would do. She'd have no choice, as several of her neighbors would be able to make the identification, too. At that point, my false documents would only confirm my guilt.

With a shock of horror, I remembered that Ilmira and I had taken pictures of each other with our cell phones. When the police questioned her, would she produce images of my face to be broadcast on local television and published in the newspaper? Or would she keep them back, and afterwards delete them from her phone?

I mindlessly retraced the path I'd taken the day before. One of the city's mangy stray dogs trotted beside me in strange companionship until I came to the battered door of the Evenki Cultural and Historical Museum. It was just past one o'clock, and the museum didn't open until two, so I prayed a little as I pressed the buzzer, and was relieved to hear the halting scrape of the second-story window. Tolya peered over the ledge, reading glasses on his nose, tufts of white hair sticking out like the horns of a centaur's helmet.

"I was wondering if I could talk to you about my cousin," I called up.

"Surely. Come up. The door's open."

I glanced up and down the street of small businesses, where people were going about their day in the warm drizzle. No one appeared to be paying attention to me. I stepped inside.

Tolya took my wet hat and jacket and made room for my bags inside the door of his small apartment. He offered tea, and set about preparing it before I had a chance to accept. "Have a seat. Emmie's at work."

"Actually, I wanted to talk to you. I need your help to go to Death Valley." It made perfect sense once the words were out of my mouth. I would be safe in the wilderness, at least for a while, and I'd be on the path to finding Misha, if he was still alive.

Tolya set the tea things on the table, sat across from me, and smiled in his untroubled way, his hands resting easily in his lap. "To look for Mikhail Tarasov?"

"It's his last known location. It's possible something happened there—I have to check it out."

He nodded thoughtfully. "And you need help getting there."

"Yes. I hope you don't mind that I came. I didn't know who to ask."

"Well, I can get you started. It's a long trip—about six days on horseback. But you can get there in six hours if you go by air. Helicopters go out to herders' camps every week or so with supplies. I can probably find a pilot who will take you, but it will cost a lot."

"How much?"

"Depends when you want to go."

"Today. I'd like to go today."

"That's not possible. Maybe tomorrow or Monday, but it will cost you more."

"I'd really like to go today."

"Why so urgent?"

"I'm heading back to the States soon. This is kind of a last-ditch effort."

The kettle whistled, and he got up to shut it off. Over his shoulder he said, "You have cash with you?"

"I have some. I also have a credit card."

"Okay, I'll make some calls, see what I can do."

He spent the next half hour on his cell phone, speaking in his native tongue. I understood nothing but the few Russian and English words he used. *Amerikanka* occurred frequently, and every time it did, I winced. I didn't need people knowing my nationality.

The first few calls were short, but the last one went on for five or six minutes. He was increasingly pleased, smiling and nodding his head. He jotted some figures on a notepad before hanging up.

"Tomorrow is the earliest. You go first thing in the morning. You'll have a very good pilot, Roxana Amasova, who's very experienced. She's flown anthropologists, oil and gas men, even people from *National Geographic*. She's just back yesterday from taking tourists to see the woolly mammoth graves. She really gets around! Says there isn't much to see at Death Valley, but she'll take you if you really want to go. She's a very good shot with a rifle—that's good to know."

"Thank you so much, Tolya. I really appreciate it."

"It will cost sixty thousand rubles, including fuel and provisions for one night camping. Cash only. Paid up front."

That came out to about $930 USD. I'd come to Mirny with a lot of cash in rubles, not knowing if I'd be able to depend on bank withdrawals or my credit card. But after having left Misha's back rent for Ilmira, I had only about 13,000 rubles, or $200 USD, left. I rummaged in my purse for Oleg's thick stack of rubles and thumbed the notes, quickly counting.

"Can you do it?" Tolya asked, reading my expression.

"Would she be willing to take fifty thousand rubles?"

Tolya pursed his leathery brown lips. "Hmm. Let me ask." He got on the phone again, and engaged in another lengthy conversation. I could hear Roxana's voice on the other end—first strident, then firm, then considerably softened. The end of their discussion involved a surprising amount of laughter. Tolya grinned as he hung up. "Done!" he said, raising his tea mug.

I clinked my cup against his in relief.

The museum was soon to open. Emmie arrived home in time to apply eyeliner in front of a little mirror hanging on the closet door, and to brush her long hair into a silky sheen. She stepped carefully into her beaded white regalia, allowing me to help with the hook-and-eye clasps down the back, then set her silver headdress carefully on her head. She slipped her feet into dainty reindeer fur slippers and her right arm into the strap on the back of the reindeer skin shield, then stood before me proudly, transformed from just another third-world girl into a kind of arctic goddess.

"You look amazing," I said.

She struck a three-quarter pose, her chin tilting up with queenly haughtiness, the gleam of supreme confidence in her dramatically darkened eyes.

I smiled indulgently.

After some moments in this posture, she petulantly asked, "Don't you want to take a picture of me?"

"Of course, what am I thinking?" I scrambled for my phone—no, Anne-Marie Phipps's phone.

At two o'clock, Tolya ceremoniously unlocked the front door, and hung the "open" sign. No one was waiting outside. Emmie sank to the floor in a magnificent white puddle to play Candy Crush on her phone. Tolya, looking dignified in his suit jacket, string tie, and beaded cap, read the newspaper. Neither seemed concerned by the museum's lack of visitors.

A half hour before closing, a small herd of Japanese tourists gathered outside. They were led up the stairs by an English-speaking Russian guide. Closing their umbrellas, they filed respectfully into the cramped museum space, dividing themselves into three fairly regular rows.

Emmie performed beautifully, jabbering an insouciant mash of Russian and English—mostly Russian—which the guide gently rendered into pure English for the visitors, who occasionally whispered translations to each other in Japanese. Emmie proceeded to teach the visitors an Evenki greeting, and soon the Japanese were reciting it in unison, and everyone seemed quite pleased. In the end, the visitors showered Emmie with applause, and further gratified her by snapping countless pictures of her, Tolya, and practically everything else, no prompt required.

Tolya and Emmie were in fine spirits as they changed into casual clothes. I felt awkward hanging around for so long, but I didn't dare show my face on the street. To buy more time, I offered to help Emmie with her English. She was thrilled, and we sat at the table for over an hour discussing simple subjects in English, with me making gentle corrections and writing English words and sentences on a pad of paper. Soon it was dinnertime, and they asked me to join them. Afterward, I mentioned that I'd checked out of my hotel and needed to find an inexpensive room for the night. They graciously encouraged me to stay with them, in a sleeping bag they would unroll for me on the museum floor. We passed the rest of the evening in pleasant conversation. They were as eager to learn about my life as I was to learn about theirs.

Later, I tried to fall sleep in the darkness among the shelves of Evenki artifacts, the handmade ancient saddle straddling its log post, and all the weather-beaten faces gazing down from photographs. The rain had stopped hours before, and the street below was quiet. *Safe*, I thought. *For now.* I was fairly certain that I hadn't told Ilmira about my previous trip to the museum. And Tolya and Emmie, in their charming simplicity, didn't watch TV. They didn't even have one. Tolya might learn about the murders in the next day's paper, but unless the story was accompanied by a photo of the prime suspect, he probably wouldn't suspect me right away, as we'd grown to be friends, and he wasn't the suspicious type.

I thought about Vera. I couldn't call her on Anne-Marie Phipps's phone. If I were captured, the call would be discovered and my cover, as pitiful as it was, would be blown. I wouldn't ask to use Tolya's for the same reason. The fewer connections he had to me, the better. It was about 1 p.m. in Maryland now. Vera would be worried and heartsick at not having heard from me for another evening. Eventually, she'd panic and start trying to reach me any number of ways—my cell phone, Lena, the hotel in Yakutsk, anything she could think of. But nothing would work—my cell phone was probably decommissioned by now, Lena couldn't be reached, and the hotel would say I'd checked out days ago. When her anxiety got intense enough, she'd probably contact the US State Department, but they wouldn't be able to help either. As far as the Western world was concerned, I'd fallen off the map.

I closed my eyes, needing desperately to rest. But it was useless: my brain was practically on fire from stress. I was guilty of murder, if not directly, then by association. If I were caught, I had no defense whatsoever. Even giving up my CIA handler—an act of treason I would never commit—wouldn't exonerate me: it would only add the charge of espionage.

Giving up on sleep, I got up and quietly pulled a chair next to the window. The sky was murky black, letting no starlight or moonlight through. A couple of electric lights flickered on the street below. I sat by the window like a sentry all night long, my ears straining for the wail of approaching sirens or the thumping of police boots on the pavement. Those sounds didn't come. But every once a while a group of Saturday night revelers passed below my perch, their young voices rising in boasting or gaiety, the tips of their cigarettes winking like fireflies in the dark. And somewhere nearby a dog kept barking furiously—sharp, jagged warnings that went on intermittently for hours.

᛫ ⁚ ᛫ ⁚ ᛫ ⁚ ᛫ ⁚ ᛫ ⁚

At a private airstrip early the next morning, I waited in a one-room office. Not an office, really, more like a public shelter from the elements. The window onto the runway was grimy, its view of tethered helicopters and biplanes distorted by a torn polyurethane covering. Across the way, at the edge of woods, was a narrow outhouse on a raised platform, several steps on each side leading up to separate doors for women and men.

A white Ford Explorer pulled into the lot, and a woman got out. She looked to be in her mid-fifties, with a strong, compact body and a long braid of coarse graying hair. Wearing a canvas hunting vest and hiking boots, she introduced herself as Roxana Amasova and confirmed the price and details of the trip. There was a flinty light in her coal-black eyes as she appraised me. I assumed she was judging me for travel-worthiness, estimating just how much of a pain in the ass this lily-skinned American doctor would be.

The Mi-8 helicopter rose at the first streak of dawn—straining and balking at first, then letting go of the earth with a sudden powerful exhalation. As Mirny disappeared from sight, a portion of the tension I'd been carrying fell away. My lungs expanded as the helicopter's glass nose filled with cloudless sky. Below, the dark green taiga, still nearly black in the shadows, rolled away evenly on every side.

Over the loud noise inside the cabin, Roxana shouted out a flight plan that meant nothing to me. Though the needle of the speedometer hovered at 138 miles per hour, it felt like we were drifting. The sun was rising far off in the yellowing southeast, like an event happening elsewhere.

An hour later, a ridge of snow-covered mountains appeared to the south. Forests of larch ran up the slopes as far as they could go, before surrendering to rock fields studded with craggy outcroppings of shale, which, in turn, gave way to wide snowy basins and white-capped mountain peaks.

Tiny rivulets plummeted down the slopes, merging into swelling streams that fell into a swollen river that rushed headlong across the floor of a narrow valley. The water was perfectly clear, no doubt icy cold, clogged in places by the branches and slender trunks of saplings that had been ripped from the low banks during spring floods. I looked for bear and wolves without success, but could make out flashes of fish scales in the water. The day blossomed into something brilliant; the sky turned Aegean blue.

Roxana guided the helicopter along the curve of the river, which grew wider and slower over the next hour. She occasionally consulted a rudimentary map affixed to a clipboard. At the fork of a large tributary, she banked north, and we followed a slender blue ribbon that curved through endless green forest. The larch morphed to pine, then birch, then back to larch—all of it uniformly dense. Rocky patches appeared and disappeared, and there were sudden glimpses of sparkling streams. Distant foothills were shrouded in a smoky haze.

Soon we were rising into hills again, and eventually crested a ridge. Now an entirely new terrain appeared: rocky mountains with round gray tops crowded close together. A shallow valley opened up. It was covered in places by short trees and underbrush, in others by carpets of moss and gold-flecked lichen. Patches of dirt and rocky fields made up the rest.

Four crumbling stone structures occupied the far end of the valley—several small ones, a larger building set apart. Doors and windows were missing, and portions of walls had collapsed into rubble. A number of open-mouthed tunnels dotted the surrounding hillsides, and running everywhere were the remnants of wooden tracks. There were no electrified fences, no razor-wire, no sentry towers—nothing to identify it as a prison—yet a shudder of fear passed through me anyway. I could almost see the single-file lines of malnourished inmates staggering into the underground shafts.

Roxana set the helicopter down on a flat area at the edge of the valley, far from the prison camp. I was confused by this choice—it would have been easy to land closer to the site. When the engine was turned off, I asked why we were so far away.

"Radioactivity," she said without perceptible emotion. "I'm going to stay with the helicopter and set up camp, so you'll be going on alone. You'll have at most three hours of daylight to hike to the site, take pictures or do whatever you want to do there, and return."

"How high are the levels?" I heard the tremor of fear in my voice.

"You'll be okay as long as you have this." She presented me with a bright orange plastic instrument with a digital display—a Geiger counter. It was surprisingly light, fit in the palm of my hand. A couple of AAA batteries fit into a slot on the back. Not only did the rate of beeping increase when radiation was detected, Roxana explained, but the background of the digital display turned color as well: green for safe, yellow for risk, orange for danger, red for critical.

"Make sure it's turned on," she said, indicating a tiny switch on the side.

I turned it on. The display lit up and *83 mSv* appeared against a green background.

"A few hours' exposure at the lower levels isn't dangerous. Just stay out of the danger and critical zones," she said.

I wasn't sure I believed her, but I wasn't turning back.

It took about an hour of hiking across uneven terrain to reach the camp's perimeter. Three small buildings, about the size of cabins, lay scattered across the lower valley. Through the gaping doors and partially collapsed roofs, I could see that vegetation had invaded them. I decided to bypass them and go on about another quarter mile to the largest building, which occupied a higher plateau at the valley's eastern end.

All along the Geiger counter had been bleating a slow rhythm. As I came abreast of two heavily rusted fifty-five-gallon drums at the side of the trail, the beeping turned frantic, and the digital display jumped to 530. *Danger*. I raced past the barrels and didn't slow down until the Geiger counter did.

An enormous hawk swooped down in front of me, blasting a loud, shrill caw. I was already unnerved by the Geiger counter, by the place, by just being there at all—and my heart raced as wildly as if the large bird had knocked me down. The hawk flew up and away, cresting the hill on wide, crooked wings. I looked around to see if there were others. There were none. In fact, I saw no signs of birds or animals—not so much as a fallen feather or dried scat. The place was eerily quiet, sunk in a thousand-year radioactive sleep, in the cool, bright air of a perfect day.

The large building abutted a steep, rocky hill dotted with the puckered black mouths of the mines. It was an imposing ruin—four stories tall, constructed of massive stones. Rusted metal grillwork still covered some of the windows, so I took it to be the barracks where the prisoners had been housed.

All furniture had been removed from the first floor, and large portions of the outer walls were gone as well. Piles of rubble and fallen concrete rafters claimed the long open space, which was protected from rain and snow by the upper levels. A fine yellow dust had sifted through the broken windows and accumulated thickly on the floor. Here, at last, were signs of life. A mother bear and her cub had made a circuit of the room, leaving clover-shaped footprints behind.

I ascended a flight of stairs on the eastern wall. The second floor was bisected by a long corridor with small rooms along each side. The floor was damp and buckled; I didn't venture far for fear it would collapse. Golden shafts of sunlight pouring through gaps in the ceiling gave the place an ethereal air.

The steps leading to the third floor were rotted. Startling blue sky hung at the top of the stairwell, indicating that the stairway to the fourth floor and the eastern portion of the roof had given way. I'd gone as far as I dared.

From where I was standing, I could look through a blasted window onto a pond of thick yellow water at the base of the hill. The pond was circled by a wide band of hard-packed, sulphurish dirt, which had somehow managed to bubble up in places, creating low moguls of a uniform size. At regular intervals, man-made holes about four feet across, lined with what appeared to be tin, dotted the sand. Together, the moguls and holes looked like swelling pustules and ingrown blackheads in a case of terrestrial acne.

After passing the radioactive drums, I'd slipped the Geiger counter into my jacket pocket to muffle the beeps, reasoning that if I started checking the instrument every time there was a mild fluctuation, I'd soon be a basket case. I was here in Death Valley now—whether it had been a wise or foolish decision to come remained to be seen—and I needed to focus on what I was doing without being distracted by fear. But, of course, I'd been listening to the beeps nonetheless, and had been aware of their steadily rising rhythm as I ascended the low hill and entered the barracks. Now I took out the instrument and checked the display: 750. *Danger.*

Time to go.

As I turned away from the window, something caught my eye in the clay-like sand around the golden pond. Shallow indentations in the roughly oval shape of…footprints. Could that be? Yes, there was a vague memory of footprints in the bank. Blurred by rain showers, but not completely washed away.

I sprinted down the stairs, crawled through an opening in the eastern wall, and found the place where the footprints began. Death Valley's human visitor had been wearing boots with a hi-tech rubberized tread. Larger than mine, but not by much. I tracked the prints as they approached the yellow sludge, hoping that the person had dropped something or left some other clue. About twenty feet from the water, the Geiger counter went completely crazy. The beeps came so fast that they were one continuous screech. I glanced in panic at the instrument in my hand. The digital display was bright red. *Critical.* I turned and ran faster than I'd ever run before.

· ⋰ ·⋰ ⸳⋰ ⸳⋰ ·

I didn't stop until I was at the bottom of the rocky slope, and the Geiger counter was bleating as weakly as a half-dead lamb. Doubled over and gasping for breath, I asked myself what the hell I was doing there and why I hadn't gone home when I had the chance. An image of Misha's closet rose unbidden in my mind. The boots on the floor, the yellow dirt. Were those his footprints circling the pond? Could their traces have survived since his likely early summer excursion? Or had he been here more recently?

I had to figure out my next move. The helicopter was more than an hour's hike away. The sky had faded from its former brilliant blue to a gunmetal gray, and fumes of frigid air seemed to be seeping out of the ground and flowing down the hillside from the darkening ridge. When days got shorter in the arctic autumn, they did so quickly. But there was still time to investigate the crumbling outbuildings that lay in the lower valley.

I followed the rocky remnants of a path to the first structure, made of timber—a single square room about fifteen feet by fifteen feet. The roof was completely gone, and there was nothing left to suggest what the building's purpose had been. A rotted wooden floor plank broke under my foot. I snapped some pictures and headed to the next building, half hoping there would be nothing there either so I could start hiking back.

The way was strewn with rocks and rubble. Shadows were lengthening, so at first I didn't realize that the whiter, oddly shaped stones were actually bones. Human bones. Shins, ribs, clavicles, tibias, spines. Small finger bones, pelvic dishes, discs of vertebrae. Thousands of bones littered an area the size of half a football field. All detached and mixed together with dirt and dry weeds in a vast open graveyard that I was inadvertently walking upon. The cold had made the bones brittle so that they crunched like seashells under my feet.

Was this what Misha had discovered and reported? Radioactive contamination, mass graves? These things were certainly disturbing. But it was a well-known fact that the Soviets had processed uranium and conducted hundreds of nuclear tests across Siberia. And that for over seventy years, forced labor camps had brutalized and murdered millions. Death Valley, for all its horror, was just another link in the gulag chain.

I was walking quickly now, skirting the open cemetery as best I could, eager to finish my job and get out of there. But something small was bothering me—a niggling little observation that kept slithering away.

The roof of the next building was collapsed in one corner, the stone wall under it tumbled down, and the inner concrete wall turned to dust. Where the roof had held up, the interior was intact: a long metal table in the center; a sink and counter along one wall; several tin buckets in a corner; spread out on the counter, an array of knives, vices, and saws. I primly told myself that this building was nothing more than a tool shed, but a moment later I was flooded with a dread so powerful it nearly buckled my knees. I'd suddenly realized what I'd seen—or not seen—in the bone field: there were very few skulls.

I crossed the makeshift surgery to a back door, wide open to a vista of darkening hills and lowering sky. The skulls had been thrown in an enormous ditch. They'd been sawed cleanly in half. The rounded top parts had landed either face up, like white bowls supplicating for rice or rain, or face down, like smooth, gently cracked bike helmets one might pick up and wear. The bottom halves were gawky configurations in comparison—just a mash of jaws and teeth and mandibles severed at the joint.

Back at the museum, Emmie had talked about the Evenki belief that souls haunted the places where they died. If that were true, then the air over this pit must be crowded with ghosts, and for a few hallucinatory moments, I felt the victims of Death Valley circling me feverishly, passing through my solid body with their non-substantial forms, clutching at me desperately, begging for justice or revenge. What did I have to give them? What could I do? I held out my hands to show my emptiness and grief.

Had they been alive when the experiments took place? When the scalp was peeled off the skull like a useless husk? And who had done this work? Sixty years ago, what monster in the guise of a doctor had been standing where I now stood?

I circled the pit slowly, snapping photos the whole time. Inside, I photographically recorded every wall and corner of the operating room, and every implement in it. Finally, I headed back the way I'd come, picking my way carefully along the rim of the graveyard, taking pictures intermittently, feeling nothing in particular, just a gaping hole in my body big enough for the wind to blow through. I knew myself then to be naked and defenseless, and realized that I'd always been this way. Only vanity had made me imagine otherwise. All my life I'd coasted along on the pumped-up self-esteem that came from living in an environment that I could, for the most part, control. While in reality, just the thinnest of veils—of time, space, luck—separated me from the victims whose desiccated bones were cracking under my heels. Their protests had no doubt been loud and clear; their tactics, resourceful; their hearts, brave and strong. But when madmen came to power, none of that mattered. Flocks of demons flew out of their hiding places, and humans by the thousands, by the millions, ended up bull-dozed into cadaver piles.

Roxana was in the clearing, hacking slender branches into firewood with a small ax. I ran up from the trail head and breathlessly insisted that we needed to get away from there immediately and find another place to pass the night. Pausing in her work, she coolly replied that flying at night was unwise: too easy to get lost. Morning would come soon enough. Then she instructed me to gather underbrush for kindling, to strip any leaves and stack the shorn branches in a pile, next to the two-person tent she'd set up while I was gone.

Night happened swiftly, and with it, the temperature dropped. We ate in silence in our coats, faces scalded by blasts of heat from the burning wood. Bread, butter, sardines, canned stew, and vodka. The flames writhed and stretched, turned pink and livid orange. The smell of smoldering flesh seemed to rise into my nostrils with the smoke. The massed flames danced a ritual of death.

Roxana handed over a tin mug of hot tea, jarring me out of my morbid reveries. "What did you find?"

"High levels of radioactivity, an open mass grave, evidence of medical experimentation. Traces of footprints approaching…I don't know what to call it…a pool of uranium sludge."

"Belonging to the person you're searching for?"

"Possibly."

"You say the footprints approached the pool. Did they return?"

"I didn't see that."

"A suicide?"

"I don't think so," I said quickly. But it was only horror at such a death that made me deny the possibility.

"Maybe the footprints went another way," she said reasonably, sweeping the idea away for now. Pulling a pair of reading glasses from her pocket and settling them on her nose, she said, "Let's see the pictures."

I handed over my phone, and she carefully studied each of the more than fifty photographs I'd taken. No comment, no perceptible emotion. She sat quietly for a few moments before telling me a story.

"A few days before I was born, the sky turned red and stayed that way for hours. A gray snow fell to the ground but didn't melt—a fine, light snow, like dust. The children played in it all day. Later, their skin blistered where the snow had touched their bodies. Many of them died soon after, my older brother among them. We thought that angry spirits from the Below World had killed them. It wasn't until the 1980s that we learned the truth: the Soviets had been testing atomic bombs, and the snow was radioactive fallout."

"I'm so sorry," I said, staring hollow-eyed into the fire.

She seemed about to say more, fell silent instead.

The hills and valley beyond the circle of firelight were silent as well—a cold, inhuman silence. A burning log collapsed, disintegrated to red hot cinders.

Roxana turned her ruddy face toward mine, and for a moment we looked into each other's eyes. She said, "There are only seventeen thousand Evenki left in the world. We're going extinct."

Extinct. A word that described animals.

There was nothing I could say in response, nothing in my experience that gave me the right to comment. Even my compassion, to the extent that it was useless, had no meaning here. Voicing it would be nothing more than a comfortable arrogance I would be using to distance myself.

"For four thousand years we had a way of life that gave us what we needed and took nothing from the land. Then the Soviets came and killed the shamans, forced men and women to work apart from each other, and snatched children from their parents to go to boarding schools far away. Our traditions were outlawed. It wasn't long until we depended on the state for everything, as it required. When the Soviet Union fell, we were left without the support they'd forced us to rely on, and tried to return to a way of life that had been practically destroyed." She recited the history matter-of-factly, hardship itself having become the Evenki way of life. "Cancer rates are high among our people, but that's the least of our problems."

I prodded the charred embers with a stick, setting off a cascade of sparks and a whoosh of combusting wood. The incited flames strained skyward, shrunk back; a flare of heat reached my face and receded. The fire was engaged in its own demise, having consumed what it could.

"Do you have children?" she asked.

"No."

"A husband?"

"No."

"You still have time."

I almost laughed bitterly, remembering Vera's admonition. Had I really come halfway around the world to be reminded once again that eggs grew foggy and forgetful long before their hosts? Was Roxana trying on a maternal role? I was no child. And what business was it of hers anyway?

"Not every woman needs to be a mother," I said, imagining the ghosts in the valley, how they'd been children once.

She didn't reply, and after a while I worried that I might have pushed her away, which was the last thing I wanted to do in this lonely place. "You? Do you have children?"

"Three daughters. Five grandchildren." She pulled a crisp photo out of her wallet and handed it over. A swaddled newborn cradled in the arms of a smiling, bleary-eyed woman. "That's Vitaliy. Vitya, we call him. Three months old."

The infant's face was wrinkled and squint-eyed. "Ah, lovely. Blessings on Vitya." I hardly knew what I was saying. I gave her back the picture, and got up to drag some underbrush over to feed the languishing flames.

"Who exactly are you looking for, and why do you want to find him so badly?" Roxana asked when I sat down.

I told the story of my missing cousin, the magazine article, and the two men who had come to the apartment.

"Secret police," she said.

"Yes, probably." She'd jumped to the same conclusion as Ilmira, but for completely different reasons. Moisture in the cut branches sizzled and popped in the fire, and there was a deep, sweet smell of burning sap.

"What are you going to do with the photos from the camp?"

"When I get back in the States, I'll turn them over to someone who'll know what to do—catalog or publicize them, whatever. It will be a way of honoring my cousin, I suppose."

"So you think he's dead?"

"I don't know. Until I learn otherwise, I'm going to assume he's alive." I flashed on an image of the footprints in the yellow sand. None had returned from the sickening pool. But they might not have been Misha's.

I paused, decided to risk more. "Roxana, you might as well know that I need to keep a low profile right now."

"Trouble with the police?"

"Yes. I believe they suspect me of something very bad. Falsely. But there it is."

"In Russia, it makes no difference what's true or false. Just ask the skeletons down there."

She began gathering up the dishes and containers of food. "Your cousin could only have come here the way you did—with a guide in a rented helicopter or plane. If an Evenki took him, I can find out who it was. I'll have an answer for you soon."

Roxana called around on her radio to the pilots she knew who ran supplies out to the herders. There was one who remembered ferrying a young man out to the brigade of a man named Ivan Nikolayevich on July thirteenth. A huge weight fell from my shoulders with the news. There was a good chance Misha was alive, and if he'd remained with the herders he might even be safe. Early the next morning, the Mi-8 rose into a temperate blue sky, banking away from the stone ruins and bone fields of Death Valley. Below, the sparkling Sakhandja River curved through thick taiga that swelled and dipped over the earth's crust like a green undulating sea. The river would lead us north toward its source in the snow-capped peaks ahead.

Roxana had to shout to be heard over the whine of the rotor blades: "Ivan Nikolayevich and his family guide their herds through these mountains all year long. They tend to follow the rivers—moving upstream in spring, back to lower ground in fall. They make, oh, maybe twenty or thirty camps a year. During the summer, the herd is feeding constantly, so they have to change camps every two or three days. Right about now, late August, they're probably at the highest point of the migration, or maybe they're already coming back down through one of the passes. The reindeer will be fattened up and moving slowly. The trick for us is to follow their route up the river until we find them."

A bright stab of sunlight glanced off the window. "How many reindeer?" I asked.

"Between fifteen hundred and two thousand, I'd say."

"Hard to miss."

"Wait till we get up a little higher, you'll see."

A half hour later, she pointed down. Two flat wooden platforms were built high among tree branches—one partly covered with a bright blue tarp lashed over bulky objects, the other wrecked and decaying with damp and mold. They were the first signs of human activity we'd seen since leaving Death Valley, and I found their presence reassuring.

"The high platforms protect their stores from wolves, but nowhere is safe from bears," Roxana said.

In time, the helicopter rose over the edge of the forest and coursed over bare slopes covered with moss, bushes, and dwarf willows and birches. There were crags and promontories, deep ravines, shallow blue streams tumbling down to meet the river, grassy basins opening toward the sun. Each cliff face fell away to another world, another vista; the river, smaller now, clung to a more twisted path. It led us to a small sapphire lake at the foot of a mountain, traces of a campfire on its bank.

"They've crossed," Roxana yelled. "Over the pass. There."

The helicopter swerved toward the mountain, threaded its way between the steep rock faces of a canyon, over a bare, stony corridor. Roxana shouted, "It's hard for the reindeer here. No water, no place to rest. And the sharp stones cut their hooves."

The pass opened suddenly to a wide alpine slope that rolled down to a narrow, sunlit valley. Here, another lake spawned rivulets that fed a bog, which contracted at its eastern edge into a fast-moving stream that spilled through a narrow gorge. On the other side of the gorge, the ground dropped away dizzily. Far below, the river turned sharply around a rocky bank, and five white tents popped into view on a grassy plateau.

"There they are!" Roxana shouted.

She brought the helicopter down some distance away from the camp. Two men jogged out to greet us. They might have been in their twenties, thirties, or forties. Their broad, weather-beaten faces and grimy clothing hid their age. One had stringy hair and a long, curling mustache; the other pressed his cap on his head against the stiff wind whipped up by the spinning propeller blades. Roxana cut the engine, and we stood up stiffly, tossed our bags onto the grass. The men picked them up and began carrying them back to camp before we'd clambered down from the cabin to stand at last on the welcoming firm ground.

We went first to pay our respects to Ivan Nikolayevich and his elderly mother, Sofia, kicking off our boots before entering the largest of the tents. Ivan Nikolayevich was sprawled at the back, propped on folded bedding and a stack of padded jackets. Sofia was tiny, gnome-like, with black eyes that beamed alertly out of a deeply wrinkled face. She was perched on an upturned log beside her cook stove, smoking a cigarette with nicotine-stained fingers. Ivan hailed Roxana warmly, and they spoke in Eveny for some minutes, with Sofia following the conversation attentively, every once in a while punctuating some comment with a hearty, toothless laugh. Her gray hair still had some black streaks in it, though she looked to be over eighty years old.

A woman about my age entered the tent, carrying a bucket of blueberries, trailing two high-spirited girls about seven and eight years old, dressed in pink and purple sweatpants and heavy sweaters. The girls stopped short when they caught sight of me, an unexpected white visitor; they stared with rounded eyes and mouths agape. The woman smiled an apology, spoke briefly to them in Eveny, and they ran out of the tent as blithely as they'd run in, breaking into peals of laughter that carried on the cold air.

The woman introduced herself in Russian as Lidia, and inquired about my trip. I described the relative ease with which we'd found the camp. Lidia said that Roxana was an expert guide, that another pilot might easily have missed the brigade's winter campsite at the mouth of the Sakhandja River and wandered far afield.

She explained that Ivan suffered with arthritis. His unsteadiness in the saddle had proved dangerous on several occasions, so he didn't go out with the herd anymore, a fact that seemed to pain him more than the disease itself. This visit from Roxana, a distant relative, was therefore a boon, which he'd happily anticipated all day. With a wry smile, Lidia warned that at some point, when he and Roxana had exhausted the family news, Ivan would no doubt turn his attention to me, prodding me unrelentingly for my political opinions and stories about the United States.

Lidia mentioned that several men were out with the herd. They would be driving the reindeer back to camp within the next hour or so for the evening roundup.

"Roundup?" I asked.

"That's when we see to any animals that are sick or hurt. We milk the nursing mothers then too."

I assumed that Lidia knew the reason for my visit, but I didn't say anything about Misha just then, and she didn't bring him up. I sensed a certain etiquette at work: personal topics would be raised at appropriate times. The camp was dedicated first to its demanding work—nearly two thousand reindeer couldn't be put on hold—and the needs of visitors were, of necessity, a lower priority.

As we talked, Lidia had been making tea. Now she poured the dark liquid into mugs and handed them around. By then the two men who'd ferried the luggage had slunk noiselessly into the tent and were sitting cross-legged on reindeer skins laid along the perimeter. They accepted the tea without fanfare, while Sofia watched everyone keenly from her corner, smoking her cigarette down to its nub.

More introductions were made. The men were called Gosha and Nikolay. A warm, friendly feeling prevailed. When the tea was consumed, Roxana produced a bottle of vodka from a pocket of her commodious field jacket.

"We must feed the fire!" she announced in Russian with a theatrical flourish, and there was hearty agreement from Ivan and a murmur of assent from Sofia. The stove was a covered rectangle made out of sheet metal, its chimney rigged to protrude from a hole in the side the tent. The tea kettle and two pans sat on its flat top, and a hatch door opened on one end. Sofia leaned over to open this door with her tiny, wizened hand. I could see the low fire murmuring inside, casting a yellow-orange glow across the blackened inner walls.

Roxana poured vodka into her mug, then splashed it across the fire. The flames leapt instantly, consuming the flammable liquid in a few crackling moments of intense heat. There was silence in the tent, then smiles of approval, and the mugs were held out for Roxana to pour a round of celebratory drinks.

Dimly, the sound of bells reached us inside the tent, and everyone went out to watch the herd. The reindeer were coming uphill from a valley, moving with surprising speed along both sides of the river, kicking dust into a low cloud. Men rode reindeer—domesticated reindeer called *uchakhs*, Roxana told me later—along the edges of the herd, keeping them headed in the right direction, while the tiny figures of dogs darted about. The herd looked to be about a mile away, an undulating sea of fur. As it drew closer, the ground trembled under the impact of thousands of hooves.

The advance guard of reindeer burst onto an enormous trampled meadow and started filling it, milling around. Soon, hundreds—then, impossibly, many hundreds—of animals were swirling counterclockwise, creating an enormous whirlpool of fur, muscle, and clattering antlers. The air reverberated with their grunts and short, rasping barks, as well as the high-pitched shouts of women and children who dashed about the periphery, waving their arms to drive back animals who were veering away from the group.

Gosha, the man with the ropey locks and long mustache, strode with a devil-may-care attitude among the jostling mass of long snouts and bony haunches. He looped halters around the necks of several and led them to milking stations where Sofia, Lidia, and another woman relieved stretched, heavy udders.

Other men stood by restlessly, scrutinizing the herd, fingering lassos, and soon the sizzling whir of hurled rope was added to the general cacophony. The men shouted with pleasure at a catch, moaned in disappointment at a miss. If a captured animal resisted being pulled to the outside, the herder pulled himself to it hand-over-hand. I saw one man twist an animal's antlers until it fell with a heavy thump onto its side, whereupon children dashed in and sat on the writhing body. The man knelt by the reindeer's side, pulling a small bottle out of his pocket and placing it on the matted grass.

"What's he doing?" I asked Roxana, who stood alongside me.

"Looks like he's about to clean out a hoof wound or an infected cut."

"Really? What kind of disinfectant is he using?"

"That's probably potassium permanganate. I've seen them use an antibiotic powder, too."

I craned my neck to watch the operation, but the swirl of reindeer kept getting in the way.

Not far away, Ivan Nikolayevich—the portly, white-haired grandfather of the group—squinted attentively at the choreographed work, occasionally taking long draughts on a short pipe cupped in his muscular palm.

At first, in all the commotion, I hadn't even thought to look for Misha, but as the processes of milking and caring for the enormous herd dragged on, I scoured the faces of the six or seven men in constant motion among the animals—all of them grimed with kicked-up dirt and streaks of muddy sweat. A younger man worked without a lasso, in clothes less worn and filthy than the others, but I wasn't close enough to notice any resemblance to the Facebook photo I'd seen weeks before.

Eventually, the long-legged reindeer were led out of camp, haunches rolling under dense brown hides, hooves ringing dully on exposed rocks, leaving the trampled meadow clotted with flattened pads of fresh dung.

His shoes gave him away. The others wore rubber waders folded down at the knee, while he strode in Nike sneakers like the ones on the floor of his closet in Mirny. He knew I was there to see him—that was clear from the dark, searching glance he gave me as the last of the animals cleared the area. Apparently, he'd been informed of my visit.

"Mikhail Tarasov?" I said as he approached.

He nodded.

"Natalie March." He was tall, like Vera and me. Dark like his Sakha father. Thick, unkempt hair flowed over the shoulders of his camouflage jacket, twigs and dirt caught in its knots. His features were strong, handsome. He walked with his chest high and shoulders back. Just as his sister had weeks before on the steps of the Capitol Building, his strong, supple grace drew my eyes and left me mesmerized.

"What do you want?"

"Meredith Viles hired me to find you."

"And you have." He frowned slightly. "How?"

I told him about the letter from the magazine and my call to the editor, the trip to Death Valley, and how Roxana Amasova had tracked him down through the helicopter pilots.

For a moment, we were silent. There was a lot to say, but it wasn't clear what should come next. It dawned on me suddenly that Misha might not know about his sister's death. I might have to tell him, and that news would need to come before anything else.

"I met your sister in Washington," I began. I explained how she'd travelled to the US on a cultural visa after he disappeared. When it became obvious that he hadn't been aware of her trip, and therefore probably didn't know about her death, I said I had some very bad news.

"About Saldana?"

"Yes."

He seemed to guess immediately. His face darkened, and he braced himself. "What is it?"

"She is…I'm sorry to tell you this…" How many times before had I given this news? Usually standing in a gleaming white corridor or a muted waiting room, the family members already stricken, having gleaned the truth from the somber look in my eye or the set of my jaw. There was no easy way to say it.

"She's gone. I'm very sorry."

His eyes closed. A few moments later, he said, "How?"

"Murdered."

He winced, stood firm. "Tell me."

I explained the police's theory that Saldana had surprised a burglar in her hotel room. Because I knew he was going to ask, I described the manner of death, the fact that it would have been over in minutes.

His face was a mask of anguish. "Does my mother know?"

"Yes. She stayed in Yakutsk to wait for you in case you showed up there, but after your sister's death, she returned to her village to be with your grandmother."

He remained silent, staring into the distance. I imagined his mind circling warily around the new reality in his life—rejecting it, accepting it. He drew a ragged breath. He'd gone quite pale suddenly; his lips were nearly white. "You're sure it was Saldana?"

"I identified the body."

A strangled noise erupted from his chest. Then, nothing. He stood rooted like an ancient tree, motionless. I imagined sheer destruction, like a blitzkrieg, happening on the inside.

"I'm so sorry," I said again, feeling the uselessness of words.

8

That night, in honor of the visitors, two mountain sheep were slaughtered and cooked on an open fire in the middle of camp. The meat was fatty and tender and fell off the bone, and I ate it greedily. The huskies, who had devoured their portions raw, lay down on the blood-soaked peat among the gnawed bones, and blinked their blue eyes contentedly before nodding off.

Sofia observed me from the other side of the campfire, not unkindly, but I started to feel discomforted by her steady gaze. I had a feeling that nothing escaped the old woman's notice. Sofia called Roxana over and whispered in her ear. Roxana returned and squatted at my side to relay the message. "Sofia says the meat of mountain sheep is especially good for the eyes."

On the other side of the wavering orange flame, Sofia reached up and gently tapped the corner of one eye. I smiled my thanks.

Misha didn't appear for dinner. He had stalked off after I told him about his sister. I had the sense that everyone in the camp had heard the terrible news. There was a gentle somberness in the way they treated me, and what ought to have been a festive event was fittingly subdued. The Evenki, who lived in such close quarters, were delicate about space and privacy, Roxana had explained. They entered conversation slowly, paused at the opening of a tent to be invited inside, were not given to intrusive questions or abrupt displays of feeling. But for all their modesty and gentleness, they were hardly strangers to violence and sudden death: two of Sofia's sons had died before they were thirty—one in a barroom knife fight, one by falling through ice.

After dinner, a couple of herders put up a small tent at the edge of camp for Roxana and me. It was tall enough to stand inside, with space for sleeping on either side. The canvas edges were folded under and secured with rocks the size of fists. It quickly filled with the warm, smoky smell of the reindeer skins the men had dragged in. The fur was coarse and surprisingly dense—each thick hair distinct and vaguely tubular. It felt alive under my stroking fingers, which soon picked up a hint of animal oil. The poplar branches under the hides were still springy with sweet-smelling sap, and these smells mixed with the dank, muddy river and the aromas of blood and cooked meat and vodka that clung to my clothes.

I badly needed rest. But I had a strange sense of disorientation that came from not being sure exactly where I was on planet Earth. I recalled the map Roxana used in the helicopter and tried to mentally pinpoint our present location—somewhere in the Verkhoyansk Mountains—but the exact spot hardly mattered in such vastness. There was a small stove in the tent, a mini-version of Sofia's. I loaded it with kindling and lit it—partly to take off the chill and partly to give myself something useful, tangible, to do with my hands.

In the glow and warmth of the heated stove, I fell asleep quite easily, almost too quickly, as if I'd tripped and tumbled down a grassy slope that led to unconsciousness, and when I picked myself up and looked back the way I'd come, a mountain ram with magnificent curled horns was standing on a rock promontory a hundred feet above me. The ram was angry. The atmosphere crackled with its rage. I understood the way one did in dreams that the anger was directed at me—although it encompassed others as well, possibly many others—and that it was urgently up to me to placate the powerful animal before it did great harm. I started trudging uphill, the earnest words warbling in my throat being stolen by the wind. It came to me that I was doing it all wrong, everything. Even my straining legs were making no progress; they only rolled like bicycle tires in the selfsame groove. The ram lowered its head, glowering down at my puniness and ineptitude, and its horns unfurled into black banded spears. I grew slower, thicker, dumber, as the bloody meat congealed in my stomach swelled to twice and three times its size.

Roxana woke me—I'd been thrashing. "You're having a bad dream."

I sat up. The dream had been so vivid that I had to tell someone. I half believed that somewhere in the jagged peaks that ringed the valley there really was an angry ram, and everyone   not just Roxana, but all the herders—needed to be warned.

Roxana listened closely, without surprise. "That's Bayanay."

"Who?"

"He's an old man, the keeper of the animals. He owns them—we're like his children—and he also *is* them. You made him angry somehow."

"Why? What did I do?"

She glanced around the tent. "Did you feed the fire?"

"You mean with vodka?"

"Did you?"

"No. But you can't be serious."

"You must do it now." She pulled a bottle of vodka from the pocket of her coat. Only an inch or so of liquid remained at the bottom. "Take it. Pour the vodka on the fire."

I felt shocked, oddly betrayed. I'd thought of Roxana as educated, rational, yet now she was insisting I perform this superstitious trick. Worse—the dream was still holding me hostage, and I found myself eager to obey. Anything to appease Bayanay. I grabbed the neck of the bottle, splashed the last of the vodka straightaway onto the smoldering, blackened boughs inside the stove.

When the flame leapt almost as high as my hand, I dropped the bottle with a cry of surprise and fear, as if a creature of the netherworld had reached out to capture me.

The bottle landed dully on the peat and rolled a few inches.

"There now," Roxana said, laying her palm on my shoulder. "Things will be better for you now."

Wordlessly, I staggered to my feet and squeezed through the tent flap. I half-walked, half-ran to the tree line, where I vomited violently onto a fallen, moss-covered trunk. Wiping my mouth with the back of my hand, I glanced back toward the tents. I didn't want Ivan or Sofia to know how I'd handled their generous feast. Gosha was sitting on a stump, whittling larch wood. He glanced away discreetly, in a way that made me feel forgiven.

Roxana met me on the way back, carrying my jacket, which she wrapped around my shoulders. "Don't worry. You'll sleep well now. Bayanay won't come again tonight."

She was wrong. I didn't sleep at all. I lay awake while she snored softly a few feet away. I couldn't get my head around anything—not where I was, what had happened, or what I'd done. The image of Tanya playfully shushing the bright, noisy parrot kept dancing through my mind. Followed by an image of shrouded bodies in a Syrian village, laid out in rows on the dusty street. Meredith with her brilliant, flashing ring. Saldana in her yellow dress.

In time, bright seams of light appeared along the edges of the tent flap. I rose and stepped outside into a dense, dreamy arctic dawn, the sky suffused with a dusky blue radiance so mute and softened that it felt like a caress. A sliver of silver moon shone down on glowing snow-capped peaks.

There was a surprising amount of activity in the camp. Children were playing kickball, and Ivan and a younger herder sat cross-legged on the moss, deep in conversation. Lidia was rinsing out what looked like long, sinewy animal innards—intestines, organs—in the cold stream, while Misha split wood at the edge of camp with the vigor of a man exorcising demons.

I could smell the fresh green of the hewn logs as I approached.

He saw me coming and laid down the ax.

"Could we talk?" I said.

We walked to higher ground, eventually coming onto a rock promontory overlooking the valley. It seemed exactly the promontory on which the ram in my dream had stood. We sat cross-legged near the edge. Reindeer were scattered like toy figurines far below, drowsing, swaying a little, facing into a mild breeze. Small, colorful blooms dotted an alpine meadow, and the air was crystal clear and cold.

"I found the skulls at Death Valley," I said. "It looks like human medical experiments took place there. I assume that's what your article exposed, why the camp was never part of the public record, and why you became an enemy of the state. But there's one thing I don't get: why did you go there in the first place? I mean, before you knew there was anything to find. What were you looking for?"

He was hunched over, running his fingers across a pad of golden lichen by his feet. "Revenge."

After a few moments, when he hadn't said anything more, I prodded, "Revenge... Against who?"

He gave a long sigh, seemingly reluctant to talk. Finally he said, "A lot of bad things happened to my grandmother...our grandmother...in the work camp."

"What bad things?"

He gazed over the valley with his head slightly turned away from me. "She was raped—many times—and the child she gave birth to was murdered."

I gasped in shock. "That's awful."

Misha picked up a pebble and lobbed it over the rock ledge. The earth was so far below that its landing made no sound. "The guy who did it—the camp director. His name was Leonid Kosloff."

"Kosloff," I repeated. "Did Katarina tell you that?"

"No. She didn't talk about those times. My mother did, though. She told Saldana and me that Grandmother had been in Camp #34 in the Kolyma Region from 1949 to 1951. So I went to Moscow and searched the State Archive, where the gulag papers are kept. I found out that the director during those years was a medical doctor named Leonid Kosloff. He was transferred to a camp called Butugychag in 1951, and returned to Moscow when Stalin died in 1953. He taught at Moscow University for the rest of his life, published a bunch of important scientific papers on human radiation sickness in the late 1950s and early '60s. He ended up a world-renowned expert in that field."

Misha turned to me. "I asked myself the obvious question: Where did he do his research?"

"Butugychag?" I said, my stomach twisting with disgust.

Misha nodded. "Camp #34 produced lumber and cleared roads, so Butugychag was the only possibility. I'd planned to kill him for what he did to my grandmother, but he died of cancer in his fifties, so I couldn't have that satisfaction. But now I figured there might be another way to get revenge. If I could pin the crime of human medical experimentation on him, I could destroy his reputation and get some justice for all his victims, not just my grandmother.

"I needed evidence, but I couldn't find a single mention of Butugychag in the official records. The only place it was named at all was in Kosloff's personnel file. As far as the rest of the world was concerned, Butugychag had never existed."

So Misha checked out all Kosloff's scientific articles on radiation sickness from the library at Moscow University. In the footnotes, he found repeated references to an unpublished monograph that supposedly gave a complete account of Kosloff's experimental procedures. That monograph was kept in a government archive as classified material. To get a look at it, he had to bribe a clerk with free tickets to the Kirov ballet, which he coaxed from a dancer friend. He photographed every page of the monograph—number of cases, patient charts, methods of exposure, causes of death, along with Kosloff's handwritten notes.

"It was all there," Misha said. "Everything." He paused. "Do you want to know why the barracks at Butugychag was so small?" He didn't wait for an answer. "Because the average life span of a prisoner was two to three weeks."

"They didn't live long enough for the barracks to fill up."

"That's right. New prisoners were constantly being shipped in. Three hundred and eighty thousand of them, by Kosloff's own count. Not one survived. They weren't just mining uranium. They were forced to breathe radioactive fumes from the drying vents and to swallow radioactive metals."

He pitched another pebble over the cliff.

He said, "Butugychag's location wasn't mentioned in the monograph. I scoured every source I could think of for a clue to help me find it, and came up empty-handed. Then, soon after I arrived in Mirny, a story came out in the local paper. A herding group had driven their reindeer into a valley by the Dentin River and discovered an abandoned prison camp—one that wasn't on any maps. The reindeer got sick from eating the grass, so I figured it had been a uranium mining camp.

"I decided to go there on the chance that it might be the lost Butugychag. You know what I discovered: the drying vents, the mass graves, the surgery. No sign that identified it formally, but everything else fit."

"So you wrote the article and sent it off with your photographs."

"By then, it wasn't just about Grandmother or Kosloff's other victims anymore. It had become something much bigger for me. The monsters who ran the gulag prisons were never punished. Even today, lies are still circulating about what really went on in them. Until we Russians face our history, we'll never go forward—we'll just keep going round and round like a cat chasing its tail, making up new lies when the old ones don't work anymore."

Another pebble arced above the valley and disappeared without a sound.

He went on, "I sent my story to the most liberal newspaper in Russia, hoping they would have the courage to publish it. Before I'd heard back, two FSB agents showed up at the chemical plant where I worked. They said my facts were wrong. Kosloff's monograph was a fake. Butugychag didn't exist. And the photographs were photoshopped. They accused me of being a spy for the West—which happened to be true, only not in the way they thought.

"I figured they were going to arrest me—if not that day, then very soon—and I couldn't risk that. I knew that if I didn't stand up to the interrogation, I could end up leading the FSB to my own mother's door. I managed to slip away on a pretext, and snuck out a back entrance of the plant. I hid outside my apartment and, sure enough, they showed up not long after to search it. I saw them leave with my computer, and knew I couldn't go back."

I said, "The editor tried to warn you. He said that the newspaper was closely monitored, that he'd disposed of your article and photos, but the FSB must have got hold of them somehow." I paused. "Did you ask Meredith Viles for help?"

"I didn't bother. I knew what she'd say. The CIA only cares about current issues. Old Soviet crimes are irrelevant to them, unless they can be used to blackmail someone they don't like."

I thought about it for a few moments and decided to confess my role. "I know about the work you were doing for Meredith. About Mayadykovsky, I mean. I met Bohdan Duboff and Tanya Karp. Did you know they were smuggling sarin?"

"Are you sure?"

"I found cannisters of OPA and DHA in their apartment."

He gave a wry smile. "Smart of Meredith to get you to finish the job."

"I'm not sure how smart she is."

"What happened to Bohdan and Tanya?" The couple's first names fell easily from his lips.

"Dead. Assassinated."

He gave a mirthless laugh. "Yeah, that sounds about right."

"I'm not sure what you mean."

"Spies, the CIA. That's the kind of thing they do, isn't it?" He straightened his spine, looked up into the sky. "It's too bad. We had some good times together. Why the hell were they smuggling sarin? That was stupid of them."

"Misha," I said gently, aware that I was talking to a teenager. "Why didn't you tell anyone you were here, safe? Your mother's very worried."

"I wanted to. But the only communication out here is by radio. The herders use the radio to talk to people in Mirny about supplies, weather, and family stuff. I would have had to find someone in Mirny who would take a message from me and pass it on to my mother. That was too risky: it would expose my location to a third party I didn't trust. And there was also the possibility that the FSB was monitoring my mother's communications, so it was safer for both of us if I didn't contact her at all for a while."

"What about Meredith?"

"She was very strict about how we communicated. Cell phone was my only option. Until I had service, there was nothing I could do."

He squeezed his eyes shut, pinched the bridge of his nose between two fingers, as if to stop headache pain, or maybe tears.

"You okay?" I asked.

He folded up his long legs and hugged them to his body, placed his forehead on his knees. "Do you want to know why my mother agreed to let me work for the CIA?" He didn't wait for my answer. "Because she was more afraid of what might happen to me if I kept digging into Kosloff's background than what might happen to me if I spied for the United States. Think about that. What kind of country is that afraid of its past?"

"It sounds like she knew you'd been to Moscow, and what you'd found there."

"I showed her everything. I thought for sure she'd support me when she saw the evidence. But just the opposite happened: she begged me to stop. She kept insisting that if I put my name on an article about medical experimentation in the Stalin era, I'd be arrested. I told her Grandmother deserved justice. 'She's never asked for it. You're the one who wants justice, not her,' my mother said. She was upset, and I was sorry for that. But I told her she was wasting her breath.

"Then she told me something I never would have guessed: she was an informer for the American spy service, the famous CIA. I laughed. It was ridiculous. My mother the secretary, who was always yammering at us about schoolwork and dressing warmly? This person was a spy? I didn't believe it.

"But when I met Meredith Viles, I started to listen. And when Meredith told me what she wanted me to do, I agreed right away. I wanted to strike back against the government any way I could. I promised my mother I'd give up my vendetta against Kosloff when I went to Mirny, so she grudgingly agreed to let me go. I didn't mean it, of course. I only said it to put her mind at rest."

The sun was warming the valley now, and a single herder was riding out on the green meadow, holding his coiled lasso. The reindeer opened a path for him, like subjects scurrying before a king.

"They say mothers are always right," Misha said resignedly. "Turns out, she was. When I see her next, it'll be hard to admit I lied to get her off my case."

"She probably just wants to know you're safe."

A breeze lifted a lock of his hair. "We used to fight so much, her and me. She was always preaching caution, staying quiet, holding back. I used to resent her. It felt like she didn't want me to be myself. Now I understand she was just trying to protect me."

He turned to look into my eyes. "Out here in the mountains, everything's different. Simple and peaceful. I like it here."

"It's very beautiful. This is the most beautiful place I've ever been."

It was true. The early morning moon had slipped behind a ridge, yet tiny, dim stars were still sprinkled across the sky. Perched so close to the edge of the promontory, with nothing but soft, pearly light all around, I could almost sense the globe twirling on its axis. I imagined the north pole canting toward and away from the sun through successive seasons, each single day lasting a long, lovely time, while the years passed quicker than you could count.

I said, "Misha, I think you are a remarkable young man."

He threw back his head and laughed. "That is such a nice thing to say, Dr. March!"

"You can call me Natalie. We're cousins, after all."

"Cousins," he repeated, a smile spreading across his face. "And here we are together in this amazing place. Two people from different parts of the world. Who would have guessed this would happen? It's a miracle, isn't it?"

It was a miracle. One I could never have foreseen, taking place against all odds. A deep joy settled in me. I knew it would be there all my life.

"What are you going to do now?" I asked.

"I promised Ivan and Sofia I'd stay until October, when some of the herders will drive a small group of the weakest reindeer to the slaughterhouse on the other side of these mountains. I'll stop over in the town there. Helicopters go in and out, and horse caravans. If I think it's safe, I'll head to grandmother's village. If not, I'll find some work in the town and spend the winter there."

"But in the long run? How will you make out?"

He shrugged. "I'm a fugitive. I'll spend my life on the run."

"Come to the States," I heard myself saying. I wanted to help him, to give him what I hadn't given Saldana. Safety, another chance.

He smiled ruefully. "And how will I get out of Russia?"

"The CIA," I said rashly. "They ought to do that much for you at least."

"It's too bad they don't see it that way." He stood up, brushed off his jeans, leaned down, and offered me his hand. "Come on. I'll show you how to get to Cherkeh."

"Cherkeh?"

"Grandmother's village. You still want to go, don't you?"

"I absolutely do."

The hand that pulled me to my feet was warm and strong.

The camp was quiet. The rest of the men had ridden out to gather the herd for the day's nomadic grazing in the lower part of the valley. I washed at the river, the cold water gently splashing over the smooth rocks at my feet, boughs softly creaking in the stand of poplars nearby. From Sofia's tent came the clatter of tin pots and merry children's voices. A tail of smoke plumed from the stove vent into a mass of heavy clouds that had materialized without warning.

Roxana bustled into the tent as I was dressing and told me to start packing. We would be leaving in an hour. The temperature was falling. If it changed too quickly, the reindeer risked pneumonia, so the herders would drive the animals to lower ground that day. The camp would be dismantled within hours. Unless we wanted to travel down the mountain with the group, we had to go.

We took apart the bedding, stove, and tent, folding and storing everything according to a detailed process Roxana knew. Sofia gave us tea, bread, and a fatty reindeer broth, which I merely sipped. Her face crinkled into a smile when I thanked her for her hospitality. She pressed my hand between her leathery palms when she said goodbye.

I took a few pictures: the little girls grinning and waving, Lidia standing beside the tent in a green headscarf, Ivan lumbering on his cane to the edge of the clearing to see us off. But there was little time for extended farewells. Rain was headed up the valley, and we needed to beat it back to Mirny.

Misha appeared to help carry our bags. He was subdued, his eyes averted, and his face was pale. I assumed that the terrible work of grieving his sister had begun. He silently hoisted our bags into the back of the Mi-8, then thrust into my hands a sheet of heavy brown paper folded into a square.

"Here are the directions I promised," he said quietly, so that only I could hear. "I drew a map for you, too. And there's...something else. Don't read it now. Wait until you're in the air."

After the usual whining and shuddering, the helicopter rose into troubled gray skies. I waited a long time, until the clouds dispersed at the western edge of the Verkhoyansk range, before I opened Misha's map. A folded slip of white paper fell into my lap—his note. I decided to keep that for last.

First, I checked the map. Cherkeh was a dull pencil dot in a vast blankness traced by a few twisting rivers. For the life of me, I couldn't see how such a rudimentary drawing could be helpful. Fortunately, he'd written out the directions in detail: I was to board a ferry in Yakutsk, cross the Lena River, and get on a van that stopped at various villages. There might be eight or ten others in the van—as many paying customers as could be crammed inside—with the driver making stops according to each person's needs. Depending on who else was riding that day, the trip might take anywhere from five to ten hours. Once in Cherkeh, I could ask any passerby for directions to Katarina Melnikova's house. There was a little message at the bottom: *Thank you for everything. I hope we will meet again someday.*

Finally, I opened the slip of white paper and read these words, scrawled in pencil:

It's my fault Saldana died. I sent her the files in case something happened to me. Kosloff's documents, the pictures from Death Valley—everything. The FSB would have found the email to her on my computer. They broke into her hotel room to steal her laptop and killed her when she came in.

There was no signature.

I refolded the note, thinking, Don't do this to yourself, Misha. *Just don't.* In his grief and rage, he was clearly overreacting, blaming himself, as family members often did. That explained his ashen look and trembling hands when we'd said goodbye. If he'd given me the chance, I would have urgently tried to talk him out of guilt. There was nothing good in it, nothing to be gained. It would only hurt him in the long run, more than he could guess. He'd been very smart to send me on my way before that conversation could take place.

But as my emotions settled, the details of the crime that had bothered me from the beginning came back into focus. The fact that the killer took Saldana's computer and not her money. And the murder weapon—the wire garrote—had always seemed the tool of a professional killer rather than a common thief. Those details had thrown the NYPD's hasty burglary-gone-bad thesis into doubt, at least in my mind. But they hadn't been enough to prove that the Russian government was behind the murder. Now all that was changed. If the FSB knew Saldana was in possession of Leonid Kosloff's monograph, they had a plausible motive for silencing her that, ironically, had nothing to do with either her plan to defect or her family members' CIA connections.

So Misha could be right. It *was* his fault—if he wanted to look at it that way, which I really hoped he wouldn't. One thing I'd learned as a doctor was how perfectly useless guilt is. There had been countless times in my career when I'd wanted to scream at bereaved family members: Of course the baby wouldn't have died of SIDS that afternoon if you hadn't put him in his crib for a nap! Of course grandpa might have lived a little longer if you'd taken him for a check-up sooner than you did! But now the baby's dead, and so is grandpa, and you're alive and well—so far—and you have no right to ruin your own god-given health by imagining you're a worse person than you really are!

Luckily for my patients, I'd learned not to say everything on my mind.

In a few hours, the helicopter touched down in Mirny. Roxana gave me a ride downtown in her Ford Explorer, waving off the extra money she was owed for the extended trip. It was just as well, as I didn't have much cash left. I copied her address into my phone, promising to write when I was back in the States.

"What about the police and the trouble you're in?" she asked.

"I'll be okay," I said, having no idea. "Just remember that what you might hear about me isn't true."

In a busy cafeteria, alive with the smells of coffee and cinnamon and the thrum of conversation, I bought a coffee and potato pastry and a local newspaper at the counter. Taking a seat as far away as I could get from the big window onto the street, I shoved my conspicuous luggage under the table. The paper gave no mention of the murders on Barrikad Street. There was nothing in the online edition either, not even on the day the murders had taken place. I had no idea what to make of that. A cover-up? Business as usual in the Russian Far East? More likely, the investigation had passed into the hands of the security forces, who played by their own rules and thrived on secrecy. In any case, I needed to get out of town right away, avoiding the airport if possible.

There was only one taxi company in town. I called the number, explained to the man who picked up the phone that I wanted a driver to take me to Yakutsk as soon as possible.

"That trip takes eight hours one way," he barked. "And you have to pay round-trip."

"How much?" I would have paid any price, but it would seem suspicious if I didn't barter.

"You have cash?" he asked slyly.

"Sorry. Credit card only."

"All right. Maybe I have a driver for such a long trip, maybe not. I will have to let you know. I will call you back in one hour."

"Half an hour."

"Maybe. I'll see what I can do."

I waited thirty minutes, pretending to read the newspaper. I bought another coffee and waited another thirty minutes. What was taking so long? Had my American accent sounded an alarm? Even though I knew it was stupid, and probably not even possible, I imagined the phone call being traced to my precise location and a flock of squad cars with blaring sirens swooping down on the little café.

I rummaged in my duffel for Ilmira's rain hat and put it on, along with my sunglasses. Then I gathered up my luggage and walked out of the coffee shop into a cool, overcast day. In a park where children were playing, I sat down on a bench and dialed the taxi service again. This time, a woman answered.

"I'm waiting to hear about a driver to take me to Yakutsk."

"What? We don't have taxis going there. It's much too far away."

"Are you sure? I spoke to someone at your company an hour ago who said he could find someone to take me."

"Who was it? What was his name?"

"I didn't ask."

"It must have been Boris. He is the only one stupid enough to have said such a thing."

"Does this mean I can't get a taxi?"

"Of course not. What do you think? The only way to get to Yakutsk from here is by plane."

I thanked her and hung up.

I'd meant to stay away from the airport. Too many people with badges hanging around; too many gates to get through. But it looked as though I'd have to risk it, as there was no safe place for me in Mirny. Imposing on Tolya and Emmie again was out of the question; I'd already put them in danger by having had contact with them at all. Roxana would probably have sheltered me if I'd asked, but that would have put her in danger, too.

I pulled up the airport on my cell phone. A shuttle to Yakutsk left daily at 2:15 p.m.

I had a passport and credit card in the name of Anne-Marie Phipps. All I had to do was buy a ticket and board the plane. I'd be fine as long as Ilmira hadn't shared my photo with the authorities, and even if she had, I could still slip through if the airport personnel were uninformed or lax, as they tended to be. The trick, I decided, would be to arrive at the airport close enough to the time of departure that I wouldn't have to wait around in the terminal, drawing attention to myself. Once I landed in in Yakutsk, I could disappear fairly quickly into the countryside.

A taxi brought me to the airport. There was no sign of police, and the official who remembered my name the last time I was there wasn't in sight. Ticketing went smoothly. I was one of the last to board a small commercial jet. Seats were not assigned, and the passengers had spaced themselves out so that I couldn't get a row to myself. I chose an aisle seat towards the back, next to a pleasant-looking woman in her sixties. As I sank gratefully into the worn upholstery, I let out a sigh of relief. The CIA's fake documents had done their work; with any luck, they'd take me all the way home.

In one of those random coincidences that travelers often experienced, my companion was an American from California, a solo traveler like myself. Hip green glasses perched on her snub nose, and her silk scarf combined all the colors of the rainbow. She wrote a blog called "Alice in Wanderland," full of tips and itineraries for the adventurous empty-nester. Thrilled to meet a fellow American, she regaled me with stories of her adventures in far-flung parts of the world. Though her determination to lead an interesting life was perhaps a bit too strident, she made delightful company. I found myself laughing unguardedly for the first time since I'd been in Russia, pleasantly homesick for my comfortable life in Washington —especially for my deep, downy couch, where I vowed to curl up for as many days as I wanted upon my return, wearing sweatpants and woolly socks, eating chocolate and ice cream, watching old Audrey Hepburn movies while guiltlessly blowing off work. If there was one thing this experience had taught me, it was that the medical center that used to be my entire universe was actually just a tiny microcosm, that I could exist outside its boundaries—and needed to. Vera would be proud.

The plane touched down in Yakutsk after a mere ninety minutes in the air. Alice and I crossed the tarmac with a couple dozen other passengers, and entered the familiar, dismal terminal building. There were the native faces waiting peaceably behind the rope line; there was the baggage chute and rotating carousel. We planned to continue our conversation over dinner—a luxury I'd decided to afford myself before I set out the next day for Cherkeh—so I waited for Alice to claim her luggage, a large red Samsonite that she needed help pulling off the belt. I had my duffel already, which held nothing decent for me to change into. My clothes smelled of reindeer skin and smoke, and were smudged—as I myself was, I realized—with Verkhoyansk Mountain mud.

As we were leaving the building, two uniformed security officers came upon us suddenly, and asked to see our documents.

Alice gave a loud sigh and rolled her eyes. "They always go for us foreigners." Seeing my face, she added, "Nothing to worry about. Just a random check. Happens all the time."

I showed my passport with what I hoped was a friendly smile. *Just a random check.* The official thumbed through it and came to a page at the back.

"Where are you coming from?"

"Mirny."

"What was your business there?"

"Tourism."

"Where do you live?"

"Washington, D.C."

He flipped to the front of the passport and studied the photo, glanced up and down several times, comparing it to my face. I tried to relax.

Meanwhile, Alice had been cleared. She pointed toward the entrance, indicating that she would wait for me there, and trundled off in her jaunty scarf, trailing her huge, eye-catching suitcase.

"What brings you to Yakutsk?" the officer asked.

I hesitated. *Why was I in Yakutsk?* "I thought I'd visit the Permafrost Institute."

"Are you traveling with that American woman?" he said, nodding toward

Alice's retreating figure.

My face grew warm. I wanted to say yes so that he might be inclined to let me follow her toward the terminal's main door. But if they checked with her, I would be caught in a lie. "No. Alone. We just met on the plane."

I felt as if I were making mistakes, tiny ones, even though I was pretty sure I hadn't so far. But the situation could spin out of control very quickly if I wasn't careful. It felt like the giddy moment when the roller coaster started to drop, and the best you could hope for was to ride it out.

The official was Caucasian, tall, narrow-shouldered—really just a boy with soft fingers and smooth cheeks, dressed up in a smart black uniform with a billy club hanging from his belt. His expression was so perfectly flat and impersonal that he must have practiced it in the mirror at home. He continued thumbing through the passport, even though we both knew the pages hadn't changed since the first time he looked.

Having traipsed back to me, travel-savvy Alice in Wanderland hovered close at my elbow, peering up at the tall boy. "What's going on here? What's this about?" she asked in high umbrage. I sensed that she'd had a lot of practice at performing entitled Western outrage in foreign hotels and restaurants. Her Russian was terrible—the *Gde tualet?* of the tourist class.

This seemed to give the boy a new idea. He looked at me with a flicker of interest. "You speak Russian very well for an American."

"My parents are Russian...I mean, Russian immigrants...American citizens, actually. I learned Russian at home."

"Ah," he said meaningfully, and I was left to wonder what meaning he'd gleaned. He flipped casually to the last page of the passport.

"Where did you stay in Mirny?"

"The Zarnitsa," I replied without hesitation, having prepared the answer beforehand. This was the nicest hotel in the city, where a wealthy Westerner would be most likely to stay.

"And when did you check out?"

"This morning."

"There's no registration stamp."

"Oh. That must be a mistake. On the hotel's part." How stupid of me to have forgotten about the governmental registration process, whereby a hotel verified a guest's stay, presenting a date-stamped form for the traveler to show officials if asked. But the situation could be finessed, I thought, as an inexperienced traveler might easily overlook the formality and the hotel must also neglect this duty once in a while.

The young man looked coldly into my eyes.

I added, "A silly mistake. But what can you do? Everyone makes mistakes."

He snapped the passport closed, and I watched it disappear into his pocket. "Come with me."

My heart plummeted. The blood rushed out of my head. Alice blinked rapidly behind her owlish glasses. "What's happening?" she asked, having been unable to follow the conversation in Russian.

"I'm not sure. Probably just a routine check," I said, eager to have her gone, as she seemed a liability now, with her clumsy self-importance.

"I'll wait for you," she said steadfastly.

"There's no telling how long it will take. You might as well go to your hotel, and I'll call when I'm done here."

The uniformed boy led me to the far end of the terminal, through a door, down a corridor, into a blue-painted room with a table and some plastic chairs scattered randomly about. The lighting was poor. There was a scrim of grime everywhere and the smell of mold.

I'd read somewhere that innocent people reacted with anger when they were unjustly accused. I hotly demanded to know why I was being detained. "You have no right to hold me against my will," I said with righteous outrage, not knowing if that were true.

"Wait here." The boy left the room.

A few minutes later, a short, heavy woman entered, and asked me to place my luggage on the table. She had blue-shadowed, droopy eyes, thick lips, and a lazy demeanor that the black police uniform, straining across her buxom chest, did nothing to offset. She pulled out my clothes, all dirty, ran her fingers through the duffel's interior pockets. She found Misha's map, and stared at it curiously without requesting an explanation. Then she extended a hand, palm up, and asked for my phone. I refused to give it on the grounds that it was an invasion of privacy. This response elicited no visible reaction, and she left the room.

There were no surveillance cameras in the room, one of the few benefits of Siberian poverty.

I opened Anne-Marie Phipps's phone and started deleting all the photos I'd taken of Tolya and Emmie, and all the ones from Death Valley. Also Roxana's name and address. There was practically nothing left on the phone after that—no contacts, texts, or emails; no apps or photos of family and friends. Only the calls to the taxi service and the airport search remained. Anyone who examined the phone would know it was a fake.

Don't panic. Think. Had news of the double murder in Mirny trickled down to Yakutsk? Did the fact that the crime wasn't mentioned in the Mirny paper mean that it was unknown here? If so, I could still slip through this net if my cover held. But if it didn't?

First off, I needed to contact someone, anyone, who could help an American tourist who'd been unlawfully detained. That meant the American Consulate. The nearest was over a thousand miles away in Vladivostok. I attempted to bring up their website, but there was no wi-fi and the cellular connection was unbearably slow. The blue line crawled a quarter-inch across the screen and died.

I went to the door of the stuffy room. It was locked. I shook the handle.

"Hello! Is anyone there? Hello?" When no one answered, I banged on the door with my fists. "I demand that this door be unlocked!"

The heavily made-up woman returned. "I will wait with you," she said, as if doing a favor for a friend. "There's no trouble. They are just checking something. It won't be long."

My things were still scattered on the table, the duffel yawning open. I folded and repacked my clothes like someone who fully expected her journey to resume, while all the while my brain was racing to concoct my story.

I was Anne-Marie Phipps. The passport gave me an age of thirty-nine and an address in Georgetown. Fine. But what about the rest? Where did I work? Was I married? Did I have kids? Anything I told them could easily be checked. What had made me decide to tour northeastern Siberia? Why Mirny, of all places? I didn't have diamond jewelry to show from my excursion, and the hotel Zarnitsa had no record of my stay. I couldn't talk convincingly about anything I'd done there. Mentioning Roxana Amasova and Death Valley would lead my questioners to Tolya and the Evenki Museum, and thus to Mikhail Tarasov, who had lived in the apartment on Barrikad Street where the murders took place.

My mind raced in circles, looking for a narrative that would hold up. I soon realized there was no way out of the mess, no thread I could find the end of and pull into a clean, innocent story that would withstand even the most casual scrutiny. The Anne-Marie Phipps identity was destined to dissolve within minutes, and if and when it was discovered that I was actually Dr. Natalie March, I'd be in the kind of trouble you couldn't talk your way out of.

There was only one option for me, I realized: silence. I would give no information at all, thus nothing that could incriminate me. If I wasn't mistaken, when Americans were arrested abroad, the host country was required to notify the American Consulate. I would demand that this be done immediately, and refuse to speak another word until a representative of my government was present and had assumed my defense. I'd keep to this strategy no matter what, without the slightest deviation, regardless of what happened or how long it took until a friendly face arrived to rescue me. I had no idea whether Russian law allowed a suspect to plead the fifth under questioning. But that hardly mattered; I would do it anyway. Silence wouldn't save me, but it would keep me safer than anything else I could think of at the moment.

I said to the guard, irritated, "Can't you get them to hurry? I have dinner plans."

"I'll see what's taking so long." She obligingly waddled to the door.

"And get me some water, please."

"Yes, ma'am."

Amazingly, she left the door ajar. I gave her a few seconds to disappear before I poked my head into the miserable little corridor. Should I run? I wouldn't get far in Russia without the passport that the young security officer had slipped into his pocket, and I'd never be able to board a plane. Besides, there was still a chance that the fake passport would check out and I'd be released from custody with an apology from my Russian captors.

But the dread in my gut said the chances of that were very slim.

So, *yes*. Yes, I should run.

I emerged from the blue room just as the boy officer appeared at the end of the corridor, holding a paper cup of water. He advanced toward me quickly, that terrible flat expression on his face. I still had a chance, I thought wildly, if I bolted in the other direction. I took a step, but before I could take another, water was dripping down my face and wetting the front of my shirt. I was pushed backwards violently, into the blue room, and then I was sprawling on the cold linoleum floor. The door slammed shut, and a key turned in the lock.

I picked myself up and wiped my dripping face with the short sleeve of my V-neck cotton shirt. I was shaking with fear and from the shock of the cold water. The cup had looked small, but it had held a lot. My shirt was soaked. I unzipped my duffel and rooted around until I found the cleanest T-shirt I had. Unfortunately, it said *GW Colonials* on the front. I stuffed it back and picked out another, a navy silk button-down with tiny white dots that I'd been keeping for nicer occasions. I stripped off the wet V-neck, and put on the silk.

I sank with a groan into one of the plastic chairs, my head falling into my hands. You can get through this, I told myself. Stay calm.

An hour went by.

The fat police woman returned, pulling a chair to a far corner of the room as if to emphasize her role as observer. She sat down and began thumbing listlessly through a magazine. I made an effort to engage her in conversation. Her name was Olga. She lived in Yakutsk. She gave one-word answers to questions of minimal complexity—she was as dumb as a post.

Another hour went by.

"I need a bathroom," I said.

"What?"

"I need to use the goddamn bathroom."

"Oh." Hips rolling under her stretched uniform pants, Olga led me back down the corridor and into the terminal. Recently disembarked passengers were clustered around the creaking, jerking carousel. Two uniformed security guards were standing against a wall, impassive, no doubt supremely bored. The scene appeared completely normal. Who was checking my passport? What door were they hiding behind?

A long line of women were waiting outside the ladies' room, luggage piled beside them, some with children straining to get away or staring into space. I took my place, Olga hovering at my elbow.

"For Christ's sake, I'm not going to run away," I said.

The line inched forward, the women pushing or pulling their luggage along. Finally, I was sequestered in a stall. I sat on the toilet, took out my phone, and checked the service. Again, I tried to bring up the website of the American Consulate; again, the blue line crawled and stopped midway.

One of Olga's lazy eyes appeared in the crack between the stall door and the frame. "What are you doing in there?"

I tucked the small phone in the snug of my palm. It was dim inside the stall; perhaps she hadn't seen. I said, "Do you really want to know?"

She grunted. "Well, hurry up!"

I decided to try reaching Alice in Wanderland, but I hadn't taken down her phone or email. I could call the hotel she was staying at, but I couldn't get the number off the internet, and if there was such a thing as directory assistance in Yakutsk, I didn't know that number either. I was out of ideas.

When I finally emerged from the stall, Olga was glowering.

"Thank you for waiting," I said politely, washing my hands as slowly as possible just to make her mad.

Back in the grimy, badly lit room, Olga turned the pages of her magazine with a desultory air. Time went by slowly; each minute felt like the cranking of an ancient rusty wheel. At some point that evening I demanded dinner, and was served an airplane tray of rubbery chicken, a tiny salad, and cranberry juice. Olga's shift ended; another woman arrived to watch over me. Older, with a harsh glare and a face of stone.

At about 10 p.m., two men in dark, ill-fitting suits entered the room. Instinctively, I stood.

One of them said, "Dr. Natalie March, you are under arrest for the murders of Bohdan Duboff and Tanya Karp, and for acts of espionage against the Russian Federation."

9

I was taken by van to the Yakutsk police station and left alone in a dingy basement room. I yelled indignantly and pounded on the locked door for a while because that was what I would have done if I were innocent. When no one came, I sat down and tried to tamp down my panic. There was a metal table, two aluminum chairs, and a third chair in a corner. My phone and luggage had been confiscated. All was quiet except for water pipes behind one wall that gurgled noisily when the toilet on the floor above was flushed.

Some time later, two men entered the room. They were not the same ones who'd arrested me at the airport. The taller one was wearing a black police uniform with a rubber truncheon and handcuffs clipped to his belt; the other was a florid-faced runt with a gleaming bald head, a squashed nose, and flaccid cheeks. The officer took the seat in the corner behind me. The pig-ish man in the shabby suit sat down across from me and began to question me calmly, almost indifferently. I could tell that calmness was not his true nature, because his eyes were darting and eager, and there was a twitch at the corner of his mouth, an excitable muscle not entirely in his control. He was a high-strung, volatile person who was pretending to be benign in the hope of eliciting my cooperation.

He would have no such luck. Ignoring his questions, I proceeded to verbally assault him with blistering shock and outrage, promising all manner of retribution when the US State Department found out about my clearly illegal detention. "Given how serious these trumped-up charges are, I refuse to speak without a representative of my government present. I demand that the American Consulate be contacted immediately. What, by the way, is your name and title?"

He was Chief Inspector Bogdonovich.

"Well, Mr. Bogdonavich, you'd better prepare yourself because you're going to have a lot to answer for very soon."

A glow of pleasure lit his eyes. The game was on, and he couldn't wait to see me crushed. He explained that for several days I'd been the guest of Ilmira Nikulina, that I'd visited the deceased in their apartment two days before their deaths, that I'd been spotted on the balcony above theirs with a rope over my arm, that I'd fled Mirny on the morning of the murders. When he asked how I would like to respond, his short fingers drummed the table in excitement.

I was sweating profusely; nausea curdled my stomach. It felt like my skin was crawling with tiny squirming bugs of terror and dread. I said, "You've twisted these facts to suit your agenda, and I have no doubt you'll continue to twist and distort whatever else I say. That is why I refuse to engage in a conversation with you or any other Russian official until I've obtained qualified legal representation from the American Consulate."

. : . . . . : .

The nightmare began then and continued, as far as I could tell, for over a week. I was interrogated for twelve, maybe sixteen, hours a day. With no clocks on the wall and only artificial light, it was impossible to keep track of time. My tormentors deprived me of food and sleep, and doggedly tried to confuse me with myriad accusations and gibberish strings of names and dates. They alternately whispered and bellowed outlandish espionage plots I'd allegedly confessed to, producing printed interrogation transcripts signed in penmanship that looked a lot like mine.

Bogdonavich was the grand inquisitor, though substitutes sometimes took his place. He seemed to relish his role: if I nodded off, he slapped his small pink hand on the desk to wake me, or picked up a metal chair and hurled it at the wall. Sometimes his contorted face was only an inch from my own, and his spittle landed on my lips. I gagged on the smells of his last fetid meal. I expected to be beaten senseless or worse at any moment, but all he did was slap me across the face if I started to lose consciousness.

When the questions confused me, which was often, I said the same thing: *I am an American citizen, and I demand to speak to a representative of my country.* My stubborn consistency was remarkable even to me, especially since, much of the time, I was barely coherent. On several occasions I keeled over suddenly, literally clobbered by sleep, and had to be picked up and set back on the chair. At other times, as I was being escorted out of the interrogation room, my legs gave way—I collapsed straight down like a dynamited building and had to be dragged by my limp arms back to my cell.

My resistance was aided by an old, familiar nemesis: migraine headaches. The headaches reached points of such excruciating intensity that I believed the pain would rival whatever might be inflicted on me through other means. They reduced me to a helpless, senseless, nearly paralyzed state in which any utterance, no matter how diabolically encouraged, was practically impossible. Bogdonavich's voice swelled inside my skull to thunderous proportions, pounding with such deafening force that I couldn't even make out the words. Light from the overhead fixture felt like hot needles sinking into my pupils; even the red glow that played across my closed eyelids was tortuous. The best I could do was long for unconsciousness, which I did with all my might.

Occasionally, I had the blissful experience of rising out of my body on a warm soft cloud that hung suspended in an upper corner of the room, from which I could gaze down upon the wretched, ignorant ritual being experienced by my earthly self. *Buck up, dear Natalie,* I whispered. *It's only luck that brought you here, and luck will take you home.*

I came to pity Chief Inspector Bogdonavich for his state of perpetual agitation. If only he knew how hard and how frequently I had to fight the urge to give him some little morsel, some insignificant detail, that might quench his rage, but I knew that any weakness I displayed would dangerously flatter him, whetting his appetite for more revelations, and prolonging the agony for us both. Thus, it was with a kind of sad affection that I refrained.

Silence was my mighty fortress, my saving lord. It was the best and only card I had to play. I eventually stopped making any noise at all—I didn't beg for water, food, or sleep; I didn't cry. My voice retreated so far inside my body that I worried I would have a hard time finding it again if I survived. I became a sack of flesh, feverish and insensible, yet complete unto myself.

Next came a long, bone-jarring ride in the back of a windowless van. I didn't know where I was going, or why, or for how long—which hardly mattered, as I wouldn't have believed anything I was told.

Eventually, the van stopped, and they dragged me out. My clothes were filthy; my delicate silk shirt had lost all its buttons and was stuck to my flesh by sweat and grime. My hair was tangled and matted. One eye was swollen shut, my hands and fingers had deep cuts I didn't remember getting, and, as I was prone to frequent waves of vertigo, I lurched as much as walked.

All around the gravel yard where I was left standing while the police officers conferred with prison personnel, there were high wooden towers and soaring chain-link fences topped with tumbling spools of razor wire. I didn't dare hope that my situation was going to improve; for all I knew, I was about to be dragged before a firing squad. Nevertheless, for a few sweet moments my deadened spirit revived because cool fresh air was filling my nostrils, and bright sunlight was spilling about my feet and warming the top of my head.

In a room with narrow benches on three sides and a big window facing a sere brown meadow, the officers presented a sheaf of papers to two prison officials, both women, seated at a wooden table. There was much shuffling and stamping of forms; then angry words were exchanged. Something was out of order, and one of the women left the room. The problem must have been resolved, because after a long wait, I was ushered to a lavatory with a toilet and rust-stained sink where, under female supervision, I stripped and washed my body in cold water that dribbled from the spigot, using a scrap of soap and a ragged cloth supplied by the guard. Neatly folded pants and a button-down shirt of dark green canvas were handed to me. Also, underwear, socks, rubber-soled shoes. I dressed, and after another long wait, a nurse arrived to perform a medical examination.

"I'm a doctor," I whispered to her, because I wanted to hear myself say it.

"So? You expect a medal?" she snapped, and I smiled slightly because her rudeness was so ordinary.

. ⸰ . ⸰ . ⸰ . ⸰ . ⸰ . ⸰ .

The compound was called Female Prison 22, the name itself a punishment of sorts, as if even the words used to refer to the place had to be stripped of ornamentation and clad in drab, utilitarian garb like the nearly six hundred women shut behind its walls.

Roughly the size of two football fields, it was divided into two main sections: one for living, one for work. The living area—many of the terms were cruelly ironic—included a two-story administration building, guard quarters, an infirmary, a social hall, and a large kitchen and dining facility. Dormitories were set in rows along the western perimeter. They abutted a so-called recreation yard and a common washroom consisting of ten spigots and ten usually plugged toilets where inmates competed with each other animalistically for the right to piss and shit.

Every morning at 5:45 the prisoners lined up in a massive grid in the recreation yard. Under the eyes of armed guards in sentry towers and a dozen more guards, many of them female, reining in lunging German Shepherds, we jogged in place and did shoulder rolls, leg lifts, and stretching exercises as the pale, watery light of the rising sun crept across the yard. The air was cold; summer was long gone. We exhaled our stored warmth in moist puffs of breath that quickly dissipated.

We labored for ten hours a day, six days a week, on the industrial side of the compound. I counted eight buildings, more or less. I couldn't be sure of the number because my work group was escorted into and out of a textile and sewing factory under armed guard. Along the way, all I could see was a garage that housed a couple of vans and a tractor, several crumbling, unused structures without roofs, and another large factory where other inmates made *melkii veschii*—trivial goods such as toys and plastic household products.

During the first week of my incarceration, I tried repeatedly to get information from the guards. How long was I being held? Under what charges? When would I be granted a lawyer or a phone call or anything? They told me either to ask the bosses or shut the fuck up. But there was no way for a prisoner to contact the administrators. Their offices were in a building at the front of the compound, beyond the guard house and fences. I'd glimpsed it only once, when I was let out of the van that brought me from Yakutsk. Its white paint and pretty window boxes had been a taunting reminder of normalcy. Apparently, the work of managing the prison did not require the bosses to venture into the compound's industrial or living areas, or to come into contact with the inmates in any way. They remained unseen yet ever-powerful, like Greek gods who tinkered with poor mortals' fates from atop Mount Olympus.

Several times, in desperation, I tried to push my way through the well-guarded gate that led to the pretty white house; when stopped, I pled my case fervently, until I was roundly ridiculed and roughly turned away.

I eventually gave up trying to get answers, and reluctantly submitted to the camp's routines. Yet wherever I went, I remained acutely conscious of the soaring metal fences that marked the compound's perimeter. The nearest was about twenty feet high. There was another a short distance beyond it. Beyond that, another. And another. Four fences total, the upper portions sloping inward at forty-five-degree angles, so that it looked as if their grotesque steel-barbed crowns were in danger of tumbling off. Warning signs at fixed intervals indicated that the chain-link was electrified; given the ancient look of the things, the derelict way they swayed and buckled, I suspected the claim was false.

By the end of the second week of my incarceration, those fences had become the central fact of my existence, my single stark reality. Because of them, I was separated from all I loved, and therefore from myself. The loss of freedom was acutely painful, but what was just as terrible was the erasure of identity. I felt myself shrinking into a primitive being intent on nothing but survival. I supposed that was the point—to be psychologically destroyed so you could be built again. Rehabilitated.

Back in Yakutsk, during the endless days of my interrogation, I hadn't actually believed that Chief Inspector Bogdonovich would accede to my demands and contact the American Consulate. But I'd kept it as an article of faith that Meredith Viles and her cohorts at the CIA would somehow figure out what had happened to me and get me out of the vile little precinct basement where I was being tortured and abused. The minute I didn't show up at Langley as I was supposed to, I'd reasoned, the alarm would sound. There would be pressure on Meredith to figure out where I was, especially given the sensitive information that was stored in my head. She was good at her job. I'd chosen to believe that, although I had no proof. And she had the resources of the world's most powerful spy agency at her disposal. I'd chosen to believe that as well. She herself had told me that. If there was any solace for me in those days of horror, it came from picturing myself being stolen away from my captors in a stunning covert operation carried out by Navy SEALs.

Now, though, with the month of September winding down, and the doors of Female Prison 22 bolted behind me, that Hollywood dream was in tatters. But still alive. I simply could not accept the possibility that I was going to rot in a Siberian prison, or undergo a mock trial followed by a real execution, or whatever the Russians had in store for me. I had to believe that help would arrive. Every minute of every day, as I went through the dreary motions of prison life, I was quietly waiting for my deliverance, in whatever form it might come, at whatever time.

. .   . .

At night, in the hour before bed when prisoners were allowed to talk, read, or write letters home, the dormitory of nearly sixty women was a noisy, crowded place. A fight might break out suddenly, accompanied by yelled curses and accusations. It was a time for petty thievery. With nothing to steal, I was spared that particular harassment, but I felt hostile eyes on me all the time. As a foreigner, an anomaly, I was closely watched. Eventually, there'd be a reckoning.

A woman named Yvonne slept in the bunk above mine. She was twenty-five years old with tightly curling blond hair, wide Slavic cheeks, and a deeply cleft chin. Sweet and open, she seemed younger than her years. She wore no make-up, but somewhere she must have had tweezers because her brows were plucked to pencil-thin arches that floated too high above her eyes. The women usually didn't discuss their crimes and punishments, but Yvonne confided that she'd been caught with a few pills of Ecstasy on her and sentenced to five years. She'd done three so far and seemed proud of the fact, as if it were a legitimate accomplishment, which I supposed it was. Her mother and younger sister lived more than two thousand kilometers away in a village on the western edge of the Ural Mountains. The distance was so great that they couldn't afford to visit, but they sent letters and photographs regularly. She stashed the photos under her pillow and took them out once in a while to gaze at them.

One night, she offered me half a chocolate bar her mother had sent. I thanked her sincerely for the little luxury, and we sat cross-legged on my bunk and ate the chocolate together rather solemnly. As we were licking our fingers, Yvonne offered me some advice.

"You must try to blend in more, Natalya. You're drawing too much attention to yourself."

"Why? What am I doing?"

"It's nothing specific. You just don't act like everyone else."

"How so?"

"It's the way you are."

"You mean I act like an American?"

"Maybe. I don't know. You're just very…um, confident. You walk with your head up all the time. You look straight at people, and ask too many questions. It seems pushy, arrogant. The worst thing is, you act more important than the guards. That's a dangerous habit. They can do anything they want to you, Natalya. So let them think you're afraid of them even if you're not." She paused. "Have you heard about Svetlana yet?"

"No. Who's that?"

"She's the boss. Like a mafia boss. She lives in another dormitory, but she works in the textile factory like we do, only in a different room. A lot of people work for her. You can never be sure who they are. If you have something she wants, she'll take it. You have to let her, or they cut off your hair and take what they want anyway. They do worse things, too, much worse. So be careful, okay?"

Prisoners were paid three hundred rubles, a bit less than five dollars, a day for their labor, given not in cash but in credit at the prison canteen. I used my credits to buy stationery, stamps, and a pen. I'd been denied phone calls and internet access, but letters flowed freely in and out of the prison. I wrote to my mother, saying that I'd been detained by the authorities in a minor mix-up that would be straightened out soon. After asking Yvonne to procure the addresses for me online, I produced an avalanche of letters to the US State Department, my Washington, D.C. congresswoman, and the American Consulates in Moscow, Vladivostok, and Novosibirsk. The letters asserted my innocence, proclaimed the terrible injustice that had befallen me, and begged for their intervention. Since the letters would undoubtedly be read by prison officials before they were posted, I couldn't say any more than that.

The temperature dropped day by day. Brisk winds shuddered the frail buildings. Bulbous clouds hung heavy, and drenching downpours turned the prison yards to mud. Field mice scrabbled under the perimeter fences, squeezed through holes in the floorboards and chinks in the pine walls. They scurried about in the sewing room, making off with scraps of fabric, which they ferreted away in hidden nests. Some women threw shoes at them; others put out precious crusts of bread.

One day, I saw the inmate at the sewing machine in front of mine cough up blood. She was old by prison standards—mid-sixties probably, but possibly much younger, as years of malnutrition and depression had undoubtedly taken their toll. Her back was narrow and stooped, the vertebrae a line of shallow knobs mounding under the dark green shirt. Her gray hair was cut short, nearly covered by a white headscarf, and the tendons of her scrawny neck stood out. She'd been coughing intermittently since my first day, the guttural hacking nearly drowned out by the clatter of dozens of sewing machines.

I noticed the blood when she stopped working for a few moments to wipe it quickly off the side of her sewing machine with a wad of the blue camouflage fabric that we were using to make army uniforms. I didn't say anything. The medical staff was supposed to handle such issues, and I was determined to heed Yvonne's warning and keep a low profile. But I watched the woman anyway; I could no more ignore the situation than I could cut off my own hand.

I soon realized that she was bringing up blood regularly, sometimes in large quantities. Most of the time, she successfully covered her mouth with her blue handkerchief, hunching over until the spasm ceased. Then she quickly stuffed the balled fabric, darkened and damp, into the patch pocket on the front of her tunic shirt, using it again within the hour.

After a few days of this, I couldn't help myself: I got behind the woman on the march back from the factory, and made a note of where she went. It turned out that she was one of the sixty women in my own dormitory. Her bed was at the back end, close to the rear door. I slipped after her into the narrow space between the bunks. She looked surprised, then fearful, and craned her neck to see who might be watching.

"Don't worry. I'll make this quick. Have you seen a doctor?" I said.

"They told me I was fine." Her dull eyes swam in gray-blue pouches of flesh. Her face was deeply lined, with long vertical creases around thin lips on which there was an uneven stain of red.

"Did you tell them about the blood?"

"Of course. What do you think?"

"And they said what?"

"That I have nothing to worry about."

"Well, I'm afraid that isn't true."

"What do you know about it?"

"I'm a doctor. There's a chance you have tuberculosis. You need to be tested right away."

The woman gave a mirthless laugh that caught in her throat and erupted into another coughing jag. She reached for the blood-soaked rag in her pocket and hacked into it violently.

"Shut up, Olga," someone said wearily from a nearby bed. "You keep us up half the night."

Olga wiped her mouth roughly with the back of her hand and hissed, "I don't need an American doctor to tell me I have tuberculosis."

I was stunned, then angry. "All right then. If you're so smart, you must know it could kill you. And that you're exposing everyone around you each time you cough, spit, or exhale."

Her expression remained stony. "I told you, didn't I? They examined my lungs and found nothing wrong. What more do you expect me to do?"

On Sunday, the prisoners' day off, I went to the infirmary, where the sharp tang of antiseptic sent up a wave of nostalgia. The lighting was good inside, bright and clean, and the temperature was comfortable—welcome changes from the dimness and perpetual chill of the buildings where I spent my time.

Six or seven prisoners sat on benches near the door, looking like a row of aging, decrepit schoolchildren in their dark green uniforms and black shoes. I approached the nurse's station, where a hawkishly thin nurse bluntly ordered me to go to the back of the line and wait. I explained that I wasn't ill: I was there on another matter, and needed to speak to the doctor in charge. A brief, futile conversation ensued, and I ended up taking my place on a bench.

Almost three hours later, I was ushered into an examining room, where, over my protests, my weight and vital signs were recorded on a chart. The doctor who shuffled in a half hour after that—barrel-shaped and bosomy, with thick calves encased in nude hose and a pouf of orange-ish hair—appeared worn-out but efficient. Her name was embroidered in black thread above the pocket of her lab coat: *Dr. Polina Chereshkevich*. She picked up my chart and skimmed it. "What's the problem?"

"I believe a woman in my dormitory has tuberculosis."

Chereshkevich glanced up in surprise. "So why are *you* here?"

"Because she won't come herself. Apparently, she was examined earlier and told she was fine." If Chereshkevich was a true doctor, she wouldn't get defensive; she'd be more interested in stopping the spread of the disease.

Her eyes lit up at the sound of my accent. "Ah. You're the American. A physician, I was told."

"You've heard of me?"

"You're only the third foreigner we've had in the time I've been here. One Chinese and one German came before you. Both spies like you."

I saw no point in correcting her. "What happened to them?"

She pressed her stethoscope's cold disc to my chest. "The Chinese died of pancreatic cancer—a quick death, but very painful. The German spy was transferred to Lubyanka. You've heard about Lubyanka, no? The KGB prison in Moscow—very harsh. You're lucky to be in this place instead. Here, the staff are local villagers who care mostly about collecting their pay, so things are easier for the prisoners. As long as you don't make trouble, you're left alone."

She pocketed her stethoscope. "What's your specialty?"

"General surgery."

"Are you board-certified?"

"Yes, of course."

She pursed her lips, holding back something she wanted to say, then she picked up a stainless steel tongue depressor and aimed it at my mouth. "Open."

"Really, Dr. Chereshkevich. I'm not here for me. I only came to bring a possible case of TB to your attention."

"You might as well let me look."

I opened my mouth.

"Uh-huh. The beginnings of periodontal disease. Very common, given the poor nutrition. If I could make one change for the health of the prison population, it would be adding a vitamin supplement to the diet. But that will never happen. We don't even have money for basic supplies." She laid the tongue depressor on a tray, leaving me to wonder whether it would be properly sanitized before its next use.

"Now, what makes you think it's tuberculosis?" she asked.

"I saw the woman coughing up blood."

"Her name?"

"Olga. I don't know her last name. She's in my dormitory and sewing room."

Crossing to a sink to wash her hands, Chereshkevich said without surprise, "It's good that you came in. Tuberculosis has remained a problem for us. We have to be especially vigilant at a facility like this one, where there's overcrowding and inadequate sanitary facilities."

With damp fingers, she began to palpate my lymph nodes. "You probably find it alarming that a case may have slipped by us, but you have to understand the situation we face. All the prisoners want to have TB. They appear in the infirmary day after day, coughing pitifully and exaggerating their symptoms. One clever woman put menstrual blood on her handkerchief and claimed it came from her lungs."

"Why would anyone do that?"

"Because a TB diagnosis gets them shipped to the hospital in Krasnoyarsk, where they rest in bed all day in a special TB ward. The food there is very good, I'm told—fruits, vegetables, meat, tapioca pudding—and they're allowed to watch television for as long as they want."

She picked up the chart and began making a notation. "Don't worry. I'll see to that woman, Olga. Now, do you have any symptoms you want to discuss?"

"Other than boredom and fatigue?" I wouldn't admit to terror and despair. Her reaction was humorless, but not unkind. "Medical problems, I mean."

"No, nothing."

"Then it seems we're done here. Now, if you don't mind, I'd like to have you look at someone."

The patient was a woman in her forties with a tumor the size of a golf ball protruding from the side of her neck. The skin over it was pinkly inflamed, stretched to a thin, gleaming smoothness like plastic wrap.

"Petra, this is Dr. March, come all the way from America to examine you," Chereshkevich said in the loud, falsely cheery voice that people use among the dying.

Petra looked at us with drowsing, pain-glazed eyes. Emaciated, a thin branch under the wool blanket, her hair a wispy halo on the pillowcase. She moved her hand slightly in greeting.

Chereshkevich stepped aside to let me examine her.

"Hello, Petra. I'm Dr. March," I repeated, because it was better to make soothing noises than to be quiet. "I'd like to feel your neck for a moment. My hands might be a little cold. Any pain here?" I gently pressed the tips of my fingers against the top of the tumor, then around its sides, all the way down to its base. It was hard and round. It could be malignant, but, given its uniform structure and consistency, I suspected it was benign. In any case, it ought to be removed immediately, as there was a danger that it would obstruct the throat if it got any bigger.

Petra denied feeling pain.

"Good," I said with a smile. Straightening up, I realized that a number of eyes were trained on me. Patients in nearby beds were watching curiously, and a young nurse who was feeding an elderly woman was gaping at the unusual sight of a prisoner examining a patient.

"Show's over, everyone," Chereshkevich said loudly, and we moved out of the ward and halfway down a corridor, where we could confer out of earshot. "Petra's on a list for surgery at Krasnoyarsk, but they're very backed up, and they put prisoners on the bottom rung. It could be months before they get to her.

Meanwhile, her esophagus is narrowing. As it gets more painful to swallow, she eats less. By the time she gets to surgery, she may be too weak to endure it. I'd like to get that tumor out of there as quickly as possible. The operation, if you agree to perform it, will have to be done here, with the basic surgical supplies and medicines we have on hand."

"Anesthesia?"

"Only morphine. I'll be there to assist."

"Risk factors?"

"High blood pressure and early stage congestive heart failure."

"If something goes wrong?"

"She'll be transported by prison van to the emergency room in Krasnoyarsk, and I will take full responsibility. No one will know you were involved."

"Or that you enlisted the aid of a prisoner."

"Correct." Chereshkevich smiled slightly at having her daring exposed.

"Why are you doing this?"

"Because I'm a doctor first; a Russian second."

I looked gratefully into Chereshkevich's tired, intelligent eyes. It was a pleasure to join forces with someone who still had ideals and was willing to take risks for them. "When do you want to do it?"

"Early tomorrow morning. Nurse Latypova will be on duty then by herself. I don't know what they teach in nursing school anymore—nothing, it seems like. She's worse than useless, and takes no interest in learning. I'll give her the night off, saying I have paperwork to catch up on and will sleep in my office, as it will be too late for me to drive home by the time I'm done. She'll leap at the chance to spend the night with her boyfriend. The two of them rival Romeo and Juliet with all the sighing and yearning they do."

The mention of Shakespeare, the way it connected us despite our differences, made me smile. I sensed that Chereshkevich was building a bridge on purpose, in order to enhance our teamwork in the operating room.

"What's your plan for me? How will I get away from my barracks?" I asked, enjoying the conspiracy.

"I'll give you a diagnosis now and put you in a bed overnight. What would you like—exhaustion? Pneumonia? Mental breakdown? You can stay in the ward afterwards for a few days' rest. That will be your payment."

My heart was banging against my ribcage in excitement. Merely to sleep and rest, undisturbed, in a clean, warm environment would be heaven after what I'd been through. But the chance to work in an operating room doing the work I was trained for and that I loved—that was even better. After so much degradation, it would go a long way toward making me feel whole.

She saw the answer on my face and smiled. "You like this good deal? Isn't that what Americans say—*let's make a deal*?"

"Yes, doctor. We've got ourselves a deal."

I peered carefully into the incision and saw that I'd made a mistake. I'd cut too much of the patient's hyoid bone. The relatively simple Sistrunk procedure to excise thyroglossal tumors required that I remove only a couple of millimeters in the bone's mid-section, enough to allow removal of the thyroglossal duct. But, as the patient was merely heavily sedated, not unconscious, she couldn't help making tiny movements in response to pain, despite the fact that Dr. Chereshkevich was holding her head steady, firmly turned to the side so that one cheek was pressed flat against the table. A single quiver of the neck muscle had been enough to make my tiny scalpel slip, and now the opening in the hyoid was too wide, with little bone left on either side.

I raised the scalpel away from the bone, and held it a few inches above the wound, as if to prevent it from doing any more harm. My fingertips throbbed inside the blood-smeared surgical gloves. I had an urge to step back from the operating table, to take a good, long moment to tamp down my anxiety, but I couldn't risk losing focus, and I didn't want Chereshkevich to see me falter. So

I merely fed myself several slow, deep breaths as I mentally prepared for the next step, which was clear. There was nothing to be done now but remove the entire hyoid bone.

With a small tweezer, I lifted out all three pieces, placing the bits end-to-end on the sterile green pad beside me. Re-assembled, the entire bone was half the length of a toothpick and about as wide. Returning to the surgical site with a cauterizing scalpel, I worked carefully around the larynx and thyroid to slowly free the thyroglossal duct up to the base of the tongue. My concentration regained its purity; the mistake was no longer in my mind. Within a few minutes, the duct, a useless embryological structure, was tugged out of the patient's neck in one long, thin, flaccid piece, and placed on the pad next to the bone.

The tumor was now completely freed from the surrounding tissue. A portion of its smooth, glistening surface was visible under the last layer of yellow subcutaneous fat. With the first two fingers of my right hand, I dug into the slit rather roughly, needing to propel the tumor from the back. It virtually popped through the incision, bright pink and slippery, almost perfectly round, about five centimeters in diameter. I palpated it softly, curiously, to feel for any abnormalities in its inner jello-like texture—there were none—before plunking it into a metal bowl that Chereshkevich held out. In the vast majority of cases, these cysts were benign. As the tissue wouldn't be analyzed in a lab, we would never know for sure. It was enough that it had been removed.

I closed with three layers of stitches, the last one everted. A warm loosening spread by degrees through the muscles of my body as I worked, and my attention gradually widened, bringing me back into the tiny exam room. Now I could hear the noises that had been in the background all along—the patient's shallow breathing, the electrical hum of the lights. My mood grew steadily lighter, almost euphoric, as I moved smoothly through the operation's final steps.

"Good work," Chereshkevich said, keeping her voice low. It was three o'clock in the morning; patients were sleeping in the ward nearby

"Thank you," I said with pride. The hyoid was not attached to any other bone, and had no purpose in the body. Like the duct, it was a relic of embryonic development, and its loss would not affect the patient in any way.

.· .· ·. .· . ·. ·. .· . ·. ·

Chereshkevich gave me little luxuries: soap, toothpaste, shampoo. I was allowed to take a warm shower, alone. Afterwards, I donned a clean gown and traipsed barefoot in the dark past twenty cots, most of them occupied, to the end of the ward, where an empty bed lay waiting, white and ethereal in moonlight spilling through the window, more vision than real. I sank into it as if dropping safely at last from a sheer rock face where I'd been dangling by my fingertips. The warmth and softness were paradisiacal. I drifted off quickly, and slept for almost fifteen hours

The first heavy snowstorm struck that night. White flakes whirled in blackness; sudden gusts buffeted the windowpanes; a high-pitched howling rattled the pine rafters. In the morning, the world was virginal, pristine. Smooth white drifts peaked the sentry towers; little cottony tufts perched atop the rolls of razor wire. A deep, perfect silence rang out like a benediction across Female Prison 22. I lay comfortably in my bed by the window, feeling a sense of peace that I knew was fleeting and unwarranted. I savored it nonetheless because another perfect moment might not come my way again for weeks or months, or ever.

Later, inmates outfitted in wool caps with Velcro chin straps and rubber wading boots began shoveling the yard. A Jeep with a plow attached pushed the snow into piles. All day long, ragged lines of poorly-clad women plodded in one direction, then another, back and forth outside the infirmary. The snow slowly darkened with the tramp of feet, and the guard dogs' yellow urine marks.

The medical center was desperately understaffed. During the day, there were at most two nurses on the floor to care for the hospitalized prisoners and to help Dr. Chereshkevich examine the dozens who presented themselves with various complaints. Nurse Latypova worked solo on the graveyard shift. Showing a lot of leg and deep cleavage to no one in particular, she perched sleepily at the front desk, chain-smoking illicit cigarettes while flipping through fashion magazines illuminated by a task lamp's electric halo, no doubt praying to be spared medical emergencies she was unqualified to handle. An old, bald doctor from the village showed up on Chereshkevich's day off. The nurses inundated him with the usual questions, which he responded to in a disgruntled manner. His primary function seemed to be to deny both the existence of illness and the need for any medical treatments beyond aspirin and cough syrup.

I observed all this with interest as the days went by. Chereshkevich conferred with me on a few matters, and I offered to help with routine care. I'd been given the diagnosis of "mental breakdown and physical exhaustion," which required no particular physical symptoms, and no expectation of a quick release. When I began changing catheters and IVs, the nurses took it in stride. I made sure that I was first on hand to quickly and cheerfully perform all the most unsavory tasks, such as cleaning vomit and feces, draining wounds, and spoon-feeding the elderly woman with dementia who pushed the food back out with her tongue. The industriousness I managed to display, despite my allegedly weak, demoralized state, was lauded by all.

It was soon past the time when, by my estimation, I ought to have been sent back to the textile factory. Nothing had been said about the unusual situation; I sensed that no one wanted me to go. I'd become indispensable around the infirmary, which was exactly what I'd been hoping for.

One afternoon, Chereshkevich came to me. "Are you feeling better, Dr.

Marchova?"

"If I say yes, will I be sent back to the factory to sew uniforms?"

"No, as it so happens. I've had you transferred." Before I could say anything, she added, "You needn't thank me. This is the Russian way. As Marx taught us, *From each according to his abilities...* And your abilities are put to better use here than in the factory."

My new job was less exhausting than the repetitive, eye-straining factory work. I had time to sit down once in a while, though I was careful not to be caught loitering. Lunch was delivered to the medical workers from the staff dining hall each noon, so my diet improved. My spirits did, too. It felt good to care about others once again, to feel that my work made a difference in some small way. But this slight rebuilding of my splintered heart was oddly painful, as it reminded me of everything I'd lost. I'd received no replies from any of the letters I'd sent. What tortured me most was thinking about Vera. I would have paid any price to speak to her just once: *I'm fine. Don't be afraid. I love you very much.* Except I wasn't fine. And neither was she—alone among strangers, confused, incontinent, unable to swallow, relying on nurses for scraps of superficial kindness, preparing herself for a solitary death.

One evening, I returned to the barracks to find a small cardboard box on my bed. Inside were all the letters I'd posted—to Vera, the congresswoman, the US State Department, and the several American Consulates. There was no note, no explanation in the box. But the message was clear.

Deeply demoralized, I finally understood and accepted that my faith in Meredith Viles and the CIA was misplaced. The idea that they would somehow steal me away was nothing more than a fairytale I'd been telling myself to help me survive what couldn't have been borne otherwise. In reality, it was likely that Meredith, not being actually omniscient, had no idea where I was. It was also possible that she knew full well and had turned her back on me, just as she'd turned her back on Misha, either out of indifference, or because she'd made a calculated decision that I wasn't worth the risk. It didn't really matter which explanation was correct. Either way, I was on my own.

The October days rapidly grew shorter and colder, as if winter, having gotten off to a slow start, was making up for lost time. The morning exercise routine took place in utter blackness theatrically pierced by glaring white floodlights. It wasn't until a couple of hours later, if I happened to glance out an infirmary window, that I would notice trickles of lavender seeping across the snow-patched meadow beyond the fences. One morning, a four-legged apparition appeared in the smoky dawn. As I watched, transfixed, it clarified into a wolf, a lone wolf exhaling puffs of breath into the icy atmosphere. The slanted sunrays illuminated warm gold tones in its wind-rippled fur. Raising its snout, it sniffed the air in several directions, froze for a few seconds, as if momentarily spellbound, then quickly turned and trotted away, becoming progressively smaller until its form blended into the dark line of the taiga.

As I thought less often of Meredith Viles and even of my mother, Katarina Melnikova became more real to me. Time and again, when I closed my eyes, I would picture her as a young woman, toiling in a gulag prison, enduring repeated rapes, giving birth in squalor. Whatever horrors she'd experienced since being deported from her home in Kiev, nothing would have compared to witnessing the murder of her infant. This event would have changed her utterly, down to her marrow. It would have stolen her sanity, stripped her of fear, turned her part animal. And somehow, from that cold, desperate place, she'd found the wildness, the reckless strength, required to escape.

10

One night, I returned to the barracks to find that the frail old woman who slept in the bed beside me was gone, and a new woman had taken her place. She might have been anywhere between twenty-five and forty. It was hard to tell because she was so gaunt and bony, with sagging bluish pouches under her eyes and raw, scaly patches on her face and neck. Her red-rimmed eyes teared continuously, while a clear, watery mucus ran from her nose. When I tried to talk to her, I was met with such a murderous side-long glance that I quickly shut my mouth.

There was the usual yelling, arguing, and coarse laughter as the prisoners settled in for the night. The young guard patrolling the aisle, while lasciviously watching the women undress, rattled his Kalashnikov along the metal bed frames to prove that he could be the loudest of all. Crude gestures were aimed at his retreating back. Eventually, the dormitory was quiet but for stereophonic snoring and whispered conversations. The window across the aisle from my bunk was blackened by a moonless night; a dim bulb near the door emitted a yellow glow that fell across the scuffed pine floor.

The new woman sleeping so close beside me—only about two feet separated the bunks—began thrashing as if in the throes of a nightmare. She kicked off the blanket, slapped her hand around to find it, and yanked it over her shoulders. Soon, she started to moan. The moans grew louder, then quieter, then loud again. A while later, I heard gurgling, choking noises, and a familiar, noxious smell reached my nose. I looked over. She was lying on her side, her face pressed into a puddle of vomit. With each inhale, she was sucking it back through her nose.

I threw off my blanket, knelt in the cramped space between the beds, and tried to lift her head of matted dark hair onto a pillow, gagging reflexively on the fumes. Her eyes flickered open. An arm flailed out, smacking me in the neck.

"Stay the fuck away from me."

"You need to get your head up or you'll drown in puke," I said.

She raised herself on a bent elbow, stared at the circle of vomit seeping through the sheet. The retching started again, but after several heaves, all she had brought up was a clear viscous liquid that dripped down her scabbed chin. She flopped onto the mattress in exhaustion, a forearm shielding her eyes.

"Here. Roll to one side so I can pull off the sheet," I said.

"Fuck you. I don't need your help. Go away."

"All right. If that's the way you want it." I lifted myself off my knees, preparing to return to bed.

Her body stiffened and began shaking violently. Her head jerked from side to side; she seemed on the verge of a seizure. I pressed my hand gently on her shoulder, and she reacted as if tasered, jerking her bony knees up to her chest and curling into an egg shape. At the same time, her bowels released. The stench instantly filled the air.

She stared up at me with hugely dilated pupils. Her breathing was shallow and fast. The symptoms coalesced in my mind and dovetailed with her haggard appearance. The runny nose and watery eyes clinched the diagnosis. Drug withdrawal. Some kind of opioid.

"Are you a drug user?"

No answer. Her bent legs jerked convulsively, but the worst of the spasm had passed.

"Can you hear me?"

"Leave me alone," she moaned.

"You sure? You don't want to get cleaned up?"

"Get the fuck out of here." She yanked the blanket up to her face with such force that her calves and feet were left exposed. The sour smell of diarrheic feces intensified, and was joined by another foul odor, one familiar to medical workers: a suppurating wound.

Pools of pus were lodged between three toes on the woman's left foot, and there was a hard, red swelling on the inside of her ankle. Wrapping my fingers in the edge of the sheet, I separated the infected big toe from its neighbor, wiped away a plug of pus in the crease to reveal a deep puncture wound with ragged pink and yellow edges. Something glinting inside—the tip of a needle.

She jerked her foot away. "What the fuck?" But it was a half-hearted protest. Maybe she was demoralized by the fact that she was lying in puke and shit, or maybe she was just too miserable to care what happened to her anymore.

"Some of your injection sites are infected," I said. "A needle broke off in one of them."

She muttered something in an irritated tone, covered her face with her hands.

I tore a long swath of fabric from the bottom of the bed sheet. It made a loud ripping sound, which drew somnolent murmurs and curses from surrounding beds. I wrapped the foot carefully, noticing as I did fresh and faded needle marks on the inside of the swollen ankle. The other foot had similar tracks but was not infected.

The woman in the upper bunk leaned over groggily. "Did someone shit the bed?"

"Whoever did that better clean it the fuck up," a nearby voice announced.

The upper-bunk woman saw the mess on the lower bunk. "Oh god. That's disgusting. Get her out of here!"

I didn't want to be there when the dormitory awakened en masse, as it probably would. I leaned over and spoke calmly to the sick woman, who had wet vomit on the side of her face. "I'm going to help you sit up. I want you to swing your legs over the side of the bed and put your arm around my neck. Then we'll go to the infirmary." It was late. Irina Latypova would be on duty by herself. She would let me throw the woman into the shower, take her vital signs, and put her to bed.

"I'm not going anywhere," the woman insisted, suddenly sure of herself.

"Fine. But if you choose to remain where you are, these ladies are going to toss you out in the snow."

"I don't give a shit. Go away and let me die."

"Sorry. Withdrawal won't kill you. You're just going to be sick for a while, and then you'll be good as new. Now come on. Swing your legs, and I'll help you get up."

The dormitory was slowly erupting in shouts of disgust and condemnation. "Somebody clean that up, for god's sake!" "Get rid of her!" "Where the fuck is the guard?"

I had the sick woman on her feet and was guiding her out of the narrow space between the cots when the young guard with the Kalashnikov appeared in the aisle. He raised his rifle and pointed it straight at my chest. "Where do you think you're going, Prisoner Marchova?"

"This woman is ill. I'm taking her to the infirmary."

"Leave her alone and return to your bed."

"She needs help."

He took a couple of steps forward, until the rifle butt was jammed against my breast bone. "Return to your bed, I said."

I unhooked the sick woman's arm from my shoulder and sat on the edge of my cot. The woman teetered, but managed to hold herself erect between the bunks.

The guard took one-eyed aim at her down the long barrel, which he swept in the direction of the door. "You. Go."

She stood directly in front of him in her shit-caked pajamas. "Shoot me," she said.

He waved the barrel toward the door again. "Go."

"Don't be scared, little man. Shoot me. Pull the trigger."

His chest heaved, and the gun barrel rode up a few inches, until it was pointed at her throat.

"Pull the trigger. Don't you see that I'm an escaping prisoner? Do your duty. Mow me down. What's the matter? Are you a pussy?"

"Go. Do as I say."

She smiled a little, slipped a hand inside her pants and removed it covered with the stain of diarrhea and a clump of crap. She moved toward him, her palm extended. "Here, pussy. Eat my shit."

The guard drew back. "Stay back, or I'll shoot."

She continued gliding toward him, bringing her hand within inches of his face. "Don't be scared. No one will blame you if you shoot me."

The young man appeared frozen, one eye squinting down the barrel, a finger on the trigger. In slow motion, she smeared the shit along the side of his face. "Shoot the fucking gun, will you? What's taking you so long?"

For a few long seconds, he didn't move. Then he lowered the Kalashnikov, twirled it like a baton to grab the barrel, swung it in a wide arc, and smashed the heavy end into the side of her head. There was a loud crack when the rifle butt met her skull. She collapsed instantly and laid inert on the wooden floor.

⁘ ⁙ ⁘ ⁙ ⁘

The guard stalked out of the barracks. There was silence for a few moments, until the prisoners started murmuring to each other. I knelt to check the sick woman, who was conscious, moaning. A minute later, the front door was thrown open, smacking loudly against the wall behind it, and heavy boots pounded down the aisle. The guard had returned with a middle-aged woman who shrieked orders to the awakened prisoners, telling them to be silent and stay in their beds, that anyone who left her bed would be shot. I stood next to my bunk. The male guard proceeded to drag the injured woman by her arms toward the door. As she was pulled across the uneven floorboards, the wrapped bandage on her wounded foot came undone, unfurling into a white cotton trail.

Staring at me with bald hostility, the female guard pointed to the sick woman's empty cot. "Clean up this mess," she ordered.

When they were gone, I stripped the bed and rolled the dirty sheets into a ball, covering my mouth and nose with a hand. I had no idea how to "clean up this mess." There was a tiny bathroom at the back of the dormitory with a perpetually backed-up toilet and a spigot that dripped cold water into a stained sink. The central washroom was bigger, with about the same level of functionality. The prisoners were responsible for laundering their own bedding and uniforms, which was impossible given the time we were allotted and the ludicrous facilities, so few items were ever washed. As far as I was concerned, there was no point in even trying to clean the soiled sheets.

I felt eyes on me, prisoners watching to see what the American spy would do. It came to me that I was dog tired of being scared and cautious, of keeping my head down. The job in the medical center had given me a certain status that I was willing to trade on now. I slipped my feet into my rubber shoes and shrugged on my parka.

"Where are you going, Natalya?" Yvonne whispered from her upper bunk.

"To get clean sheets."

"No, Natalya. Please don't go outside! If they see you, you could be shot."

I stuffed the balled sheets under my arm and headed down the aisle toward the door. An old veteran started to cackle. A few women urged me on; someone else laughed mockingly. They had no idea what I was doing; they were just hoping for another dramatic scene.

The night was pitch black, moonless; the frigid air was like a million tiny icicles pricking every centimeter of my skin. Powerful floodlights illuminated the recreation area, but the edges of the compound were completely dark. Strangely, there was no one in sight. I cut to the rear of the barracks, and trekked north along the row of evenly-spaced dormitories, running my hand along the back of each building to guide myself. At the last one, I turned east, headed back toward the center of the compound, guided by a light over the entrance to the long, one-story infirmary. A couple of filthy dumpsters behind the building overflowed with trash. I found my way to them carefully, stumbling in the pitch dark, and tossed the sheets onto a hulking pile. My teeth were chattering, and my tear ducts streamed in the fierce cold.

I waited in the shadows near the entrance until the two guards left, having deposited their human package, then I strode inside with confidence. "I've been sent to help look after the new patient," I informed Nurse Latypova, who was slouching at the desk.

She shrugged as if to say *better you than me*, and gestured toward the ward. "She's down there, on the right. She needs to be cleaned up."

Wide awake and still in her filthy pajamas, the sick woman was lying akimbo on top of the blanket, as if she'd been dropped there from a considerable height.

"How are you feeling?" I asked.

"My head hurts."

"I'm not surprised."

Her wild black hair made a dirty halo around her head. I took a closer look at her face. She had widely spaced eyes of a strangely golden color, the whites tinted dull yellow. High, jutting cheekbones. A long, flat nose with flaring nostrils. Thin, flexible lips that seemed on the verge of movement. A disappearing chin.

"Can you walk?" I asked.

"Yes," she said in a tone of mild offense.

"It's this way to the shower."

"Are you an English woman?"

"American. Dr. Natalie March from Washington, D.C. And you are?"

"Zara Chernovskaya. From Krasnoyarsk." Her eyes narrowed. "Why are you trying so hard to take care of me?"

"Habit, I suppose."

While she was in the shower, I got the key to the storeroom from Latypova. I selected a hospital gown, bandages, and three sets of clean, folded sheets. I recorded the patient's vitals, picked the needle tip out of the flesh between her toes, cleaned and dressed her wounds, ordered bed rest: no reading. Right now, I was more concerned about a possible concussion than the drug withdrawal process. Latypova sat up front with her magazines and cell phone, happy to be oblivious.

More slowly this time, given the bulky load zipped inside my parka, I retraced my steps to the barracks, keeping well away from the floodlit recreation yard. At one point, I stumbled on uneven ground, and a frenzy of deep-throated barking erupted from over by the guard house. Three or four dogs were going wild, but they didn't close in on me; they must have been chained.

A few women were still awake. They watched as I swayed down the aisle, and dumped the fresh sheets on my bed. One gave a low approving whistle; another chuckled quietly.

Yvonne's sleepy head popped over the edge of the top bunk. "Oh my god. Where did you go?"

"I didn't go anywhere, sweetheart. I was here all along. Wasn't I?" I said, shivering mightily from my sojourn in sub-zero temperatures.

She leaned over, nearly rolling off the bunk. "What's that?"

"A present for you." I passed a set of sheets up to her, and she received it with a muted little squeal. When her delight subsided, she said, "Be careful,

Natalya. You're playing with fire."

"Don't worry. I've become a model prisoner, thanks to your advice. People at the infirmary are quick to say how useful and obedient Prisoner Marchova is."

I put a set of clean sheets on Zara's bed, made up my own bed, and fell, exhausted, onto it. I refused to worry about the risk I'd just taken, refused to second-guess myself. That little lick of freedom had made the blood sing in my veins. And I'd gained crucial knowledge: the prison was poorly lit and poorly guarded in the dead of night. I didn't know what I was going to do with that information, but having it made me feel powerful.

Zara was expelled from the infirmary first thing the next morning, as Dr. Chereshkevich had no tolerance for addicts, whose suffering during the withdrawal process was, in her opinion, not only well-deserved, but also an effective deterrent to future drug use. Meanwhile, the other patients on the ward were in an excited buzz. Apparently, Zara Chernovskaya was no stranger to Female Prison 22. She'd been released from the prison six months earlier after serving five years for possession of narcotics. She and Svetlana had ruled opposing gangs, and it had only been Zara's release that had allowed Svetlana to rise to unopposed dominance. Zara's unexpected reappearance promised a return to hostilities—the news was flying around the camp.

The word was that Zara's former loyalists had gone on to make other alliances, some with Svetlana herself. So Zara was completely unprotected. The patients on the ward agreed that she had little chance of surviving more than a few months. Murders within the walls were rare, but not surprising. The administration raised a cry afterwards while doing little to prevent them.

That night, as we were undressing shoulder-to-shoulder in the narrow space between our beds, Zara spoke to me in a low voice. "Do you know who

I am?"

"I heard." I made a point of sounding unimpressed. So far, I'd managed to avoid Svetlana's corrosive attention, and I intended to stay far away from this piece of bad news as well. Where Svetlana was sadistic and stupid, which made her fairly predictable, Zara was rumored to alternate periods of hostile solitude with sudden bouts of impulsive, crack-pot craziness, the latter of which I could certainly attest to, having witnessed her suicidal taunting of the guard the night before. She'd been linked to two deaths inside the walls, both times managing to hide her tracks.

"And what do the rumors say about me—that I'm not an angel? Does that make you scared?" Zara said.

I turned to meet her gaze. I was afraid of Zara, as any sane person would be, but I wasn't going to submit. "People say you've got some problems, and given the way you behaved last night, I have to say I agree."

She cackled at the unexpected honesty. "I do! I've definitely got some problems! You want to be one of them?"

"No. I really don't."

"Good. So the next time I tell you to leave me the fuck alone, that's what you will do."

We stared into each other's eyes. We were exactly the same height. My heart was clanging against my ribs. I willed myself into my long-practiced clinician's role, noting that the raw, scaly patches on her skin were less inflamed than they'd been the night before. But there was still a sour odor coming off her body, and she was holding herself too stiffly, as if disguising pain or tremors. She'd probably never been strong, even when she was well. Her frame was too slight. It would have been intelligence that brought her into power, and that was what I saw glowing in her tawny eyes—an alert, predatory shrewdness.

I said, "Believe me, Zara Chernovskaya, I have no desire to mess with you, now or ever. But if there's ever a medical emergency, I'll act as I see fit."

"Ah, well said! You are a true humanitarian. The world needs more people like you." She continued undressing. Under the dark green tunic was a filthy tank top, something silver glinting on a leather cord between small, high breasts.

A few moments later, she asked, "How did you get to this place, Natushka?" The endearment was confusing. A prelude to friendship? A power play? A veiled threat?

"They think I'm a spy."

"Are you?"

"No."

Her lips quivered into a smile. "You are a very bad liar, my friend."

She turned to her cot, yanked the tank top over her head. A multi-colored tattoo, well and intricately drawn, covered her entire back. A Siberian tiger, just its head, with mellow, complacent eyes staring out from her shoulder blades, and short, erect ears that twitched when her shoulders moved. Another tattoo—a twisting vine of roses, the thorns as big as the blossoms—ran the length of her right arm. There was something small on the back of her neck, too, just under the hairline, that I couldn't make out.

She pointed to the folded sheets on her bed. "Who did that?"

"I did."

"Why?"

"They ordered me to."

A pause. A tilted head. "How did you wash them so fast?"

"I didn't. I stole a new set from the infirmary."

She nodded thoughtfully, as if what she was hearing was strange, but not too strange. "I've heard that Americans go all over the world taking whatever they want."

"And you believe that?"

She said with an amused lilt to her voice, "You're the first American I've met. And so far, you are proving it to be true."

She made her bed and climbed into it naked, her hips narrow and frail-looking, her buttocks drooping like an old person's jowls. Folding her legs tightly into her chest as she had the night before, she shrank into a compact lump under the blanket. The great Zara Chernovskaya. A little pile of lunatic flesh and bone.

The first of November came and went. The temperature dropped below zero during the day, occasionally as low as twenty-five degrees below. The sun was a dimly glowing yellow orb that briefly traversed the southern horizon, vanishing each day by three o'clock. Snow was scarce, but what fell remained. Beyond the web of perimeter fencing, a thin, white crust glittered on the meadow, where the wolves occasionally strolled like kings.

The scant mental and emotional resources that had remained to me after I'd given up hope of being rescued by the CIA withered away. I became increasingly despondent. At times, the mental pressure got so great it felt as if my brain itself was burning up. In silent agony, I did in fantasy what reality wouldn't allow. I mounted passionate defenses to invisible committees; imagined squinting down the barrel of a stolen Kalashnikov, calmly picking off the guards in the sentry towers, one by one, as if it were a carnival game, then evacuating the prisoners en masse, and blowing the whole place up.

An ugly, croaking voice took up residence in my head: *You're going to rot in this place. Rot like a living carcass, until you're shriveled and dry, your only remaining pleasure masticating twice-daily pieces of stale bread. Until you don't know who you are anymore, and don't care. Until insanity is your refuge, and death looks like a sweet release.*

My dreams turned into a regular shop of horrors: deafening volleys of machine gun fire, bubbling lakes of yellow sludge, sky-high piles of human skeletal remains. Balls of fire in the night sky, torrents of burning rain, the seared flesh of children peeling off in ghastly, glowing bands. Things lost, things abandoned. Myself lost and forgotten in a desolate environment at the farthest edge of the civilized world, where the only religion was gross inhumanity and death. On waking, I didn't experience the dreamer's relief at finding myself safe and sound in a cozy bed. I woke to find the nightmare true.

Then one morning I woke to find everything changed. My mind was sharp and supremely focused; my emotions were as smooth and glassy as the surface of a resting lake. My anguish had dissolved and disappeared during the night, as if it had been mere illusion all along, and a new diamond-hard clarity had taken its place. I had the impression that even my eyesight had improved.

I started to observe my surroundings closely. A truck being packed with boxes of finished uniforms. Local men in torn coats unloading eggs, potatoes, and loaves of bread from the back of a small van—good food that never showed up in the prisoners' dining hall. Uniformed guards with shoulder-slung guns standing stock-still, like painted wooden toys, in the watch towers, their fur *ushankas* with the fiery red insignias perched high on their heads. They must drowse on their feet at least some of the time, I thought, numbed by cold and drugged by colossal boredom.

Usually, the main gate was closed and the mechanical arm was down. Once, I noticed that the door to the sentry house was ajar, the guard huddled outside it to puff on a cigarette with a thickly gloved hand. Any lapse on the part of the staff, however tiny, was a point of interest to me.

While I was working, giving sponge baths or mopping floors, I compiled mental lists of potentially useful items: forks, light bulbs, a German Shepherd's leather harness, the hook-and-eye closure on a door. From the infirmary: scissors, needles, gauze pads, medical tape, a patient's gold cross on a chain. My mind listed and sorted compulsively.

I didn't dream anymore; I barely slept. Night after night, I lay rigidly on my bed, breathing the fetid smells of sixty unwashed women, while my mind coolly and methodically kneaded the pertinent facts: it was fifteen kilometers to the village; I had only prison garb, no money, and it was rumored that the villagers were paid handsomely to return escapees. Heading in the opposite direction, into the frozen taiga, would be certain death. The only viable strategies, it seemed, were to stowaway in a van or truck, blackmail a worker, or take one hostage. Or something I hadn't thought of yet.

I had one mantra, which I repeated over and over whenever my thoughts strayed. *I will escape from Female Prison 22.* I had no idea how it would happen, or when; only that it must and would. I believed the dream completely, worked at it constantly, and my perfect faith and dedication kept my terror and despair at bay.

I told myself not to force anything, not to overthink it. The plan would come together in its own time, and I'd know when it was right. But I couldn't wait too long, as winter was setting in. Afternoons had become a long limbo of twilight during which objects blurred and eventually disappeared. Then blinding blackness descended, and the cold got even deadlier. One night, it snowed again, a fine mist falling softly through the auras of the floodlights. In the hushed barracks of sleeping prisoners, I lay awake on my cot, listening to the melancholy howls of the wolves in the forest. Soon, I would be on their side of the fence.

Films were screened in the dining hall on Sunday nights at 8 p.m. The long refractory tables were pushed aside, and about a hundred folding chairs were set in rows, facing a pull-down screen. Attendance varied depending on the film. Tonight, it was an educational documentary about the unusual creatures of the Galapagos, and only about a third of the seats were filled.

Zara, Yvonne, and I slid into the empty last row, following Zara's lead. She was much better, steadier and stronger, with some color in her face. To my surprise, we'd become friends, to the extent that friendship could exist without privacy or trust, in an environment of constant threat. Zara was a talker, it turned out. She liked to brag about all the friends she had back in Krasnoyarsk, where she was born and had spent her life. Apparently, during her last incarceration, she'd received visitors every single month for five straight years.

Yvonne whispered peevishly in my ear that she'd rather be sitting at the front of the hall. We both knew she wouldn't dream of crossing Zara; no one did, except me. I'd made a point of standing my ground with the former warlord, and seemed to have been granted a kind of special adviser status as a result, a role I hadn't courted and didn't want.

As we waited in the gloomy hall for the movie to start, Zara rather secretively showed me a photo of her son—a fearsome-looking adolescent with his mother's wide cheekbones and thin lips. His expression was ominously flat and vacant, which made him look older than his sixteen years. Yet she was as proud as any mother, displaying the photo without letting me touch it, as if it were too precious to be entrusted to another person's grubby paws.

When the opening credits rolled and the sound came up, Yvonne leaned over and whispered, "Why didn't she show me? She acts like I don't exist." She was jealous of Zara in a touching way, like a little sister forced to share an adored older sibling with an unworthy interloper.

Soon, slow-moving tortoises were lumbering over jutting island rocks, and an even slower Russian voiceover was offering scientific commentary. The smooth sand beach and sapphire ocean were the best things I'd seen in months. I imagined salt air filling my nostrils and a warm breeze stroking my face.

Partway through the film, Yvonne nudged me. Two huge black iguanas were butting their tufted, leathery heads on the screen, while a heavy, short-necked, buzz-cut blond was strolling down the center aisle. It was Svetlana, and behind her was another woman, so fat that she rocked side-to-side as she walked. Yvonne pointed in the other direction, where two more women were coming down the side aisle, not bothering to hide the fact that they were carefully scanning the spectators' faces, obviously looking for someone. Heads were turning to follow the gang's progress; a low buzz was building in the hall.

"It's happening," Yvonne said tersely.

I glanced behind me. The laptop showing the movie was unattended. The rear half of the hall was vacant, no guards in sight. It was a straight shot to the doors.

I leaned over and whispered to Zara, "You've got some friends coming."

"Shh. This is the best part." The iguanas were starting to fight.

"Zara. You've got to get out of here now."

She frowned, then spied Svetlana and the others. To my surprise, she exploded from her seat like a rocket, and screamed over the soundtrack, "You bitch. You afraid to fight me alone? You need your friends with you? Well, fuck you, you stinking piece of lesbian cunt. You want me, here I am!" She scrambled over my knees and Yvonne's, emerging in the center aisle about eight feet from her rival.

Svetlana stopped, feet planted wide apart, and puffed up her chest; the fat woman hovered at her elbow. The two other gang members appeared behind Zara—how they got there so fast was anyone's guess—and one of them shoved her hard between the shoulder blades, so hard that she lurched toward Svetlana, who tripped her and stepped aside adroitly to let her fall. Svetlana's minions were upon her in an instant, kicking her viciously in the stomach, back, and head. The air filled with their grunts of exertion and the thud of heavy shoes impacting tissue and bone.

The iguanas were quickly forgotten. The prisoners streamed out of their seats and crowded around the assault, many of them silent and aghast, many more cheering and yelling encouragement. Standing close to the action, hands on hips, Svetlana watched fixedly.

I was frozen in place. Zara was supposed to have tough companions who would come to her aid, but she didn't. Only Yvonne and I were on her side, and then only tentatively, by proxy, and, in any case, we were obviously not battle-ready. In fact, Yvonne was tugging my sleeve, urging me to run. She seemed to think that the casual association we had with Zara put us next in line for attack.

I shook her off, and just kept standing there in impotent horror, my ears filled with the ugly sounds of the beating, while my eyes were glued to Svetlana's smug face. Then, without warning, a fiery rage surged from the deepest ground of my being like an eruption of molten rock.

Roughly pushing my way to the center, I reached Svetlana in a few swift steps, using momentum to shove her off balance, just as skinny Zara had been shoved. Svetlana staggered, managed to catch herself, quickly found her equilibrium. Fists raised, she squared off to me, a satisfied smile playing across her lips.

The ring of onlookers expanded to accommodate us. The thugs working Zara drew back, their attention lured by the surprise attack. Svetlana waved them off. She wanted the American doctor for herself. The next thing I knew, one of Svetlana's fists had powered into the pit of my stomach, and the other was smashing the side of my face. My torso spun in a bent-over position, falling across my own stationary feet. I landed on my side on the floor next to Zara, and immediately sensed shadows converging on me, the minions closing in. There was no time to get up. I covered my face with my hands and stiffened my abdomen against what was going to happen next.

Which took place very quickly. Zara sprang up, attached herself like a monkey to the fat woman's back, and started raking her eyes and cheeks with stiff fingers bent like claws. The woman swung from side to side like a powerful blinded animal, trying to throw the monkey off. A glinting knife emerged from someone's pocket, and was plunged into Zara's side. She slid off the fat woman's back onto her knees, where she wobbled at dwarf height, unprotected. I spied the bloody knife in a lowered hand, and staggered to my feet, ready to knock it away, but it vanished before I could get to it. All this happened silently. Then a sudden roar reached my ears: the hollering of prison guards and the stomping of heavy boots. The crowd dissolved, Svetlana blending in with the others. The empty seats were quickly re-populated. By the time the guards reached the scene, the prisoners were paying rapt attention to phalanxes of mottled red crabs swarming by the thousands across a white sand beach.

I knelt at Zara's side. My fingers slid under the heavy tunic to gauge the severity of the wound. The knife had slashed the top layer of skin but hadn't penetrated beyond that. Nevertheless, there was a lot of blood; a sticky pool was spreading across the pine floorboards.

Zara struggled to sit up; she appeared confused, dimly enraged. I pushed her firmly onto her back, leaned down, and brought my mouth close to her ear. "You're in no danger. It's a superficial wound. If you want to get out of this place, shut up and do exactly as I say." Then I rocked back onto my heels, yelling, "She's bleeding out! Hurry! Get a bandage! Quick!"

There were only two guards standing near me—they had sounded like a herd—young men from the village with no appetite for blood and guts.

I screamed at them, "Get a stretcher! What are you waiting for?"

They both ran off a few paces, until one, realizing he wasn't needed, doubled back.

"A bandage, for Christ's sake! Hurry!" I shrieked.

Yvonne, to her credit, hadn't run away. Her eyes wild with terror, she pulled off her tunic top and tried to rip the stiff fabric.

"Just give me the whole thing," I said.

Together, we lifted Zara's torso and cinched the sleeves around her waist. When Zara tried to say something, I quickly pinched her lips closed. "Don't talk, not a word until I say so. You're in shock. You're going to need CPR, IV fluids, and life support. Now try to fucking act that way."

I removed my fingers, and Zara obediently kept her mouth shut, while Yvonne's eyes widened in confusion.

The guards returned with a stretcher, with Nurse Latypova—would-be sex goddess, sneaker of cigarettes, and connoisseur of fashion—bringing up the rear.

"Isn't anyone else on duty tonight?" I asked in a voice of desperation.

"Just me. What difference does it make?" she said sullenly.

"Oh, for god's sake," I muttered, hoping to exacerbate her lack of confidence.

Zara was heaved onto the stretcher, her head wobbling as if no muscle was controlling it. She was either passed out or doing a good imitation. The guards carried the stretcher toward the exit, Latypova following in a sulk. The moviegoers took precious little interest, acting for all the world as if the Galapagos had them enthralled. Yvonne fell in behind me, walking practically on my heels. I whirled around and said sharply, "You stay here."

"Please. I want to come."

"No, Yvonne. You have to stay."

"No, no, Natalya. I can't bear to be here for two more years. It'll kill me, I swear. I don't care what the risks are. I want to go with you."

I drew close beside her and lowered my voice. "Listen to me. Two years is nothing. You'll have your whole life to forget about this place. Now go sit down. Get away from me."

"Please, Natal—"

"Did you hear me? I said *go*. Get the fuck away from me."

She stood still and mute as I followed the stretcher out the door.

. ⋅ ⋅ ⋅ ⋅ ⋅ ⋅ ⋅ ⋅ ⋅ ⋅ .

I hovered over the bed on which Zara lay, applying a large gauze bandage to her superficial wound, while furiously barking orders to a stony-faced Latypova. Loitering near the door, the brash young guards seemed eager to bolt out of the pee-smelling sick house; only the opportunity to ogle the lovely Latypova was holding them back. In the shadowy beds along the ward, patients slept or quietly observed the crisis. The stale aroma of Latypova's cigarettes hung in the antiseptic air.

"She's lost a lot of blood," I bellowed to Latypova. "Blood pressure's low and falling. Abdominal swelling suggests heavy internal bleeding. We need to get some fluids into her fast, but it probably won't be enough. If she doesn't get to a hospital soon, she'll die."

Latypova stared blankly for a few moments, until her brain shifted into low gear. "I'll call an ambulance."

"Not enough time. She'll be dead before she gets to Krasnoyarsk."

The nurse looked horrified. I got the sense she'd never seen a patient die before.

"What's wrong with you? Call for a prison van!"

"I should ask Dr. Chereshkevich first," she said hesitatingly.

"Well, for god's sake, do it now!"

The doctor was home with her family, about a thirty-minute drive from the prison. It was 9 p.m. on a Sunday night, and the temperature outside was in the teens. After a brief conversation in which Latypova offered tentative, mumbled answers, Chereshkevich asked to speak to me. I summarized the patient's critical condition in rapid-fire medical talk. We agreed that emergency surgery might be required, and that a trained medical worker should accompany the patient during transport to administer CPR if needed. I didn't have to add that we couldn't wait for an ambulance to arrive; Chereshkevich said it herself. She got Latypova on the phone again, and the nurse listened, not saying anything, just nodding her head. After hanging up, Latypova repeated her boss's instructions like a robot. "You are to take the patient to the hospital under guard. I am to stay here and supervise the ward."

"Well, let's go! Hurry up!"

She made another call, this one to the guard house, while I grew frustrated trying to find a healthy-enough vein in Zara's arm for the IV. Five minutes later, we were loading the patient's stretcher into the back of a prison van. I piled in after, and set up the IV drip. Zara lay motionless, her face blank and chalky. It was hard to tell how much of her unresponsiveness was an act and how much was real. I worried that there had been internal damage after all.

When one of the guards pulled out handcuffs, I responded in high umbrage. "How the hell can I take care of a patient while wearing handcuffs? Do *you* want to be the one to administer CPR when she goes in to cardiac arrest?" He contented himself with slamming the heavy metal doors, plunging the back of the van into darkness.

"You still with me?" I whispered.

"You are very bad with the needle, my friend. Someday, I'll teach you how to do it right," she whispered back.

⠂⠄⠂⠄⠂⠄⠂⠄⠂⠄⠂⠄⠂⠄

The guards were in high spirits, having lucked into an off-campus jaunt. Pop music blared out of the crappy speakers and echoed in the cavernous back of the van, mixing with the loud engine noise. Every once in a while, the vehicle's rear end fishtailed on a patch of ice, and Zara's IV bag swayed precariously on its jury-rigged holder. There was no heat in the back, as well as no light. Zara was covered with two thick blankets from the ward, but I had only my parka over the prison uniform, and the metal floor was like ice. I wouldn't let Zara give me a blanket in case one of the guards slid open the panel on the wall separating us and took a look back.

After about forty-five minutes, the van shuddered to a stop and the doors swung open. The first thing I saw was a beautiful yellow crescent moon suspended in a velvety black sky, just above a concrete building about the height and width of a battleship—Krasnoyarsk Hospital. The waiting room was crowded and overheated, filled with adult moans and the whining of children, thick with the smells of sour bodies and damp wool. It was hard to tell the sick from the well as everyone appeared to be suffering.

Zara was carried in on the stretcher. When the triage nurse came, I spoke to her out of earshot of the guards, who seemed discomforted at having found themselves crammed among the injured and infirm. I described the patient's condition as stable, and the nurse instructed the guards to place Zara on a hospital bed at the end of a corridor. The dozen or so beds parked along the way were occupied by other patients awaiting treatment. With any luck, it would be a long time before a doctor got to us.

Once Zara was transferred to the bed, the two guards and I were pressed together awkwardly in the narrow corridor. What to do now? Should we just leave the patient there and return to the prison? Should someone stay with her? For how long? No one had thought this far ahead.

An orderly pushing a wheelchair tried to get past us, but the guards were blocking the way with their large bodies and the unwieldy stretcher, now empty. Once the wheelchair had squeezed by, I suggested that they go and sit in the waiting room, while I stayed with the patient until the doctor came. They happily complied.

Minutes went by   ten, maybe fifteen. White-coated medical staff popped in and out of examining rooms; the triage nurse seemed to have forgotten about the stable patient with the superficial knife wound at the end of the hall. I was keenly aware that the minute Zara passed into the control of hospital personnel, my presence would be superfluous. I'd be forced to return to the van, and shunted back to Female Prison 22. I couldn't allow that to happen, but there seemed no way to break free. I was wearing a blood-smeared prison uniform, and there were too many people around.

A few minutes later, Zara solved the problem by insisting she had to pee.

"Of course you do," I said. "Here, let me help you up."

She sat straight up, rising like Lazarus from the dead. Wincing at the pain in her side, she threw off the blanket, and viciously yanked the IV needle out of her arm.

Laying a firm hand on her shoulder, I hissed, "Take it easy. Act like you're injured. Walk."

I helped her carefully off the bed, pulling one of her arms across my shoulders, and we staggered toward a sign marked *tualet* at the end of the hall. Next to it, there was a metal door with a push bar topped by a red exit sign. I glanced back to see if we'd drawn any attention: the corridor was empty but for the line of hospital beds. We passed the bathroom at a snail's pace, then slipped through the heavy door, finding ourselves in a gloomy, unheated stairwell. Up or down? In wordless unison, we descended, moving fast now. The stairway ended abruptly after one flight. We faced another metal door, which we pushed open, emerging onto a concrete platform, into bitterly cold air. It was a delivery bay; a couple of trucks were parked for the night under an overhang. There was a narrow access road, well-ploughed; banked snow along one side reflected the crescent moon's pale light.

We raced quietly along the access road, then along the far edge of the parking lot, to an exit that dumped us onto a wide thoroughfare with a median strip. A couple of cars sped past, heading toward the lights of Krasnoyarsk, but overall there was little traffic. It must have been midnight, maybe later.

Zara darted across the lane, clambered over the snow mound on the median strip. I followed. Turning south, she sprinted along the shoulder; I was right behind. The snow bank to our right was waist-high; behind it, a row of evenly spaced evergreens; beyond that, utter dark. We ran full-out on the pavement for a long time—too long to be so exposed. A couple of cars overtook us, tires spewing grainy mud. Once the news of our escape was out, would the drivers remember seeing two women running on the side of the road? Could they make out our prison uniforms, or was it too dark?

Finally, we came to a turn—an unlit road disappearing into woods. As we jogged along it, the highway drone faded and was replaced by the rhythmic thudding of our feet. A park, I thought.

"Wait," I called to Zara. I stopped, doubled over, and tried to catch my breath. My lungs were on fire.

Zara's face was a haggard pale oval not far ahead. "Don't stop yet. Hurry, hurry."

I broke into a sluggish jog, willing my legs to pump faster than they wanted to go, intent on keeping Zara's shadowy form in sight.

The road wound at its leisure through a pine-scented forest, and the night grew darker, quieter, colder. An icy wind sighed in my ears, carrying the tang of fresh moisture.

Zara slipped on a patch of ice, let out a cry. I reached her and helped her up. If her wound opened, what would I do?

"Come on, we're almost there," she said, walking now, canted sideways, pressing her palm into her side.

The road ended in a cul-de-sac around a tall stone obelisk and some snow-topped shrubs. Beyond that, an enormous empty field glowed with dull phosphorescence in the moonlight. Only it wasn't a field; it was a river snaking gently northward, losing itself in the sparkle of not-too-distant city lights. The sky above it was satiny black, the crescent moon hanging crisply in one corner, like a yellow paper cutout. The scene might have come from a book of Russian fairytales.

I was shivering. The instant I'd stopped moving, the sweat on my body had begun to freeze. The shivering quickly became violent, until I felt like a jangling skeleton. Neither of us had coats.

"What now?" I asked.

Zara gazed at the river with strangely rapt attention, her black hair streaming out in the frigid wind sweeping across the ice.

"There must be someone you can call," I prompted, my teeth clattering like castanets. Krasnoyarsk was Zara's city.

"With what phone?" she said sarcastically.

The rising wail of a siren reached us. We didn't move until the vehicle had sped past the park entrance and the sound had died away.

"We've got to get out of here," I said, my voice rising in panic.

She continued to observe the river silently, her face tilted slightly up, like a wolf sniffing the air.

It occurred to me that she could simply leave me there. Her life would be a lot easier without an American spy in tow. Maybe that was what she was contemplating—whether to abandon me in the park.

The shrill scream of another siren was fast approaching. Again, we waited wordlessly as the noise expanded into a blare and shrank to a whine. I was convinced that the next patrol would discover us; my imagination teemed with searchlights, megaphones, police cruisers, dogs.

"We've got to get out of here," I repeated in near hysteria.

Zara turned to me and smiled, one tooth catching a gleam of moonlight. "Cheer up, Natushka. You're free."

The ice wasn't solid. It was composed of large chunks that bobbed and bumped in the current, and flat sheets that ground against each other like tectonic plates. Zara had led the way to the river's edge, where we now stood, listening to the quiet lapping of moving water and, further out, a creaking like the straining timbers of a wooden sailing ship.

An inch of snow blanketed the shoreline. She turned and loped along it with surprising speed. I struggled to keep up, not entirely trusting her, but scared of being left behind. I'd tucked my bare hands under my armpits, but it did little good. I couldn't feel my fingers, toes, or face.

She stopped at a paved landing where, in a different season, small pleasure boats were eased into and out of the river. Here, the shallow water was frozen solid. She stepped onto the ice mantle easily, like stepping onto a ramp, and I followed her lead. The edge crumbled a little, but held our weight. The ice was covered by a layer of granulated frost, a good, rough surface that crunched under our rubber-soled shoes. We walked out as fast as we could, staying ahead of the chorus of sharp, percussive cracking that accompanied our steps.

In the middle of the river, the wind died down mysteriously, and the temperature seemed to rise. I was cold to the core; my thoughts were sluggish. Sensing the slight temperature difference, I greedily imagined more warmth than was really there, and, just like that, my misery eased. I stopped in my tracks, and, with a sense of wonder at where I'd found myself, gazed first at the sweep of night sky, where the lantern moon appeared low enough to swing on, then to the river's far shore, where a hopeful green light was twinkling. Was it possible that we would make it all the way across? Would we really escape?

My feet tingled with the sensation of encroaching wetness. I looked down at a puddle of slush deepening around my shoes—the black river was rising quickly through thick but porous ice. I lurched forward, all my terror returned. Up ahead, Zara was a murky running shadow on the verge of disappearing, her ghostly arms outstretched like wings.

Further on, the ice sheet broke into large moving floes that swayed and dipped precariously under our weight as we jumped heedlessly from one to the other. I hardly knew what I was doing. I had one thought only: to get to the other side.

We were almost there. Now nothing but a stream of quickly moving liquid water, about seven feet across, lay between us and the beach. Zara didn't hesitate: she backed up a few paces and took a running leap, splashed into the river, found her footing, and staggered onto dry land. For the first time since our wild dash began, she turned to wait for me, pant legs dripping, hands on hips, long hair whipping across her face.

I knew better than to think. I made the same gangly leap, plunged into the heart-stopping ice-water. I was beyond shrieking, beyond pain. The water was almost to my waist, the current flowing fast along a rocky bottom. I stepped, teetered, almost fell. Zara waded in, grabbed my hand, and pulled me onto shore.

11

We scrambled up a low rise. We were wet from the waist down in freezing cold, and I assumed we wouldn't survive. I couldn't feel my legs at all, though I must have been moving them, because a dark, looming embankment was coming closer all the time. I huddled momentarily at its base, protected from the wind. I had an urge to stay there, to curl up, conserving whatever warmth my body still retained, but I didn't dare indulge it. I followed Zara up the steep rise—part ice, part mud—crawling on all fours, slipping and regaining ground. We reached the top at roughly the same time, clambered over a guard rail, found ourselves on a deserted two-lane road. Moonlight illuminated the snow-dusted pavement. We crossed over, hid ourselves in a copse of trees where the underbrush sticking out of the snow was sharp and brittle with ice. I set about trying to strip off a low branch with my chafed, numb hands, thinking to make a rough shelter that might trap our combined warmth after we'd stripped off our frozen pants and shoes.

"What the hell are you doing?" Zara hissed.

"We've got to get warm."

"Not that way."

She lurked at the edge of the forest, quietly observing the empty road, seemingly unaffected by cold, panic, or fear—or even the wound in her side. What choice did I have but to follow her lead? I didn't know the territory, there wasn't a soul in a thousand miles who would help me, and the first few words out of my mouth would peg me as a foreigner. Zara's dash across the icy river had been insanely reckless, to be sure, but somehow, we'd made it, and now, thanks to her, we had a chance—if we could make it to warmth.

In due course, a car filled with people whizzed by. The next car had two passengers inside.

"What are we waiting for?" I asked.

"Someone driving by themselves."

"There," I said a few minutes later. A small pick-up truck was barreling down from the north, one head behind the wheel and none on the passenger side. Zara stepped into its path, waving her arms. The driver pulled over, popped open the passenger door, yelled out, "You need a ride?"

"Sure do," she yelled back.

We climbed into the cab. There was no backseat, so we crammed together on the passenger seat. "Boy, are we glad to see you," Zara said, sounding folksy and innocent—an actress playing a part.

He pulled away. "What happened?"

"We skidded on a patch of ice back there. Went right into the river. Just a few feet luckily, so we were able to get out. But we're soaked, need to get warm fast." She rubbed her hands in the stream of hot air coming from the vent. "God, that feels good."

The cab was dim, the Samaritan intent on the road. There was a whiff of alcohol about him, but he didn't seem drunk. It was unclear whether he'd noticed that his passengers were dressed in the same institutional clothes.

"You live around here? I can take you home," he said.

"It's kind of far. We need to get out of these clothes right away."

"Well, I live just up the way. I could take you there."

"Hate to impose on your family."

"No problem. I live alone."

Zara picked up one of my hands and rubbed it briskly between her own. "Don't worry, Petra. We're going to be all right," she said in a nurturing tone. Then, turning to the driver, "I think my friend here is in shock."

Now I didn't have to speak.

The Samaritan's cabin was in the woods, a few hundred feet off the road. There was a light over a side entrance, but the rest of the place was dark. He fumbled a bit with the lock, while Zara and I huddled behind him on the stoop. Once inside, he flicked a switch, revealing a small, homey kitchen with a hand-hewn pine table, cheerful red curtains, a stove with a kettle on top. Iron pans hung from hooks on the wall; a grimy tool box lay open on the counter.

"I'll turn up the heat and get a fire going. I've got sweatpants and T-shirts you can borrow," he said, heading toward a front room.

Zara grabbed a hammer from the tool box, and, following swiftly on his heels, raised it high, and smashed it onto the crown of the man's head. The crack of bone was audible; he collapsed instantly.

"For god's sake, what are you doing?" I screamed, sprinting across the room.

Before I could get there, the hammer slammed down a second time on the back of the man's skull. It rose once more, but this time I was there to grab it. I yanked it out of Zara's grasp, shrieking at her to stop.

She stood back, eyes wild and gleaming, a drop of spittle lodged at the corner of her mouth.

"Wat the fuck! Are you trying to kill him?" I dropped to my knees beside the face-down, inert form. Two bright seams of blood were bubbling through the crew-cut hair. There was something, some sixth sense I had, that told me the man was dead.

My right hand was still curled around the warm wood shaft of the hammer.

My grip loosened, and the hammer tumbled to the floor. I placed two fingers on the side of the man's neck, hoping… But no, he was gone. I rolled back on my heels, my hands fallen helplessly to my sides. "Oh my god."

I looked up in baffled amazement, into Zara's mad, glittering eyes. "You killed him."

Her mouth curved into the hint of a smile.

"And you liked it," I said in horror.

"I had to do it. He would've called the police."

"You didn't know that."

"When he heard about the escape, he would have had no choice."

"We would have thought of something." I stared at her, hard. "You didn't have to kill him."

She wavered, muttered, "I didn't think he'd die."

"Oh, come on. He was down the first time. You hit him twice."

"I'm not going back to prison. Not for anyone."

"So you murdered someone?" I shook my head at the enormous stupidity. "Now you go away for life. We both do."

"Not if we escape."

"That's a big *if*," I said.

A circle of blood was spreading under the sprawled form. I rolled the man over. He had a high-boned face and a small mouth. His open eyes were glassy, unmoving. I closed them with two fingers, one after the other, wondering what his name was, if he'd had children, what kind of work he'd done.

"He's dead," I said again, still not believing it.

"What did you think would happen?" she taunted.

"I don't know. Not this."

"Stupid cunt," she said with a smirk.

Wearily, I said, "If you think this makes me afraid of you, you're wrong. I actually don't give a shit about you right now."

"Be careful what you say. Don't forget that I got you across the river. You need me."

"You need me more. Not just because I got you out of prison, and out of the hospital. But because you're fucking crazy, Zara. Full-blown insane. You take stupid risks, and you like killing people. You could so easily fuck this up."

She stiffened; a haunted look entered her eyes. She knew I was telling the truth. A few silent seconds passed, during which I didn't take my eyes off her haggard face. Not until she looked away.

"We make a good team, Natushka. You and me," she muttered.

She stepped gingerly over the body, knelt before the fireplace, and started piling logs on the grate. Like a good Girl Scout, she arranged them carefully for maximum draw. She had grown preternaturally calm, as if the killing had already drifted into a murky past. I recalled the rumor: two brutal murders behind the walls attributed to Zara Chernovskaya. How many more had happened outside them? How many were yet to come?

She could easily kill me, too, I realized.

Stiff-limbed and shivering, we took off our wet, icy clothes and wrapped ourselves in blankets from the bed. Sitting as close to the fireplace as we could get, we silently watched the new flames lick the bottoms of the logs, cleave to them, begin to rise up their sides, and finally cover them like a shroud. The room filled with the crackling of dry bark and pops of boiling sap. Soon, our cheeks and hands were burning with heat, and when the Samaritan's pooling blood came too close, we staunched its flow with towels from the bathroom.

After a while, we dressed in the Samaritan's clothes, padding the toes of his huge boots with socks and rolling up the bottoms of his jeans. We dragged the body into the bathroom and closed the door. Wiped the floor and tossed the bloody towels in the bathroom, too. I rolled our water-logged prison uniforms into a ball and stuffed them in a garbage bag to take with us in the pick-up and eventually throw away. No point in leaving calling cards.

We worked together smoothly, wordlessly, with an uncanny mutual understanding of all that had to be done. Zara piled whatever might be useful by the door: the toolbox, a hunting rifle, a box of bullets, a kerosene lamp. I emptied the refrigerator and cupboards of anything edible that would keep. I yanked out a succession of drawers until I found a wad of rubles stuffed in the back of one. In the pocket of the Samaritan's parka, my fingers curled around a cell phone. I took it out, carefully studied the scratches on the screen and its worn rubber case. Evidence of *him*, his individual life. Not long from now, it would start ringing. Friends and family—a girlfriend maybe? a son or daughter?—would start calling, wondering where he was. Why hadn't he shown up at work, or called his brother, or picked up his kid? First, the callers might be angry, then concerned, then...

I dumped the cell phone back into the parka's commodious pocket as if to give it refuge from the coming ordeal. I wanted to say I was sorry—it had happened so fast I couldn't stop it—but who would give a shit about my meager excuse?

It was after two a.m. by the time we were ready. We took hats and gloves, shut off the lights. On her way out the door, Zara swiped a bottle of vodka off the counter. I grabbed the keys.

"Give them to me," she said imperiously, holding out a hand.

"Forget it. I'm driving. From now on, we're doing things my way."

Snowflakes fell softly in the blackness. It was not as cold outside as it had seemed before. I backed the Samaritan's Toyota pick-up to the end of the driveway, stopping when I got to the road. "Which way?"

"Any way," Zara said with a shrug.

"Come on. You're from this town. You must have friends."

"That's the first place they'll look. I have to get out of Krasnoyarsk, and stay away, maybe for a long time."

"Okay, but where?"

Zara's mouth puckered. "Irkutsk? We can get on the Trans-Siberian Railroad there or go over the border into Mongolia."

"How far away is that?"

"Fifteen hours."

"That's too far."

She gave a snorting laugh. "Where do you think you are? Ohio?" She named the state with odd glee, as if proud of remembering her grade-school US geography, then screwed the top off the vodka bottle and held it to her lips. Before she took a swig, she said, "Go left, west. Hurry. We've got to get out of here."

The road curved lazily with the river. Flurries waltzed in the headlights, as the wipers waved laconically across the windshield. We pulled over at a steep embankment, and Zara went right to the edge in the darkness, hugging the trash bag stuffed with our uniforms to her chest. She heaved the bag into the current, and the blackness over the river was so thick I didn't even see it fall.

The road was taking us closer to the lights of the city. I said, "There'll be checkpoints, so we should stick to the back roads. They'll be looking for two people, so if you see headlights, duck out of sight."

"Yes, ma'am," Zara said with a hint of sarcasm. She tipped up the bottle again and started guzzling.

"And put that thing away. I need you sober."

She wiped her mouth roughly with the back of her hand, seemed on the verge of making some retort. But she screwed the top on the bottle, and tossed it onto the pile of blankets in the back. The tires slipped on a patch of hard ice under the dusting of snow, and I steered into the skid to keep us from sliding off the road.

The Samaritan's odor of pine wood and sweat filled the cab, and the heater finally started spewing enough hot air that I could take off his large leather gloves.

We skirted Krasnoyarsk without incident and drove for hours on narrow forested roads, occasionally speeding through tiny sleeping villages, where the headlights swept over shabby, unpainted houses with dilapidated barns out back and muddy yards for chickens and cows. Close to six o'clock, we came upon a large, gently curved snow mound on the side of the road. It was a car, I realized, craning my neck as we went by. Covered in a thin snow blanket, its front end tipped into a shallow ditch. I stopped and drove in reverse until the abandoned car was in front of us, illuminated by the Toyota's headlights. Zara hopped out, lifted the tool box out of the back, wiped the snow off the car's rear license plate, and started to unscrew it. I grabbed a screwdriver and started removing the Toyota's plates. Ten minutes later, the abandoned car's plates were on the Toyota, and the Toyota's plates were buried about a hundred feet in the woods under a layer of snow that would only get deeper as the weeks went by.

"Come on, hurry up," I said, glancing up and down the deserted road.

Ignoring me, Zara strolled back to the abandoned car. She had the hammer in her hand—unwashed, glinting red in the headlights from the Samaritan's blood. Just the sight of it was enough to set my blood racing. Before I could ask what the hell she was doing, she tried the door and, finding it locked, used the hammer to shatter the passenger side window. Then, reaching through the broken glass, she popped open the door, slid inside, and started rifling through the glove compartment.

"Fuck," I muttered. We'd been there much too long; a car was bound to come along at any moment. Still, I was hoping she'd find something—money, a license. I got into the Toyota and cranked the engine so we could make a quick getaway.

A minute later, she climbed inside the cab. "Nothing," she said in disgust.

Just after seven o'clock, we rolled into a small town. Not a town, really, more like a handful of buildings. Grocery, laundromat, post office—all deserted. A sign on the door of the Sibneft station indicated it wouldn't open for another hour. The Toyota was very low on gas, and there might not be another town for hundreds of miles. I didn't want to chance it, so we parked behind the station, turned off the engine and lights, and waited. Zara hauled a bag of food from the storage area behind the seats. We smeared raspberry jam on crackers, passed a carton of cold milk back and forth. Zara cracked a raw egg and tipped it down her throat. I hesitated, then followed suit. We finished up with a tin of pickled herring and a couple of radishes.

"Where the hell are we?" she said.

"I thought you knew."

She fished a map out of the glove compartment and studied it. "I'd say we're around here," she said, pointing to a blank spot southeast of Krasnoyarsk and west of the Lena River. The only thing nearby was the highway to Irkutsk. To the north there was a huge expanse of nothing, a wilderness the size of Canada, stuck in the middle by the pinprick of Yakutsk.

"How far to Yakutsk?" I asked. The idea of heading to my grandmother's village on the Tatta River crossed my mind; Misha had told me how to get there, and my relatives, I trusted, would take me in. But if they refused, what then? I'd be stranded in the middle of nowhere. And if they did give me shelter, what would I do there, other than hide? Besides, I doubted Zara would agree to that plan, so I'd have to get rid of her first, and I didn't want to do that. I needed her to speak for me in un-accented Russian, at least until we got to a place where Westerners were less conspicuous.

I'd been thinking as we drove, and I'd concluded that my best bet was, again, the American Consulate, where I could throw myself on the mercy of my countrymen, and trust that the CIA would care enough about me—their captured fugitive spy—to smuggle me out of Russia. Vladivostok wasn't the closest city, but it was a better choice than Novosibirsk, as it was smack at the end of the Trans-Siberian Railroad, where Zara and I were presently headed in the only mode of relatively safe transportation currently available. If Zara decided she'd rather go with Plan B and hop the border into Mongolia, I was open to that idea, too. Anything, as long as I got out of Russia fast.

"Four thousand kilometers to Yakutsk, roughly. About a fifty-hour drive," she said, folding the map and putting it away.

That was too far anyway, which happily justified the decision I'd already made.

"Getting cold in here," Zara prompted.

I turned on the engine, and soon the fan was blowing hot dry air into our faces. I leaned my head against the head rest. The pickled herring was not sitting well, or maybe it was the raw egg. My stomach heaved, and I swallowed down the acid. The ghostly thin-lipped face of the dead Samaritan—eyes wide open in either the shock of being murdered or the shock of death itself—floated on the other side of the windshield. I blinked away the image, but another one quickly appeared—my hand wrapped around a small scalpel, a thin seam of red bubbling on a smooth white neck.

A brutal loneliness washed over me, as vast as Siberia itself, a feeling that I was nothing and nowhere, that I'd somehow ceased to exist. Like a drowning person, I tried to propel myself back to the surface of sanity, back to whatever I used to know that might still make sense. I tried to mentally retrace the events that had gotten me to where I was, but the pieces dangled, unconnected. The steps that had taken me from my bright, busy office in Washington, D.C. to this dark, vacant lot were numerous and bizarre. I couldn't possibly recall them or link them logically. So many small and large decisions. What should I have done differently, if not everything? Where had I made my mistakes? And how would I ever crawl out of this below-zero place?

"You okay?" Zara's feet, swimming in the Samaritan's wool socks, were propped on the dashboard, and the vodka bottle was pressed between her skinny thighs.

"Why would I be okay? Are you?"

A crooked, bashful smile played across her lips. "Yeah. I'm fine."

"A man is lying dead back there."

Zara said calmly, "Isn't this what you wanted? To be free?"

I pondered the question. *Is this what I wanted?* As if watching a grainy time-lapse film, I saw murky images of a woman, Dr. Natalie March, getting old in Female Prison 22, the years ticking by slowly, her hair turning gray and her skin falling into wrinkles, as she mopped floors and changed bedpans and learned to sleep like the dead. Before my eyes, she grew ever more sallow and stooped, until her steps were mere shuffles, and her eyes didn't leave the floor. Someone had needed to care about that woman, to try to save her from a fate as bad or worse than death. If not me, then who? So if everything had to happen the same way, if the Samaritan had to die to free my future self, would I do it again? It shocked me to realize that I would.

"Did you always want to be a doctor?" Zara asked quietly.

"Always. Ever since I can remember."

"Why?"

I grimaced in the dark. "I've forgotten."

"You wanted to help people. That's what most people say."

"Yeah. I suppose that was it." The Samaritan's head bumped softly against the windshield like a beach ball hitting the side of a pool. The eyelids I'd pressed closed flickered up and down. There was nothing behind them but dark water flowing fast.

"You have it good, you know," she mused. "You put on your white coat and your stethoscope, and you get respect. I bet you believe what you see in people's eyes, don't you?"

"Not always," I muttered.

"Me? I have to fight for respect, always have, since I was a kid. People always told me what was wrong with me. Total strangers, who didn't know me from crap. Yet they all agreed how fucked up I was. I've been hearing what a piece of shit I am all my life." She paused, put her hand out to touch my sleeve briefly. "Don't be scared, Natushka. You're going to get out of this one way or another. You'll go back to having money, being somebody, living in a nice place. You'll see. You're not like me."

There was nothing I could say to that, so I asked, "What did you want to be when you were a kid?"

"A photographer. I used to take pictures for my friends—weddings, graduations, babies. Happy times. I could have done it, I think. I was pretty good."

"Why didn't you?"

She shook her head in bewilderment. "I honestly don't know."

"When this is over, Zara, things will be better for you. Just stay off the drugs."

She gave a sarcastic laugh. "You make it sound so easy. But you don't know what it's like. I've got a mental problem, Natushka. My head doesn't work like other people's. I think I'm god sometimes; no one can hurt me. I play chicken with trains. Then the next day I want to kill myself. I think about hanging, how my body will swing on the rope. By the way, if I ever do it, that will be how." She turned her tawny eyes to me. There was nothing but calm acceptance in them, resignation to a fate. "I need the drugs. That's how I survive."

"No. You need to see a psychiatrist. You're probably bipolar. It's nothing to be ashamed of—a lot of people are. There are very good meds these days for people like you."

"In Russia? Good meds in Russia for people like me?" She gave a bitter laugh. "I can just see it: I walk into a hospital. Say, 'Oh, excuse me, I'm crazy. May I have some good meds, please? Like they have in the United States?'"

"You have to try, Zara. There are doctors out there who will help you, I'm sure of it. Maybe in some little town. If you really try, you can figure it out."

She rolled her eyes. "You're as crazy as me."

Maybe she was right. I put my hand out for the bottle, and she handed it to me. I felt like getting drunk, but that wasn't going to happen: the bottle was too light. I guzzled the last of it and said, "If I could claw my way through the fucking planet to get out of here right now, I would."

I felt her smile in the darkness. "My, my. So dramatic."

"What? Aren't you scared, Zara? Just a little?"

"Mmm. No, not me. I don't get scared."

"Bullshit. Everyone does."

"Oh, maybe once in a while. But it doesn't bother me too much because I know I'm going to die soon. Maybe today, maybe tomorrow, maybe in five or ten years. Death is not far off for me. I don't fight it, so I don't worry. Simple." She turned to me with a sad half-smile. "Take my advice and don't worry, Natushka. Every life ends the same way."

"If you get to Mongolia, if you get away—you have a good chance, you know. You could make a better life."

She punched my shoulder playfully. "What are you up to now? Trying to curse me with hope? Don't you know I'm Zara Chernovskaya? I don't need hope or dreams. I don't need anything. If I'm still alive ten years from now, I'll mail you a postcard. It will say, *Dear Dr. Natushka, It's me. The same fucked-up Zara with the same shitty life. Thank you for believing in me anyway.*"

.· .· .· .· .· .· .· .·

We gassed up when the station opened, and continued our journey east. The sun rose, burning off the haze. Signage appeared, indicating that P-258 to Irkutsk was ahead.

"You ready for civilization?" I said.

We merged onto the highway, stayed within the posted speed limit. The traffic was light. In a few miles, Zara said, "There's a truck stop coming up. Pull in; we need more money."

I took the exit, parked at the rear of the lot, facing outward. A couple of big rigs came and went, the drivers getting out to stretch their legs and piss into low, dirty snowbanks. They glanced at the Toyota pick-up with two women inside, but climbed back inside their cabs. Finally, the driver of a cement mixer saw us parked there and headed over, zipping up his fly. He had a bristle of short white hair, and a pink, small-featured face.

I rolled down my window.

"What are you girls doing here?" he said in a tone both sour and amiable.

Zara leaned over. "Looking for work."

"Oh, yeah. Just one of you, or the both at once?"

"Whatever you like."

"How 'bout…" His glance slid from me to Zara and back. "How 'bout you?"

I shook my head. "Sick, very sick. Venereal disease."

"Fuck you," Zara whispered.

Looking confused, the driver said to Zara, "Okay. So…so how 'bout you?"

"You got enough? I'm not cheap."

He looked her over. "You're nothing to write home about."

"Just for that, you're gonna have to pay more."

"Come on. Didn't mean nothing by it."

She followed him to his truck, which was parked about fifty feet away. I could see his head in the cab, but not hers. I averted my eyes, settled in to wait.

It didn't take long. A few minutes later, Zara pulled open the passenger door and hopped into the pick-up. "Hurry up. Drive!"

I shifted into gear, accelerated, merged onto the highway. She peered through the back windshield until the truck stop was out of sight. "Good," she said, flopping back around.

"What happened back there?"

"You don't want to know."

"You didn't do anything, did you?"

"I didn't suck him off, if that's what you mean."

"No, I mean…you didn't hurt him, did you?"

"No more than he deserved."

"Jesus. What'd you do?"

"Don't act so surprised."

"I'm not. Just…just tell me what you did."

"I got us a whole load of cash, that's what."

"But what'd you do to *him*?"

"Don't worry. He'll be fine." She thumbed a colorful stack of rubles under my nose, and I shut my mouth.

The idea of boarding the Trans-Siberian Railroad wasn't sitting well with me. Word of our escape would be all over the place by now, and train authorities were likely to be on alert. Zara might be able to slip by, but for me, with my American accent and no passport, it was a bad idea.

Attempting to sneak into Mongolia didn't seem like such a good idea either, on second thought. There would be a checkpoint at the border crossing, and, even if we got through, what would we do in Mongolia with winter setting in, other than encounter a whole new set of problems while trying like hell to get out of there to someplace that was bound to be just as sketchy?

The more I thought about it, the clearer it seemed that driving to Vladivostok was still the best plan for me. Travel by car felt relatively safe now that the Toyota had different plates and we had a wad of cash for gas and food. And one thing I was willing to trust about the roughly 2,500 miles of sparse, untraveled roads between here and that far-eastern city was that they were probably not rife with local cops lying in wait to issue speeding tickets or to pull over Toyota pick-ups matching a certain description. There was always the chance, much too slim to be relied upon but an active hope of mine nonetheless, that neither the Samaritan's body nor the stolen truck had been discovered yet. I pictured myself walking into the American Consulate in Vladivostok—in my imagination, it was warm and plushly carpeted, with an urn of fresh coffee and a silver tray of cookies set out for visitors—and being greeted by friendly Americans who gave me food, sympathy, nice clothes, and a place to rest before I was spirited off, secretly, to a small plane bound for the US.

I told Zara what I was thinking, and she admitted it made sense, but she was still bent on Mongolia. She thought she could make it from there to Turkey, where she had friends. So it was time for us to split up. We ought to do that anyway, she said, as we would each have a better chance alone.

"We can split the cash, but who gets the car?" I asked.

She didn't answer right away, and the silence took on an ominous quality. I had the same thought I'd had in the park. What was to stop her from getting rid of me? Maybe a hammer blow to the head, or a push out the door in a remote area. Then she'd have the car and all the money, and could probably get herself across the border in a day.

"Zara. You have to talk to me. We can work this out."

A few more moments passed before she said, "You take it, Natushka. I can get through without it. But you, you stick out like…I don't know…like an iceberg in the desert."

"You sure?" I asked in concern. *Oh, just shut up and take the fucking car,* another part of me was saying.

She cocked a plucked eyebrow at me. "Surprised?"

"I don't know. I guess I thought you…" I faltered.

"You thought the evil side of Zara would fly out of her cave to kill you, too."

"Well, yeah. It crossed my mind."

"If I wanted to do that, it would have happened a long time ago, Natushka. At the river, maybe. I could have left you there."

"Why didn't you?"

"Because you went after Svetlana like a baby tiger. Claws out—*grrrrr*." She curled her fingers at me, enjoying the tease. "And you got me out of that shithole, where those stinking bitches would have killed me eventually. Now they won't have that satisfaction, and I have the satisfaction of remaining the great Zara Chernovskaya who escaped from prison. My legend is even bigger now." She paused with a satisfied smile, then went on more thoughtfully. "If you are ever in trouble, Natushka, you come straight back to Russia and talk to me, okay? If you can find me. Or maybe I should visit you in Washington, D.C., huh? I'd like to see the tomb of Abraham Lincoln. Did you know he was a famous khomus player?"

"Funny. My mother told me that."

"Your mother is a very wise woman whom I would like to meet. But tell me, seriously, if Zara Chernovskaya showed up at your fancy house in Washington, D.C. one day, would you take her to see the tomb of your greatest president?" She cocked an eyebrow at me in a challenging way.

"I would. Definitely. We'd go there and a lot of other places, too. And we'd eat and drink like queens."

A glorious smile spread across her face. "Yes, that is just what we'll do, Natushka. We'll visit the Lincoln tomb, the zoo, the Congress, and at the end of the day, we'll sit in a bubbling hot tub sipping the very best champagne. With Russian caviar and Cuban cigars." Her tawny eyes sparkled at me wickedly in the pick-up's gloomy interior. "Do you believe it?"

"I do," I said, not really lying.

"Good. You must always believe that, my friend, even on the very last day of your life."

⠂⠄ ⠂ ⠄ ⠂ ⠄ ⠂ ⠄

We split the cash, and I dropped her off at the next rest stop. Our conversation was brief, as she seemed eager to be gone. I figured her mind was already working on the challenges ahead, as mine was. But before she strolled off toward the line of parked trucks, she tossed this at me: "See you in Washington."

"I'll be waiting," I said, playing along.

As I watched her walk away, I had to remind myself several times that she could take care of herself.

I got out the map and unfolded it. Irkutsk, not far ahead, was the only major metropolitan area on the way to Vladivostok. After that, it was open road. If I stopped only for gas and food and a few hours' sleep when I needed it, I'd be smelling the salt breeze off the Pacific Ocean in two and a half days.

Traffic thickened as I approached the Irkutsk city limits. I ought to cut over onto back roads, but I didn't need to do it yet. Right now, it was good to hear the tires humming over smooth highway pavement as the Toyota ate up the miles.

An exit ramp appeared and disappeared. There would be another one soon. I switched on the radio and played with the dial until a local news show came through clearly. I listened for a while, hearing nothing about escaped prisoners. Maybe what happened in Krasnoyarsk wasn't news in Irkutsk. It might be okay to stay on the highway that went straight through the city after all—a faster route—instead of taking the back roads.

Another exit ramp went by. Then, just like that, the traffic slowed to a crawl. Up ahead, flashing lights; a blockade had been erected, narrowing the highway to one lane. Police officers were stopping cars, asking for licenses, opening trunks, waving drivers through one-by-one. My heart thudded and nearly stopped. Already, three or four cars were queued behind me; there was no way out. The line of vehicles inched forward. Not far ahead, a huge rig was stopped on the shoulder. I swerved out of the lane and pulled behind it, letting the other cars pass. The Toyota was now hidden from view, at least until the truck resumed its journey. My palms were damp on the steering wheel, and I could barely breathe. I was ready to bolt out the passenger door, dash across an apron of field into the woods, but I would certainly be seen, and even if I wasn't, the Toyota would eventually be searched or towed; it would become clear soon enough that the Krasnoyarsk escapee was in the vicinity on foot. Searchers would go out. How long could I expect to last?

At that moment, I would have given anything to have been trekking across Mongolia with Zara, or to have taken the exit I'd just passed. I glanced back. I could still see it there, the sign outlined against a leaden sky. It wasn't too far.

I jammed the transmission into reverse. The pick-up bobbled along on the uneven pavement of the break-down lane, accelerating as it went. I didn't look back, didn't glance to the side, just kept the tail end pointed at the back of the sign. Once there, I had to swing out into the lane to get the truck headed in the right direction. An oncoming car swerved around me, blaring its horn. Then I was off, speeding down the ramp, taking the turn at the end—away from Irkutsk—headed god knew where, with no intention of slowing down.

Slow down, I whispered to myself, *slow down*. My foot eased off the accelerator. There was no one in the rearview mirror, hadn't been for a while. Gradually, my heartbeat slowed. I passed through a tidy suburb: the homes had pretty carved gingerbread shutters and window boxes stuffed with sprays of evergreen and holly. There was some traffic, a police station with a cruiser parked outside. I kept my eyes facing forward like a model citizen, until the village disappeared behind me, and rolling pastureland opened up. Low hills rose under the steady grip of the tires, and gently fell away.

Travelling east on back roads, I eventually came out somewhere past Irkutsk, and zigzagged my way to P-258, which ran along the southern shore of Lake Baikal. The lake was huge, oceanic, a bewitching dark blue color, with steep snowy slopes and towering fissured crags. Its vast surface unbroken by boats, its coast with no trace of human activity, it maintained a primordial majesty. I drove white-knuckled through the afternoon, while the sun melted ever closer to the horizon, growing wider, redder, and duller all the time. Eventually, I came to a decent-sized town with a gas station. I filled the tank, purchased three plastic gas containers, filled them, and stashed them in the back of the pick-up. The clerk eyed me with interest but didn't ask questions; I handed him bills and accepted my change without uttering a word.

Back in the cab, I had to count my remaining cash several times. My brain was foggy, overstressed, and the sky-high numbers on the dirty rubles in my hand made no sense to me anymore. With effort, I came to understand that I was in command of the following assets: one full tank of gas, three containers that may or may not equal a tank, money enough for one more tank and, possibly, a meal. Blankets, sundry food items. An enormous, empty landmass to traverse, and an unknown amount of time until the first blizzard made the roads impassable.

The police blockade outside Irkutsk had spooked me, and now Vladivostok no longer seemed safe. A national manhunt was probably underway; how could I have imagined otherwise? And what fond insanity had made me think that the American Consulate would provide sanctuary anyway? I was an escaped convict, accessory to a murder, in addition to being an accused spy. No doubt international law required that I remain in Russia to stand trial. Why would the consulate endanger its relations with its host country by flouting that rule? And if the CIA had washed its hands of me once, why wouldn't it do so again?

I checked the Samaritan's map. Misha's directions to Cherkeh came back to me—four or five hours southeast of Yakutsk, east of the Lena River. At this point, Yakutsk was 1,200 kilometers up the Lena Highway, but I wouldn't have to go that far. There was a place I could stop along the way, a town called Aldan, about six hours south of Yakutsk. It was possible that someone there could direct me to the unmapped village on the Tatta River where my grandmother lived, where my aunt was in hiding, and where I might find refuge for a while.

I continued east. The headlights switched on automatically in response to the creeping dusk. At a tiny town called Never, the road intersected the Lena

Highway. I turned north, drove through miles and miles of vacant, snow-dusted fields, low mountains hulking in the distance. Then the taiga took over, butting right up to the gravel shoulder, as if unwilling to cede even a few extra yards to the asphalt cut across its face.

The radio signal jittered and periodically failed. I switched off the static, and in the deep silence that ensued, felt my terror churning like a monster just under the level of consciousness. I mustn't give in to it, mustn't let it out of its cage. I turned the radio back on, and played with the dial until a few bars of a Michael Jackson tune were recognizable. *Thriller*. In spite of everything, I smiled. I started to sing along. I sang as loud as I could, doing my best to carry the familiar melody through the periods of hopeless static. It seemed important to do this.

Eventually, the radio was completely useless, and a pitch black night set in. There was nothing but the steady strum of the revolving tires and the pavement disappearing hypnotically under the headlights. The next thing I knew, I was jolted awake by the sensation of tires jouncing across loose gravel. I jammed on the brakes right before the Toyota slammed into a tree.

Shaken, I climbed down from the cab and stood trembling on firm ground in the frigid air. As if to fool myself into thinking that I hadn't really fallen asleep at the wheel, but had been meaning to stop all along, I moved into the forest beyond the glow of the headlights and peed. Survival seemed to have become a matter of playing these little tricks on myself. I then emptied two of the plastic containers into the tank, holding the third in reserve. During this short time, the cold invaded my clothing efficiently: its dainty fingers crawled up my sleeves and curled softly, insistently, down my neck. I was shivering mightily as I steered the pick-up off the shoulder and onto the ribbon of dark highway that was guiding me ever deeper into the wilderness.

Sunrise was tentative and teasing, a gradual offering of lavender and pink before the spill of yellow. The highway was ghosting a frozen estuary. It was a lovely landscape—snow patches dotting the black ice, answering the morning rays with friendly sparkles. On a hill overlooking the river, tall red letters spelling out the word *pectopah*—restaurant—stretched across the roof of a low building. Trucks and vans were parked in the lot, and well-built wooden outhouses were available in the back.

Inside, there was warmth, bright light, and pleasant human noise, as well as the gorgeous aromas of meat pies and baking. I piled dishes covered in plastic wrap onto my tray one after the other. This was the kind of glorious feast I used to dream about in prison, food the likes of which I hadn't seen in months. I had to put most of the plates back when I remembered the skimpy roll of rubles in my pocket. Still, I reached the register with fruit cup, shepherd's pie, and hot coffee on my tray. The hands that paid for the meal were dirty and trembling. They didn't look at all like mine.

I joined a young woman, elderly gentleman, and little girl at one of the long tables. The little girl had a pink barrette fastened in her silky hair. She was sucking tapioca pensively off a spoon, her narrow eyes trained unflinchingly on the mystery of a lone white woman in an oversized flannel shirt.

"Anna," her mother whispered, reproaching her daughter for the impolite stare.

"I don't mind," I said, taking comfort in the sight of a child, and in the safe world her presence connoted.

The woman bashfully averted her eyes; Anna kept staring.

"I'm new to this area," I said unnecessarily. "I was just wondering…maybe you could help me. I'm looking for a village that ought to be…well, somewhere around here. It's called Cherkeh. Have you heard of it?"

The woman looked doubtful, turned to the leathery old man. They conferred briefly in Sakha. The old man shook his head.

"We've never heard of it," the woman said.

"Are you sure?" I pleaded, as if urgency could make her remember.

The woman spoke to her father again, and this time the conversation went on for quite some time. Finally, she turned back to me. "Yes, I'm sure."

I thanked her and returned to my meal. Tendrils of panic fanned out from my gut to every part of my body. What if I couldn't find Cherkeh? What then?

Well, in that case, a sensible voice in my head piped up, you'll simply think of something else—a Plan B, or C, or whatever the fuck letter of the alphabet you're on. If you've come this far, you can go the distance. So stop belly-aching and eat your shepherd's pie.

But my heart didn't believe it. The moment when my luck was due to run out felt long overdue.

I finished the meal, bussed my dishes to the tray station, and went outside. The sky was bright blue like a child's painting. People were ice-fishing on the estuary, the children tumbling about in colorful hats and mittens, chased by lively dogs. It was ten degrees below zero, and no one seemed to care.

Towards evening, I reached Aldan, a gold-mining town, population about twenty thousand, according to a friendly cashier who instantly pegged me as a visitor and took the last of my money for half a tank of gas. She presided over a treasure trove of things I could no longer afford: candy, gum, soda, cigarettes. I was surprised to see an indoor restroom, and asked to use it.

In prison, I hadn't dared look in the handheld mirrors that some of the inmates had, and the washrooms weren't outfitted with such decadent items. So when I noticed a mirror over the sink, a flicker of fear rose in me. I sidled into my own view by degrees. A wild woman glared back at me warily from the glass—her gaunt face was limed with dirt; her hair hung in greasy, matted clumps; her lips were pale and cracked. I searched for signs of myself, Dr. Natalie March, in my reflection's eyes. But the being looking back was more like an animal.

I washed my face, rinsed my mouth, removed the Samaritan's clothes, and splashed my emaciated limbs with water. A layer of dirt trickled away. My legs were bruised, and stubborn dirt was caked between my toes. My body, like my face, was largely unrecognizable. I'd lost twenty pounds at least.

I did what I could with my hair, pulling it back and knotting it at the nape of my neck. But I had nothing to pin it with, so it fell out as soon as I took my hands away.

It was hopeless. I felt that I'd never again be clean, presentable.

Once more, I pulled on the dead man's clothes, which were still infused with his masculine smell. *I'm so sorry*, I whispered to him and the woman in the mirror, as if they were one and the same.

When I came out of the restroom, the attendant asked nervously, "Are you okay?"

"Fine," I said, straining to find a smile. I went to the counter and spread out my map. "I'm looking for a village called Cherkeh. It's supposed to be around here." I swept two fingers across an admittedly large, perfectly blank region to the east of Aldan and slightly north.

"What's it called again?" she asked.

I repeated the name, and in my broken, weary mind I saw her mouth curling into a sneer and heard her saying acidly: What, are you crazy? There's no village by that name; there never was. That was just a story they told you to make you do what they wanted, and like a fool you believed it, because you wanted an end to your pain and guilt, to all that had gone wrong, and your stupid faith in their lie took you straight to hell, and now you're just another empty soul stumbling about in the wilderness.

But she didn't say that. She gave me directions. Told me to hurry, as snow was in the forecast.

I folded the map quickly, pressed it to my chest. "Have a nice day!" I said, because she seemed like a nice person, and I wanted her to think of me as a nice person, too.

. : . . . . : . .

At some point the next day, I pulled off the road and tried to sleep for a few hours bundled in blankets. But it was too cold. I had to turn the engine on to warm the cabin every fifteen minutes or so. Eventually, I gave up, steered the car back on to the pavement, and drove through another pitch black night. Flurries of snow swirled occasionally in the headlights, and were swept away by a bitter wind. At about two a.m., the highway turned to dirt, and the ride got bumpy. I didn't mind, because the jolting kept me awake. I worried about hitting a deer, but, on the cusp of dawn, it was a wolf that obstructed my way. A magnificent pale gold creature with glimmering dark eyes pricked by red. Its ears twitched with what might have been a question, or nerves—it had, after all, been caught dead-on by two rapidly approaching beams of light. But it didn't give way, didn't yield to the invader. I had to stop the truck and wait patiently until it had made its dominance clear, until it moved out of the spotlight willingly, lanky haunches rolling with slick grace.

In mid-morning, a hand-painted sign announced the village of Cherkeh. I couldn't quite believe I'd arrived, and soon started to wonder whether the entire place consisted of a sign and nothing more, because for a few miles all I could see out the window was a flat, snow-covered plain melting by degrees under a harshly burning white sun. Finally, some dilapidated wood-frame houses came into view. Smoke curled from chimney pipes; silver satellite dishes refracted the sun's brilliant rays. A little bandy-legged man trundled along the side of the road.

I pulled over and rolled down the window. "I'm looking for Katarina Melnikova. Do you know her?"

He seemed embarrassed, shook his head.

"Lena Tarasova?"

He pointed. "Brown house. Not far." His skin was like grainy brown leather, and he was missing his front teeth.

Further on, a billboard warned about the dangers of alcohol; the next presented a huge color-intensified photograph of a smoker's diseased lung. Unambiguous messages from the Department of Public Health.

The town hub consisted of three buildings: a meeting hall, general store, and Sibneft station. A couple of beat-up cars and an old tractor were parked outside the store. No one was in sight. A little further along, I came to a brown house with a green painted door, bigger and in better shape than most of the others I'd passed. Beside it, set well back from the road, there was a large barn, unpainted but in fairly good condition, with a snow-spattered, fenced-in yard of frozen mud.

I was seized with nerves as I parked on the snow-packed street. What if it was the wrong house? What if it was the right one, and Lena didn't want to take me in?

I sat in the car, nearly paralyzed with dread, trying to make out if anyone was home. There was no car in the deeply rutted driveway, but a tendril of smoke was curling above the roofline from a chimney at the rear of the house. The house itself was one-story, with small windows flanking the front door, each framed by the fanciful carved shutters endemic to the region, and underlined by window boxes filled with snow-dusted sprays of pine and spruce. In the front yard, there was a sloping earthen mound the height of a short man, a wooden door set into its face. It probably went to an underground vault cut into the permafrost where food could be kept frozen all year round. The entire lot was enclosed by low, unpainted, nearly rotted post fence.

A movement in one of the front windows caught my eye. Someone had let a lace curtain fall back across the glass. It was time for me to go and introduce myself.

The wooden gate wobbled, didn't open all the way, so I sidled through it and made my way up the shoveled path, feeling horribly conspicuous. At the front door, I hesitated, letting the frigid air sting my cheeks, until I found the courage to knock.

12

The door was opened almost immediately by Lena Tarasova. I easily recognized her short, blunt haircut and heavy, black-rimmed eyeglasses. In tasteful, well-made clothing, with an erect posture that made her seem taller than she really was, she had the polish of an executive secretary. Pleasant yet cool; friendly yet distant. She kept half her body hidden behind the door, as if prepared to shut it at a moment's notice.

"May I help you?" she asked.

"Hello, Lena. I'm…" choking on the intimate words *your niece,* I settled on, "…from America."

Her eyes flicked behind me to take in the Toyota parked on the street.

"Come in, Natalie," she said calmly.

She ushered me in to a quaint living room, indicating pegs where I could hang my coat and a space beside the door where I could leave my boots.

"Misha said you might come. But that was months ago." She took the Samaritan's monstrous parka from my hand as I kicked off his obviously oversized boots. There was a watery pink stain at the toe of one of his baggy socks that was either his blood or mine from a blister. Lena glanced at the boots and socks doubtfully.

"Where have you been?" she asked.

I was speechless. Lena's house was so warm and cozy, and she herself seemed so reliably normal, that for a moment I wondered whether my experiences were real and true, or just a long nightmare I was finally waking from.

She seemed to sense my distress and bustled off, leaving me to follow. "Come to the kitchen, and I'll make some tea. Have you had a long trip?"

"Yes, very long," I was able to say. A million agonies long. Longer than I'd ever dreamed.

The kitchen was at the back of the house. A row of square windows overlooked the side of the barn and a flat snow field running toward a hazy white horizon. Radiating heat from a corner of the room was a wood-burning stove of dun-colored clay, the irregularity of its conical shape attesting to the fact that it had been made by human hands. A blend of residual aromas hung in the air—fried eggs, maybe, and cream.

"We were worried about you," Lena said with a hint of admonishment as she filled the kettle.

"We?"

"Misha and I. He said you were planning to come here after you left the herders' camp. When you didn't show up, we assumed you'd gone back to the States."

"I didn't go back," I said, remembering the moment in the airport when I'd made that choice.

"Where were you?"

"I was arrested."

"Arrested?" She turned to me with a frown. "For what?"

"The murders of Bohdan Duboff and Tanya Karp, and acts of espionage against the Russian Federation."

Her eyes widened in shock, then just as quickly contracted in fear. "Did you say anything?"

She was asking if I'd given them up—her and Misha and Meredith and Oleg. "Not a word."

"You're sure?"

"Positive."

"And you've been…?"

"In prison."

She shut off the tap without saying anything. She seemed to be thinking.

"I escaped," I added.

Silently, she lit a burner on the stove and put on the kettle. I saw her struggling with the news, perhaps not sure what or how much to believe. She motioned to the table. "Sit down. Tell me everything."

I wondered if I should trust her—everyone I met seemed capable of duplicity to me now—but distrust was too arduous for me at that moment. I had no energy left, and no place else to go. So I recounted everything that had happened since my arrest in the Yakutsk airport, including the murdered Samaritan and the hot car presently parked outside her house. She questioned me with great specificity, circling back to clarify points, and, with subtle skill, worming out of me information about the Russian authorities I didn't even know I had. It was an unofficial debriefing carried out by a pro. It lasted a couple of hours, through several cups of strong black tea. In the end, she was clearly satisfied, and went off to make some phone calls in another room, leaving me with a bowl of warmed-up borscht, which seemed pathetically anti-climactic, a culinary pat on the head, not that I didn't devour it.

"Don't worry about the car, we'll get rid of it," she said brightly, sweeping back into the kitchen.

"And the guy—the dead guy?"

She gave me a quizzical look. "What do you mean?"

"The guy. He's dead."

Leaning down, she put her hands firmly on my shoulders and stared deeply into my eyes. "It's over, Natalie. Let it go."

I drew a deep breath. Could it really be that easy? Should it? I was no fan of guilt, but I felt it nonetheless. An innocent man was dead, and I had played a part. I was guilty, wasn't I? Or was it only Zara who had murdered? Or was the past so far behind me now, so beyond anyone's reach, that it practically didn't exist?

"Can I call my mother?" I asked like a child.

"Not as long as you're in Russia. We have to assume her calls are being monitored."

"How about Meredith Viles? Can I talk to her?"

"I already let her know you're here. Don't worry. We'll find a way to get you back to the States."

"I have no passport, no money. Not even my own clothes."

"Let us take care of that." She smiled at me warmly, a look of respect in her eyes. "You're a survivor, Natalie, like your grandmother. You've got her courage and her luck. You'll do fine."

"Is she here?" I asked, startled. I'd almost forgotten about Katarina Melnikova, who'd been the whole purpose of my trip.

"I'll introduce you later. For now, wash, rest, eat. You made it. You're safe."

The words produced a dizziness in my brain. I was suddenly a child again, whirling in the teacup ride at the amusement park, where you spun crazily in two directions at once. Now the ride was ending; the teacup was knocking lazily back and forth in its metal track before coming to rest. There was the sound of the buzzer that unlatched the safety gate. But I was still jumbled internally, too disoriented to exit the ride.

"Where's Misha? Is he okay?"

"He's here in Cherkeh. He'll be very glad to see you."

I somehow dredged up the hardest words. "I'm so sorry about Saldana."

Her eyes softened. "I know you are. But let's not talk about that now. Let's just be thankful you're here. We'll have a few days to spend together before you have to go, I hope. I want to know everything about you and your mother, and your life in Washington, D.C."

"That seems so far away."

"You'll be back there soon. You will."

"I find that hard to believe."

"One thing at a time. First, let me get you something to wear."

It turned out that Cherkeh was home to a modern replica of a traditional Sakha settlement that had been built years ago to attract tourists, though few had come. Lena said that a group of patriotic Poles had ridden all the way to Cherkeh once in a rented van to visit the tiny restored cabin of the Polish exile Petr Alekseev, who'd started a school for the native children and was much beloved. But that was all so far; no other tourists of any nationality, not even Russians, had been willing to traipse so far across the Siberian steppe for the pleasure of sleeping for a small fee in a *babarnya*, the traditional octagonal dwelling of the formerly nomadic Sakha people. They hadn't been enticed by the chance to sit inside the sturdy log meeting house, tucked ingeniously inside a shallow hill, so as to be insulated from the cold by the earth itself; neither had the cleverly engineered horse-powered water wheel seduced them. Or the one-room houses with scuffed plank floors, complete with authentic tools and fishing gear, wooden buckets with woven horsehair handles, and fur-draped sledges for winter travel.

This lonely ghost town, a half-mile trek from her house, across a meadow and along a forested path, was where Lena led me as daylight waned. She carried fresh sheets and towels; I carried a shopping bag of groceries: crackers, a bottle of fresh milk, a block of cheese, and a tin of sardines. Apparently, the babarnya had become the village's unofficial guest house.

It was a good-sized structure with thick log walls and a clean plank floor.

A large, elevated fire pit occupied its center, directly under a wide, circular opening in the domed mud-and-thatch roof. The air inside was dry and woody-smelling, and felt quite warm after the stinging below-zero temperatures outside.

A man was there, busily splitting a pile of logs into firewood. He'd already gotten a small blaze crackling in the pit, the smoke rising straight up to meet a swath of twilight sky. He was in his late thirties or early forties, dressed in jeans and a dark sweatshirt, so intent on the thudding rhythm of his swinging ax that he didn't hear us come in.

"Dmitri," Lena said. "This is Natalie."

He laid down the ax and turned to us. "Welcome," he said, extending his hand.

I put the bag of groceries down and shook it. He was an inch or two taller than me, broad-chested, dark-skinned, with a firm grip. I glanced at Lena, questioning her with my eyes. How much did this man know?

"Dmitri is a friend. Anything you say to me, you can say to him."

I met his eyes—narrow, dark eyes with sparks burning in their depths.

"Dmitri will get it warm in here in no time," Lena said. "I'll send someone out to let you know when dinner's ready. In the meantime, just relax." As she let herself out through the screen door, she called back to me, "You'll want to shut the heavy door behind me so the heat doesn't escape."

As I did so, Dmitri went back to his log-splitting. I walked around the babarnya curiously. Wooden sleeping pallets covered in animal skins were built into six of the eight walls; various primitive artifacts hung on hooks. Into this authentic indigenous habitat, a full-sized modern picnic table had been dragged. Also two big coolers and a collapsible card table displaying various items of convenience—two kerosene lamps, a couple of flashlights, fat candles in silver holders, boxes of batteries and matches.

I found myself quietly alarmed. Was I really supposed to stay here, in some kind of failed tourist experiment deep in the woods, with no lock on the door? I remembered the billboard warning against alcohol abuse. No doubt the village was full of carousing drunks. And god only knew what was in the forest. Bears, probably. Odd, of course, to have survived a filthy prison cell and crowded, disease-ridden barracks only to quibble over these vastly improved, if rustic, accommodations.

Dmitri was loading split wood onto the fire, and it was answering him with bright licks of flame.

When I asked if he lived in the village, he explained that he was an engineer who'd been working on an oil rig in the arctic until recently. Which didn't answer the question.

"Did you grow up here?" I pressed.

"I come from Ulan-Ude. That's a city south of Lake Baikal, on the Trans-Siberian Railroad."

"So what are you doing here?"

He gave a close-mouthed smile. "Vacationing."

"Not one for a typical tourist spot, I see."

He threw another log onto the fire, and switched the topic. "Lena says you're a doctor. Better be careful: if word gets out, there'll be a line of patients outside your door."

"I'd be happy to see them, though I don't know what I could do without basic supplies. I'm actually not planning on staying long." I wanted this to be true.

He picked up the ax and resumed chopping.

Raising my voice over the dull thudding, I said, "If you won't tell me what you're doing here, maybe you could tell me how you know Lena."

He stopped his work and regarded me thoughtfully. Finally, he said, "Lena and I work together." He paused, seemed about to speak again, but didn't. "It's better if I don't say any more. All you need to know about me is that I trust your government more than I trust Putin's, which isn't saying much."

Feeling reassured, I let out a long sigh. "Do you really think you can get me out of Russia?"

"It will take a little doing, but we'll figure it out."

I wanted to believe it, but I couldn't. "You know, for a long time in prison, I was convinced that the US State Department would suddenly show up to demand my release."

"You were disappointed," he said in a neutral tone.

"I suppose the fantasy kept me going for a while, until I realized I didn't want to wait any longer to see if it was really going to happen."

"So you got yourself out."

"With one fuckload of luck."

"There was probably more to it than that."

I shook my head ruefully. "I'm not so sure. Things could so easily have gone another way." I could still feel the ice floes dipping under my weight, sense the speed of the moving river, see the rotating blue lights of the police cruisers on the highway outside Irkutsk.

"True, but that doesn't change what you did."

He set a log on its end on the chopping block, swung the ax, and split it cleanly down the middle. He took one of the pieces and set it on the flames. The fire was burning steadily now, throwing out plenty of heat.

"There's enough split wood here to get you through the night. If you need more, let me know." He leaned the ax on the wall by the door and lifted his parka off a hook.

"How will I reach you?"

"Lena knows where I am." I must have looked doubtful, because he added, "Don't worry. You're perfectly safe."

"Really? There must be bears in the forest," I said lightly, as if it were a joke.

"There are. But they stay away from people."

"In the States, you always hear stories about bears wrecking campgrounds, searching for human food."

He shook his head a little, gently amused. "These bears have plenty to eat in the wild."

I gave a tight, embarrassed smile. "Okay. Just nerves, I guess."

He paused, re-hung the parka on the hook, and came back to perch on the earthen lip of the fire pit, his arms loosely crossed. "I don't have to go just yet."

"Oh. Well, really, it's okay if you do," I said, hating that I'd come across as needy. But why try to hide it? I wasn't ready to be alone out there with night falling and nothing to occupy my mind. In prison, I'd never been alone, not even in the toilet.

"Have you ever been to the States?" I asked.

"Never been outside Russia. I'm a single guy with no kids, so it's almost impossible for me to get a visa. Putin's government is afraid I won't come back."

"Are they right?"

"Maybe."

"Well, the US is a great place to visit if you ever get the chance," I said, aware of how lame I sounded. "I grew up in Rockville, Maryland, which is near Washington, D.C...." His eyes were patient and tolerant, and I found myself going on. And on. Blathering my life story, as if it were important news. Maybe he was just that type—the quintessential *poputchik* to whom people poured out their hearts on a train or plane. Or maybe I just needed to talk, to try as best I could to resurrect the old Natalie March, the person I'd been before I got split into a hundred different parts.

"I'm probably boring you to death," I said after a while.

"Not at all. I enjoy hearing about your life."

"I usually don't talk so much. I'm more of a listener, actually."

"Whom do you listen to?"

"My patients, mostly. I have to figure out what's wrong with them, which isn't always that easy. They tend to bury the important facts—not intentionally, of course. Maybe it's just human nature to hide your vulnerabilities. So sometimes I have to draw them out, until they find what they want to say."

"Like a detective."

"I guess so. Only in medicine, the bad guy always wins in the end."

"By bad guy, you mean death?"

"Yeah, death. The big D. We throw everything we've got at it—medicines, technologies—and we can do a pretty good job sometimes of postponing it for months or years. But it always wins in the end." I realized I was echoing Zara's words: *Every life ends the same way.*

"You fight it anyway," Dmitri said quietly, firelight glowing on the side of his face. "If you stop fighting, what's left?"

I felt uncomfortable suddenly and went to the door. I opened it to the frigid air, gazed across a low, snowy meadow. It was dusk, and the sky and snow had blended together into a fog of muted lavender. In the distance, a group of shaggy ponies emerged as gray shadows, mixing smoky plumes of breath.

"When do the horses go back to the barn?"

"When they want to," he said.

"How is it they don't freeze to death?"

"They've made a lot of adaptations over the centuries, like reindeer."

"Clever of them."

"Very." There was a smile in his voice, as if I'd gotten an answer right.

I turned, wanting to see his expression, but he was stooping to pick a log off the woodpile. When I looked out the door again, a little boy was running up the path, making fast time despite his puffy pants and heavy boots. He skidded breathlessly through the door I held open for him, and fairly shouted at me, "It's time for you to go to dinner at Lena Tarasova's house!" He stared in excited wonder at the American visitor for a few moments before bolting away.

. . . .

Lena's kitchen was filled with warm cooking smells, but what riveted my attention was the old woman seated at the table.

"Mother, there's someone here to see you," Lena said.

The woman raised faded blue, milky eyes. Her face was narrow and very pale—so unlike the Sakha faces. In comparison to theirs, her nose seemed abnormally long and thin. Wisps of steel-gray hair strayed from a headscarf, her shoulders hunched forward, a hand-knit afghan covered her lap. She seemed to have collapsed into herself, the way the ground might sink over time into an unused mineshaft. But a strong jaw hinted at former beauty, and there was an appealing inquisitive tilt to her head as she tried to fathom the unfamiliar person in her line of sight.

"Do you remember the baby daughter you told us about—Vera—who stayed with your brother in Kiev? Well, this is *her* daughter. Her name is Natalie, and she's come all the way from America to see you."

The rheumy eyes flicked over my face. There was no understanding in them.

I crouched to be at her level. "Katarina?"

She seemed befuddled.

Lena shook her head. "No, don't call her by her first name. You should call her *Grandmother* out of respect."

"Grandmother," I said gently.

She reached out a gnarled hand and patted my arm.

I glanced to Lena for help.

"It isn't clear how much she understands," Lena said.

"Does she recognize you?"

"Sometimes, I think. It's hard to tell."

The old woman continued patting my arm gently.

"Grandmother," I whispered, looking for signs of Vera in the aged face, signs of myself.

She smiled, showing grayish, worn-down teeth.

"She fades away day by day," Lena said sadly. "There's less of her all the time." The table was set for three. There was a pot of boiling water on the stove, and sliced tomatoes and cucumbers arranged on a serving plate. Lena placed a steaming mug of tea on the table. "Here, this will warm you up."

I sat next to Katarina. "How long has this been going on?"

"Ten years, I'd say."

"Has she seen a doctor?"

"I offered to take her into Yakutsk for treatment when her symptoms first started, but she refused to go. She'd actually never been to a doctor before, at least not in Siberia. During Stalin's time, it was too risky. Her European features, no ID—anyone would have figured it out. Even after the Soviet Union collapsed, there were still plenty of former Communists around who would have seen her as a criminal. She said she'd come this far in her life without medical treatment, and didn't need it now."

"It's probably Alzheimer's."

"That's what I figured. And since there's no treatment for it anyway, there seemed no point in forcing her to go."

I looked into the bland, vacant eyes of my grandmother, and tried to control my disappointment. In all this time, it had never crossed my mind that Katarina Melnikova would be incapable of welcoming me and reaching out to my mother. I thought back to what Saldana had said when I asked about Katarina's health: *She has the problems old people have.* I'd been willing to leave it at that because, unconsciously, I'd already started writing the story of a happy family reunion, of my mother at last receiving a measure of the love she'd lived so long without.

Lena was ladling small fish the length of my hand out of the boiling pot, and arranging them on a serving plate. The entire fish, including head and tail.

She brought the plate and a bowl of cooked pasta to the table.

"These little fish come out of our shallow lakes and streams that are fed by rains, which filter through the meadows. They're very mild; I think you'll like them. But you have to watch out for the bones." She pulled the body of a fish apart with her fingers. The flesh fell away easily, exposing a tiny skeleton and dozens of nearly translucent filaments. She picked out a fleshy piece and sucked the meat off a needle of cartilage. She smiled at me. "You try."

I did. The fish was soft and sweet.

"Now," she said conspiratorially. "You won't be a real Siberian until you've eaten the tongue."

I tried to look interested as she dug her fingers into the head, pushing out the little eyeballs and then, with a slight grimace, hooking her finger around something that she yanked out with a flourish—a small pink muscle the size of a fingernail.

"This one's for you," she said generously.

"No, please. You go first."

She popped it in her mouth and started the same operation on another fish head. In a few seconds, I was given my very own tongue. I pinched it gingerly between two fingers and held it up to the light. It had a little crease down its center, just like a human tongue. "Bottoms up," I said, and dropped it into my mouth.

It was actually quite tasty.

"Good, isn't it?" Lena prompted.

"Very."

"You want another?"

"Sure."

She smiled. "We were raised on these fish, along with fresh milk and meat from our cows, and, if you don't mind me bragging a little, we don't have anywhere near the rates of illness you have in the West."

"And we're getting sicker all the time, I'm afraid."

"Whenever I come back to the village, the purity of the air and water just astounds me," Lena said.

She began cutting pieces of fish, pasta, and tomato into bite-size pieces on a separate plate, and scooted over to be closer to her mother. "I used to feed her first, but my hunger would make me impatient. Now I eat a little first, so I can take my time with her." She held out one small spoonful after another.

Katarina's mouth opened and closed like a baby bird's.

I watched the domestic ritual in wonder. Was the old woman in the rocking chair really my grandmother? I wanted to know everything about her, but her stories were locked inside her. Or more likely, given the advanced stage of her disease, they weren't there at all anymore. Her past, gone; her memories, vanished or sketchy at best; she herself only a shadow of what she'd been. It hardly seemed fair that the jaunty young wife in the belted jacket, who'd once cradled the infant Vera in her arms, who'd suffered so terribly and survived by risking all, who'd bravely made a life in this foreign place, should have come to this. I wanted her to have a clear victory, a sweet revenge, a happy ending—to be surrounded for just one perfect moment by people who understood the enormity of her struggle and the magnitude of her success. I wanted her to feel unique and powerful, and deeply loved. To know in her heart that her humble, painful life had been the most exquisite paean to beauty and truth. That, despite outward appearances, she'd been part goddess all along.

That was what I wanted. But fate hadn't stopped to inquire about my wishes. If it had, I probably wouldn't have lobbied only for Katarina, but would have made the same request for Vera—and everyone else in the world, for that matter. Even myself. Why not? Why shouldn't we all have grace in abundance?

Katarina's plate was clean. Suddenly, she frowned. "Where are the berries?" she asked in a querulous voice.

"I'll get them for you." Lena stood up and took a plastic container out of the refrigerator. "She loves these," she said over her shoulder. "We pick bushels of them in the summer and have them all year long." She dished some small red berries into a bowl and added a splash of thick cream.

Katarina smiled with delight when the bowl appeared in front of her.

"She had a hard life," Lena said later, as we sat by the living room fire, sipping wine she'd kept for a special occasion. Katarina was in a rocking chair between us, the afghan covering her lap. "She spent two years in that camp. Escape was practically unheard of; it took a lot of courage for her to try. She was found not far from here just about this time of year, early winter, with a head wound she'd packed in snow—so frozen she could barely walk. A hunter from the village found her and carried her back in his arms."

Katarina's presence in the village had been controversial, Lena explained. If the Soviets found out that an escaped prisoner was being harbored in a village, men, women, and children were taken out of their houses and shot. If the villagers turned the prisoner in, they got a reward. So when word got out that there was a convict in the hunter's house, a lot of people demanded that she be surrendered right away, while others mocked them for believing the Russians' promise. They said that Russians weren't likely to give money to the Sakha, whom they despised, and that if they did, the sum would be so small it would be an insult. After some discussion, an uneasy compromise was reached: the European woman would not be turned over to the Soviets, but she wouldn't be allowed to stay in Cherkeh either. She'd be given clothes and food and sent on her way, to fend for herself.

"People would have known in their hearts that this solution was actually a death sentence," Lena said. "Because if the coming winter didn't kill her, the Russians eventually would. Escaping from the gulag was high treason; Stalin's henchmen were known to spend years tracking down escapees. Even if she managed to make it out of Siberia, she wouldn't be able to return to her home and family without eventually being re-arrested and probably shot."

"So they changed their minds and let her stay here after all?" I asked hopefully.

Lena gave a deep sigh. "Not exactly. Mother couldn't say where she'd come from or how far she'd travelled. All she knew was that one day when she was being driven to the camp director's house—apparently, it had been built outside the prison grounds—she suddenly got up the nerve to grab the driver's gun and shoot him with it. She pushed his body out of the car and drove south on dirt roads as far as she could before the gas ran out. She pushed the car into the woods and tried to cover it with brush, but everyone knew it was only a matter of time until the vehicle was discovered and soldiers fanned out across the area. Finally, someone suggested that the best way to solve the problem was to bring the search for her to an end."

"So what happened?"

Lena leaned over and lifted the afghan off Katarina's lap. Katarina's right hand was intact; her left one was missing. There was only a stump.

I recoiled. "I don't understand."

"The Soviets had a long-standing agreement with herders across Siberia. If they found the body of an escaped prisoner in the taiga, they were to cut off the left hand and bring it to the authorities for a reward. Once the hand was turned in, the search was called off." Lena let the afghan fall across Katarina's lap.

Katarina had become agitated: her eyes roamed from my face to Lena's.

"It's all right, Mother," Lena whispered to her gently.

"So they..." I said with dread.

"The option of losing her hand was offered to her, and she took it. After the hand was frozen in the snow, it was presented at Camp 34, the only prison camp within the distance she'd presumably travelled, and the herders were given their reward."

We were silent for a while. Night had fallen and, with it, the temperature. The windows were covered by an insulating clear plastic, yet a sharp cold emanated from them nonetheless, as well as from the entire outer wall of the living room. At the same time, waves of heat radiated from the low fire burning in the hearth. Fire and ice—each force deadly in itself. We occupied a tiny circle of safety in a vast, potentially lethal environment. How fragile and tenuous our position was.

Finally, I asked, "Was she happy here?"

"She tried to be, I think. My parents had affection for each other, but there was always a gap between them they couldn't cross. I don't think Mother ever felt safe in the village either: anyone might have turned her in. She tended to stay home, sent me to the store for her as soon as I was old enough. She had a kind husband, a child, and books and art supplies my father brought back from his trips to Yakutsk."

"Art supplies?"

"Mmm. She loved to paint. But even that wasn't enough. How could it be? She'd been raised in a modern European city with education, music, museums. She'd lost everyone she ever loved: her parents, her first husband, a baby daughter. And her life in the gulag—if you can call it that—had been unspeakable. I remember waking in the night to her screams. She would startle at anything—a mouse running across the floor. Her face would have such a look of horror—I'll never forget it. It was clear that the memories tormented her. I don't believe I ever saw her truly happy. I did my best when I was a little girl; I loved her very much, and all I wanted was to see her smile. But I know now that there wasn't much I could have done for her."

Lena leaned over and tenderly stroked her mother's cheek. Katarina's eyes were closed. She'd fallen asleep by the fire.

"In a way, this disease is a blessing. It's taken away the bad memories. I like to think she's found contentment at last."

I thought of Vera. What would I tell her? *Your mother is alive, but she doesn't remember anything. She doesn't remember you.*

"Do you see that picture over the mantel?" Lena said.

It was a watercolor of two children running in a bright snowy meadow, a sense of motion in their flapping coats and wind-whipped hair, a frozen stream in the foreground and ponies in the distance. I easily recognized Saldana and Misha.

"Mother did that," Lena said in a tone of pleased reverence.

"It's lovely."

"Come. I'll show you some others."

She led me to a small room on the other side of the house, where there was a washer and dryer, household cleaners on plastic shelving, and a side door that went out to the barn. Propped between the washer and the wall were dozens of canvasses stretched on wooden frames, and on a high shelf that went the length of the room there were stacks of rolled watercolors.

She began to pull out the canvasses. Most were children at various ages, caught in natural poses. "That's me," Lena said, pointing to a girl with long black hair and bangs cut straight across her forehead. I recognized Lena's square face and sturdy stance in the child she used to be.

"And that one?" I asked, pointing to a taller willowy girl with a long nose and a curl in her dark hair.

"That's Vera," Lena said. "Mother painted her almost as often as she painted me. Of course, she could only imagine what Vera would look like. Can you tell if she was far off?"

With a lump in my throat, I studied the various paintings. Vera at five years old, at ten, at fifteen. "It does look like her," I said finally.

"Mother is religious, you know—or was. That's unusual around here. I grew up saying secretly, *God bless Father, Mother, and Vera.* I dreamed of meeting my older sister someday."

"Why didn't you try to find her?"

"We did. But my uncle had moved, leaving no forwarding address."

"They were still there, still in Kiev. That's where Vera grew up!" I spoke urgently, as if the mix-up could be solved at last, and the reunion could still happen.

Lena shrugged sadly. "Mother couldn't find him. And he wouldn't have been expecting to hear from her. People didn't return from the gulag." Lena slid the canvasses back into place beside the washing machine. "And soon, she had me to think about. And my father, of course. She talked a few times about going to Kiev, but we didn't have money for trips like that."

So Katarina *had* tried to find my mother. And when she couldn't, she'd painted her alongside Lena—two sisters playing together. The older one with paler skin and curling hair.

Grateful tears stung the backs of my eyelids. "My mother has to know this. You've no idea how much this will mean to her."

Lena smiled, flicking off the light to the laundry room. "Oh, I think I do. Never fear. We'll make a video for her. I have some nice pictures of Mother when she was younger, and a couple of videos taken before she became ill. The kids have tons of pictures and videos, of course. Mother was usually in the background of those." She looked over her shoulder as she led me back to the kitchen. "You'll take some of her paintings home with you. Yes?"

"That would be wonderful," I said. A few of Katarina's paintings, and the story of how she'd tried and failed to find her abandoned daughter, would be enough to show Vera that she'd been loved.

I woke the next morning with the terrible conviction that I'd slept too long and missed my chance—that my rescuers had arrived in the village and departed, unable to find me, or that the entire village had packed up during the night and moved away, reverting to their nomadic ways.

I ran to the door of the babarnya and opened it, expecting to see a deserted land, but there were the pretty Sakha ponies, scattered as usual across the snow-blanketed meadow. Smoke was curling lazily from the chimney of a distant house, and the sky was a pale blue wash of innocence. I must have slept a long time for the sky to be this bright.

They won't find you here, Lena had assured me the night before. *They don't know this place exists.* But what made her so sure? If I could get to Cherkeh, anyone could.

I breathed the frigid outdoor air, sucked it down into my lungs, trying to expel the ghostly filaments of panic the dream had left behind.

The fire inside was down to ashes and smoldering embers. I piled wood into the pit and waited, shivering, until the licking flames coalesced into a blaze. The outhouse was too far away, so I pulled on Lena's borrowed boots, trekked to the point where the clearing met the woods, and peed in the snow.

Then I wandered further into the forest, into a cathedral of hushed, soaring pines, and it was as if I'd crossed into another world. The sunlight filtered down in distinct white-gold spears, and the air was immaculate, soothing to my lungs. Frozen crystals on the branches were as bright and sharp as diamonds. Toadstools had a second, perfect downy cap. It was so silent that, when I stepped on a twig, the crack resounded. I came across a trail of animal tracks, and knelt to examine them. Fox, I thought. The rounded indentations of the pads, the delicate piercings of the claws. I wasn't alone out here.

Back in the cabin, with a blanket draped over my shoulders, I drank water made from melted snow, munched crackers and cheese, and watched the friendly, dancing spits of flame for a long time. The forest had calmed me with its beauty and order, and now the fire was lulling me into a peaceful trance. By degrees, a strange euphoria came over me. What if Lena was right, and I was safe? I just might make it home.

Lena's kitchen was bright with sunshine; the old conical clay stove radiated heat, quickly dispelling the blast of frigid air that had accompanied me through the door. There was bread on the table, with the deep-hued berries Katarina loved, and cream so thick that the wooden serving spoon stood straight up in the bowl. Lena told me to help myself. She said that Katarina was at the community center where there were activities and exercises for the elderly. A woman from the village took her over there most mornings, stayed with her for a few hours, and brought her back. The arrangement gave Lena a few hours to herself.

Lena poured coffee that she'd brewed especially for me and sat down across the table. It dawned on me that she'd heard every detail of my awful story, but I hadn't asked about her ordeal.

"How have you been with…everything that's happened?" I said kindly.

She dropped her eyes to the table self-consciously and began fiddling with the salt shaker. She seemed to sense that I was offering her an opening—caring for the caretaker. It clearly made her uncomfortable, but she took the opportunity.

"It was awful when Misha went missing. I was in agony. I couldn't bear to think what might be happening to him, and then there was the possibility that Saldana could be in danger, too. I found a cultural exchange opportunity online, and bribed her dance company to send her to New York. I even bribed a government official to get her visa approved. I can tell you that when I put Saldana on that plane, my broken heart was breaking one more time. The only way I could bear the pain was to convince myself that Misha would return, and that we'd join Saldana in America, where we'd be a family again, safe. I promised Saldana it would happen. I could tell she didn't believe me, but she sensed my desperation and was willing to do what I asked."

She looked so sorrowful and defeated that I placed my hand gently on top of hers.

"She was always good that way," Lena said softly. She went to the sink and ran the water, and I knew that was the most she could say.

That afternoon, Misha stopped by the babarnya. We embraced warmly. I was very happy that he'd made it to the village from the herders' camp, just as he was greatly relieved to see me. But he admitted to feeling restless. He couldn't return to Yakutsk or Mirny or, for that matter, go anywhere in Russia as long as he was a wanted man. He was relatively safe in Cherkeh, but the thought of spending years there doing odd jobs and farm work depressed him mightily. It felt as though his life was over before it had begun.

"You should come back to the States with me," I urged again.

"There's no way that can happen," he said morosely.

"Oh, yes, there is. If that's what you want, I'll make it happen. Believe me."

"How?" He looked hopeful and doubtful at the same time.

I pressed my lips together and shook my head. What I had to say to Meredith Viles would be between the two of us. "Just think about it carefully, Misha. If you leave Russia with me, you won't be able to come back."

"I don't have to think about it. There's no life for me here."

"All right. Let's talk to your mother," I said.

Lena must have seen us through the window because she opened the door before we knocked. Her face was tense and fearful, reflecting the expressions she saw on ours. The conversation went on for an hour. At the end, mother and son were embracing and crying together. It had been decided that Misha would come with me.

If the CIA agreed.

The sun was setting outside the window in gold and pink. The last rays glimmered on the frozen crust of the snow field. Lena's hand trembled as she poured us tea. After losing her daughter, she had just agreed to surrender her son. I didn't envy her.

On the practical level, she wasn't convinced that the CIA would agree to the plan. "They'll go to any length to get *you* out of Russia," she said, nodding in my direction. "But not Misha. Why would they go to such trouble for him? He isn't important enough."

"Tell Meredith Viles I need to speak to her," I said.

Lena gave me a doubtful look.

"You can get her on the phone for me, can't you?"

She nodded. "Tonight."

"Thanks."

Late that night, Meredith and I hammered out an agreement. She already knew my basic situation from having spoken to Lena. Now she was forced to hear me recount the ugly facts we both knew, the facts I hadn't told my aunt: that she and the CIA had betrayed both Misha and me. That when I'd managed to uncover clues that might have led to my missing nineteen-year-old cousin—too young and inexperienced to have been recruited in the first place—she'd brushed them aside, preferring to trick me into completing his mission, which was much more dangerous than she'd let on. Then when I finished the job she gave me, instead of taking me to my Russian family as she'd promised, she tried to put me on a plane back to the States instead—all without bothering to mention that that very morning I'd become a wanted criminal in Russia. And when I was finally arrested, she'd sat back and let my dismal fate unfold.

"You must have known what happened to me," I told her icily, though at that moment I still wasn't sure.

"Natalie," she said, "there's no use in—"

"Yeah, you knew," I interrupted. I couldn't bear to hear the rest of whatever patronizing brush-off was about to cross her lips. "You knew, and you let me rot."

"We didn't know all the details."

"Did you try to find out?"

"You had murder charges against you. There are things the CIA can't fix."

"Murders you committed."

There was a pause on the other end of the line. I had no idea where she was calling from. It could have been next door, or Moscow, or Washington, D.C. Finally, she said, "You had your orders, Natalie. You should have gotten on that plane."

"Well, maybe if I'd known…" I let it drop. The conversation was pointless.

What remained were my demands: Misha would come with me to the States and would receive political asylum. Lena would be offered the same opportunity, if and when she wanted it. That would be my payment for having kept my country's secrets safe through torture and imprisonment.

Meredith agreed.

The next night, there was a potluck dinner in the meeting hall in my honor. About thirty residents of Cherkeh gathered to welcome Lena Tarasova's niece from America. They brought their favorite meat pies, casseroles, and baked goods. After dinner, costumed children performed a skit dramatizing the epic hero Nyurgun Bootur deftly slaying monsters from the Below World, where all the ills that beset humanity originated. They recited their lines as children did everywhere—some with exaggerated brio, some in frozen terror—while a teacher whispered prompts when necessary, and parents beamed. Dmitri was there. He offered to translate the Sakha into Russian for my benefit, but I said I'd rather listen to the music of the language and watch the actions unfolding on the stage.

Afterwards, I found myself in Lena's living room, discussing culture and comparative politics with a small group of adults who were eager to understand the West and the Western mindset. Katarina was there in her rocker, wearing red lipstick—the first lipstick I'd seen on anyone in months—and a pretty floral headscarf. She smiled benignly at the hub-bub, the end of her left arm tucked under the afghan on her lap. Dmitri didn't say too much, apparently enjoying the evening's second performance: me fielding questions on topics such as American presidential elections, social security, health insurance, and the weather. Towards midnight, Lena shooed everyone home.

I realized I'd forgotten to bring the flashlight from the babarnya, and Lena offered hers for the walk back.

"I'll go with you," Dmitri offered.

"It's okay. I know how to get there," I said, independence being my habit.

"Don't you want some company?"

I glanced at Lena, not sure what I was looking for. Her face was neutral.

"Yeah, sure. That would be nice," I said, hearing stiffness in my voice.

The stars were extraordinary, more than I'd ever seen, a million shimmering sequins on the black satin sky. The hard-packed snow of the trail crunched dryly under our boots. All around, there was a faint whispering, as if from ghosts.

"Do you hear that?" I asked.

"It's the wind in the branches."

"I don't feel a wind."

"It's very light tonight. You have to stand still."

So I did, closing my eyes. The gentlest of air currents caressed my cheeks.

At the door to the cabin, he said, "So I'll leave you here."

A bit of panic fluttered in my chest. I was suddenly afraid of the deep, starless night, the killing cold, the strange angles of the babarnya. I wanted to make the fire bright, and fill the shadowy space with conversation before I was left alone.

"No, come in. I mean, if you have time."

"Let's see. I don't think I have any appointments."

I looked to see if he was teasing. The crinkles at the corners of his eyes said he was, and a hot flush crept up my face. Were we flirting? It had been a while since I'd done that. I'd almost forgotten how. Maybe I never knew.

Inside, he built up the fire. Then, without asking, he carried some logs from the stockpile near the door and began splitting them into firewood, replenishing my already sufficient stock. I couldn't take my eyes off him. Not just because he was a man not wearing a uniform and not carrying a gun, but simply because he was there. With me. In an eight-sided cabin in a village not found on any map, in a far-flung region of one of the world's most remote territories. What were the chances of that? It was almost a miracle. *What if...*

The thought dissolved before it was half formed. I didn't know what to think anymore, didn't want to think at all. The simple truth was that I wanted someone to hold me. Just that, nothing more. I barely knew him. There were a hundred questions I ought to ask. But I had an anxious sense of time slipping by, running quickly like an underwater current—unseen, practically unfelt, sweeping me along to a point in time when there would be no more chances like this.

When he put down the ax, I went to him and rested my head on his chest. He folded his arms around me, touched his lips to the top of my head. The warmth of his body and the glow of firelight disarmed me. Tears formed, and fell, and he kept holding me. I cried for a long time, longer than I wanted to, then stepped back, aghast.

"I'm so sorry," I mumbled.

"Do you want me to stay?"

"Oh, no. I'll be fine."

"I didn't mean…"

"No, I know you didn't."

"I could sleep on one of the beds on the other side of the cabin. If you don't want to be alone."

"Yes, maybe. No." I looked at him helplessly. "I don't know what I want."

He hesitated, bravely trying to decipher me, as if it could be done. "I'll stay."

"No, no. Please go. I'm fine, really I am." Yes, this was the right answer. Anything more would be…too much.

"You sure?"

"I am. Thank you for helping me…for the wood and everything. And the hug. Thank you. I really mean that."

"All right." He went to the door and shrugged on his heavy parka. "If you need anything…"

"I will. Thank you. Thanks again."

From the doorway, I watched his flashlight beam wobble along the line of ghostly trees, growing ever dimmer until it was snuffed out.

The next morning, I built the fire into a glorious blaze. It was a much bigger fire than I needed—its flames yearned openly for the circle of sky; its heat warmed the darkest shadows; it glowed across all eight walls. I went outside and piled snow into a bucket, and set the bucket on the edge of the fire pit. When the snow had melted to slushy water, I stripped, splashed my face, wet a towel, and washed my naked body slowly, methodically. Then I raised the bucket over my head and tipped it, so that the now-cool water coursed through my loose hair and splashed a puddle around my toes. The whole time, Dmitri was on my mind.

I dressed, boiled water, prepared tea, ate crackers and dried fruit.

In time, I heard a step outside. The door opened, and it was him, ushering in a blare of sunlight and a blast of icy air. Snow crystals sparkled on his parka; his face was ruddy with cold. He took off his gloves, his hat, his coat, his boots. I smiled, thinking, *Siberian striptease.*

He came to where I was sitting at the picnic table, and knelt before me. "Is it okay that I'm here?"

"It's perfect."

"Did you think I'd come?"

"I hoped you would."

I touched his wide-boned face, ran my fingers through his hair and along his neck, tenderly traced his smooth, satiny lips with my fingers. He let me, waited for me. Finally, I leaned down and kissed him. I felt the tensing of the muscles in his arms and back, the heat of his skin radiating through his rough wool sweater. We undressed each other slowly, and slowly began to move together, to press together, in the ancient dance. Our love was urgent and careful, our closeness unfamiliar, worthy of respect. And what had started the night before didn't end for hours.

Lena received word that the CIA was sending a helicopter. The flight plan hadn't been disclosed, but she guessed they would take us north, possibly to Magadan on the coast of the Okhotsk Sea, where private planes were known to fly back and forth to Alaska. I was to be ready to leave at any moment, but Lena said it could take weeks.

I spent the days with Lena, swapping stories of our lives. Together, we made a documentary for my mother, splicing in old photographs and videos, and mixing it all with family stories told by Lena and Misha. A whole portion of our little film was devoted to Katarina's paintings, especially the ones of her lovingly imagined child, Vera.

When Lena was busy, I read to Katarina from books I picked out of the bookcase. Tolstoy, Chekov, Pushkin, Pasternak. Whenever I stopped, Katarina would urge me to continue, saying that I had a lovely voice. She kept calling me Saldana, and I kept correcting her, hoping that one of those times it would stick.

"I'm your granddaughter Natalie," I would say. "My mother is Vera, the baby you had to leave behind. Do you understand?"

The first dozen times, nothing registered, then, all of a sudden, Katarina looked straight at me and said, "Vera?"

"No, Vera is living in America now. I'm her daughter."

My grandmother furrowed her brow. She seemed to be lost for a while. Then a glorious smile spread across her face. "Vera!"

There was more force and recognition in her eyes than I had seen in her before. Sensing that this was the best her brain could do, I saw no harm in indulging her. I embraced her, and she hugged me much tighter and longer than I expected from so frail a woman.

After that, I was Vera, and Katarina wouldn't let me out of her sight for long. Now when I read to her, I sat close beside her, with her fingertips resting on my arm.

During the night, I was with Dmitri, in a separate universe that existed for us only, outside of time and place. Our lovemaking grew bolder and more assured as the days went by, until it surpassed anything I'd known. I had no words for it, and didn't try to find any. There was just him, the fire blazing or burning low in the background, the texture of animal skins under my naked body, and the smells of pine smoke and snow.

One day, when I was in the babarnya by myself, a little boy appeared at the door. Lena had received news that the helicopter was about to arrive, and I was to pack quickly and come to her house. I folded up a couple of things—there wasn't much—and headed down the well-worn snow path in a biting arctic wind. I didn't want to go. My life in Cherkeh was well-ordered and beautiful; I lived each day as if it were a gift. I dreaded saying goodbye to Lena and Katarina, but it was the thought of leaving Dmitri that I almost couldn't face. He'd told me he would never leave Russia, and we both knew I wouldn't stay. Not just because of Misha, but also because I didn't belong there. My life was with my mother and my patients in the States. Beyond that, we hadn't talked about my going—what more was there to say? Better to keep what we were sharing untainted by the world, almost sacred, untorn until it had to be.

The helicopter touched down at noon in the meadow, scattering the ponies, and sat idly in the bright snow, looking foreign and ugly, like a giant mechanical gnat. The men came into Lena's house to get Misha and me—one a Russian pilot, the other an American CIA agent wearing arctic blue sunglasses and a vivid red mountaineering parka with numerous zippers and snaps. They filled her tiny kitchen with their big egos and restlessness. Misha wasn't there, making Lena and me worry. But he soon showed up, looking dazed by the significance of what he was about to do, with clothes spilling out of his backpack and some books under his arm.

"You're coming, right?" he said anxiously to his mother. "To America?" As if she might forget.

"When I'm ready," she said calmly. Which meant, when Katarina was gone.

I kissed my grandmother, hugged my aunt. My bag was stuffed with food for the journey, gifts, including one of Katarina's paintings, and a thumb drive with photos and our video on it. I was dragging my feet, hoping Dmitri would arrive in time to see me off. But he didn't come, and I couldn't delay forever. I told myself he was staying away on purpose, to make it easier, and Misha and I followed the men out to the helicopter in the stinging cold. I climbed inside, belted myself into a contoured leather seat in the back, with just a tiny window to my right. Misha sat close beside me in the cramped space, his face pressed to the tiny window on his side, where his mother was waving goodbye. I could only imagine what they were feeling.

The rotors whirred faster and faster, the noise of the motor grew shrill and deafening, the craft lifted with a reluctant juddering and peeled away from the earth.

There, on the road not far from Lena's house, I saw him. His car pulled over, the door flung open, him standing tall in the middle of the road, peering skyward, shielding his eyes against the glare. He raised his arm and waved slowly, in a wide arc, back and forth; I waved back, hard and fast, though I doubted he could see me. The shadow of the helicopter passed over him. The aircraft banked; he came into sight again, slightly behind me. He turned his body to follow the line of flight; he kept waving and so did I. Seconds later, he was gone from my sight, and the village, too, had disappeared. The helicopter raced over a vast snow field, gaining altitude all the time. I placed my hands protectively over my belly as the aircraft lurched into a blinding sky.

13

Just as Lena had predicted, the helicopter brought us to an airfield outside icy Magadan, where a small private plane, a single-engine Piper Cherokee, was waiting. The pilot was American through and through, with his ready white smile, and his way of making the hardship of twenty degrees below zero feel like a brisk adventure.

He shook my hand firmly though our puffy gloves. "I heard you had quite a trip," he said, laughing at his own drollness and the crazy ways of Lady Luck, who had spit me out of her incomprehensible whirlwind onto the unlikely shores of the Bering Strait.

"Very," I replied.

Misha said hello in English, *hello* being one of the several English words he knew.

Next, we landed at a US Army base somewhere in Alaska, where more American men vigorously shook my hand, and a few of them went on to pat my back with enough fond energy that I had to brace my feet. Misha valiantly practiced his hellos. I quickly forgot the men's names. What I remembered was their high spirits, the brilliant sunrays piercing off the wings of the Cherokee, and the damp, muddy smell to the air. I did learn the name of one of the mess hall cooks, a fresh-faced Jeb from Columbus, Ohio, who served us cheeseburgers and fries.

I wouldn't be allowed to call Vera until after my debriefing at Langley. That took several days, during which Misha and I stayed in separate rooms at a local motel with a pervasive chemical smell and depressingly bland art. Two taciturn, well-muscled agents picked me up every morning at eight a.m. and delivered me back to the motel at precisely five p.m. During those long days, while the leaden skies of December hung motionless outside the institutional windows of CIA headquarters, I spilled every detail of my true story and, in return, was provided with a detailed false story to relate to family and friends. At night, after dinner with Misha, I leaned back against thin pillows and a flimsy headboard, watching episodes of *Friends* and *Frasier* until the raucous laugh tracks lulled me to sleep.

Finally, it was time to see Vera. Agents had already been to the rehab to break the news of my return to her in person. They'd answered her questions with the official story, which I'd sworn to dutifully repeat.

I was nervous as the sprawling facility came into sight. I was driving my own car and wearing my own clothes. My hair had been cut by a stylist, and I'd put on a few pounds. The gifts for my mother from her Russian family and the video that Lena and I had made were stowed in my bag. But I didn't feel right. The world I was now inhabiting was strangely brilliant, busy, and lavish. Everything seemed to be moving at twice the normal rate of speed. I'd referred to myself as Anne-Marie Phipps several times, and on a couple of occasions had glanced down and imagined that my feet were encased in heavy, blood-stained socks. I wondered if I'd ever fit in to my old life again.

Vera was waiting in her usual place, just inside the glass doors of the main entrance, when I came up the path. A pretty scarf was draped over her shoulders. She looked an awful lot like Katarina in that moment, except for the fact that both her hands were visible in her lap. The automatic door opened for me with a gentle whoosh, and I went to her.

"Hi," I said, crouching down to be on her level.

"You didn't have to take so long to come home," she said, trying to be old-lady peevish.

"I found Katarina Melnikova," I said excitedly. "I have so much to tell you."

"Not yet. First, let me look at you."

In the silence that followed our eyes met and filled with tears.

"I'm so sorry, Mom," I said.

"For what?" She seemed surprised.

"For everything." For leaving her alone so long. For making her worry. For spending so many years of my life believing that every cruel disease I encountered, every pain and unhappiness, most of all her own, was somehow mine to cure.

"Oh, Natalie. What are you thinking? I'm the luckiest woman alive."

My nameplate was still on the door to the suite at the George Washington University Medical Center, and my office was dusty but intact. My sickest patients had scattered, of necessity, to different doctors, but many of the people who saw me only once or twice a year hadn't even noticed I was gone. A lighter workload seemed to be the main effect of the more than three months I'd been away.

At the end of my first week back, I met with Joel to review the files of the patients I'd referred to him. Our discussion was brisk and to the point, peppered with the medical language we both spoke so well. Out of nowhere, I experienced a sense of déjà vu: everything I was hearing and seeing—his melodic voice, his familiar urgency, the precise way he tilted his head when he posed a question, the very words coming out of his mouth—had happened a hundred times before. He had been such a vital part of my younger life. I realized what an unparalleled blessing it was to have loved a person you also greatly admired.

As he straightened the folders, he asked a bit hesitantly, without quite looking at me, "How are you doing, Natalie?"

"Very well," I said.

"Really?"

"Uh-huh. I stayed in Russia a little longer than I expected to."

"I know."

"I met my grandmother."

"Really?" He perked up at this because it put us on safe ground. "And how was that?"

"It was excellent. A bit taxing emotionally because she has Alzheimer's. But my aunt and a cousin were there, too, so I learned a lot about her life from them. Mother's thrilled, as you can imagine."

"Of course." He knew my family history better than anyone. "I'm happy for you."

"Thanks." I drew a breath. "And you. I hear congratulations are in order."

He smiled. "We're delighted. It's still early, of course. We're just through the first trimester."

"I hope all goes well. You'll be a wonderful father, Joel."

He looked at me kindly, and I saw that he was trying to find some words. But there was nothing more to say.

There was no pregnancy for me, which was disappointing at first. But as I reconnected with colleagues and patients, I came to believe it was for the best.

A week or two later, I called Detective Ruggeri, who informed me that there'd been no progress in Saldana's case. Soon after, I received a package in the mail—a large, slightly crushed cardboard box with an NYPD return address. Inside was a jumble of athletic wear, street clothes, and miscellaneous items. Saldana's personal effects. A note from Ruggeri stated that the items deemed to be evidence in the homicide investigation had been bagged and stored at precinct headquarters. The remaining items, having not been claimed by the Russian Consulate as was customary in such situations, were being shipped to me as next of kin. The impersonal tone of his message sounded distinctly like a wrapping-up.

Neither Misha nor I could bear to go through the box, so I re-folded the cardboard flaps and stashed it on the floor of the hall closet. At that point, Misha was staying in my spare bedroom. He was enrolled in an English immersion course at GW that he was about to flunk for lack of attendance. Instead of going to class, he spent his time making friends in the Russian community in D.C., an activity at which he excelled. He worked evenings doing valet parking at a fancy downtown hotel, another activity at which he excelled, if you could call driving very expensive cars very fast up and down the narrow ramps of a city parking garage excelling. Misha was perfectly maddening in his way: he absolutely refused to take his future seriously. But he was also very good company, always positive and energetic. He did what no one had done for a long time: he made me laugh.

Soon, the winter holidays were just a week away. The temperature hovered around freezing, and precipitation came down as either rain or snow, sometimes as both. Dirty slush was packed against the curbs, and the air had the kind of damp, penetrating chill that quickly seeped through woolen coats and scarves.

One night, I dug out my ceramic Christmas tree with the flashing colored bulbs and set it up in its usual place on the end table next to the couch. Then I wrapped the gifts I'd bought for my mother and stacked them by the door in preparation for the holiday. I knew that the terrible ache inside me was my longing for Dmitri, but I wasn't allowed to contact him, not ever again. I had tried books, television, even the medical journals that once so reliably occupied my mind. But nothing had been able to quell my lonely restlessness. Sometimes when I closed my eyes, I could feel his warm, smooth skin under my fingertips, and I wondered if anything that true and good would ever happen to me again.

It got late, past the time that Misha usually went to bed, yet his light was on in his room, and I could hear louder-than-usual noises coming from inside. I was curious about what he was doing, but I wanted to give him his privacy, so I didn't say anything. Then I heard a sharp cry that sounded like pain and joy combined.

I went to his door and knocked. "Misha, are you okay?"

The door opened. His face was red and his eyes burned with intensity. Laid out on his bed were woolen leg warmers, worn-out ballet slippers, and a couple of pairs of toe shoes wrapped with pink satin ribbons. Sweaters, jeans, old rubber flip-flops, a beaded make-up bag, and toiletries with Cyrillic labeling. A Russian-English pocket dictionary and a zippered vinyl binder of language-learning CDs. The box from the NYPD was open on the floor.

"Oh, Misha. I'm so sorry," I said, assuming that the sight of Saldana's belongings had spurred a fresh round of grief.

He shook his head to tell me I was wrong and wordlessly handed me a laptop I had loaned him. I perched on the edge of the bed to read the document that was open on the screen. It was in Russian, a lot of lists, and I was too tired to decipher it myself.

"What is it?"

"It's the monograph. Kosloff's monograph," he said excitedly.

I looked closer, at a column of names and dates—1952, 1953.

He said, "They're all here, all the files I emailed Saldana, including the photos of the prison camp."

I looked up at him, incredulous. "Where did you find them?"

He picked the vinyl binder of language CDs off the bed and waved it in front of me. "In here. She copied everything onto a flash drive and hid it in here, in one of the pockets where you put CDs." As if I wouldn't believe him, he opened the binder and showed me how the CDs fit into tight plastic sleeves.

"Do you think she knew what was in the files?"

"I have no idea. I labelled them as choreography for different pieces. I thought for sure she wouldn't open them. She always hated to learn dance that way."

I checked the title on the menu bar. *Choreography, Grande Pas de deux, Paquita.*

I said, "She must have opened them and realized they were dangerous."

He nodded, too overcome to speak.

I shut the laptop and placed it gently on the bed among Saldana's things. How brave she was, I thought, to have copied the files and hidden them away. As if she knew something might happen.

"What are going to do?" I asked.

He smiled broadly. "I'm going to send my article to the *Washington Post*."

Of course. It was so like him not to miss a beat. "You'll have to translate it first," I reminded my young truant.

We'd always spoken to each other in Russian, but now he switched to English. "You will be help to me, no?"

I looked at him standing there, so full of vitality and purpose, and something deep inside me opened. "I'll always help you," I said.

THE END

NOTES & ACKNOWLEDGEMENTS

The research for this book ranged across an assortment of apparently random topics such as surgical procedures, weapons treaties, and Russian drinking toasts, to name just a few. Anyone checking my computer search history while I was writing this book would have been puzzled and perhaps a bit worried about my state of mind. When I needed a more in-depth understanding of important subjects such as the gulag, nomadic cultures, and Russian prisons, I relied on memoirs and scholarly works. A bibliography of fascinating books on these topics and others related to Siberia is available on my website.

I never would have attempted writing about Siberia without having visited there first. My deep appreciation goes to my generous Russian hosts in Yakutsk and Cherkeh. Thank you for opening your homes and sharing your stories and smiles with me.

Though I did not make it to the other settings mentioned in the book—Mirny, Butugychag, or the Verkhoyansk Mountain Range—I stayed as close as I could to available facts when describing them. In Butugychag especially, there is a rich photographic record. However, whenever there was a conflict between reality and the demands of novel writing, the fictional world naturally took precedence. The alert reader will note that I added a chemical plant to the city of Mirny, revised the date of Butugychag's discovery, and no doubt made numerous errors regarding the murky (to the layperson) art of intelligence gathering.

I am lucky to be blessed with wonderful friends and colleagues who helped me transform what started out as a half-formed idea into an actual book. Writers Linda Barnes, Shannon Kirk, Holly Robinson, Leonard Rosen, Hank Phillippi Ryan, and Joanna Schaffhausen took the time to nudge early drafts into progressively better shape. It is a pleasure and an honor to share this journey with them. Thanks to my sister, Dr. Carolyn Harrington, who signed off on the medical details. And I am ever indebted to my agent, Esmond Harmsworth, whose faith in me and my work is an invaluable gift. To Jason Pinter and the good people at Polis Books—thank you for every large and small thing you did to bring this book to life. Finally, my love and gratitude eternally flow to the three special people who bring color and warmth to my world: Robert, Ben, and Ellen Sophia.

ABOUT THE AUTHOR

Elisabeth Elo is the author of *North of Boston*, chosen by *Booklist* as a Best Crime Novel Debut of the year. Published in six countries, it was also an Indie Next Pick and a Book of the Month/Literary Guild selection. Elisabeth grew up in Boston, graduated from Brown University, and earned a PhD in English at Brandeis. She worked as a children's magazine editor, a high-tech product manager, and a halfway house counselor before starting to write fiction. To learn more, visit www.elisabethelo.com.

31901064669874